# DEAD MEN DON'T FLIP

## BOOK 3 IN THE MARTIN AND OWEN MYSTERY SERIES

### NINA CORDOBA

Art director: Sierra Acy

Original cover art: Kostis Pavlou

Editor: Jennifer Bray-Weber

❀ Created with Vellum

# CHAPTER ONE

**Rika Martín**

When I parked my Honda Fit in front of the duplex in Reseda, it was only seven-thirty in the morning.

I scanned the area.

The street was pleasant enough with mature trees and even some new construction. The house—my target—was craftsman style, probably nice when it was first built, but now the paint was chipped and what remained could best be described as "dirty eggshell."

I hoped my client, who owned the place, was a house flipper because, otherwise, I might not be getting paid for this job.

The property was enclosed in chain-link, but the gate was unlocked, just as I'd been told it would be. I lifted the U-shaped clasp to let myself into the yard, coming to a dead stop when the hinge creaked.

Since the street was eerily quiet, I might as well have sounded a foghorn. The creak bounced off the neighboring houses and echoed back at me.

I glanced around, again, looking for doors opening or curtains moving in the homes nearby.

No movement.

I listened for several long moments in case I'd alerted a neighbor to my presence.

Not a sound.

My job was to search the left side of the duplex. The owner had assured me no one would be in either side this morning. She knew because she currently lived in the right side of the duplex.

I stepped quietly onto the cement porch and approached the front window, cupping my hands around my eyes to see through a slit in the curtains. Nothing was moving in the living room. I detected no noise coming from inside. The only sign of life was a potted cactus to the left of the door.

I reached into the pocket of my jeans, intending to fish the key out, but a wave of anxiety hit me.

I'm not the most suspicious person in the world—that title already belonged to my grandmother—but I wasn't born yesterday on a turnip truck, or however the saying goes.

After considering my options, I did a one-eighty and tiptoed down the porch steps to slip along the left side of the house. I had plenty of time, and I didn't want to walk into an unknown house without checking it out for myself first.

There were several windows on the side of the house, but without a porch to stand on, they were too high for me to see into.

I'd worn my best running shoes in case I needed to flee the scene. They had a lot of squish in them, which meant they made me about five-five, instead of my usual five-four-and-a-half, and, hopefully, bouncier.

I crouched into a semi-squat and jumped, but my eyes only made it to the bottom of the windowsill. I tried again, this time putting more energy into it. As I sprang up, I got a quick glimpse of the back wall of the living room and part of the hallway, which was also devoid of humanity.

Moving farther back on the property, I paused and assessed

the next window. This one was smaller and higher. I wasn't sure I could manage the jump.

*You're only as short as you feel. You're only as short as you feel*, I chanted in my head. Then, I tried to picture myself in a Lakers uniform about to dunk the ball into the net, but couldn't really relate, so I closed my eyes and imagined being the Seeker in a Quidditch game.

I'd fallen down, down, down, but was about to rally and swoop high in the sky on my broomstick.

Crouching, I put every ounce of spring I had into the balls of my feet and jumped. Then something strange happened.

I made it all the way up to the middle of the window, which turned out to be the one for the bathroom, and I sort of hovered there like I was in a martial arts movie.

*Have I finally gotten my superpower?*

I'd never thought of the power to hover outside bathroom windows as a superpower before—more like a misdemeanor peeping power—but I'd wanted to be at least a little supernatural since I was a kid, so, at this point, I'd take what I could get.

All that went through my head in a split-second while the logical part of my brain tried to point out that what was happening was impossible. Well, impossible unless there were a pair of large hands gripping my waist, which there were.

"New hobby?" One of Nick's hands slid lower and cupped my rear end.

"Put me down," I said, mostly annoyed to learn I was still superpowerless. I tried to ignore the warmth that was radiating through my jeans from his hot palm.

I checked his face for signs of strain but didn't see any, which was a relief considering I'd spent my teenage years shaped like a very short linebacker, but without the wide shoulders.

Nick set me gently on my feet and I turned around to face him.

Even though it was late January, Los Angeles had been experiencing a heat wave for the past few days, and he was wearing a navy, short-sleeved t-shirt that fit him like a glove. This meant I couldn't miss the recently flexed muscles in his arms and chest. His jeans were kind of distressed, but not in that pre-distressed way I often saw in L.A.

I knew from the time I spent at his house in Bolo, Texas that Nick's jeans were legitimately distressed from actual manual labor. Manual labor he sometimes did shirtless.

*Mmmmm...hmmm...*

Damn, he was distracting. I forced the mental picture of half-naked Nick out of my head. "You're late," I hissed.

"The address you sent me was off by one digit," he replied. "I was up the block at another house until I decided to drive the neighborhood and spotted your car. You should check your texts."

"Okay, whatever." I was annoyed that I might have messed up something as simple as an address, and even more annoyed at his insinuation that I wasn't as tech—or in this case, text—savvy as he was. When I met him, he was using the oldest iPhone I'd ever seen in person.

Anyway, this was my—I mean "our"—first official job as private investigators, and I didn't want to screw it up.

"Wanna tell me why we're here?" he asked. "And why you've turned into a peeper? Not necessarily in that order."

"I was just making sure the house was really empty before I entered."

"Are you entering as in 'breaking and entering'?"

Oh, jeez. Maybe I should have asked Eli to join me in the biz instead of Nick. Eli was my self-proclaimed stalker, but at least he wouldn't have all these scruples about sneaking around and spying on people.

I put my hands on my hips. "Yes, Nick," I said in a snooty tone. "I've decided to start my career as a juvenile delinquent at the age of twenty-four."

"I think you might have started it when you and LeeAnne climbed the fence at the Microtology VIP center."

*Ugh!* Why in the world did I partner up with a lawyer? He had an argument for everything.

His biceps flexed again as he reached out and lifted a lock of hair from my face—that must have fallen there while I was doing my Michael Jordan impression—and smoothed it back where it belonged.

*Oh, yeah. Because he's hot as all hell and he does sweet-sexy things, like smooth the hair out of my face.*

I pulled out the house key and showed it to him.

"Okay..." He put his hands on his hips, which was much more impressive than my hands-on-hips move because it made him seem even bigger. He was well over six feet tall and broad shouldered. I found his size both arousing and aggravating, considering I'd planned to grow a lot taller than I did. I'm not sure why I had those expectations since nearly all the women in my family were around the same height or shorter, except for my cousin Sofia, who was two years younger, but outgrew me when I was seven.

Nick's curious blue eyes stared down at me, clearly waiting for an explanation.

"I'll tell you when we get inside," I said, trying not to let his gaze affect me.

I muscled him out of the way, which meant he let me pass because there was no way my muscles could out-muscle his muscles. His eight-pack alone could bring a woman to her knees. I mean, seriously, his torso looked like it had been airbrushed.

He followed me up the front steps, his cowboy boots clomping on the porch.

"Could you be a little quieter?" I asked.

"Why do we need to sneak around if the owner of the property gave you a key?"

I wanted to tell him he was making too many assumptions. I

hadn't told him the owner was the one who gave me a key. But if I challenged his assumption, he'd challenge me right back. Then, I'd have to admit it was, indeed, the owner who gave me the key, and he'd be able to give me his *I was right* look, which I didn't want to see at the moment.

Furthermore, I did not need his backtalk today. I was stressed already. Unlike Nick, it was my life's goal to be a private investigator, and I didn't want to mess up my first official case, even if it was just a jealous girlfriend who'd hired me.

When I unlocked the door and let us into the living room, my nostrils were assaulted with a very male smell. Not like a locker room or a men's bathroom—*gag*—more like an auto repair shop.

Nick stood in the middle, his eyes sweeping over the meager belongings. The furniture was sparse—an old brown, reclining love seat, an old, non-flat-screen TV and two scratched wooden end tables on either side of the love seat. However, what the house lacked in furniture, it made up for in tools. They were scattered everywhere—manual ones, like hammers, wrenches and screw drivers as well as a few elderly power tools, like drills and saws.

Nick took the place in, then tilted his head and looked at me. "What's going on?"

"It's our first official case," I announced. When I called him and told him to meet me here, I'd intentionally been vague about the reason. In fact, I might have implied I was doing a favor for a friend.

"First case?" Nick repeated. "We don't even have our office space yet."

This was a bone of contention between us. I wanted a starter P.I. office over a Chinese restaurant—that's how I'd always imagined it—while Nick kept pointing out that we'd have to sign a three-year lease, therefore, might as well get something we'd want to spend three years in.

My problem with this was two-fold. One, I was used to

earning the things I had and didn't want a fancy office until I'd earned one. Two, Nick was financing the office, and I wasn't comfortable with him spending so much money on something he never would have considered if it weren't for me. Sure, he didn't want to be a criminal lawyer anymore, but private investigation was my dream, not his.

He'd countered my objections by pointing out he had plenty of money and wouldn't miss the monthly rent coming out of his pocket, even L.A. rent, which was sky high. To make me feel better, he'd argued that I was the partner with the know-how, and he was the one putting the money in, a common business arrangement.

I still felt weird about it. In all honesty, I'd never imagined Nick being a part of the P.I. firm I'd always wanted. Not until I was desperate for an excuse to keep him in L.A. after my dad's situation was resolved. Then, the words just popped out of my mouth with no thought as to how it would all work.

Now, I felt awkward and stressed, desperate to start making money so I didn't have to feel as beholden to Nick. He was a great guy, but the balance of power in most relationships seemed to come down to who had control of the money, and I didn't want any man to have control of my life, especially after the fiasco with my ex-boyfriend Brandtt.

I might make mistakes, but I learned from them. Besides, I was pretty sure my grandmother and aunts' mistrust of ninety-nine percent of men in the world had rubbed off on me, at least a little, and I wasn't entirely sure that was a bad thing.

"We don't need office space to start our P.I. work," I said. "All we need are these." I pulled a card from my pocket that read, "Martin and Owen Private Investigations" and handed it to him.

Nick took it and examined it. His eyebrows lifted. "You left the accent off your name?"

*Ugh.* That was a pet peeve of mine and he knew it. "I needed to get them printed cheap by one of those online services.

7

Apparently, they don't do accent marks, even if you submit it with one."

"So, you're just plain old Martin, now." Nick's lips quirked in a teasing grin.

"No, I'm still Rika Mar-*teen!*" I replied testily. "I'll get new cards as soon as we can afford them."

Nick's eyes softened and I felt the cool blue of them coating my skin, except, as usual, the coating quickly turned ultra-warm. "I can afford better cards, Rika," he said.

He didn't need to tell me he could afford better cards. I knew he could afford better cards. Thanks to LeeAnne—my new friend from Bolo and Nick's old frenemy—*everybody* knew he could afford better cards, including my grandmother, my aunts, my cousin Sofia, and my grandmother's neighbor Mrs. Ruíz.

Actually, if Mrs. Ruíz knew, everyone in the world knew.

"I don't want you buying everything." I had my pride. Maybe not enough pride to let Nick drive off into the sunset the way he'd let me drive away from Bolo, but enough that I didn't want to feel overly indebted to him.

Nick shook his head, the look on his face saying, *Who can understand the female brain?*

That look made me want to snap at him, but since he hadn't made the statement aloud, it would have seemed like an over-reaction.

"Anyway," I said. "The owner of the duplex lives next door. She's been letting her boyfriend live on this side, rent-free, but she suspects he might be two-timing her when she goes out-of-town for business, and she wants to make sure he's not just using her, L.A. rent being what it is. She's in love with him."

Nick took in a deep breath and let it out slowly. Until this instant, it hadn't occurred to me that Nick was not the kind of person who would feel good about rifling through someone else's belongings.

*Damn it.* Why hadn't I come up with another way to keep him in town? This was so unnatural.

"You don't have to do this," I said. "I can take care of it. I'm just going to look for receipts, credit cards statements, that sort of thing... Oh, and she said he was going to the doctor for some sort of medical procedure today and was planning to leave his cell at home to keep it from getting stolen, so I can check it too. Apparently, hospital personnel are pretty larcenous in the places he's lived."

I turned and left the living room, anxious to do my job and get out.

"What places are those?"

I glanced into a doorway on the left. It was the bathroom I'd seen from the outside. "Moldova, originally, but she said he's been all over the world."

Through a doorway on the right, was a combination kitchen-dining area. The appliances were old and a bit on the grimy side. The kitchen had no window because the wall was shared with the other half of the duplex. I thought this was poor planning. Most people would rather have a window in their kitchen than in their bathroom.

I felt Nick behind me, surprised I hadn't heard him this time. Apparently, he could break out his cat feet at will.

He had all kinds of superpowers.

*Annoying.*

When I stepped inside the final doorway, I had just enough time to register that it was the bedroom before my brain started screaming, *There's a man in the bed! There's a man in the bed!*

Wait, make that two men.

Wow. I doubted my client would be any happier to learn her boyfriend was sleeping with a man than with another woman.

I couldn't see the second man's face because of an extra pillow that had ended up scrunched up between their heads. But the one leg that wasn't covered had to belong to a man, unless my target was cheating with a woman who had never shaved her legs, and had very large, masculine feet.

Nick had reached out when we crossed the threshold and grabbed my arm to stop my progress in the same moment I'd seen the men.

We were both still as statues for several seconds. We needed to get the hell out of here, but I guess our brains held us there, needing to understand what we were seeing.

In a way, this was easier. I didn't need to rifle through any drawers. I only needed to tell my client I'd seen her man in bed with another man. Case closed.

But just as I was about to turn around, the sleeper closest to us opened his eyes. As it registered that two strangers were standing in the doorway of the bedroom, his mouth fell open. "What...?" He blinked his dark eyes at us like he wasn't sure we were really there.

"I'm sorry..." I began. "We thought the house was vacant." That was what I'd planned to say if the place turned out to be occupied.

He glanced toward the other man. "Grigore!" he said. As he pulled the pillow from between their faces, he pointed at us, nudging the other man with his elbow. "Grigore!"

"Look, we'll just—" I began.

The man had done a double-take and was now staring at this "Grigore" person next to him. My gaze followed his. As I stared at the scene before me, I, too, blinked several times, trying to make sense of it.

But nothing made sense.

Suddenly, he was frantic, screaming "Grigore!" over and over as he touched Grigore's face. But, oddly, he was doing it from a mostly lying position, instead of sitting up, like anyone else would.

My eyes focused on Grigore. He was lying completely still, left eye open. The right eye had a screwdriver sticking out of it.

"Oh, my God!" I said.

Nick gave a surprised gasp, then sprinted over to Grigore.

The live man, still frantic, but also still lying down, reached over with his right hand and grasped the screwdriver handle. "I get it out!"

Nick grabbed his wrist before he could touch it. "No. That could make it worse," he said.

"But..." The man turned his head frantically, looking between Grigore, Nick and me.

Nick let go of him and pressed on Grigore's neck. "There's no sign of life," Nick said. "I'm sorry."

Something seemed to dawn on the man, and he pulled to the right, flailing his arms like he was trying to get away, but all he managed to do was flop around a bit.

Was he paraplegic? Then, I noticed that Grigore was flopping around too.

Nick was wrong. Grigore wasn't dead. Nick was a lawyer, not a doctor. Why did he think he knew how to tell a dead person from a live one?

But other than flopping in unison with the flailing man, Grigore showed no sign of life.

The live man turned his face toward me, his eyes wild. "Call my doctors," he said in thickly accented English. He was reaching toward a cell phone on his nightstand but seemed unable to rise off the bed to get it.

I took a step toward him at the same moment the sheet slid off him.

My eyes caught on what should have been the space between the two men, except there wasn't any space. Their bodies were fused together from just below the shoulder to the hip. They wore what must have been custom-made underwear because it stretched around both of them and had three leg holes instead of two, with a leg coming out of each hole.

I stood there, frozen. I couldn't possibly be seeing what I

thought I was seeing.

"My doctors!" the live man yelled again. "Please help me. We have to call my doctors or I will die too!"

I looked at Nick. He had his phone to his ear and was repeating the street name, presumably to a 9-1-1 operator.

I wasn't sure the emergency medical technicians would know any better than I did how to handle this situation.

I ran over to the nightstand and picked up the cell phone. It had the charger attached, but it wouldn't come on. I checked the wall below and found the end of the charger on the floor instead of in the power outlet.

I plugged the charger in, turned the phone on and held it toward the yelling man. Still in a reclining position, he snatched it from my hand, then pressed and swiped at the screen with his shaking fingers. He put the phone to his ear.

"Dr. Duarte! It's me, Teodor. My brother's dead... Grigore... He's dead!"

Teodor—pronounced "Tay-oh-dor" by my client and by Teodor himself—was the man I was supposed to be checking up on.

He listened, still on his back because he had no other option.

"Okay... yes..." He looked up at me. "Yes, doctor, there are people here." Something seemed to dawn on him. His eyes grew wild. "Murderers!" he cried. His gaze darted from me to Nick. "Murderers!"

Nick's eyebrows rose in surprise, but he turned away, plugged his spare ear, and continued talking to the 9-1-1 operator. I stepped over to the bed and reached for the phone. Teodor tried to hold it farther away, but he was nearly immobile, still held down by his brother's very dead weight. I wedged a knee on the bed, wrapping my arm around the crook of his until it gave way.

When I got a grasp on the cell, I peeled his fingers off it.

"Doctor?" I said.

"Yes, who is this?" A woman's voice asked.

"This is Rika Martín. I'm a private investigator. There was kind of a mix-up." I couldn't divulge information about my client and there was a mix-up since Teodor wasn't supposed to be here. "We thought this house was empty until Teodor woke up and started screaming," I continued. "The man, um, *attached* to him is dead. There's a screwdriver in his eye."

"All right," she said so calmly I figured she must have spent a lot of time in the emergency room. "I'm getting into an ambulance, right now. It's Geary Ambulance Service. Teodor lives a few blocks from the hospital. Don't let anyone else pick him up. If they take him to a different hospital, he won't make it."

"Okay, no problem," I said. "Anything else?"

"Yes. Hold on to Teodor's phone until I get there so we don't lose touch."

"Alright. Is there anything we should do for him...them?"

"Are they losing a lot of blood?"

"Not a lot," I replied. There was some blood, but I'd seen Alberto Viera's crime scene photos a couple of weeks ago, and I knew what a lot of blood looked like.

"Okay, don't remove the object from his eye," she said. "And don't let anyone else remove it either."

"Grigore!" Teodor cried. Then he shouted several words in another language. I couldn't understand the meaning, but the emotion was clear. I'd never heard anyone sound more distraught.

"We're on the way," Dr. Duarte said into my ear. "Please comfort him and don't let him move around too much."

I sat on the edge of the bed near Teodor. "Dr. Duarte is on her way," I said. "She wants you to be still."

"*Fratele meu*," he said in a language I wished I could understand. "*Fratele meu*..." It turned into a chant, the same two words over and over. Teodor's eyes were wild, and I wasn't sure if he was grieving or trying to say something to me.

"I don't understand," I said gently. "I'm sorry."

"My brother," he rasped in a voice that already sounded exhausted. "My brother." He closed his eyes and lay still as tears poured down his temples.

I heard sirens outside and ran to the front door. Two squad cars had stopped out front. An ambulance came screeching up at the same time as an unmarked police car. They were coming from opposite directions and for a split second, I thought they might collide.

A woman in a white coat, who I assumed was the doctor, rushed out of the ambulance. Detectives Hertz and Winchell began getting out of their car at a leisurely pace.

*Really?* Out of all the detectives in L.A., it had to be the ones who tried to put my father away for a crime he didn't commit?

They looked the same as the last time I saw them, both wearing dark slacks and blazers, Hertz with her blonde hair pulled back in a no-nonsense ponytail, Winchell with dark hair, cut short in a military buzz.

Maybe it was a result of my experiences with them, but the pair always looked shifty to me. I wouldn't trust them to get a cat out of a tree, much less with a murder scene as unusual as this one.

The presumed doctor hurried toward me, a pleasant yellow blouse and brown slacks under her coat. The sun glinted off the small gold cross that hung around her neck. "I'm Dr. Duarte," she said quickly. "Where's Teodor?"

I pointed inside. "In the back of the house," I said as a couple of other people in scrubs jumped out of the same ambulance carrying medical equipment. "I'm Rika, if there's anything you need."

"Thanks," she said as she started to move past me.

Unfortunately, the dirty duo had made it onto the porch. Detective Hertz placed a hand on the doctor's shoulder and pulled her backward.

"This is a murder scene," she said. "We can't have people

traipsing through it."

"My patient is in there!" she cried.

"Look, miss..." Winchell began.

"Doctor!" Dr. Duarte and I said in unison. I had a feeling it wasn't the first time she'd had to remind people she was a doctor. She was a Hispanic female who might be middle-aged but still looked youngish and attractive. Men probably underestimated her all the time.

"Okay, *Doctor*," Winchell said mockingly. "This is still a murder scene and we can't have people mucking it up."

"There's a live man in there!" I said.

"And he'll die if I don't get to him right away," Dr. Duarte added.

"Oh," Winchell said. "Then be careful not to disturb the other body."

"That's not possible." Dr. Duarte moved to pass by, but Winchell grabbed her arm, stopping her again.

I heard Teodor screaming inside the house, and I'd had about enough. Seriously, if it had been left up to Hertz and Winchell, my father would be in prison and his former sous chef's killer would never have gone to jail.

I don't know why I thought my five-four-and-a-half-inch self could take on the LAPD, but I made meaningful eye contact with the doctor as I threw myself against Detective Winchell.

It worked a little too well. I'd expected to shove him over a bit to make a hole big enough for the slim doctor to rush through. Instead, there was a domino effect. My body smashed into Detective Winchell's. Detective Winchell's body slammed into Detective Hertz. And all three of us fell, a pile of tangled arms and legs.

Jeez, if there were two people in L.A. I did *not* want to have an accidental threesome with, it was Hertz and Winchell.

Winchell and I got up. Hertz shrieked and at least five different expletives rushed from her mouth.

*Uh-oh.* I'd forgotten about the cactus.

# CHAPTER TWO

**Rika**

A few minutes later, I watched Nick emerge from the door, helping to carry one of the two stretchers. He, Dr. Duarte, and the hospital people who'd come with her had to move slowly as they attempted to keep the stretchers side-by-side with one twin on each. Grigore was covered with a sheet, but it had slid down enough to expose the top of his hair which was dark brown—identical to his brother's.

I would like to have helped, but I was sitting in the back seat of the unmarked cop car as Detective Winchell brushed dirt off his slacks and a young male medic from the second ambulance—the one sent by 9-1-1—plucked cactus needles from Detective Hertz's ass with a large pair of tweezers.

She was only a few feet away from me, and after every "Ouch! Dammit!" she'd twist her head and give me a dirty look.

I hadn't meant to knock her into it, I swear. That part was just a happy accident.

A nurse was carrying an IV bag that had already been attached to Teodor's arm by a needle. The doctor was talking quickly on the phone as she boarded the ambulance behind the stretcher.

As the doors closed and the ambulance drove away, Nick glanced around the front yard.

"Nick!" I called through the crack in the window the detectives had allowed me.

Nick turned and squinted in my direction. When he saw me, he didn't seem the least bit surprised. He threw me a chin lift, then approached the detectives. "You've got my partner in your car," he told Detective Winchell.

Winchell straightened and glared at Nick. "She assaulted an officer of the law."

"She's ninety pounds soaking wet."

I definitely weighed more than ninety pounds. In fact, I was nearly ten pounds over the weight I wanted to be. But if Nick thought I only weighed ninety pounds, did that mean I could get a Krispy Kreme on the way home? Finding a half-dead set of conjoined twins and getting arrested was pretty stressful, but nothing that couldn't be fixed by a jelly doughnut or twelve.

"Size doesn't excuse her from obeying the law." Detective Winchell's face was tight, his eyes narrowed. He was still pissed at us for solving Alberto Viera's murder, which was ridiculous. We couldn't help it if we were smart and resourceful while he and his partner were idiots.

Detective Hertz sent a furious glance in our direction, just as the EMT was about to extract another needle.

He pulled.

"Fuck!" Hertz yelled as she turned, lightning-fast, and slapped the EMT in the face. He lifted his palm to his injured cheek, his expression resembling that of a kicked puppy.

Detective Hertz rolled her eyes and said, "Pass that on to her! It was her fault!" She pointed at me, and the EMT's eyes followed. Now she, Detective Winchell and the EMT were staring at me accusingly.

*Damn it!* I was going to jail. If I'd known this would happen, I'd have picked up some scary temporary tattoos, including a couple of teardrops for my cheek.

I always heard prison gangs divided themselves by ethnicity. Were there Colombian gangs in California prisons? Maybe I should pretend to be Mexican because I wasn't going to pass for Asian and definitely wouldn't make the cut for the Aryan Brotherhood. Or, I guess, in women's prison, it would be a sisterhood, which sounded kind of nice, if you took off the Aryan part.

Nick looked at Detective Winchell then Detective Hertz. His brows squeezed together as he watched the medic grasp another cactus needle with his tweezers.

Nick's lips twitched once before he got them under control. His eyes shifted back to Winchell. "Do you really want to go in front of the judge for this? Because the men they just took away in the ambulance are Siamese twins—"

"Conjoined!" I called from inside. "They're called 'conjoined twins,' nowadays."

Nick flicked his eyes at me, and I realized I'd interrupted something it was not in my best interest to interrupt.

I pulled my lips in to show him they were sealed and I wouldn't be adding any more commentary.

At least until I was out of this car.

"As I was saying," he gave me one more *Are you sure you're not going to interrupt me again?* side-glance. "Those men are conjoined twins, and she was trying to save Theodore's life." I squelched the urge to correct his pronunciation of the name Teodor. "Do you want to be the assholes who were getting in her way?"

Detective Winchell's eyes widened at the thought. He looked like he'd changed his mind already. Detective Hertz, not so much.

Of course, she still had at least three more needles that needed to be extricated from her ass, so...

"Fine," Nick said. "It's been a few months since I was in a

courtroom. This will be all over the news." He shrugged. "It'll be fun."

Both detectives stared at him threateningly. Nick didn't look the least bit threatened. He folded his arms on his chest and leaned against the car as if he had all the time in the world.

Finally, Detective Winchell turned and opened my door. "We're letting you off with a warning, this time," he said. "In the future, don't try to interfere with a police investigation."

Nick pulled himself away from the car. "What about saving lives?" he asked. "Should she keep trying to save lives?"

Neither detective answered.

"Oh, wait. Wrong people to ask. If she saves too many, you're out of a job." He shrugged. "But there's always vice."

Detective Hertz shot him a death glare. Detective Winchell unlocked my handcuffs and it hit me that, after living a quiet life for most of my twenty-four years, I could now say I'd been handcuffed twice in the last eight months.

Although it was a scary thing for me to be handcuffed and thrown in a cop car, I didn't want to give these two the satisfaction of knowing that.

I plastered on my biggest smile. "Thanks, you guys!" I said in the same tone I might use to thank people for having me over for dinner, but more sarcastic. "I'll see you around."

"Yeah..." Detective Hertz said, her eyes ice cold. "Watch your back."

~

**Nick Owen**

No one left at the scene seemed to know which hospital the twins had been taken to. I used my GPS and started driving toward the nearest one while Rika called to make sure we were going to the hospital Dr. Duarte had come from.

After several transfers, she got confirmation.

At the next light, I glanced over and noticed something unusual peeking out the sleeve at her wrist. "What is that?" I asked.

She looked down as if she'd forgotten what was on her arm. "Oh!" She brightened. "It's from Assassin's Creed, the video game."

"Yeah, I've played it," I replied.

Her brown eyes glowed with excitement as she pulled her sleeve up to reveal the leather arm guard and metal blade on her arm. "The geek site sent it to me to review." With her left index finger, she pushed a button and the blade snapped forward. "Cool, huh?"

"Dangerous, is more like it," I said.

"It's not even real metal." She ran her finger along the edge of the blade. "It's for cosplay at the gamer conventions. But doesn't it look great?"

Truth be told, I didn't get "cosplay," and I didn't think it was safe to go around wearing any fake weapon. For one thing, it could get her shot by the cops. "The detectives didn't take that away from you?"

"They didn't even notice it." She shook her head. "I don't understand how those two keep their jobs."

"Regardless, if you're serious about your new job, I think you should stop playing around with fake weapons and get a license to carry a real one."

"A real knife?"

"A real gun. You've been shot at and attacked several times since I met you. You're a tiny little thing." Her eyes narrowed at the word "tiny," but this was too important to let go. "And your geek toys aren't going to do you any good when it counts."

"Excuse me?" she said testily. "One of my 'geek' toys saved you from men with guns just a couple of weeks ago. And stop calling me 'tiny' and 'little'. They're redundant anyway."

I'd noticed she seemed to have a thing about her size, like it bugged her that she wasn't taller. Personally, I didn't understand how she could look in the mirror every morning and see anything but perfection. Sure, she was no Amazon, but she had the perfect little body. Perky breasts I couldn't wait to get my hands on. A nicely rounded ass—just the right size as far as I was concerned. And I kind of liked how her hands and feet were so slender and delicate compared to mine.

Damn, I wanted to take her back to my hotel room and—

"It's right there."

"What?" Had I accidentally driven her to my hotel while I was daydreaming?

She leaned forward and checked my face for signs of intoxication. "The hospital?" she said. "Where they've taken the half-dead set of conjoined twins?"

Yeah, when she said it like that, it seemed ridiculous they'd slipped my mind, but that's what being around Rika did to me.

I parked as close as I could to the emergency room entrance.

Once we got inside, we were directed to a waiting room on the fourth floor near the O.R. where surgeons were working to separate the dead twin from the live one.

We found a machine and bought coffee. It was the consistency of mud and tasted like it was cut with mulch.

Rika made herself comfortable on a gray vinyl couch. I wasn't ready to sit yet, too keyed up from the morning we'd had, and not the least bit okay with all the information she'd withheld from me. While I considered how I wanted to handle this, I watched a bricklayer spread mortar, then carefully place a brick on top of the ones he'd laid before.

From this vantage point, it looked like the new wing of the hospital we'd caught a glimpse of on the way in was nearly done.

Funny, when I decided being an attorney wasn't for me, I'd considered construction work. I didn't need to work for money, but a guy had to do something with his time and construction just seemed like a simpler, more fulfilling job. At least, when you were done, you'd have something you could point to and feel proud of.

But that wouldn't keep me around Rika every day. I looked down at her. "Do you want to start from the beginning and tell me what the hell is going on?"

"Just a second. I'm trying to reach Erissa."

She inhaled deeply and I realized, from up here, I could see right into her V-neck "Hermione Granger for President" long-sleeved t-shirt.

The shirt was charcoal gray, her bra cups white, but my eyes stuck on the tops of her breasts as they rose and fell with her breathing.

I felt a twinge below. Clearly, there were parts of me who didn't care how annoyed I was with her.

To avoid a full-scale hard-on, I averted my eyes and recalled the TV show the Delacruz women were watching a couple of days ago when I walked into Rika's grandmother's house to pick up "my" dog Gucci. The TV surgeons were fixing a woman with botched breast implants. Rika made room on the couch for me, but I declined, saying I didn't want to watch.

"It's a show about boobs," Rika's Aunt Madi said, the typical mischievous look in her eye. "What guy wouldn't want to watch that?"

"Any interest I have in fake boobs is of the post-op variety," I replied.

Madi was always busting my chops, but I liked her. I liked all of Rika's family. I was never one hundred percent sure where I stood with them, though, especially her Aunt Margo and her grandmother.

Since I'd come to help Rika find her dad a few weeks ago, their attitude toward me had morphed from extreme suspicion to extreme gratitude with a light aftertaste of suspicion, which Rika claimed was nothing personal and all about their experiences with men.

She expelled a frustrated breath, which reminded me what we were talking about. "I met Erissa in a Starbucks," she said. "She was complaining to the barista that she suspected her boyfriend was sleeping around whenever she left town, but she loved him and didn't want to accuse him if it wasn't true. She was afraid she was being paranoid. I gave her a card."

"Okay..." I prompted. I was having a hard time visualizing Teodor having sex with a woman while his Siamese—excuse me, *conjoined*—twin was right there in the bed. Wouldn't being conjoined automatically make all your sexual experiences a threesome with your sibling?

I grimaced at the thought. I didn't have a brother, but I had a little sister, and, in my mind, she not only would never engage in a threesome, but was also still a virgin, despite having been married and divorced.

"So, a few days later, she called me," Rika continued. "She's been letting her fiancée Teodor Vatamanu stay in the other side of the duplex she owns. She wanted to make sure he wasn't just using her for a place to live and a green card."

"Are you saying the fact that he had another person, literally joined at the hip to him, didn't come up in your conversation?"

"You'd think it would, wouldn't you?" Rika said. "But she didn't mention it."

"And how was this little escapade supposed to go down this morning?"

"She told Teodor she had to go out of town. He was supposed to leave around six this morning for a medical procedure and be gone all day. She wanted me to check for anything suspicious."

"Do we know what the medical procedure was?"

"I didn't ask," Rika said. "It seemed too intrusive."

"And digging through his belongings didn't?"

"That's different. We were getting paid to do that as professionals."

I shook my head slowly, then sat on a set of *conjoined* plastic

23

chairs at a right angle to the couch she was on. Now that I'd confirmed she was also in the dark about the twin situation, I went back to the other issue at hand. "I still don't understand what possessed you to have business cards made when we don't even have a business address yet."

"We're going to need to earn money to pay for the office space."

"Not really," I replied.

She huffed out an annoyed breath. We'd been having this argument for the past two weeks, ever since I agreed to be her partner.

We'd hired a commercial real estate person to find us space to lease and he'd shown us some nice offices.

But Rika wouldn't have them, convinced we should start out in a dive and work our way up to the nicer place.

I didn't understand why it was necessary for her to suffer in a building with a questionable roof, questionable air conditioning and a dank smell when I had plenty of money for nicer digs.

For once, I didn't even know how to argue the point because I'd never partnered with a woman who wanted to spend time in a crappy place when she could have a fancy one.

Of course, the women I'd spent the most time with were my mom and my three ex-wives. Since I met Rika, I'd been coming to the realization that my past relationships didn't represent a sufficient cross-section of womankind. In fact, it concerned me that my tastes had been so limited. Made me wonder about myself.

"Help!" a woman screamed as she flung herself out of the elevator.

A young nurse with dark pigtails, who happened to be walking by, jerked, spilling pills out of the mini paper cup she was holding.

"Fuck!" she said before she caught herself. "Um, sorry." She looked at the panicked woman. "What can I do for you?"

"Where's my fiancée!" the woman asked. "Where's Teodor?

Teodor Vatamanu?" she added as if she thought the place was teeming with Teodors.

So, this was the girlfriend who hired Rika.

"Oh!" the nurse said, her eyes widening as she realized which patient the woman was asking after. "He's in surgery. It may be all day. You know his brother has, um, passed?"

"I know. Dr. Washington called me. I just want to know if Teodor is going to make it!"

"I'm sorry," the nurse said with a shrug. "He just got here a half hour ago. Even the doctors won't know enough at this point to give you an update."

The woman's shoulders dropped and she stood there, breathing hard, seemingly at a loss as to what to do next.

"Erissa," Rika called.

The woman turned around. When her eyes focused on Rika, she rushed over.

"Dr. Washington told me there were people who called the ambulance. Was that you?"

"Yes, it was us," Rika said. "Erissa, this is Nick Owen, my partner. Nick, this is Erissa Fisher, Teodor's fiancée."

I reached out and she laid a cold hand in mine. "Wish we could meet under better circumstances," I said. "I'm sorry for your loss."

"Loss?" Her lips quivered and she blinked faster. "Did you hear something? Is Teodor dead?"

"No," I replied. "I was referring to your future brother-in-law."

"Oh." She breathed a sigh of relief. "We didn't get along. He was just holding Teodor back, anyway."

I'd never seen anyone react so coldly to the death of a person she knew. Erissa Fisher had just jumped to the top of my suspect list.

*Suspect list.* Huh, I was getting as bad as Rika. This wasn't a case we needed to solve. We'd been hired to investigate a cheater,

25

not a murder. But it was hard not to be curious when you actually found the body.

"Why wasn't he already at the hospital?" Erissa asked. "He should have been here much earlier."

Rika gave her a sympathetic shrug. "Maybe he forgot to set his alarm?" she offered.

"But this was so important to him," Erissa said. "I can't imagine..."

"Wait," Rika said. "I just remembered. Teodor tried to use his phone when he woke up and the charger wasn't plugged into the wall outlet. Did he use his phone as his alarm?"

Erissa was nodding before Rika finished. "Yeah. That explains it," she replied.

I wasn't sure how Rika felt, but I was uncomfortable hanging around here. Sure, we were the ones who rescued the twins, but we'd gone there to rifle through Teodor's things. I wasn't totally okay with it when he was a possible cheater. Now that his twin was dead and he was fighting for his life on an operating room table, I felt downright smarmy.

Rika didn't seem to share my discomfort. "Do you have any idea what might have happened?" she asked.

"No." Erissa shook out her hands like she was trying to rid herself of nervous energy. "I was staying at a friend's house because I had told Teodor I'd be out of town..." She cocked her head. "Wait, I thought you were there."

"Yes and no," Rika said. "We walked in right before Teodor woke up and started screaming. We didn't witness the murder."

"Oh," Erissa said. "Yeah, I guess that makes sense." She seemed kind of bewildered, but I figured it was normal to be dazed and confused under these circumstances.

"So, Grigore?" Rika said. "Was that the victim's name?"

"Yes. Grigore Vatamanu."

"Was there anyone who might have wanted to hurt him? Did he have enemies?"

Erissa shrugged. "He didn't have a lot of friends. Grigore seems shy when you first meet him, but, once you get to know him, he's kind of an ass... I mean *was* kind of an ass to me. He wanted me out of Teodor's life." She pressed her palm to her forehead. "I guess you're not supposed to badmouth a dead person. It's just hard to wrap my head around."

I nodded. Hell, I was having a hard time believing what we'd witnessed this morning. I'd never even seen a set of conjoined twins, except on TV, much less a half-murdered set.

"I have to eat something," Erissa said. "I'm diabetic." She thrust out a hand and steadied herself on a chair. I reached out and put a stabilizing hand on her back as I grabbed her elbow.

At the same time, I thought I saw a strange look come over Rika's face, but it was in my peripheral vision, so I wasn't sure what it was about. Not that I normally knew what Rika was thinking. Or any woman, for that matter.

While holding Erissa steady, I glanced around and found the sign I was looking for.

# CHAPTER THREE

**Rika**

Nick reached for his wallet. "I can get you something from a vending machine," he said. "Will that work?"

Typical Nick. Always eager to rescue a damsel in distress. I examined Erissa more closely.

*Hmmm...* Until now, I hadn't thought about how tall and blonde she was.

Totally Nick's type.

Nick gave me an *I'll be right back* chin lift and went to get directions from a nurse. While he was being Erissa's glycemic knight in shining armor, I decided I'd take advantage of her weakened state and ask her more questions.

Considering the major fact she'd left out of Teodor's story when she hired me, namely that he had another whole person attached to him, I didn't trust her to tell me the truth once she had her wits about her again.

"So... surely you can think of someone whose been angry with one of the twins." I figured it would be easy to confuse identical twins when they were sleeping. Maybe the killer was dyslexic and had intended to kill Teodor.

"No," Erissa said. "Neither of them had any real enemies. Of course, it could have been a psycho fan."

"Fan?" Nick repeated as he walked up and handed Erissa a Snickers and a cup of water.

"Yeah. They're performers in a circus," she explained. "It's called Cirque de Sorbet. It's kind of a cross between a regular circus, Cirque du Soleil and a comedy show. Their whole family does this flying contortionist act."

Nick sat in the same place he'd been before. "Even the twins?" he asked.

"Oh, yeah, they were a big hit. They've been doing this since they were babies. They can—I mean could, I guess— make all kinds of interesting shapes with their body."

I tried to imagine the two men contorting their shared body to the applause of a crowd, but I couldn't get past the image of Teodor, virtually immobile on the bed, and the screwdriver in Grigore's eye.

I closed my eyes in a prolonged blink and took a moment to push that image aside for the time being. I couldn't allow myself to be overly empathetic if I was going to be a good private investigator.

Besides, I needed to keep my head clear and figure out exactly what Erissa had involved me in. In hindsight, she'd acted pretty sketchy, not even mentioning the unusual situation her supposed boyfriend was in. Maybe I should go back to what started all this. "So, you're dating Teodor seriously?"

Erissa nodded. "We're planning to get married, just like I told you."

"But you thought he might be seeing someone else," I pointed out. "Do you think that person could have gotten angry at Teodor or Grigore and—"

"No," she said. "There isn't a person. I mean there could be, but there's no one specific I know of."

"Then why did you hire me?"

Erissa blew out a frustrated breath. "Look, I've been burned before and I swore I'd never be an easy mark again. Teodor had wanted to live in the U.S. for a long time. His visa is temporary, and he doesn't have a lot of money. I'm not mega-rich, but I am an American with rental properties in L.A. and Vegas. He's from a poor country I've never been to and has never made a lot of money. His dad kept a tight rein on the contracts with the circus and whatever money they made. I just needed reassurance."

Okay, maybe that made sense. I'd never owned property or had much money, but I didn't doubt that, if I had, I might have been easy prey to a charming opportunist. Honestly, after feeling like a romantic reject for years, I was a little too grateful that Brandtt wanted me. The more time I had to consider that relationship, the more embarrassed I was that I'd fallen for him.

And, from what I'd seen, smart women make dumb relationship decisions all the time.

Regardless, this situation was so unusual, I just had to ask, "Did you know both of them...intimately?"

Out of the corner of my eye, I saw Nick's torso jerk forward. His lips parted.

That jackass was tempted to jump in and save her from answering my question! I wasn't sure if I was more jealous that he had the urge to shelter another woman from me, or more incensed that he would throw a monkey wrench into my murder investigation, official or not.

"Do you mean was I screwing both of them?" Erissa asked.

I winced at the word and shrugged.

"Jeez, if I had a million bucks for every time I've been asked that question."

We watched her, waiting for her answer.

"No!" she said loudly. "I'm not some weirdo with a thing for circus freaks! I fell in love!"

"Sorry," Nick said in his calming voice. "My partner was just—"

*Oh, my God!* Was he apologizing for me?

*Jerk!*

Erissa raised her hands in a conciliatory gesture. "I know," she said. "Everyone is curious, but the two of them were used to doing their own thing, you know, tuning out each other's activities."

"How is that possible?" I asked. "I mean, while you and Teodor were, um, *intimate*?" Apparently, "intimate" was the only word I knew for the act that didn't sound completely out of line under the circumstances.

"Grigore was usually reading. In fact, I'm pretty sure he was either gay or asexual. I was all over his brother, inches away from him, and he never even got a hard-on." She seemed kind of insulted.

Nick tilted his head and his lips turned up slightly. "That's hard to believe," he said flirtatiously. Maybe he was flirting to lower Erissa's guard, but I didn't like it one bit.

She smiled weakly at him. "Well, it wasn't going to be a problem much longer, anyway."

"Why was that?" he asked.

"Because of the separation. Actually..." she seemed to be thinking aloud, "this was the ideal time for the murder to happen." Her coarse words seemed to dawn on her. "I mean if it was going to happen at all."

Nick and I both leaned in. "What do you mean?" I prompted.

"The separation was already scheduled for this morning. The plans had been made. The team of doctors was in place."

My heart beat faster. I heard Nick's breathing change as he straightened. "You're saying that the twins were scheduled for a separation surgery this morning?"

She nodded.

The information I'd come across in the past about conjoined twins began to surface in my mind. "When one conjoined twin dies, the other typically dies within hours," I said. "So, if the murder had happened any other night, both would probably be dead by now."

Erissa nodded again. "That's why I was saying it was a good thing... I mean, not a good thing, but at least the surgeons were already here and ready."

Nick and I looked at each other. I widened my eyes at him. He gave me a subtle nod, assuring me we were on the same page. I was pretty sure we held the same opinion about convenient coincidences.

"Who all knew about the scheduled separation?" I asked.

She shrugged. "Lots of people. Doctors, nurses, hospital administrators..."

"No," I said. "Who else besides you and the medical personnel?"

"Like I said, lots of people. They had a documentary crew following the procedure for the Med Channel. There were a couple of articles and a few mentions on TV news, but the press didn't cover it as much as they would have because Teodor and Grigore had signed a contract with the Med Channel and weren't allowed to give television interviews. Oh, and there's everyone at the circus, of course."

My mind replayed the information again, trying to make sense of it. Who would benefit from killing one of the twins the night before they were to be separated? Wouldn't it have been safer to wait until they were separated and kill Grigore when he was alone? What if Teodor had awakened during the murder?

Unless the plan was to murder him too. If the murderer knew anything about conjoined twins, he or she might think two birds had been killed by one stone. Or one screwdriver, in this case.

Nick crossed his arms, which made his biceps bulge. A work-inappropriate tingle wiggled through me. I tore my eyes away and found that Erissa had noticed too. Her eyes were trailing down Nick's body.

Caustic liquid—hot and undoubtedly green—shot through to

my extremities. I imagined pressing Erissa's eyes back into their sockets with my thumbs.

Then, I remembered we hadn't been hired to solve a murder. We—and, more importantly, Nick—had no more reason to spend time with Erissa, and I needed to go out and hustle up more jobs. We probably weren't getting paid for this one. As interesting as this scenario was, we needed to extricate ourselves from it. "Well, I'm sorry for the way things worked out," I began.

"Did you find any evidence before he woke up?" Erissa asked.

Nick's head jerked back. He was clearly appalled that she was thinking of anything other than her fiancée's life and his brother's death right now. "As in, evidence of another woman?" he asked.

"Yeah." She nodded.

"We'd just walked in when he woke up and started screaming," I replied. "But we were counting on the house being empty. We wouldn't have stayed and looked around once we realized it was occupied, even if he'd kept sleeping."

"Oh, sure," she said distractedly. "That makes sense. Sorry, I can't always think straight when my blood sugar is off."

Nick dipped his head toward the Snickers in her hand. She looked at it as if she'd never seen it before.

Okay, maybe she was in shock rather than being the heartless bitch I thought she was. She tore the wrapper off the candy bar, took a big bite, closed her eyes and chewed very slowly.

"We should be going," I said. "Is there anyone I can call for you?"

"Oh," she replied. "No. I'll call his family as soon as I finish this." She lifted the candy bar.

"You mean *their* family," Nick said, trying to remind her that there was one man dead and another whose life was hanging in the balance.

She swallowed the bite. "Hm? Oh, yes, of course." She bit another chunk off the Snickers then set it on her thigh.

I fought the urge to snatch it up and eat the half she hadn't. I hoped she didn't throw it in the garbage. It was a travesty to waste perfectly good chocolate. No one could ever convince me otherwise.

Nick stood. "Okay... We'll get going then."

I was torn. I did feel kind of bad about leaving her all alone with questionable blood sugar, even if she hadn't seemed like the greatest person today, or when she hired me, for that matter. But she wasn't our responsibility.

I stood and stepped toward her, wondering if she'd expect a handshake or a hug.

"No," she said, holding a hand over her mouth to cover her chewing.

"No?" I repeated.

She put her free hand up in a "wait" sign, swallowed and took a quick sip of water. "Don't go yet. I want to hire you to investigate this."

Nick sucked in a slow breath. "I don't feel good about rifling through this man's receipts after what he's been through," he said.

Erissa shook her head. "No. I want you to investigate the murder."

Nick and I exchanged surprised glances. "You do?" I asked.

She nodded.

"But I thought you didn't particularly like Grigore," Nick pointed out. "Why would you pay us to investigate his death?"

"Because," she said. "My husband was murdered a few years ago. I was arrested for it, but there wasn't enough evidence and the district attorney wouldn't go forward with the case. The cops claimed they had no other leads and left it unsolved. The homicide detectives were pissed. They're going to come after me for this."

~

**Rika**

When we got into Nick's fancy black Ford pickup truck he'd ordered shipped from his house in Bolo the same day he agreed to stay, he didn't start it up right away. From the corner of my eye, I could see him watching me.

I'd asked Erissa how her husband had been killed to make sure it wasn't some sort of stabbing or impaling, or any tool-related death. She'd said "poisoning," which sounded even more like an inside job to me.

"I thought you'd be happier," Nick said. Apparently, his attempt to read my mind by staring at my brain had failed.

"Why?"

He hung his wrist over the steering wheel and knitted his brow into a quizzical frown. "Isn't this what you wanted? A big case to solve?"

Of course, I'd wanted a case, especially an interesting one like this, but he wasn't seeing the big picture. "If the killer turns out to be our client, what do you think the chances are we're getting paid?"

"Why would she hire us to investigate if she killed him?"

"I don't know. People do a lot of wacky things. And if the cops believed she killed her husband, there's a good chance she already had at least one murder under her belt before Grigore. They say it gets easier every time."

"You were suspected of murder in Bolo and you were innocent," Nick said. "The LAPD suspected your dad of murder and he was innocent."

Jeez, it was annoying when he used logic to point out I was jumping to unsubstantiated conclusions.

I hated feeling illogical. For years, I'd wanted to be like Mr. Spock from Star Trek so I could have no feelings, and act like a robot, no matter what the other kids threw at my head.

I blew out an annoyed breath. "I'm just saying this might not be the ideal case to spend time on, considering the client could be arrested and we'll probably never see our money."

"No big deal," Nick said. "Either way, it'll be good practice."

"I didn't start a business to work for free."

"I just meant that we're not under the gun. I've got it covered."

But the "it" he was talking about included a salary Nick insisted I take so I could quit my old job. I'd regretted agreeing to his proposal within twenty-four hours.

The situation made me incredibly uncomfortable. I didn't want to be another woman Nick took care of. I was *not* his helpless mother, or one of his gold-digging diva wives. It was bad enough that I hadn't had any choice but to live at his house and eat his food last summer.

"It could be good publicity," he added.

He was just trying to pacify me. We both knew most private investigators did their work quietly in the background and didn't get publicity from the cases they worked.

I was staring at the dashboard wondering if this whole partnership thing was going to backfire on me and make me lose Nick for good. We seemed to have very different ideas about how to run a business.

"Paprika..." he said. He lay a hand on my shoulder and squeezed. That little bit of physical contact made me want to lean over the console and rest my head on his chest, but I didn't. "There's no reason to be stressed. We're starting the P.I. firm you always wanted. We can afford a practice case or two."

*He* could afford a practice case or two. He could afford a lot of things, but I earned my own money, whether I was living at my Lita's house, in my own apartment, as I did the first year I was dating Brandtt, or in his apartment in New York. I paid for my own car, my own gas. I bought groceries.

At Brandtt's, I'd insisted on paying the utilities. In fact, for several months after I left New York, I got the utility bill along with my other forwarded mail. I was going to leave it unpaid as revenge for the douchy way Brandtt had dumped me but worried it could affect my credit rating. Instead, I informed the utilities I wasn't living there anymore and had everything turned off.

Brandtt, who hadn't had the decency to break up with me in person, text, email, or even Facebook—he let his doorman do it—called me and left a panicked message, believing I was in control of getting everything turned back on.

I didn't reply and let him figure it out for himself. I enjoyed imagining the look on his face when he realized he couldn't watch himself on *The Real Millionaire Bachelors of New York* that night and live tweet about it to his fans.

I couldn't help the evil grin that spread over my face every time I thought about it.

"Rika?" Nick said.

Oh, crap. He'd seen my evil grin.

"Yeah?" I replied, trying to remember what we were talking about.

"Do you want to take the case or not? Unless we have other clients beating down our door, I don't see how it could hurt."

I supposed he was right about that. We didn't have any other clients right now.

Erissa's image popped back into my head.

*Could* it hurt? What if her combination of long legs, blonde hair, and need to be saved from another murder accusation made her irresistible to Nick?

*If he's led astray by every blonde he meets in L.A., you'll never keep him anyway*, an all too perceptive voice whispered from somewhere in the back of my mind.

"I'll text her that we're taking the case," I said. "But I don't want to question her again until we've spoken to the twins' friends and family, so we have a better idea of who we're dealing with." I straightened. "Can we go to Lita's now? I'm starving and she said she was making *empanadas* this morning."

His gaze caught mine and held it. I realized he was trying to read my thoughts again and I shifted my eyes away, afraid he might develop some of those psychic abilities I didn't believe in. I didn't want him to know how jealous I was over him.

Finally, Nick quit trying to figure me out, for the moment anyway, and started up the truck.

# CHAPTER FOUR

**Nick Owen**

On the way to her grandmother's house, I was thinking about Rika. I'd been getting a lot of mixed messages from her since we'd solved the murder of her dad's sous chef a couple of weeks back.

I wanted to chalk it up to her being upset that her dad went back to Colombia. Just like before, he didn't really have a choice. The Microtologists had pulled strings to get him a quick work permit, but now that they were in jail and the religion was basically defunct, he didn't have a legal way to stay in the country. In Colombia, however, he was well-known and respected. He'd made a couple of calls and got immediate job offers.

It sucked that Rika had not only lost her mother young, but kept losing her dad, over and over.

Really, I had no idea if that's why she'd been running so hot and cold. I was grasping for straws because I didn't want it to be about me and her.

When we were together, I often felt like there was something solid between us. Mentally. Emotionally. And physically, though, something had always held us back from fully exploring that one.

In Texas, she was my client, therefore off limits, plus, there was the fact that the ink wasn't dry on my divorce yet. Then, we were finding her dad and proving he wasn't guilty of murder.

And now?

I wasn't sure how to proceed with her. Sometimes, when I put my hand on the small of her back as we walked into a building, I felt her relax, like she did that first time in Bolo. Other times, my hand would accidentally brush her abdomen or her thigh and I'd feel her tense up like...

Well, I didn't know like what. I wasn't used to getting that reaction from women, and it didn't feel right to try anything more when her body seemed to be putting up a red light. Or at least a yellow one.

I just hoped she hadn't stuck me in that "friend zone" I'd always heard about.

Damn. I'd never been relegated to the friend zone with a woman I wanted to be with.

*Ever.*

As I pulled up in front of the house, I was distracted from my mulling by the ruckus outside.

"What's going on?" I asked Rika.

"I'm not sure," she replied.

Mrs. Delacruz, Rika's grandma, was on her front porch, gesturing wildly with whatever she was holding in her hands. When we got out of the truck, she was in the middle of a rapid-fire Spanish tirade directed at two young Hispanic men on the corner.

Gucci, the ditzy Maltese my ex was kind enough to dump on me, was standing next to her.

The second Mrs. Delacruz's yelling paused, Gucci started yapping like the two of them were some kind of trash-talking tag-team.

I noticed Rika's cousin Sofia, who often took care of Gucci, had tied a tiny pink and yellow bandana around my dog's neck.

While I was wholeheartedly against dogs wearing clothes, it was a small price to pay for the free dog-sitting.

Mrs. Delacruz started yelling again, making shooing motions with her hands. The men looked like shady characters, one with a long, nearly black ponytail, the other with his head shaved. But it wasn't that or the baggy jeans and the thick chain ponytail guy was wearing that made them suspicious looking as much as it was their general demeanor.

Let's just say, whatever Rika's grandmother was yelling about, I was pretty sure they were guilty of.

She was so caught up in the drama, she didn't notice we had arrived.

We walked toward her, but when we were only a few feet away, she drew one arm back and launched what I now recognized as a cooking pot at the duo.

It flew through the air and slammed into ponytail guy's shoulder. He jumped away, then turned toward the porch and started yelling back at Mrs. Delacruz in Spanish. I didn't know a lot of Spanish, but the words *bruja vieja* were definitely in there.

*Old witch. Uh-oh.* I was pretty sure she wouldn't take that insult lying down.

Her face turned from angry to infuriated and, although she was five feet tall and probably in her sixties, I'd never seen anything scarier.

She charged down the porch steps like a mini-rhino, Gucci at her heels.

"Lita!" Rika started after her.

"Stay out of this, Paprika," her grandmother said. Rika's feet stuttered to a stop as if they weren't sure whether to obey her grandmother or her better judgment.

"*Jou* want to sell *drogas* on my corner?" Mrs. Delacruz yelled, her voice suddenly reminiscent of Al Pacino in Scarface. "*Pues,* we'll see how you do it with no customers!" Then, she launched what she had in her other hand—a small cast-iron skillet—at the bald one. It hit him in the head.

That's when I started feeling like I was in a very strange dream. The pot was iffy, but how could Rika's grandma possibly have beaned a guy in the head with a cast-iron skillet from several yards away?

Her second victim was holding his head as a trickle of blood streamed down his cheek. "Fuck it, man!" he said. "I can get my shit somewhere else." He jumped into an ancient Ford Falcon and peeled out, squealing his tires as he went.

Mrs. Delacruz—Gucci still at her side—was advancing on the drug dealer, even though she was out of cookware. Both Rika and I sprinted toward the spot on the corner where the ne'er-do-well was holding his ground. We got there at the same time Rika's grandmother did.

Gucci grabbed the hem of his jeans with her tiny teeth, growling like she thought she was with the K-9 Unit of the LAPD.

The dealer started making kicking motions to get her off him and I was afraid she was about the get her tiny skull crushed. I took a step toward her to pick her up, but a cluster of ringlets streaked by me and Gucci was snatched away.

I turned and realized Sofia had done the snatching. She was fast. I didn't even know she'd come out of the house.

"Who kicks a four-pound dog?" she yelled. "Pick on somebody your own size!" Clutching Gucci to her body, she drew back her booted foot and smashed the toe of it into the dealer's shin. She moved away but kept watching from the edge of the yard.

The dealer screamed, grabbed at his shin, then recovered enough to yell a nasty string of epithets, including calling Sofia a bitch in two languages—I'm not bilingual, but everyone in South Texas knows the cuss words.

Sofia just smiled and gave the guy a one-shouldered shrug. Rika's grandmother, on the other hand, let out a roar and lunged toward the dealer.

We both stepped forward and reached out to stop her before she got hurt. "Lita!" Rika cried just as I said, "Mrs.—" But that was all I got out before she grabbed the guy by his ponytail, reached into the pocket of her pink velour sweatpants, pulled something out, and pressed her hand against her opponent's midsection.

A strange look passed over his face.

Had she stabbed him?

Whatever she'd done caused him to go down hard on the cement.

"Oh, my God!" Rika cried. "Lita, what did you do?"

I didn't see any blood or knives, thank God. I checked Mrs. Delacruz's hand.

She held it out proudly. "I zapped him!" she cried triumphantly. Her pronunciation of the word "zapped" as "zah-pehd" would have been cute if she wasn't holding a stun gun in her hand.

"Lita, when did you get that?" Rika asked.

"I saw it on TV a few years ago," Mrs. Delacruz replied nonchalantly. "I knew those *caraculos* would be back sooner or later!" She marched over to her cooking pot and picked it up, inspecting it for damage. I picked up the cast iron skillet. It was the smaller version that my mom used for cornbread, but it was still heavy.

I'd been good at sports my whole life, but those sports were played with balls that were meant to be thrown. I was sure I'd need quite a bit of practice to throw this unwieldy object at a target yards away with any accuracy.

"Were you aiming for his head?" I asked, wondering if it was a fluke.

"I aimed for both their heads," she replied. "I was just out of practice on the first one."

*Okay, then. Note to self: Do not, under any circumstances piss off Rika's grandmother.*

I knelt next to the bad guy to feel for a pulse, but before I managed it, his eyes fluttered. He lifted his hand to his head where it had hit the sidewalk and moaned.

"You see!" Mrs. Delacruz said to her victim. "People in grass houses shouldn't throw stones."

"Do you mean 'glass houses'?" I asked.

"No. He is selling grass to pay for his houses," she said. "It's a metaphor." She looked at me like I might not be as smart as she'd thought I was, then turned and walked back to her house, murmuring to herself, "Just because it is legal to buy now doesn't mean he can sell it on *my* street."

I looked at the baggies that had fallen from the guy's pocket, instantly deciding not to tell her he was selling meth, not weed. If she knew anything about the drug, she might come back and finish him off.

Rika stood on the sidewalk, a strange look on her face. "They were true," she said as if she couldn't believe it.

"Come again?" I picked up the baggies, planning to flush their contents down the nearest toilet.

"All the stories. I assumed they were exaggerated—at least the part about her actually hitting them." She stared at the corner as if replaying the incident in her head.

I tugged a strand of her hair. "Still not sure what you're talking about."

"Lita." She looked up at me. "People around here always swore that when the drug dealers and gang bangers tried to move into the neighborhood, years ago, she would step out her front door and throw whatever she had in her hands at them. Mr. Garza said he saw her hit one right between the eyes with a cast-iron skillet. I believed she threw things at them. I just thought the part about her hitting them was folklore."

"Well," I replied. "If you'd asked me if she could pull that off, I'd have said 'hell no,' but I saw it with my own eyes."

Rika looked toward the house, then back at the drug dealer who'd managed to get up, but was veering off to one side, stumbling as he tried to walk away. I'd never been stunned by a stun gun before, but I wondered if the dealer was on meth himself because that seemed awfully fast to be up on his feet.

"Maybe we should call an ambulance," I said.

"No ambulance," he slurred without turning around.

"No ambulance," Rika repeated quietly. "He doesn't want police showing up and my grandmother..."

I couldn't help but chuckle. "Yeah, she beaned him on a public sidewalk. He could press charges."

"He won't be pressing any charges," Rika said. "He won't want to have to explain why he was standing around on the corner. And I'm sure he doesn't want to be on the cops' radar any more than he may be already."

Sofia had turned to walk back to the house, but Gucci was looking over her shoulder, barking what I imagined to be "And don't come back," in Maltese to the perpetrator.

"What are you doing out there?" Mrs. Delacruz called from the door. "Lunch is ready. Come eat!" She said the last two sentences as if lunch was the biggest event of the day, and she hadn't just, literally, tried to knock some sense into a man forty years younger and nearly a foot taller than she was.

I put my arm around Rika's shoulders. "I don't know about you, but I'm going in," I said as I swept her along with me.

"But..." she began as she twisted her head to look back at the corner. "...she just..."

"Yeah, she did, and she still has a meat cleaver and a barbeque fork she hasn't tried out," I replied. "Let's not take any chances."

Rika chuckled, then shook her head as we headed toward the front door.

As Sofia walked up the porch steps in front of us, she put Gucci's chest to her shoulder and patted her back like she was burping a baby. "It's okay, Gucci," she cooed. "You scared them away."

Gucci lifted her head to look at us, a superior expression on her tiny face.

Sofia paused on the front porch and turned to me. "Jeez, Nick, why don't you make yourself useful and open the screen?"

Gucci yapped at me in agreement, always happy to take Sofia's side.

As I opened the door and held it, the thought passed through my mind that there might be too many bossy women in this family for my liking.

Sofia and Gucci strolled in like queens of the castle. But, as Rika passed, she smiled like she had an inkling of what had been going through my mind. Her eyes beamed warmth and maybe affection, and I knew I'd gladly put up with an army of bossy women just to see that smile.

# CHAPTER FIVE

**Rika**

The next morning, Nick drove us back to the hospital. The sky was blue, and the forecast was for a perfect high of seventy-two degrees.

After lunch, yesterday, we'd spent time doing internet searches for information about the twins and Erissa. Mostly, the Vatamanu name came up in relation to their circus act. And while the press knew about the separation, the stories were short and vague since the twins couldn't give interviews.

Erissa was another matter. We found a number of stories about her husband's murder. Apparently, the police had arrested her for the crime, but the district attorney didn't go forward, which meant he wasn't confident he had enough evidence to convict.

From what we pieced together, her husband had, indeed, been poisoned. Traces of it were found in an insulated travel bottle he'd taken along on a car trip. Police believed Erissa had filled it with a poison-laced soft drink and given it to her husband as he left.

Erissa said in an interview that she had put fruit infused water into the travel bottle because her husband—who was twenty years older—was supposed to be on a healthy diet for his blood pressure. The soda he refilled it with had to have come from somewhere else, she'd claimed.

I also found a mention of fingerprints that were on it—hers, her husband's and an unknown set.

Interesting. I could see why the cops believed she did it and why the D.A. wouldn't try her.

Now, Nick and I were in their shoes with the possibility of Erissa as the killer, but no usable evidence pointing to her...yet.

Once we got inside to the hospital reception desk, we learned Dr. Choi—one of the surgeons involved in the separation—was free to see us.

When we walked into his office, I couldn't keep the smile off my face. He was an orthopedic surgeon, so I guess I'd expected to see prosthetic limbs or pictures of dissected joints on the walls of his office. I'd never considered that doctors were into science therefore might be geeks who liked the same things I liked.

But as soon as I hit the doorway, I knew he was one of my peeps. Not only did he have Star Trek memorabilia all over his office, but he had a Millennium Falcon clip holding his tie together, *plus* Gundam models—the kind you assemble yourself—all over the wall behind him, each with its own little fiberglass shelf.

I decided it was best if I took the lead this time around. "Hi, Dr. Choi?" I said. "I'm Rika Martín. This is my partner Nick Owen."

Dr. Choi stood and held his hand out across his desk as we both shook it. "Nice shirt." He gestured to my yellow Chewbacca t-shirt, not to be confused with my blue, black or pink Chewbacca t-shirts. "I've never seen anyone look so good in geek clothes." He smiled and watched my eyes for a reaction.

I couldn't help but notice he was better looking than most

doctors. When he'd stood, he wasn't as tall as Nick, but he was four or five inches taller than I was, which was plenty as far as I was concerned. He was Asian and had his hair cut in a chunky, choppy style like the heroes from my manga books.

To borrow LeeAnne's words, he was *kuh-yoot!* My cheeks heated as I smiled back at him. "Love all your geek gear," I replied.

Nick went deadly still—I could feel the tension in his body— then shifted closer to me and cleared his throat. I glanced at him. He was staring at Dr. Choi with narrowed, suspicious eyes.

I hadn't thought I needed to explain that if you look at people suspiciously right off the bat during an investigation, they're less likely to feel comfortable and open up to you, but maybe I did.

Wait, he was a really good lawyer. Shouldn't he know that already?

"What can I do for you?" Dr. Choi gestured to the seats. "And before you answer, I'd just like to point out that I'm single." He gave me a meaningful look.

Girly laughter that sounded dangerously close to a giggle burst from my mouth. I shut it off as fast as I could because I did *not* want to be the P.I. who giggled around cute doctors while investigating a murder.

I needed people to respect me as a professional. Private investigators didn't get all flattered and silly unless it was an act they put on in order to gain information.

As Nick and I sat in the chairs Dr. Choi had indicated, I decided to tell myself that's all I was doing, hoping I could get past my embarrassment and focus on the case.

"I'm here to—" I began.

Nick butted in. "*We've* been hired to investigate the murder of Grigore Vatamanu." Unlike Dr. Choi, Nick was not smiling.

And now I wasn't smiling because I'd started to say something, and Nick had just talked right over me.

*What a jerk!*

I threw an angry glance his way. He didn't notice and continued, "You were the lead physician on the separation, right?"

Erissa had texted me all the info once she learned Teodor had come out of surgery alive. Maybe I shouldn't have shared it so freely with Nick.

Dr. Choi was nodding. "Yeah." His smile faded. "Didn't turn out like I expected, though. There was every reason to think we'd end up with two live men after the surgery. As you may have guessed, I've never operated under these circumstances before."

Until now, I hadn't considered how disturbing it might be for doctors to operate on a live person while there was a dead one attached to him with a screwdriver sticking out of his eye.

I nodded sympathetically. "It must have been difficult," I said. "Did you have a lot of contact with the twins before the surgery?"

"Sure. I was the one who spoke to them initially, ordered the tests, put the team together..."

"So, you were all expecting to do the separation this morning, regardless."

"Yes and no." He picked up a stylus and bumped the rubbery end on his desk as he spoke. "Grigore called the night before last —which was the night before the scheduled surgery—saying he was having second thoughts. Then Teodor got on the phone and said not to listen to Grigore. He claimed it was just cold feet and his brother would be okay with it by morning."

*Hm. Interesting.* "Had Grigore expressed misgivings before?"

"Not in so many words, although he definitely seemed the most concerned about the separation. But that's understandable, considering..."

"Considering?" I prodded.

"Considering that his brother was expected to come out of surgery a nearly normal, fully functioning person while Grigore would be learning to walk on a prosthetic leg and might not have a functioning penis."

"The surgery could have made him impotent?"

"It was a possibility because of the way the nerves were routed. Not likely, just possible."

"What did he say to you when you told him about that possibility?"

"To tell you the truth, Grigore never really said much. Teodor did most of the talking. He pointed out to Grigore that it was a small chance of impotence and said he'd be fine. Grigore seemed to accept that."

"So," Nick began, "Teodor was going to come out of the surgery and be able to marry his fiancée and start a normal life, while Grigore would be alone and a cripple."

Dr. Choi winced. "We don't like to call them 'cripples'."

"Whatever you call it, it sucked for Grigore," I said. "He'd have no woman, one leg, and no job. What was he planning to do for a living?"

"I never asked," Dr. Choi said. "I'm a surgeon. I slice 'em and dice 'em. If you want to know more, maybe you should talk to Dr. Washington. Kenya Washington. She's the psychiatrist they were required to see as part of the process. Normally, we wouldn't be able to talk to you, but the twins signed a pretty broad privacy waiver when they agreed to let the documentary crew follow them around."

"Who else spent a lot of time with them?"

Dr. Choi shrugged. "Well, because they were mostly joined at the hip..."—I held in my snicker at the cliché that had suddenly become literal— "...and I'm an orthopedic surgeon, they spent the most time with me and Dr. Washington. Other than that, Dr. Vivian Duarte, the vascular surgeon, was with them some. She had to map out a plan to reroute their shared blood supply and they seemed to like her. Teodor brought her up often when we were talking."

"And by 'brought her up,' you mean...?" Nick asked.

"Well, when I was explaining the surgical plan and risks, Teodor would add 'and Dr. Duarte said...' all the time. Usually something positive. I'm not sure if he had a crush on her or if maybe his brother did, and he was using her name to convince Grigore to get the surgery."

"Anybody else?"

"Not really. The anesthesiologists and other surgeons who were assisting only met them briefly."

"And what about Teodor's fiancée Erissa?" I asked. "Did you have much contact with her?"

"Actually, I only met her once," he replied. "And she was listed as the emergency contact."

"Did either of the twins seem afraid of her? Or anyone else?"

Dr. Choi's brows hitched up. "I don't remember them mentioning her more than a couple of times. I didn't get the idea anyone was afraid of her." He leaned forward, lowered his voice and asked, "Do you think she killed Grigore?"

"We're just trying to rule people out," Nick replied.

"Honestly," Dr. Choi paused. He seemed to be scanning his brain for more information. Then he shook his head, "Sorry, I only get as personal with patients as is necessary. Medical history, basically. Wish I could be of more help."

"Okay," I said, standing.

Nick stood simultaneously and was fully vertical before I was, as if he couldn't wait to leave. I gave him a quizzical look. "Thanks for talking to us," I said to Dr. Choi. "Can I contact you if I have any more questions?"

His lips curved into a sexy smile. "Sure," he said. He rolled his chair around and reached toward the credenza behind his desk. His chair had been hiding an intricate model of Hogwarts from Harry Potter.

I couldn't help the smile that spread across my face. *Oh, my God!* I wanted a Hogwarts, too!

I scanned the credenza to see what other treasures I hadn't noticed when I was sitting.

A miniature Jedi Starfighter. An X-wing. A Superstar Destroyer...

*Holy mother of Zeus!* Dr. Choi appeared to have every Star Wars spacecraft depicted in exquisite detail. Not out of plastic, but some sort of metal.

I know Freud thought it was all about the penises, but I was having serious Clawcraft envy right now!

Dr. Choi turned back and held a business card toward me.

I reached out, but Nick was faster and had longer arms. He snatched the card from Dr. Choi's hand and murmured a thanks. I watched the card go straight into the back pocket of his jeans. Then, he turned toward the door.

"Thanks again for your help," I said to Dr. Choi. I didn't want Nick's borderline rudeness to burn my bridges with this guy because he clearly knew where to get the best geek stuff. I started toward the door, but turned back, remembering the thing that had pinged in my brain after one of the first questions I'd asked.

"Just, one more thing. Do you think it's possible that Teodor killed Grigore?"

Dr. Choi's eyebrows shot up even higher this time, and his mouth fell open. He shut it and cocked his head as if considering the idea. "Well... I guess..." Then he untilted his head and looked at me straight on. "I'm not really comfortable having this conversation about my patient."

"But this is a murder investigation," I said. "We have to consider every possibility, even if it's just to rule it out. I've dealt with the cops quite a bit"—I left out the part about how they were often arresting me when I was dealing with them—"and if they don't come up with another suspect, they'll pin it on Teodor, just to close the case."

Actually, I didn't know if Winchell and Hertz would even think of the possibility. They weren't the most imaginative detectives in the city. At least I hoped they weren't or L.A. justice was screwed.

Dr. Choi nodded. "Yeah, I wasn't impressed with the two who spoke to me." He chuckled. "One of them's last name was the same as a donut chain...not Duncan..."

"Winchell," I said. Strange I hadn't thought of that before, considering my love of doughnuts. But then I'd met the detectives at a very stressful time, when my father was missing and his co-worker was dead. "Yeah, I guess him becoming a cop was like a self-fulfilling prophecy."

Dr. Choi and I laughed together.

"So, you were going to say..." Nick prodded. I got the feeling he was in a hurry to get us out of here, but I wasn't sure why.

Dr. Choi sighed. "I guess it's possible," he said. "Teodor was determined to get the operation. Grigore not so much. If they were fighting about it..." He shook his head suddenly. "But it's hard to believe Teodor would plan to murder his brother. They'd been together every single second since they were born. Teodor would have to have been beyond enraged and the screwdriver would have to have been handy. He couldn't exactly ask his brother to help him go get a weapon in the middle of a fight."

That was good thinking. Maybe Dr. Choi had missed his calling as a P.I.

"There were tools scattered all over the house," I said.

"Oh, you're right," Dr. Choi frowned thoughtfully. "I forgot about that. A couple of months ago, I dropped off some things for them to fix for me and it did seem like there were tools on every surface." He shook his head slowly before meeting my gaze again. "It's still hard to imagine, though. My brother isn't my twin and he's a real asshole. He even slept with my girlfriend when we were in high school and I still didn't stick a screwdriver in his eye."

Wow. Did that mean Dr. Choi had a brother who was even

hotter than he was? I tried to imagine the sibling who could steal women from the man in front of me and found that I couldn't.

Nick was standing impatiently by the door like a kid who'd been dragged along on a shopping trip by his mom.

"Okay, thank you for your time, Dr. Choi. We really appreciate it." I walked to where Nick was holding the door open.

"My time is your time," Dr. Choi replied. "And call me Geoff." He winked.

I thought I heard a low growl come from Nick, but when I checked, his face was blank.

As we walked through the hall toward the exit, I asked, "Could I get that card from you? I may want to—"

"No."

*No? Did he just say "no"?* Because I was pretty sure it was me Dr. Choi was handing the card to. And if I started earning decent money, I'd want to know where to get one of those cool models. I'd seen lots of geek trinkets and memorabilia, but none as intricately detailed and high-quality as his.

I tried again. "But, even if we don't need any more from him about the case, I may want to—"

"No," Nick repeated.

*Jeez.* What was wrong with him?

"At least let me have it long enough to take a picture of it," I said. "I store all that stuff digitally anyway."

Nick didn't reply and didn't hand over the card. "I'm hungry," he said. "You hungry?"

He was probably just using the easiest ploy to distract me since I was almost always hungry. I was especially ravenous today because I'd skipped breakfast, hoping to drop the extra weight so Nick and I could take things further, physically speaking.

If he still wanted to.

I really hoped he wanted to have a more intimate relationship with me. The times we kissed had felt passionate in a way I couldn't imagine before I met Nick. But there was always that nagging thought that the kisses we shared could be knee-jerk horny man reactions and I was just in the right place at the right time.

"I could eat," I heard myself say.

*I guess I can lose the weight tomorrow.*

# CHAPTER SIX

**Rika**

Nick and I stopped at a cafe to eat and discuss the case.

When we got inside, he looked at the chalkboard menu hanging behind the counter and decided he wanted one of their house burritos. I stared into the glass case, lusting after the three huge chocolate-chocolate chip muffins dressed ultra-sexy in sheer white pleated muffin pan liners.

I shifted my gaze to Nick's abs—some of which I thought I could see through his t-shirt—then settled for the half-sandwich and soup combo.

"What do you think so far?" Nick asked after we sat down with our trays of food. But most of his attention was on his burrito as he unrolled it and smothered the contents in salsa from one end of the tortilla to the other.

I swallowed the bite of turkey sandwich I had in my mouth and took a sip of water. "I think Erissa did it," I replied.

"I don't know," Nick said. "That was a big risk to take with Teodor's life. What if you hadn't shown up?"

"What if I hadn't shown up?" I replied. "Of course I'd show up. It's my job."

"There was no way for Erissa to know you weren't the kind of person who blew off jobs, or overslept, or were habitually late."

"We talked," I said. "I assured her I'd be there on time. And she kept re-confirming with me. I thought it was because she didn't want to risk me being there when her boyfriend came home from his 'procedure,' but, since his procedure turned out to be getting separated from his conjoined twin, she knew he wasn't coming home that day."

Nick shook his head. "I don't know. It's hard to imagine her sinking a screwdriver in someone's eye."

"Why, because she's pretty and blonde?" I blurted.

*Crap!* I did not mean to say that aloud. But it would be just like Nick to fall for her act.

"No," he replied. "Because it was dangerous to the man she was in love with and because it's a pretty brutal crime for a woman who hasn't lost all her marbles. This would have been premeditated and women don't usually like the hands-on, 'in your face' type of murder unless it happens in the heat of the moment. When women plot a crime, they're more likely to poison."

"Which is how she killed her husband," I said, even though we both knew she hadn't been indicted for the crime. "But she couldn't poison Grigore. That would have killed Teodor for sure considering they shared a blood supply."

Nick washed down the last of his burrito with a gulp of Coke. How did he finish a whole burrito that fast? And why wasn't his stomach stretching his shirt out like mine did when I ate a burrito?

Tall people were annoying. Nick could probably eat a dozen chocolate chip muffins and never see the results on his extra-long frame.

"I didn't mean she would poison him, specifically," he replied. "I'm just saying, of all the ways to kill a person, it's hard to imagine she'd choose to stab someone in the eye with a screwdriver."

"Can you imagine *anyone* you know stabbing someone in the eye with a screwdriver?" I asked.

Nick gave a slight shrug. I took that to mean he was conceding the point.

I tasted the soup, which had a pleasant lemony flavor, then asked, "Who do you think did it?"

Nick considered the question. "Well, it's still early," he said. "But I think it's a lot more likely that Teodor stabbed Grigore in a fit of rage while they were fighting over the operation. There were tools handy all over the house. If one happened to be on the nightstand..."

"But wouldn't that be too much like stabbing yourself?" I argued. "They've shared a body their whole lives."

"From what we've learned, they were very different people. Maybe if Teodor got angry enough—"

"But, if we went with that hypothesis, we'd have to believe Teodor killed his conjoined brother, then just went to sleep," I pointed out.

"Maybe he killed him, then passed out from physical or emotional shock," Nick said. "He may have felt it, in some way, when it entered Grigore's body. And, even if he were a sociopath, seeing a screwdriver sticking out of a face that looks just like his own would be a major shock."

I considered his hypothesis while trying to chew the next bite of my sandwich faster. I found it stressful when the person I was eating with finished their food and had nothing to do but watch me eat. I'd always liked to savor my food, plus once I got heavy, I didn't want to eat in front of anyone other than family.

I shook off the discomfort and got back to business.

"I still think Erissa's instructions to me were suspicious," I argued. "Maybe she and Teodor were in on it together."

Her instructions *were* suspicious, weren't they? I didn't think much of it at the time because I was excited about my first real case.

I pictured her pretty face, her swoopy, swishy blonde hair, and her slender body that surely had never needed to struggle to get into its jeans. Then I remembered—again—how Nick had raced off to get her a snack when she mentioned her blood sugar.

*Yeah, that bitch is guilty all right,* I thought, but didn't say.

"Wow," Nick said. "You really have it in for Erissa."

Wait, had he read my mind? Regardless, his stubborn defense of her was pissing me off. "And would you like to have it *in* Erissa?" I blurted.

Nick tilted his head, his brow low like he wasn't sure he'd heard me right. "Say, what?" he finally asked.

"Nothing," I replied. "Leave me alone and let me finish my soup."

~

**Rika**

Later that afternoon, I was on the phone, trying to find out how long it would be before we were able to talk to Teodor and his other doctors while Nick herded his ginormous vehicle through Los Angeles traffic. He'd adapted well to L.A. driving in the short time he'd been here, even with the pickup truck, which bugged me. Maybe because I'd put one of his trucks in the ditch outside of Bolo the first time I drove it.

While on hold, I'd been thinking about Erissa, and whether she was trying to play me for a fool. There was something about her that rubbed me the wrong way from the first time I met her. I was trying to decide if it was the gut instinct a private investigator is supposed to have or just the fact that she was hot and bitchy, the way Nick seemed to like his women.

Okay, I didn't really *know* any of Nick's three ex-wives, but I'd seen two of them. They were definitely hot and, in my mind, they were always bitchy.

Nick pulled into a parking lot.

I looked around, not recognizing the building. Nick had claimed he needed to run an errand.

"Where are we?" I asked.

"We have an appointment."

"We?" *Grrrrrr!* Had he made another appointment to see office space without my permission? "Why are we here?" I asked.

"Just humor me," Nick replied.

*Damn it!* This was the third space he'd driven me to against my will this week. As he came around and opened my door— which was also bugged the hell out of me because if I wanted the door open, I could open it myself. I picked up my phone and started punching numbers.

"Who are you calling now?" Nosey Nick asked.

"9-1-1. This is the third time you kidnapped me this week."

He wrenched the phone out of my hand and checked the screen. I hadn't dialed 9-1-1, of course. No one should call 9-1-1 if it's not a real emergency.

"Kidnapped?" He snorted and handed the phone back to me.

"Taking a person somewhere against her will is the definition of kidnapping," I said loudly.

Nick threw his head back and laughed. The smile he aimed at me afterward took my breath away.

I couldn't seem to stay angry when Nick smiled at me. What was wrong with me? They were just teeth, for Zeus' sake!

Beautiful, perfect teeth given to him by his beauty queen mother, as far as I knew. I'd never gotten to see his father.

He held a hand out toward me and I took it. I couldn't stop myself.

It was hard to have half my brain telling me to draw the line with him and not let him treat me like a helpless female when the other half wanted to glob onto him and soak into his pores, so we'd never be apart.

As we walked toward the door, he placed a hand at the back of my neck, placating me by massaging my muscles with his fingertips while steering me in the direction he wanted me to go.

*Okay, whatever. I'll go see the stupid office.*

What can I say? A neck massage from Nick Owen is irresistible, regardless of his motive.

We took the elevator to the sixth floor of the six-story building. To the right, as we got out, were double glass doors. Nick opened one and ushered me through.

"You've got to be kidding me," I said as I stared at the half-circle reception desk. The counter looked like it was made of marble. I leaned to one side to see behind the partial wall. "This place looks huge. What would we do with all this space?"

"Once things get hopping, we'll need a receptionist," Nick replied. "And here we have a conference room to speak to clients or have our meetings in."

"We can have our meetings in your giant truck—with room to spare—without spending thousands of dollars a month on rent."

"Nick!" A woman's voice cried.

I whipped around to find a tall blonde in a white button-down shirt and pencil skirt approaching. She clearly thought "button-down" meant you were only supposed to button the bottom half of the shirt because the top half was wide open.

The sparkling statement necklace on her bare upper chest matched her bright blue eyes. She moved gracefully in four-inch spiked heels I probably couldn't even stand in.

When she reached Nick, she put her arms around his neck.

*What the—?*

Even worse, he put his arms around her back and they hugged. "It's been a long time!" she said.

"Yeah, about ten...twelve years?" Nick agreed. "Rika, this is GracieAnne—"

"I just go by Grace, now," she said.

So, she must have escaped rural Texas and reinvented herself in California. Couldn't say I blamed her for that.

"Okay, got it," Nick said. "And this is Rika Martin, my business partner."

She reached for my hand and shook it. "Martín," I corrected. "I'm Rika *Mar-teen.*" I gave Nick a dirty look. He pressed his lips together like he was trying to keep from laughing. "How do you two know each other?" I asked.

"GracieAnne—sorry, Grace—lived in the next town," Nick said. "Mom and DeeAnne knew her from the pageants. I ran into her sometimes on the weekends."

*Great.* That's all I needed. Another pageant girl to distract Nick. And was there no end to the sexy blondes who'd been in Nick's life?

"And every time his football team came to play ours," Grace said. "I rooted him on from the sidelines."

Nick gave her a perplexed look. "You were a cheerleader for the other team."

"I know." She flipped her eyebrows suggestively.

*Bitch*, I thought. Then I told myself it was wrong to judge this woman just because she was sexy, tall, blonde, went way back with Nick and was the kind of "pageant girl material" his mother wanted for him.

They looked gorgeous together and would make beautiful little blue-eyed babies.

Oh, what the hell. I hated her!

As we looked around the lovely office, I realized Nick had listened to me, sort of. This might not be the office over a Chinese restaurant I'd imagined, but it was a lot less opulent than the last office we'd visited. And the view was limited from this height.

However, Los Angeles real estate being what it was, I knew the place would cost more than we could possibly earn in the near future. Why was Nick trying to make my life so difficult?

The thought of him shouldering all the costs freaked me the hell out, every time it popped into my head. I did not want Nick—or any man, for that matter—to be my sugar daddy.

And this difference of opinion about money combined with my body issues—or maybe they were just body image issues now, I was never sure—were making me act weirder around him. I'd probably been putting out mixed signals.

Not that I wanted to, but he was so freaking hot, it was hard not to respond to his flirting sometimes.

Unfortunately, when he'd tried to take things a little farther, the thought crossed my mind that I was still overweight by almost ten pounds.

The idea of Nick seeing me totally naked at less than my best really messed with my mind. Several times, I froze and stopped breathing when he put his hand on me.

Nick was no dummy. He felt my apprehension and backed off.

And now this GracieAnne person was on the scene. My heart sank as I was sure one of them would be getting a late-night "You up?" text from the other.

I was too distracted to take in the tour Grace gave us. It was pointless anyway. I wasn't going to rent a place this big.

After we'd seen it all, we walked to the door. Nick and Grace hugged again as I fantasized about pulling all the bleach-blonde hairs from her head, one at a time. Wait, were those extensions? If she suffered from male-pattern baldness—a stupid name for it considering women could have it too—I'd at least have one advantage over her since I had a very full head of hair.

Probably just wishful thinking.

"Thanks, Gracie—um, Grace," Nick began.

"Nick," she tilted her head and gave him a wistful smile. "You know you can call me whatever you want and I'll come runnin'." Her Texas accent, which hadn't been noticeable when we first met, snuck back in on her last sentence. It made the comment sound even more suggestive. "You know, I'm not a little girl anymore," she added.

*That bitch!* She did *not* just proposition my Nick right in front of my face!

A new fantasy flashed through my mind, one in which I was shoving all the blue stones from Grace's necklace up her nose.

"Thanks, GracieAnne," I said. "We'll have to think about the space." I only told her we'd think about it because I didn't want to get into an argument with Nick in front of her.

"Sure, nice meeting you," she replied.

As we walked out, I was so angry I wanted to kick Nick in the shins like Sofia had done to the drug dealer.

Or maybe I'd aim higher. He'd clearly looked up an old love interest to act as our realtor! We'd had a perfectly good commercial realtor that I approved. Why was this Grace person showing us spaces?

"What happened to Kadar?" I asked.

"Remember? He told us he was leaving the country soon, but he'd show us everything he could until then. You weren't happy with the spaces, and now he had to go back to India and do that arranged marriage thing."

"Okay, whatever," I said.

As we got to the truck, he clicked his key fob and reached out to open my door.

"Stop!" I said. "I don't need my door opened for me!" At this point, the door was just representative of all the things I was uncomfortable with. Nick and I shouldn't be business partners, we should be another kind of partners. Going into business with him was a mistake. It was too stressful. I couldn't handle it.

"You seem a little peeved," he said.

I was not about to tell him I was jealous of his old wannabe girlfriend and was feeling the balance of power tilting out of my control in our business relationship.

He'd say I was being silly and then I'd kill him.

Because I didn't want Nick dead or myself in jail, I rewound until I found a peeve I could admit to.

"What's with the Rika Martin, thing?" I asked. I really was "peeved" every time he did that.

He didn't answer, but one side of his lips lifted in a sexy half-grin.

I pressed my lids closed to avoid being affected by the expression, got control of myself and opened them again, but aimed them at his collar bone. "You know my last name is Martín, with an accent. Why do you insist on introducing me as Rika Martin?"

He reached out and nabbed a lock of my hair, sliding his fingers to the end and giving it a little tug. Our gazes met and he was stifling a grin. "'Cause I like to see your eyes flash." He left me standing by the passenger door and walked around the truck.

A sensation passed through me, like a hot vibration, trembling down my spine, tingling its way through my appendages to my fingers and toes.

*I like to see your eyes flash.*

My heart felt like it was beating too fast. At this rate, it was going to bang its way right out of my ribs.

I pressed my hand to my chest to steady it. Now my eyes weren't the only things flashing. I was flashing all over the place, including the spot between my thighs that hummed whenever I was in Nick's vicinity.

The sound of his door slamming jarred me out of my trance. I pulled my hand away from my thrumming chest, opened the passenger door, and climbed into the truck.

# CHAPTER SEVEN

**Rika**

Nick drove us out to where Cirque de Sorbet was performing. The huge red tent was situated on a vacant lot where a couple of buildings had been demolished. One large building, probably a warehouse at one time, remained on the property, directly behind the tent.

We stepped inside the big top to find an older, dark-haired man shouting in a foreign language at a group of younger people who were contorting their bodies into odd shapes, some while hanging from ropes. They ranged in age from preteen to twenty-something—six male, six female—and all of them looked like they could be related to him. Each was dressed in a leotard with either skin-tight shorts or tights that stopped at the ankle. They were all barefoot and buff, even the two young women who appeared to be pregnant.

The yelling man was super-shredded for his age—not an ounce of fat on him— just lots of lean muscle.

*Hmm...maybe I need to join the circus.* I was tempted to bing "circus workout" and see if any gyms were offering it.

They stopped what they were doing as their eyes fixed on us. The loud man turned around to see what they were staring at.

"Get out!" he yelled in accented English. "This is rehearsal time! No show until nighttime."

"We're not here about the show," Nick said. "I'm Nick Owen and this is Rika Martin. We're looking for the Vatamanu family."

"Martín," I said automatically. "I'm Rika Mar-teen."

But the words *I like to see your eyes flash* echoed through my brain, preventing me from giving Nick the dirty look that usually went along with the correction.

Then I realized I'd deprived him of seeing my "eyes flash," whatever that meant. I wondered if I could see the so-called flashing if I gave myself dirty looks in the mirror. I made a mental note to try it next time I was in a bathroom.

"I am Anatolie Vatamanu," the man said. "And this is my family." He waved his hand in their general direction. "What do you want from us?" Then something sparked in his eyes. "Are you reporters?" he asked. "We are always happy to talk to the press."

Nick gave me one of his *WTF?* looks. I widened my eyes at him in agreement.

Grigore Vatamanu had just died. Teodor was in the hospital. But their family was here in their practice attire like nothing earth-shattering had happened.

"We're investigating Grigore's death," I said. "We had a few questions we were hoping you could answer."

Anatolie yelled something in another language at his family. They all looked relieved and hustled out the back of the tent. "Please excuse my mood," he said. "I understand that a murder must be investigated. It's just that my family and I are hanging by a thread—is that how you say it?"

"Yes," I said, even though he'd said, "tread" instead of "thread."

"How so?" Nick asked.

Anatolie took in a breath and blew out a frustrated sigh.

"Teodor and Grigore were our gold," he said. "Siamese twins who were contortionists and could work the trapeze like they were born on it!"

I had the urge to correct him about the Siamese thing, but he was their father. Surely, he knew the appropriate name for their condition.

"The twins were your big draw, then," Nick paraphrased.

"Yes! For nearly thirty years, since they were three! Then Teodor falls in love with that American slut and wants to be separated from his brother. What about the rest of us? What are we supposed to do?" He looked at us like he expected a response.

"Yeah, that's a tough one," Nick replied.

"And now, one of my daughters is *gravida*." He threw his hands in the air dramatically. "Pregnant! With no husband! So, now, we put a pregnant stomach on her sister so she can mirror her in their act. It looks to all the world like both my daughters are pregnant. And none with husband! But these crazies in L.A. love the pregnant stomachs in the act. What is wrong with you people?"

Nick's eyes cut to me. "A question I ask every day," he said.

"And, what do we do after the baby's born?" Anatolie went on. "Why will anyone want to see us then? Without the twins or the pregnant daughter, we have no draw. We will be replaced by the Bouncing Butnarus!"

Although I was dying to find out more about the Bouncing Butnarus, I reined in my curiosity. I couldn't solve his other problems, but maybe I could help him outfox the competition. "The website doesn't say your daughter is pregnant," I pointed out. "It says you are 'celebrating womanhood and the giving of life'."

"Yes?" He didn't see where I was going with this.

"After the baby's born, couldn't you just buy another pregnancy suit and have both of your daughters wear them as costumes?"

His head jerked. He turned and looked toward the exit his

family had gone through, then his gaze met mine again. "You! You are genius!" He closed the space between us, grabbed me by the shoulders and kissed me on one cheek, te other.

I tolerated his attention but was glad it didn't last very long. He smelled like cabbage and vinegar battered in Old Spice. Not my favorite combination.

"Still," he said, "it was better in the old days when we were true *calatorii*. I used to travel around in wagons with my parents and aunts and uncles." Nick and I exchanged a glance at the word "wagons." Sure, he would have been a kid in another century, but that was the twentieth century. People had cars.

Then I remembered Moldova was the poorest country in Eastern Europe and had been under communist rule for several decades before the Berlin wall fell. So, maybe they did ride around in wagons. What did I know about Roman ian-Moldovan circus people?

Anatolie was still talking, almost as if to himself. "Of course, there was some danger in the picking of pockets, and our women had to pretend they could tell fortunes, but at least it was honest work."

Depending on your definition of "honest work", I supposed. "Sounds...um...great," I said. "But could we ask you questions about the murder?"

Anatolie rolled his eyes. "Ungrateful children," he murmured. "Always causing me trouble." He didn't seem the least bit broken up about Grigore or worried about Teodor. "Go ahead."

"Was there anyone who's been especially angry or upset with one or both of the twins?"

"Yes," he replied, flinging his hands in the air theatrically. "Me!"

Nick shifted his weight and rubbed the back of his neck as I'd seen him do in times of annoyance or stress. This time, I was guessing it was annoyance. "Are you saying you killed your son?"

"Of course not! What would that do besides put me in jail? Then my useless children would have to survive on their own."

I thought maybe his family would prefer to take their chances, considering he was a total narcissist a-hole.

"Anyone else who might have reason to kill either one of them?" Nick asked with mock patience.

Anatolie shrugged. "I don't know. They didn't own anything worth killing for."

"Any romantic entanglements? Were they dating?" Nick prodded. "Besides Erissa," he added quickly, before Anatolie could refer to the "slut" again.

"Grigore never had a date," he replied. "And I disowned Teodor months ago when he told me he wanted the surgery. I do not know if he is married to the slut or dating someone new."

Nick glanced at me questioningly. I gave a slight shrug. "Disowned Teodor, but not Grigore?" he asked.

"Yes."

"How is that possible?"

"Speak to one. Don't speak to the other," he said as if it was the most obvious thing in the world. "Grigore could come eat supper with us. Teodor had to eat before he came. No plate for him!"

*Wow.* "Okay..." I took a deep breath. "Did Grigore have any close friends?"

"Yes. He and Constata were close. She is in charge of wardrobe, but not here now. She went with most of the performers and crew to matinee performance of Cirque de Soleil." He turned his wrist up, checking his watch for the time instead of a cellphone.

How retro.

"I'm sorry, but I have to get my lazy, no-good family back to rehearsal. Our contract expires in three months and, if we are not at the top of our game, we will be beggars."

"Sure," Nick said. "Sorry to inconvenience you."

"We are all just doing our jobs," Anatolie replied philo-sophically.

Nick moved as if to leave, but I wasn't quite ready. "Just one more thing," I said. "Did you get to see or talk to Grigore the night before his murder?"

Anatolie nodded. "We spoke on the phone."

"Can you tell us what he said?"

"He said he did not want to do surgery anymore." Anatolie shook his head dismissively. "It did not matter. I knew he would agree in the end. Teodor always got his way with Grigore, one way or the other."

*One way or another. Hmm...*

"Grigore..." He paused and I wondered if we were about to see his human side. He shook his head. "Grigore was weak. If he stood up to his brother when the slut put the crazy ideas in his head, maybe they would still be alive and helping their family like eldest sons should."

"Teodor still is alive," I reminded him.

He shrugged again. "For all the good it will do me. Are your questions finished? I have work to do."

"Sure," Nick said, but the look on his face was clear. He didn't approve of Anatolie's parenting any more than I did. "We'll let you get back to work."

∾

## Nick

"What a prince," I said as we walked to the truck. "He disowned a son for wanting a life and seems like he wrote off Grigore just as easily. Who acts like that?"

"Fathers have killed their own kids for life insurance money," Rika pointed out. "I even saw a story on TV about a woman who killed two husbands, then tried to kill her daughter who she claimed wrote a suicide note confessing to the murders of her dad and step-dad. Luckily the daughter didn't die, but people suck."

I wondered if Rika was thinking of her own mother's murder. If she was, I wanted to get her mind off the topic. "Do you think he killed Grigore?" I asked, even though I didn't think Anatolie was a good suspect.

"No," Rika replied. "He's awful, but if he was in a fit of rage about the operation, he would have stuck the screwdriver in Teodor's eye, not Grigore's."

We were on the same page there. "Makes sense that it could be somebody from the circus, though. Murder victims usually know their killer." We got to the passenger side and I opened the door for her, remembering belatedly that she'd asked me not to. It was a habit my Southern-fried mom had hammered into my head from the time my dad died and could no longer open doors for her.

Rika was too distracted to notice this time. "Makes even more sense that it's Erissa," she said. She started counting off on her fingers. "She arranges to have me search the duplex. She reconfirms the details a dozen times. Then, we conveniently walk in just in time to save her boyfriend from dying with his brother. It's too much of a coincidence."

"Coincidences happen all the time," I replied. Although, truth be told, this coincidence smelled fishy as hell. But I still couldn't see Erissa as a screwdriver-wielding murderer. "It would be a big risk to take. Besides, she knew the cops would suspect her."

"With good reason, since her husband died suspiciously."

"Yeah." She was in the truck, so I slammed her door shut and headed around to my side, slid in and started up the motor. "But I think we have a whole lot of people to interview before we get a handle on this case."

She pulled out her phone and started texting.

I watched, curious, but not sure it was any of my business.

She glanced up and caught me. "I'm texting Erissa," she said.

"Telling her we need a retainer if we're going to do any more investigating on this case. We'll see how serious she is about it, then." She put the phone in her lap while she fastened her seat belt.

I took in a deep breath. "Rika, I told you, you don't have to worry about money."

Her head snapped toward me and she looked me in the eye. "Do you really think I'd ask you to finance my *hobby*?" My lips parted to reply but she beat me to it. "I'm not one of your wives and I'm certainly not your mother. I asked you to partner with me in a business, and businesses have to earn a profit!"

Her eyes flashed so fiercely, I wanted to pull her to me for some impromptu sex on the reclining seat of my truck. Instead, I smiled and said, "Simmer down, Paprika Anise"—I pronounced her middle name "Ah-nees" like her family did. "We'll get there."

The use of her full first plus middle name got me another angry flash.

*Score.* Turned me on every single time.

My hand jerked toward her without permission, slid into her hair and cupped the base of her head, pulling her in my direction. I leaned in but caught myself just before our lips touched.

We were breathing the same air as she stared into my eyes. I saw surprise in her gaze and maybe something better.

My mind was all over the place, thinking about the mixed messages I'd gotten, but dying for another taste of her. It had been weeks since I'd felt her lips on mine and that seemed all kinda wrong.

"Paprika?" I whispered, needing a sign from her.

She blinked twice, sucked in a shuddering breath and jerked forward. Suddenly, her mouth was on mine, her tongue shoving through my parted lips, attacking, full force. Her hands slid up my torso and over my shoulders.

*Damn.* I wanted—no needed—her. Now. Naked, underneath

me. Or on top of me. I wasn't picky about the position as long as I could get inside her.

On instinct, my hands slid down her silky hair to her back, pulling her closer. Next thing I knew, she was in my lap in an awkward position, squeezed sideways between my chest and the steering wheel.

My mind spun, trying to work out a way for us to consummate this partnership immediately, but it was hard to think with all the blood drained south.

Her sweet round ass was pressed onto my erection as I battled her tongue back and took control.

*Now, now, now*, my body urged as my hand slipped under her shirt. Could I get her to go to my hotel with me? Or any hotel. I wasn't picky about that either.

*Tap-tap-tap.*

We startled at the sound and turned to my window, where a blonde woman was standing, wearing a security guard uniform.

Rika dove off my lap and was back in her seat in a split second, leaving me with a visible hard-on.

I tugged the bottom of my t-shirt out to cover my crotch, rolled down my window and gave the guard a respectful nod. "Ma'am," I said.

"Ma'am!" she said. "Shit, how old do I look?"

"It's what we call women in Texas," I explained for the dozenth time since I'd been in L.A. "It's a term of respect."

"Yeah, okay," she replied. "But it's not very respectful to sit out in a public parking lot and—wait, Rika Martín?"

I turned and looked at Rika. The expression on her face was one I'd expect on an embezzler who just got audited. "Um, yeah," she said guardedly.

"Remember me? Ashlynn? We totally went to school together. Damn you look—"

A glance at Rika told me she'd gone from freaked out to horrified. I wasn't sure what the deal was, but I had to save her. "Am I gonna get a ticket or something?" I asked, knowing she had no power to give me one.

Ashlynn's gaze switched back to me. "No, I'm not a cop," she said, then her eyes went back to Rika. "Damn, girl! You've changed! And you're with this hottie?" She gestured toward me. "I can't believe we used to call you—"

"I'm sorry. We have an emergency," Rika said loudly. She held up her phone. "Nick, we've got to go."

"We'll catch you next time," I said to Ashlynn.

I started up the truck and drove out of the lot, not sure what had just happened.

Whatever it was, it had totally killed the mood.

If I wasn't gonna get any, again, I thought I should at least know why. "Was she a good friend of yours in high school?"

A half-chuckle escaped Rika's mouth, but she wasn't smiling with her lips or her eyes.

Within a couple of minutes, we'd gone from hot and heavy to cold and distant. She stared out the passenger window, deep in thought...or memories, maybe.

"So, I guess this Ashlynn wasn't very nice to you?"

Rika shrugged. "She wasn't really any better or worse than the others."

What did that mean? I sucked in a slow breath, preparing myself for the rejection that I was pretty sure I was about to experience. "Wanna tell me about it?" I asked, trying to hit the right tone between casually curious and vaguely sympathetic.

I'd learned Rika was uncomfortable with heavy doses of sympathy. Hell, maybe it reminded her of the way people treated her when her mother died.

She didn't reply.

"Rika...?"

"Nope."

And that was the end of that.

# CHAPTER EIGHT

**Nick**

The next morning, Rika had called the hospital before I picked her up. Via text, she'd told me Teodor was stable, but not cleared for visitors, yet, so, we'd decided to go back to the circus and try to speak to Grigore's friend Constata.

On the way, the truck was quiet to the point of awkwardness. I took a moment while she was messing with her phone to check out her t-shirt. It was red, long-sleeved and more form-fitting than the cotton ones she usually wore, and it sported a thick yellow lightning bolt in the middle.

*Captain Marvel.*

*Damn. She's still breathtaking in red.*

"Sofia's okay with keeping Gucci all day?" I finally asked, even though we had established that yesterday.

"Mm-hm," was her only reply.

After the kiss last night, I guess I expected her to act a little different towards me this morning. Was it egotistical to think she'd forget about the Ashlynn thing—whatever that was—and remember the quick but hot make out session right before it?

If I'm being completely honest, my hope was that when she

opened her front door, she'd smile at me in a special way, or, better yet, raise up on her tiptoes for a good morning kiss.

But, minutes ago, when I'd knocked, then braced my hands casually on the door frame and leaned in, putting me closer to her height, I got nothing.

Every time I'd made this move before, it had ended in a kiss. Either the female in question would instigate one or she'd make herself available, smiling flirtatiously as I went in for the kiss.

Not today.

Rika opened the door, made eye contact for about half a second before her eyes flitted around. She mumbled something about forgetting her computer and turned back toward her room, leaving me standing there, unkissed.

Worse, was that her Aunt Madi, who was sitting on a stool at the kitchen bar, saw me, totally knew what I was up to and burst out laughing when Rika went back to her room.

Clearly, any man who spent time around the Delacruz women should prepare for a few dings to his ego.

I turned without a word from the still laughing Madi and went to sit in my truck. A minute later, Rika climbed in with a backpack I hadn't seen before. This one was canvas and leather. Pretty cool-looking although I suspected the insignia embossed in the leather was a Legend of Zelda emblem.

After several minutes of silence, I couldn't take it anymore. "Nice backpack," I said.

"I've got my computer in it," Rika replied. "I'm hoping my friend Najila from the M.E.'s office is able to send photos today."

"You know the medical examiner?" I asked.

"No, she's an intern, for now. I'm hoping she ends up there full-time, though. I met her through a forensics class we were in together."

"Isn't that where you met Julian?" I asked.

"No, I met him in a criminal justice class at community college, but the one I took with Najila was a night class at UCLA."

"How many college hours have you taken?"

She pushed her eyebrows together and listed a few courses with their credit hours before she gave up. "I'd have to check," she finally said. "Around two hundred hours, maybe?" She shrugged like it was no big deal.

"Two hundred hours?" I repeated. "That's more than my undergrad degree required. Do you have a degree?"

She shook her head. "Nope."

"Why would you take that many courses and not get a degree?"

"You sound like Tía Margo," she replied.

Apparently, it wasn't the Friend Zone I had to worry about. I was in danger of entering Auntie Territory.

"I always wanted to be a P.I. and you don't need a degree for that," Rika explained. "And I don't have unlimited funds, so, I take classes I think will help me be better at my job and run a business."

Was that "unlimited funds" comment meant to shame me about not having to worry about money for college or law school? I wasn't sure.

"What kinds of classes did you take?" I asked.

"Some criminal justice courses, a few cyber-security, forensics, bookkeeping, managerial accounting, entrepreneurship. Some I took in person, some online. I started when I was still in high school, and just took whatever classes I could afford to pay for that semester, after I took money out for my car expenses and groceries."

I'd thought I couldn't be more impressed by Rika. But, where does a girl who basically lost both parents when she was eight or nine find the will and the drive to do so much? I wanted to know more. Truth be told, I wanted to know everything about her.

"How'd you start making money in high school?"

"Actually, I may have still been in junior high," she replied casually. "I signed up for an online tutoring service. Had to lie and tell them I was eighteen, though."

Wow. The more I got to know Rika, the more awesome she was. Until her, I never knew what it was like to be attracted to a person's body *and* mind. Except, maybe once, when I was a sophomore in high school, but, if that was the case, I was too young to appreciate it.

I pulled up to a red light. "I always said you were pretty smart for a hot chick." I looked over at her, expecting to see her blush and try to fight back a smile at my sexist comment, but she was staring into her phone as if she was suddenly engrossed in her reading and had forgotten I was in the truck with her.

What was up with her? Making out with me one day, ignoring me the next.

It always seemed like one step forward, two steps back with her. I really needed to get her alone with enough time to explore this relationship a little—okay a lot—further.

But, as much as I hated to admit it, even to myself, I was afraid to ask her to come up to my hotel room. I had the feeling it would spook her. And this thing between us, whatever it was, felt like something I didn't want to mess up. Damn, even if all we could ever be was business partners, I knew I'd stay because I'd already learned how badly I could miss her.

I tried to imagine a future in which Rika and I were not going to bed together every night.

No. I was fooling myself. I could only resist her for so long. Something would have to give. But if I asked her to go to my hotel room and she refused without explanation, where would that leave us?

I'd never in my life waited this long to have sex with a woman I was interested in. And they'd never wanted to wait, but Rika... Well, clearly, Rika was very different.

When we got into the circus tent, we found several acts rehearsing. A bleach-blonde woman in a sparkly pink leotard was running three poodles and a pony through their paces as they jumped on and over each other, culminating in a pony-poodle-poodle-poodle pile on, with the tiniest poodle in a tiny pink cape on top.

Rika laughed at the sight. It was different than her usual laugh. More girly. It may have even qualified as a giggle. Whatever it was, it caused a squeezing sensation in my chest.

I shook it off, glanced past the clown sitting on the bleachers near us, doing what looked like online banking on his laptop.

*Guess even clowns have bills to pay.*

Rika was looking up. I followed her line of sight to the Vatamanu family, minus Anatolie, up in the air. Most of the men were on the high wire or the platforms on either end of it. But my eyes caught on the young Vatamanu women, each with a pregnant belly, mirroring each other, swinging by their toes from trapezes.

One called out to the other and, suddenly, they were falling. By reflex, I took a couple of steps forward to try to catch them before I noticed the net.

This was a big relief, considering I couldn't have caught them both. The only criteria for deciding between them would have been which one was actually pregnant, but I couldn't tell the fake belly from the real one.

*Savior complex.*

I really owed my buddy Gabe—now a judge in my hometown of Bolo—a *you were right* phone call. He'd diagnosed me years ago, and I'd told him he was wrong.

Of course, I wasn't going to make that call. He'd enjoy it too much, and he already knew he was right anyway.

I was surprised to see the two women running toward us as fast as their bare feet would bring them.

As they got closer, it hit me how petite and thin they were except for the giant bellies.

"You..." One of them began. She looked at her sister, her identical twin.

Holy cow! The Vatamanu family had a set of identical twin girls in addition to a set of conjoined twin boys? When they were standing right in front of us, I realized how young the girls looked. There had to be a decade between them and their oldest brothers, maybe more.

The sisters spoke to each other in a language that sounded kind of like Spanish or Portuguese mixed with Russian—okay, I wasn't much of a linguist.

They seemed to be trying to figure out how to communicate with us.

Rika whipped out her phone. "Here..." She tapped the screen a couple of times and said, "Romanian?" Then checked her phone. "Romana?" she asked them.

The women breathed a simultaneous sigh of relief and started jabbering away at Rika.

How did she know what language they were speaking?

*Oh.* She was constantly researching something on the internet. Maybe she'd listened to clips of world languages and memorized the patterns. That sounded like something she'd do.

Rika held her hand up in a stop sign, then pushed the microphone on her phone screen and held it toward the twins.

"*Sunteti politisti federali?*"

I was pretty sure the one speaking was the pregnant one, now that they were up close in leotards. "Are you federal police?" appeared on the screen.

Rika shook her head.

The sister with the fake belly checked over her shoulder nervously.

The other one looked at me hopefully. "Law-lerrr?"

"I think she's asking if you're a lawyer," Rika said. She pressed the microphone. "Are you a lawyer?" she said into her phone.

The twins checked the Romanian translation and nodded excitedly.

Before Rika could confirm that I was, I reached over and

pressed the microphone on the screen. "What is the problem?" I said into the phone.

After pushing the mic, the pregnant one began speaking in rapid-fire Romanian.

When she finished, I was surprised at how well the translation app had done its job.

The young women said their father was very abusive and they didn't want to raise a child with him. They wanted a lawyer who could help them get away from him and allow them to stay in the U.S.

Three sets of big brown eyes looked up at me hopefully, including Rika's. Damn, I wanted to help. Not just to impress Rika, but because these women were in a foreign country with an abusive father and little knowledge of English, then there was the baby...

I noticed the mix of emotions on Rika's face. I was sure she was thinking about how unkind immigration rules could be. How they'd separated her from the father she loved. How they might, in effect, force these young women to stay with a father who only saw them as a means of making a living.

*Damn.* I didn't want to disappoint her, but I had no choice.

"I specialized in criminal defense," I said. "Immigration law is very specific..."

Rika brightened. "Immigration law..." she murmured as she tapped around on her phone. She pulled up a photo of a business card, the one Diana Viera had given us when we were investigating her husband's murder. "I heard from one of Lita's friends that she's got an immigration lawyer volunteering part-time at her office," Rika said to me.

Recalling what Ms. Viera's office was like when we talked to her about her husband's death, I hoped the new attorney hadn't already been swept away by a paper avalanche. And I seriously hoped they'd been able to bring a full-time legal assistant on board to get things organized.

"Do you have a cell phone?" Rika asked the twins.

They nodded enthusiastically. "*Da! Da!*" They said.

Rika tapped the mic again. "Take my phone and send this card to yourself. Then download this translation app and take it with you to her office."

They read the translation, then the pregnant one took Rika's phone and texted the photo of the card to herself.

"Can you get away to see her?"

"*Da*," she replied, then explained via the translator that she could say she had a doctor's appointment and it was normal for her sister to go along with her.

"*Tatal vine!*" one of the Vatamanu men on the high wire called in a warning tone.

"Father..." One of the twins explained before they turned to run back to their places. Then they stopped, twisted their torsos around, and said, "*Multumesc!* Thank you!" in unison before continuing. Seconds later, Anatolie stepped in through a back door and eyed us suspiciously.

"You are back? Why are you here again? I don't want you distract *familia mea*." He didn't seem to notice he'd switched back to Romanian at the end of his sentence.

"We're just here to see Constata," Rika said.

"There." He pointed to the door he'd come in through. "Find room with the costumes. She's there, maybe."

He turned his back to us and started yelling at his family in Romanian.

"Why did we decide he wasn't the killer again?" Rika asked under her breath.

"Motive," I replied.

"Maybe being a controlling, abusive asshole is motive enough."

"Yeah," I let out a slow breath as I looked back at the twins, their eyes downcast as Anatolie berated them. "Sometimes it is."

**Rika**

Once we walked through the door at the back of the circus tent, we were in the hallway of a grungy, fluorescently lit building of unknown origin. There were doors with windows in them on either side of the hall. We started looking in each one, trying to find the wardrobe room.

The first room looked like a hangout for the circus dogs, complete with crates and toys. The divider wall between that room and the next had been opened and that space included huge bags of dog food and training treats, plus two grooming tables with various accessories.

As we continued through the hall, we saw show props, crates, and boxes, but no costumes or clothing.

The door at the end of that hall opened into a high-ceilinged warehouse full of larger props, tools, and a forklift. Across the warehouse were bathrooms marked "Ladies" and "Gentlemen." To the left were huge, open garage doors, but no one was around that I could see.

"Is there another building we missed?" I mused aloud. "I feel like the wardrobe department should be closer to the tent."

"That does seem like the logical way to do it," Nick replied. "But I have zero circus experience..." He lifted his chin toward a door he spotted to the right of us. "That one doesn't look like an outside door," he said.

After avoiding being hit by the surprisingly fast-moving forklift—with a driver who yelled at us in a Slavic language—we walked over and opened the door.

This room was much bigger than the ones in the hallway, filled with rack after rack of costumes. Maybe this is why wardrobe wasn't up front—the space requirement.

"I didn't expect this," Nick said. It was dark, so he started flipping switches, but the lights remained off. The only illumination came from two tiny windows at the top of one wall.

"Me either. Seems like an awful lot of clothes for one circus troupe." But as I squinted at the nearest rack, I noticed there were multiples of each costume.

That made sense. They'd need to be laundered, and probably repaired often.

Along one wall were signs that read, "Dry Clean, Machine Wash, Hand Wash, and Spot Clean" in large block letters. Each sign was translated into four different languages and had a large laundry cart under it. From what I could see, the many metal posts in the room also held signs indicating where the costumes for each act were hung.

"I can't get the lights to come on," Nick said. "Maybe they blew a fuse or something."

In one dark corner near the door, I noted a hot plate with a pan on it, a microwave, and a water boiler and wondered if they could affect the circuit breaker in a room this large.

Then, I thought I heard footsteps near the back of the room. Nick didn't seem to hear, which meant I was able to get in front of him and start walking down the center aisle toward the back. I didn't want him thinking he was the leader, ergo the boss, of our little operation.

Nick followed behind me without objection. "Yeah, that's not creepy at all," he said sarcastically. He tilted his head, indicating a mannequin done up head-to-toe like a clown, flanked by oddly attired dressmaker dummies. The dummies were adjusted so there was space down the center or across the middle, like a bunch of bisected torsos.

It was like the clown killed them and cut them up into pieces.

I shook off the strange feeling it gave me, telling myself things would look less creepy once we had more light.

"Constata?" I called out.

Nick checked his phone. "Maybe she's at lun—" he began, as something sliced through the air between us.

He whipped his head to his left and I followed suit. "Is that a..." He pulled something from the middle of the clown's forehead.

"Knife," we said at the same time.

A second object whooshed by us. The clown now had a second knife buried in him, this one in his neck.

"Shit!" I cried.

"Fuck!" Nick yelled at the same time.

We dove in opposite directions to avoid being in the direct path of the lethal weapons.

*Oh, my God!* Was someone throwing knives at us?

"Constata," Nick called from between two racks. "If that's you, we're just here investigating Grigore's—Ugh!"

"Nick?" I cried. "Are you okay?"

"Shhh!"

I felt my phone vibrate. It was a text from Nick.

*Ear is bleeding but I'm okay. Don't call attention to yourself.*

This knife-thrower wasn't messing around! I mentally flipped back through the Cirque de Sorbet website but didn't remember a knife thrower being mentioned.

*Get out!* my phone screen read.

*Not without you,* I replied.

*Damn it, Rika! You can go get help.*

I quickly considered the mostly empty warehouse and the long empty hallway back to the tent. And even if I got there, I didn't know if the Vatamanus would rush back here to help.

Maybe the poodles?

No, they probably weren't trained for this sort of thing.

I wasn't leaving Nick.

"Over here!" I heard Nick yell.

It took me a split second to realize he was talking to the knife-thrower, not me. He was trying to give me a chance to escape.

I heard one set of feet running, then another.

The first sounded like Nick's boots. The second sounded slower, louder and clompier.

Both were headed toward the front of the room, so I headed that way too.

Then, the footsteps stopped. I ducked into a rack of clothes in case the thrower was aiming at me. But the hangers gave way, causing me to crash through them and fall out the other side.

*What a stupid, clumsy mistake. I could use some ninja skills right about now.*

The clomping footsteps started coming my way, but Nick yelled, "You couldn't hit the side of a barn with a sledgehammer," and they moved away again.

I tried to get up but was jerked back by my hair. I turned to find I was being held hostage by a zipper on the back of a blingy, grown-up sized onesie. Somehow, a lock of my hair had gotten tangled up in it when I plowed through the rack of clothes. I knew from experience that it would take forever to sort out properly. Clutching the costume, I pulled, ripping my hair out at the roots, leaving a sizeable clump of it on the zipper.

I thought I saw the top of Nick's head moving quickly toward the front of the room. Then a knife flew through the air—more awkwardly this time—hit the wall where he'd *just* been and fell to the cement floor with a clatter.

*Holy mother of Zeus!* We were in a fight to the death with the murderer!

No way was I running away and leaving Nick with this person. He or she had already come close to hitting Nick several times. I imagined him with a scar on his forehead and that wasn't bad at all. Then I imagined a knife sticking out of Nick's eye, like poor Grigore with the screwdriver.

Rage swept through me, triggering adrenaline that shot up to my brain, nearly blowing my head off.

Nobody—and I mean *nobody*—was going to mess with Nick's beautiful eyes!

I kicked off my tennis shoes and ran toward the sound, noiselessly, in my stocking feet. I made it to Constata's kitchen corner just in time to see a hand, holding a knife, sticking up above a clothing rack, poised to throw at the opposite corner.

The opposite corner where Nick was standing, looking the other way, probably searching for me.

I was close enough to touch the cooking paraphernalia, so I reached behind me and grabbed the closest thing I could find. Lifting the heavy object, I threw it with such force, I stumbled forward before regaining my balance.

I heard a heavy thud, followed by a clunk, as the cast iron skillet fell off the head of our attacker, who was facedown on the floor.

Nick and I walked over to my victim. We stood there, staring in surprise at the full-figured, gray-haired woman moaning at our feet.

When I looked up, I realized Nick was now looking at me, his expression more shocked than I'd ever seen it. "You did it," he said. "You threw a cast-iron skillet across the room and beaned her."

"I..." No that wasn't possible. I was a five-foot-four—and a half—geek. "I don't know how..." My voice drifted off again. How *did* I do that? "Well, it wasn't a big skillet," I said.

"It's cast iron," Nick pointed out. He shook his head in wonder. "Looks like you inherited your grandma's superpower."

# CHAPTER NINE

**Nick**

If I hadn't seen it with my own eyes, I wouldn't have believed it. I was pretty sure my college physics professor would deem it impossible. Somehow, Rika had thrown a cast-iron skillet over twenty feet and hit her target in the head. Just like Mrs. Delacruz had.

It wasn't a fluke. It was more like a freak genetic ability, the likes of which I'd never seen before.

"Did you know you could do that?" I asked.

"No," she replied. "I told you I thought they were making it up about my Lita all these years. I certainly didn't think I could do this... whatever 'this' is." She stared at the skillet, looking genuinely bewildered.

The groaning woman rolled to her back, saw me standing over her and started yelling in several languages before she got to one I could understand.

"Help me!" she was screaming to anyone but us. She was wearing an emerald green vest over a long-sleeve white shirt. Her full skirt—same color as the vest—was tangled around her legs.

"Nick," Rika said. She tossed her head, directing me to step back and let her handle this.

I guess she'd handled it pretty well up until now. I kicked the remaining knife away from our would-be assassin, took two steps back, and rested my hands on my hips, interested to see what Rika would do next.

She knelt, took the lady by the arm and gently pulled her to a sitting position. "Are you all right?"

Not what I would have opened with. And I certainly wasn't feeling as sympathetic as Rika sounded. I touched my right ear.

Still bleeding.

The woman's wrinkled face showed surprise. She rubbed the lump on the back of her gray head. "You hit me?" She gazed down at her skillet. "With that?"

"Yes," Rika said. "I'm sorry. I just couldn't let you hurt my partner."

The woman lifted her head and stared up at me. She flipped her eyebrows. "This your partner?"

I let out an involuntary laugh. The woman's look was suggestive, but at least she was recovered from the knock to the head.

Rika smiled. "We're private investigators. We're looking into the death of Grigore Vatamanu."

"Grigore..." The woman's hand touched the heavy silver crucifix dangling from a chain around her neck. Tears appeared in the corners of her hooded, caramel eyes. She focused them on me. "I thought you his, ehh..." She searched for the right word. "Murder." Her accent sounded a lot like Anatolie's but thicker.

"You thought I was his murderer?" I clarified.

She nodded.

"Are you Constata?" I asked. She nodded. "We called out your name and told you why we were here."

"I not understand," she claimed. "My hearing is eh... *cuidat...* strange, for long time now. In old days, when I was child, my father shoot me out of cannon." She tapped her ear. "Ringing all the time. Sometimes not sure what I hear."

"A human cannonball?" I asked doubtfully. "Were they still doing that in the 1900's?"

Rika gave me an *I wish you would let me handle this* look. "A new record was set for being shot from a cannon in 2002," she said. "And someone died from it in 2011."

Was she yanking my chain?

"That is right!" Constata cried, clearly impressed with my partner's circus acumen.

How could I have doubted Rika's knowledge of random facts? She googled—excuse me, bingged—every question that ever passed through her head.

Truth be told, it was one of my favorite things about her, although I couldn't say why.

Maybe because after all those years of same ol' same ol' where women were concerned, I liked that she could surprise me.

Constata struggled to get off the floor. I pulled her up, then took her elbow and helped her over to a red plastic chair that was sitting near the sewing machine.

"Thank you," she said, smoothing the bottom half of her skirt before sitting. "Sorry for knives. I fear since Grigore die." She crossed herself.

"Why do you think they'd come after you?" I asked.

"I do not know!" She threw her hands up dramatically. "I only friend of Grigore. If he know something or..." her voice trailed off. She shook her head and let her hands drop to her lap.

"Do you have any idea who would do this to him?" Rika asked.

"This is what I think of, every minute, every day," Constata replied. "I try." She tapped her head with her knuckle. "I try remember." She grasped the necklace again. "God forgive me, I think of this for me, not only Grigore. What if they think I know?"

"Who is 'they'?" I asked.

She shrugged, her eyes widening fearfully. "I told you, I do not know. That why I throw knives."

I thought about the fact that the person who killed Grigore had no problem plunging an object into his eye. This woman had been trying to do the same to me. "Where did you learn the knife-throwing?" I asked.

She looked at me like I was an idiot. "I work in circus all my life! Perhaps you cannot see now, but I was beautiful girl. I become part of knife-thrower act..." Her eyes peered into the clothing racks as though she saw a memory there. "And when he not practicing or making love to me, he teach me throwing."

Too much information. She could have left out the "making love" part. This woman was older than my mom, and, ageist, sexist or not, I didn't want any amorous videos running through my mind starring either one of them.

"Constata..." Rika said the name softly. "Did you speak to Grigore the last few days before he died?"

"Yes... Grigore very upset."

"About what?" I asked.

Again, she looked at me like I was an idiot. "About surgery! They say, 'low risk,' but low risk for Teodor. For Grigore, false leg, all the way from here." She touched the place where her hip connected to her leg. "He woul' have...what do you call it —*terapy?*"

"Physical therapy?" Rika helped.

"Yes! Months. Years," Constata continued. "Or in wheelchair. But, worse for him was to lose Teodor. Grigore not inde..." She tapped her head again. "Inde..."

"Independent?" Rika offered.

"Yes. Grigore not independent like Teodor."

"Is there a chance someone wanted to kill Teodor and made a mistake?" Rika asked. "Or assumed if they killed Grigore they'd kill them both?"

Constata shook her head. "Teodor was a strong, eh, *personalitate*?" She didn't seem sure about the word.

"A strong personality?" Rika said.

"Yes, he make people angry, but not strangers. People he know. And these people know what twin Grigore and what twin Teodor."

"What about their father?" I asked.

"Anatolie?" Constata snorted. "Anatolie is all words, no biting." She paused. "That is how you say it?"

"All bark. No bite," Rika said.

"Yes, that is Anatolie. After my parents die, when I was nineteen, every day, Anatolie tell me he going to come into my tent that night and—"

I put up a hand. "We get the idea."

"Three nights, I sit with knife. Awake. Then, I put knife under pillow for many months. He never come."

"But his daughters seem afraid of him," Rika pointed out.

"Oh, yes." Constata frowned and touched her crucifix again. "Anatolie think family is possession. Very bad to them. Poor girls. Good, sweet like mother. God rest..." She murmured something in another language and touched her crucifix.

I realized she probably knew Anatolie's wife. Anatolie's late wife, apparently.

I started to point out to her that this contradicted what she'd told us about Anatolie being all bark and no bite, therefore, unlikely to be the murderer. But she wasn't on the witness stand and I didn't think it would get us anywhere.

"Okay, thanks for your time," I said.

Rika gave me the same dirty look she'd given me several times when we were questioning people about her missing dad and his dead sous chef a few weeks ago. I'd ignored it at the time because we had more important matters at hand and she was under a lot of stress, but it was starting to bug me.

Rika found her discarded shoes and slipped them back on,

told Constata goodbye and followed me out. We decided to exit through the open warehouse doors instead of going back through the tent. She was lost in thought, but not sharing any of those thoughts with me. I liked it better when she thought aloud.

"What are those looks you keep giving me when we question witnesses?" I asked.

"What do you mean?"

"I mean you give me dirty looks. Sometimes in the middle of questioning and often when we're about to leave."

"When *you're* about to leave," she corrected.

"What does that mean? We leave together."

"But we don't decide to leave together. You just decide you're done and thank them for their time or whatever. If anything, I should be the one deciding when we're done."

"I *have* questioned a lot of witnesses in my time," I pointed out. I didn't add that I'd probably questioned a lot more witnesses than she had, starting with mock trials in law school, then during depositions, then in actual trials.

"You have," she agreed. "But you weren't working as an investigator. You were asking as a lawyer after all the investigation work had been done."

"What does that mean?"

We'd reached the truck and she moved in front of me toward the passenger door.

"Nothing. It's just a different job. Most of the important facts of the case had been discovered before you started those trials. The lawyering part is more about marketing and semantics."

I felt my mouth fall open but got it closed before she turned and looked at me. For once, I didn't have to fight the urge to open the door for her. I clicked the key fob to unlock the doors, went around to my side and slid in.

As she climbed in, instead of starting up the truck, I turned and looked at her. "Marketing and semantics?"

"Everybody has their job," Rika said. "Detectives and P.I.'s dig up the facts. Lawyers arrange them for the jury."

"Arrange them," I replied, keeping my tone flat. "Kind of like a florist."

She considered my words for a moment. "I'd never thought of that metaphor, but it's a good one. Each piece of evidence is like a flower in the bouquet. You arrange them so the jury will be more attracted to your bouquet than the prosecution's."

I opened my mouth to argue—something I knew I was good at from my previous job. But no reply came to mind.

Apparently, I wasted all that money I spent on law school. I could have spent that time in a fucking flower shop and gained the same skill set.

Is this why I was getting mixed signals from her? Because she was attracted but didn't want to waste her time on a glorified flower arranger?

I stuck the key in, turned on the ignition, and put the truck in Reverse.

"You're mad," she said.

I shoved the gear shift back into Park and twisted toward her. "You don't think I have reason to be? I have seven years of post-secondary education and you just called me a flower arranger."

"No, you called yourself a flower arranger and I agreed with you."

*Damn it!* She was trying to out-argue me, and succeeding, with no law degree whatsoever. She was the one woman in the world I cared about impressing, and she was clearly not impressed.

I'd been a pretty confident guy most of my life, but, with just a few words, Rika had sucked the wind right out of my sails.

"I was being sarcastic when I brought up the flower arranging. I had no idea you thought I was incompetent at this job."

Her expression softened. "That's not what I meant," she said.

"This is just a different job than you're used to, but it's the one I've dreamed about and worked toward for years."

Instead of responding, I changed gears again, backed out, and rolled to the parking lot exit.

"Nick," Rika said as the traffic on the road streamed past the front of the truck.

I raised my eyebrows at her but didn't say anything.

"What did you do when you left last night?"

"What?"

"Humor me."

"Okay..." I shrugged. "I went through a car wash. Drove back to the hotel. Ran on the treadmill for an hour or so. Showered. Ate a bag of microwave popcorn while I watched TV and fell asleep."

"Do you want to know what I did?"

"Sure."

"Because I knew we'd be coming back here, I got on the internet and searched Cirque de Sorbet, again—articles that were written about it, etcetera. It's how I stumbled onto the human cannonball facts in a listing of interesting circus accidents."

Was she saying I wasn't working hard enough? I'd always been the hardest working person on the team, from high school football to the law firm.

"You think I'm a slacker," I paraphrased. "I'm not pulling my weight as a partner."

She frowned at me and shook her head. "No, you're just used to doing a different job. That's all I meant. So, for now, in this job, the leadership role should default to me. Or, we decide things together. You shouldn't be the sole decider of when an interview is over. And, for the record, I like having you as a partner. You helped me get my dad back and saved my ass more than once."

Now it sounded like she was saying she was the brains and I was the brawn. I think one or both of us had made jokes about that. Well, I'd thought they were jokes at the time.

A slow-simmering anger had filled my gut and was starting to spill out onto my other organs. I decided I needed time to chew on Rika's words before I said something I might regret later.

Still, I had to rub that bothersome tingle from the back of my neck. I'd been feeling it a lot more since I'd come to L.A. Maybe I needed to see a doctor.

"Okay, moving on," I said as I turned the pickup onto the busy street. "What do you think about Constata?"

∾

**Rika**

Nick was angry at me. He was trying to hide it, but clearly not hard enough. The tightness of his jaw caused my muscles to tense up and stay that way.

But I was also kind of proud of myself for standing up to him. My communication courage came and went, but I'd made a conscious decision recently to work on the problem.

However, I guess it was kind of unfortunate that I'd picked a moment when Nick pissed me off to say what was on my mind instead of, say, a moment when his mere presence had me so turned on, I could barely stand it, which was most of the moments.

But what would that honest conversation be like?

*Uh, look, Nick, I've been super into you since the day we met in Bolo and I'd like to rip off your clothes and give you a tongue bath. But I've gained some weight again, and I'm kind of freaked out about you seeing me naked right now. And I don't know if you noticed them that day you caught me in your bathroom, but I have a few lines on my body I'm sure you've never seen on the other women you've had. They're called "stretch marks," and I have them because I used to weigh about twice as much as I do now.*

*Honestly, I'm not sure if the stretch marks are still there. The more stressed I am when I look in the mirror, the more of them I think I see, which makes me want to eat to calm my nerves, which is why I live in constant fear of losing my tenuous grasp on my diet and gaining all the weight back.*

*And, now that I'm being totally honest, this weight gain-weight loss process may have made me kind of crazy because even after all those lost jean sizes, I'm constantly convinced parts of me are out of proportion. In fact, whenever I think someone is watching me walk away, I'm convinced I'm waddling like a duck. Oh, and if we ever do hook up for real, I probably won't be very good in bed because I'll be worried about how to keep you from getting a good a look at me.*

Uh, no. That conversation was not happening. Well, maybe on my deathbed, if he was still around for that.

"What do you think of Constata?" Nick asked.

I took in a deep breath and let it out slowly, relieved he was moving on to a different topic. "I can't imagine her murdering anyone."

Nick stopped at the red light and looked at me like I'd lost my mind. "She just tried to kill us," he replied. "Or, at least me."

"She thought she was defending herself," I argued. "That's totally different."

"We were no more of a threat to her than Grigore was. Maybe she thought she needed to defend herself against him, too."

I didn't bother to answer because we both knew his last statement was ludicrous and he was only arguing because that's what he was trained for.

My phone hummed. I grabbed it and read a text from my Tía Margo telling me to be sure to come home for dinner. Lita and Mrs. Ruíz were making a "special" one. I scanned my brain, wondering if I'd forgotten someone's birthday.

*Nothing. Oh, well, I'll find out tonight.*

When I clicked out of the text, I noticed I had an unopened email. And, it was from Julian! I went straight to it and started reading.

"We've got closeups of the murder weapon," I said to Nick.

"The preliminary report from the lab says the only fingerprints are Teodor's, and you and I both saw him grab it when he was panicked about his brother... However, the report also says the handle was likely cleaned with antiseptic recently."

"That sounds like a lead," Nick said. "Maybe it was someone in the medical profession."

His tone made me check his expression.

*A little combative... Kind of smug... and something else...*

He wanted it to be Dr. Choi! I was sure of it! Then I'd never get my super awesome Hogwarts model!

Wait, did Nick refuse to give me the doctor's card out of jealousy?

I laid back on the headrest and savored the thought before getting my brain back in the game. "That means the person didn't panic after the murder," I thought aloud. "Less likely that it was a crime of passion."

"There have been plenty of murders that happened in the moment and the killer tried to cover their tracks afterward," Nick argued, of course.

"That's why I said, 'less likely' and not 'impossible'," I replied.

"Okay, I can go with less likely," he said. "Where'd you get the information?"

"Julian emailed it to me," I said as I scanned through my mental list of suspects.

"Julian?" he said in an odd tone, but I was too busy going over the case again to pay attention.

Erissa could have pulled off the murder and kept her head together, I was sure of it. Anatolie, maybe, except he would have known if one died the other would, too.

And if he was angry at Teodor, wouldn't it have been much more satisfying to sink the weapon into his eye? Unless he wanted to torture him with the knowledge that he was stuck there in the bed with his dead brother, knowing he was next.

*Wow.* I could totally see Anatolie doing something like that.

"I didn't know you were still talking to Julian," Nick said. This time, the tone of voice registered loud and clear. He didn't approve of me talking to Julian.

"Why would I not be talking to Julian?" I asked. "He's the only contact I have who's a cop..." I thought about Detectives Winchell and Hertz. "Well, the only one who likes me," I corrected.

"Yeah, that's the problem," Nick said.

"What are you talking about?" I was a decent person, why shouldn't Julian like me?

The stoplight turned yellow and, instead of gunning it to get through the intersection, like a normal person, Nick hit the brake.

"Are you really asking me what's wrong with using Julian as your LAPD informant?"

I flipped my hands, palms up and said, "Yeah."

Nick's jaw went tight, again. He propped an elbow on his driver's side door, just below the window, his thumb cradling his chin, his hand forming a finger moustache—or fingerstache, as I call it. He sucked in a huge breath and blew it out.

I watched him, waiting for his explanation until the light turned green and we started rolling.

"Do you have any more appointments right now?" Nick asked.

"No," I replied.

"Then what do you say we head to the hospital and see if we can find anyone to talk to?" He turned and gave me a hard look. "Is that okay with you, boss?"

*Jeez!* Men were so freaking sensitive, I didn't know how they managed to fight in all the wars they started. "Sure," I said as he took the freeway entrance ramp. "Hospital sounds great."

# CHAPTER TEN

**Rika**

When we got to the hospital, we were told Teodor still wasn't allowed visitors and Dr. Duarte was in surgery. However, I knew that Dr. Washington's psychiatry practice was housed in the professional building right next to the hospital. I figured we might as well try to see her while we were in the area.

The waiting room was the coolest I'd ever seen, the focal point being a realistic undersea mural with coral, angel fish and conch shells.

Personally, I would have added a shark or two to keep things interesting, but maybe that wasn't a good choice for a place where anxiety-ridden people came for help.

When the receptionist opened the sliding window to see who'd come in, my eyes caught on her long hair, which had been dyed emerald green. I wondered if she'd colored it to match the office because she looked like she belonged in the mural. Like a beautiful, coppery-skinned mermaid.

She told us Dr. Washington was with a patient, but if we could wait about twenty minutes, the doctor would likely be willing to use part of her lunch hour to talk to us, considering what happened to Grigore.

At the appointed time, the door opened, and a man walked out briskly, avoiding eye contact.

"Bye! See you next week, Mr. Ray," the mermaid called after him. You'd think the receptionist for a psychiatry office would be able to pick up on the signs that the patient wanted to slip out as inconspicuously as possible. But, who knew, there might be studies saying a cheerful farewell increased endorphin output or something.

*Hm.* Maybe I hadn't spent enough time on psychology courses. I wondered if I could learn things that would help me create profiles of murderers or know better when people were lying to me. I made a mental note to check the online course catalogues for classes.

A middle-aged woman with mahogany-colored skin came to the doorway. She had super cool hair, with braids running up her scalp on the sides, disappearing into a wide, fluffy version of a mohawk on the top. She wore a V-necked ruby dress and high-heeled sandals. Each shoe had one gold loop on the top. The shape of the loops mimicked the top of the gold Egyptian ankh hanging from her neck.

But I especially liked the way she held herself. The combination of excellent posture and secure confidence dazzled me.

That familiar envious feeling seeped through me. Whenever I saw a woman who had her look completely together, my high school yearnings returned and I wanted to be a cool girl, despite my geek pride and love of nerd shirts.

"I'm Kenya Washington," she said, reaching out to shake our hands. "How can I help you?"

"We're here about Teodor and Grigore," I said before Nick could take over. "We've been asked to investigate the case by Teodor's fiancée. I'm Rika Martín and this is Nick Owen."

Dr. Washington's face fell at the mention of the twins. "Yes, okay," she said quietly. "Come on in."

We followed her into her office and sat on a long sofa that faced her desk. Instead of going behind the desk, she took an upholstered chair at a right angle to us.

"Normally, I wouldn't talk to you about any of this, but both twins signed waivers because of the documentary." She took a deep breath. "I never dreamed of this outcome."

"Can you tell us about Grigore?" Nick asked.

Dr. Washington stared out the window for several seconds before she focused her gaze on us. "I guess I'd describe him as a gentle soul. He was the quieter twin and seemed the most fragile. He was the one I was worried about from the beginning."

Nick and I both leaned in. "Worried about?" I repeated.

"I wasn't convinced, at first, that he wanted the surgery."

"Because of the prosthetic leg?" Nick asked. "Or losing his job?"

She shook her head. "No... granted, that was probably part of it, but it was mostly the idea of losing his brother," she said. "They'd been together constantly for over thirty years—their entire lives. Grigore seemed to have trouble imagining a life without Teodor attached to him. Teodor is the more dominant personality. He made most of the decisions. Even though they have—um, *had*—two different brains doesn't mean they weren't used to borrowing each other's. They had very co-dependent systems in place."

"What does that mean?" Nick asked.

"For instance, we first met at a restaurant near here because I wanted to observe them in a more casual setting. Teodor spoke to the waitress for both of them. Grigore was brought the wrong meal, but Teodor sent it back. Grigore didn't need to speak up because he and his brother knew each other so well."

That made sense. Even married couples did that to some extent, didn't they? The dependency had to be magnified a thousand-fold with conjoined twins. "And what part did Grigore play?" I asked.

"From what I gathered, he tended to do the quieter, more meticulous, tasks. He was the one who paid the bills. Teodor would say they needed a certain item, but Grigore was the one who did the research online and made the purchase. I think Grigore also wrote their emails."

Buying things. Paying bills. Writing emails. Not exactly the kind of high-risk behaviors that put you on a hit list. "When was the last time you spoke to him?" I asked.

Dr. Washington's shoulders sagged, her perfect posture gone. "The night before he, um..." She leaned toward her desk, pulled a tissue from a blue Kleenex box, and dabbed at her eyes. "He called me. My understanding was that he had just called Dr. Choi and tried to cancel the surgery. Teodor was determined they were having it. They put me on speaker phone, and I tried to mediate. It was a challenge. Looking at it from a typical person's point of view, if they were separated, they could have their own lives. To most of us that seems like freedom. On the other hand, they weren't children. The adjustment would be hard and Grigore would go from what he thought of as normal to being disabled to an extent the surgeons couldn't fully predict."

I opened my mouth to ask another question, but she seemed to have more to say, so I kept quiet.

She lifted her hands slightly and turned them, palms up, as if showing us they were empty. "I felt helpless," she continued. "I have a degree from a great medical school, a PH.D. in psychology and I'm a board-certified psychiatrist." She shook her head. "But nobody trains you for this. With Grigore attached, Teodor couldn't live the life he wanted. Without Teodor attached, Grigore saw a bleak future for himself. I think each of them wanted me to take their side and talk sense into the other, but how could I do that? There was no win-win. If one of them won the argument, the other would suffer permanently."

"How did you leave things?" Nick asked.

"I told Grigore all the surgical team members were here, either way, and suggested he sleep on it. I reassured him that the operation would not be done without his consent." She looked away again. "I just... If I had done more... Maybe Grigore would still..." Her voice drifted off.

"How would you doing more keep someone from killing him?" Nick asked. "Grigore would have slept in the same bed that night no matter what you did." He watched her face with the keen eye of a trial lawyer. "Unless you think Teodor killed his brother."

She sucked in a quick breath but didn't make eye contact. "I could never make an accusation like that against a patient." She steadied her breathing, but it took effort.

I noticed she didn't deny that it could have been Teodor. In fact, the expression on her face indicated that Nick had guessed what she was thinking, but never planned to say.

"No," she said as if trying to convince herself. She met Nick's gaze. "Teodor had a healthy sense of self-preservation. There's no question in my mind he would have chosen staying conjoined with his brother over risking his own death. He definitely would have died soon after Grigore without medical intervention."

I wondered again if Erissa hired me to be the intervention middleman, so to speak. What if Grigore dug in his heels and Teodor became enraged that his brother was ruining his life, they fought, Teodor killed Grigore, then called Erissa—

No, that didn't make sense. Erissa hired me days before the murder. Could this have been a contingency plan? Or did she originally hire me for the reasons she stated, then send those extra confirmation texts the night before the surgeries after Teodor called with a plot to kill his brother?

Of course, Grigore would have been right there when Teodor made the call. But he could have been asleep. Or they could have plotted by text.

I blew out a frustrated sigh. Teodor and Erissa were the only people we'd found with reason to kill Grigore, but it still seemed farfetched that Teodor would sink a screwdriver into a body attached to his.

"What if Teodor wasn't thinking clearly?" Nick asked. "What if there was more than a verbal argument? What if Teodor became enraged that his brother was refusing to let him have the life he wanted? There were tools handy, in every room of the house—"

Clearly, his thoughts were running parallel to mine.

"I'm sorry," the doctor said, holding her hand in the Stop position. "I can't participate in this kind of conjecture about my patient."

Guess I couldn't blame her for that. It was her job to help her patients, but not to help them become suspects in a murder case. "Just one more thing," I said, wanting to get my question in before she decided it was best to throw us out. "Was there anyone else in Grigore's life who had motive to kill him?"

"Not that I know of."

"He never mentioned any enemies?" Nick asked. "Jilted lovers? Seedy characters in his life?"

"I'm sorry," she said. "I went back through all my notes right after it happened. I didn't find anything like that."

"Okay, thanks for—" Nick began before he saw the expression on my face. He lifted his brows and lowered his chin in a *You've got the floor, Sherlock* gesture. You'd think a gesture couldn't say all that, but this one did. Sarcastic or not, at least he'd listened to my grievance and was abiding by my wishes... today, anyway.

I stood. "Thanks for your time." I pulled a card from my back pocket. "If you remember anything else, would you let me know?"

"Sure," she said as she stood to usher us out.

**Rika**

On the way to my grandmother's house, I brought up the idea of Erissa, or Erissa and Teodor, as the murderer again and, even though I was sure he was considering the possibility when we were in Dr. Washington's office, Nick insisted poor, diabetic, sexy Erissa couldn't be involved in this.

Okay, I added the "sexy" part in there, but he did try to bring her diabetic condition into it.

"That's the kind of thing attorneys slide into trials hoping there are people on the jury dumb enough to think having a chronic health condition automatically makes you less homicidal," I said. "Know your audience."

Nick threw his head back and laughed. I chuckled, too, then realized he was still smiling at me, giving me that warm look that told me he appreciated my mind.

Whenever he did that, my whole body felt full, in a good way, like I was sucking in helium and, at any moment, I might just float into the air like a giant balloon in the Macy's parade. Unfortunately, I'd also see my Garfield-shaped body getting caught on a building and crashing to the asphalt.

Honestly, unless we were in the middle of interviewing someone, the stress of solving the case wasn't nearly as extreme as the stress surrounding my personal life.

I was still living at Lita's, but thinking I really needed to get my own place because there was a part of me—okay, most of me —that wanted to do grownup things at my own grownup place with Nick, once I lost this extra weight, of course.

However, I couldn't get my own place unless I accepted the salary Nick was expecting me to take. He'd pointed out, repeatedly, that it took most businesses several years to be profitable. And that they were typically financed by an investor or a bank, so there was no reason for me to be "silly" about it.

But if he was paying for my apartment, wouldn't that make

me a kept woman? Especially if we were doing the mattress dance in there.

And, that wasn't my only problem. Nick's presence was really starting to get to me. The sexual tension I experienced nearly every second I was in a room with him was driving me out of my mind. We were together all day and every night until after dinner.

Lita had made it clear he was not just invited but required to eat with us or she and Mrs. Ruíz would be insulted.

As much as she hadn't wanted men around for the last couple of decades, she'd seen how messed up Nick's hands were after the fighting he'd done to get me and my dad out of trouble.

He'd also ended up with bruises on his face, but when my grandmother and Mrs. Ruíz tried to make a big deal about it, he acted like the bruises didn't bother him at all. I guess maybe it made sense, considering he'd been an athlete in school. Football players were always getting banged up.

Now, the bruises were mostly gone, and his hands looked normal. I was glad he was a fast healer so I could quit feeling guilty every time I looked at him.

But tonight, as we were sitting down to dinner with Lita, Mrs. Ruíz, LeeAnne, my aunts and my cousin, I couldn't get the comment Nick had made—the one about my eyes flashing—out of my head. There was something about that statement that made every organ in my body snap to attention.

That odd sentence had clarified things in a way they should probably have been clear to me already, considering how much Nick had done for me.

After the shock of his words wore off, I wondered why he hadn't tried harder to hook up with me. I mean, yes, I'd frozen up at least half the times he'd touched me since he'd agreed to stay in town. But if he hadn't backed off immediately, I was pretty sure I could have gotten past my body issues and fallen completely under his spell.

*Bleh!*

I'd grossed myself out with that very un-feminist thought. Men were supposed to take no for an answer nowadays. They couldn't go dragging women around by their hair and force themselves on them. Only creeps did that, and I didn't want a creep.

The ball was probably in my court. I should grow a pair and talk to him about it.

Well, growing a pair probably wouldn't be the best tactic. Nick probably wouldn't want to encounter said pair when he made it to third base. Or was it second base?

Honestly, I wasn't sure which bases were what. Maybe if I'd ever watched a whole baseball game—*snore, snore*—it would be clearer.

I glanced at Nick, saw he was looking at me then turned my attention to the beef and cheese enchiladas Mrs. Ruíz had made for dinner. Desserts aside, enchiladas were the perfect combination of fat and carbs. And the perfect food for keeping every ounce of weight on me and maybe adding a few more.

My life felt like a catch-22. I wanted to lose weight now that Nick was around, so I'd have the courage to take my clothes off in front of him. However, the stress of him financing our business venture and worrying whether he was happy being a private investigator, living in L.A., and being my business partner kept me craving comfort food and sweets, nonstop.

"Anyways," LeeAnne was saying. "When I talked to Petra, she sounded like she and Dwight were doing great. Such a relief. I love him, but I didn't imagine we'd ever get to have our own lives." Dwight was LeeAnne's brother, who was on the autism spectrum and had a not-so-endearing communication style, but somehow managed to find a woman as obsessed with spiders and Spider-Man as he was.

Come to think of it, Dwight and Petra had met each other *after* Nick and me, yet they were already living together. Meanwhile, Nick and I, who hadn't been diagnosed with any special communication issues were...

What exactly?

*You should never have made him your business partner,* a voice in my head informed me for the thousandth time.

*But, then, how would you have kept him around?* another voice chimed in.

My hands flew up to cover my ears, attempting to block out my internal thoughts.

"Something we said?" my always-snarky Tía Madi asked. I looked around the table to see her, Tía Margo, Sofia, my grandmother, Mrs. Ruíz, LeeAnne and Nick, all staring at me.

I dropped my hands to my lap. Then I raised one to pick up my fork. My other hand was still lying in my lap doing nothing.

Everyone, including Nick, was still staring.

What did I usually do with the extra hand while I ate?

*Please, everyone quit looking at me so I can remember how to eat!* I wanted to scream.

I think there was a time when I wasn't self-conscious. When I wasn't bothered by a room full of people turning their attention on me. Back when I had both my parents, alive and with me. Before I lost them and started growing in girth much faster than height. Before kids started whispering behind my back or throwing things at my face. Before my aunt and grandmother started fighting over how I should be raised.

I wondered sometimes what parts of me would be different if—

*Dammit!* There was no point in wondering such things unless someone invented a way to go back in time and stop my mother from going to her yoga class.

I forced my mind to focus on the case at hand. "I'm going back to the duplex tonight," I blurted out. I hadn't meant to tell anyone that, especially my grandmother and Tía Margo.

"It's still a crime scene," Nick mansplained to me.

"Oh, really?" I said sarcastically. "Then what interest could I possibly have in it as the P.I. hired to investigate the crime?"

Nick's lips parted and I knew an argument was coming.

"I'll go!" LeeAnne volunteered way too enthusiastically. The last time she and I went out alone at night, there were shots fired on the freeway that we *might* have been responsible for.

"No." Nick's voice sounded like he was training a dog. "No way, LeeAnne. I—"

My grandmother interrupted. "You should call Julian," she said. "He would go with you."

Now, Nick's eyes were the one's flashing and not in a good way. Against all odds, considering her decades-long disgust with nearly all men, Lita had taken a fairly quick liking to Nick and an instant liking to Julian.

"Julian?" Nick said in a voice laced with annoyance. "He's a cop. He's the one who's supposed to keep people out of the crime scene."

"Mamá?" Tía Madi said. "What is this obsession you have lately with Julian?"

Nick's eyes darkened to thunderstorm mode. Still beautiful, but kind of scary. He hadn't been in the room the other times my grandmother brought up Julian.

Julian was a nice guy who had risked a lot to send me information I wasn't supposed to have when my dad was abducted. He could have lost his job.

"It's no obsession!" Lita replied. "He is a nice boy. A policeman. He's Latino and the same age as Rika."

"Since when are you into the LAPD?" Tía Margo chimed in.

My grandmother had never had the greatest faith in cops, coming from a place where cops and crooks could be especially difficult to sort out. Then, later, it was the LAPD who failed to find the person who abducted and murdered her daughter.

"And he's not Latin," I said. "He's Italian."

"How is that not Latin?" my grandmother asked. "The Romans spoke Latin. Rome is in Italy. So, Italians are more Latin than anyone."

*Hm.* She had a point.

"Mrs. Delacruz," Nick said. "I don't think it's fair to ask Julian to do anything more to endanger his job. If you think about it, he's still a rooky cop"—I noticed he emphasized the word "rooky"— "probably without a lot of education to get another job."

Was Nick trying to position himself as better boyfriend material than Julian by pointing out where Julian was lacking?

That was so cute! God, I hoped that was what he was doing.

"Julian has a bachelor's degree," Tía Madi pointed out with a smirk. I knew she liked Nick because she was always giving him a hard time.

Nick's eyes shifted to her. "I hear a lot of people who only have bachelor's degrees can't get jobs nowadays."

I was pretty sure he'd said "only" to point out that he had several more years of education after his bachelor's degree.

*Wow.* If we could just be alone right now and he reached out and touched me, I could go all the way with him, extra pounds or not.

He didn't do jealous in the typical caveman way, and that kind of behavior would have scared me off, anyway. But his more subtle lawyer-style jealousy was a total turn-on for me.

His gaze left Tía Madi and settled on me. "I'll go with Rika." His tone said, *I'm the man and I have spoken and, thus, it will be done.*

It was kind of hot but still brought out the feminist in me. "I didn't ask anyone to come," I said. "I'm perfectly fine going alone."

"*Rika.*" His gaze was bearing down on me.

*Ha!* Nick Owen might be my business partner, but he wasn't my boss. "*Nick,*" I said back, in the same bossy tone.

"Paprika Anise Martín," Lita said. "You let Nick go with you! If you insist on doing this private investigation business, I want you to take a man with muscles with you."

I flinched at the use of my full name, then cringed inwardly at the fact that my grandmother had mentioned Nick's muscles.

*Hm.* Maybe she was pushing me toward Julian because she wanted Nick for herself.

Everyone at the table was watching for my response. Watching with concern in their eyes, damn it!

When your mom is murdered, it leaves a lasting impression on the family, let me tell you.

"Sure, no problem." I turned my attention to Nick. "Just remember, I'm the brains. You're the brawn."

Everyone at the table laughed, knowing he had at least two more degrees than I did.

Satisfied with my answer, he went back to eating his enchiladas. LeeAnne started a story about a bitchy customer who'd come into the boutique where she worked. I breathed a sigh of relief.

Then the doorbell rang.

# CHAPTER ELEVEN

**Rika**

"Rika, can you get the door, please?" Lita said, but there was a strange formality to her voice.

Wondering what she was up to, I went to the door and opened it. Julian was standing on the porch, still in his police uniform, a big smile on his face and a big bouquet of flowers in his hand.

My eyes caught on the blossoms, and I had to swallow hard to keep the bile from coming up in my throat. Although I'd been surrounded by my grandmother's floral furniture as long as I could remember, my first memories of fresh flower arrangements were of the ones that came after my mother's body was found.

They came. And they came. And they came.

Not just to the funeral home, but to our house before and after the funeral.

The crime was horrible enough to make the news more than once. We were drowning in flower arrangements for what seemed like forever to eight-year-old me.

Finally, my grandmother put a sign on the door, directing the delivery people to take all flowers to the nursing home a few blocks away.

However, since then, every time there was any sort of flower delivery, I felt sick in a way it was hard to describe to anyone else.

I swallowed hard again. "Hi Julian," I said.

"Rika, you look great!" He leaned in and kissed my cheek, proving my grandmother's assertion that he was a true Latino. "I brought these for you." He held out the bouquet.

I told my hand to take it from him, but it wouldn't budge. I felt like I'd lost the use of my arms.

My grandmother, who knew about my aversion—though we'd never discussed what had caused it—sprinted over and took the flowers. "How beautiful!" she gushed. "I'll put these in water." She hustled them to the kitchen.

"Thanks for inviting me over for dinner," Julian said. He looked past me at the table. "Am I late?"

"No, it's fine!" Mrs. Ruíz said from the table. "We were just filling our plates."

"Come. Sit down!" Lita laid an extra plate on the table. She put it at the end where my grandfather used to sit, which meant Julian would be at a right angle from me on my left, Nick on my right.

Like I wasn't stressed enough already! I didn't know how to juggle two men, even if I wasn't sleeping with either of them. And how, exactly, did *I* invite Julian to dinner? I was tempted to check my phone to see if I'd butt-texted him.

"Did you get my email?" he asked as I followed him to the table. As I sat in my chair, I couldn't miss the expression on Nick's face. His mouth formed a straight line as his eyes stared at me accusingly.

*Shit!* I did not need this tonight!

I couldn't think of a way to ask Julian exactly how he'd ended up at dinner with us without making the situation even more awkward.

He was a nice guy and I would never want to embarrass him. Not to mention that I could use all the contacts I could get at the LAPD if my new business was to be a success.

Then I looked around the table and noticed my Tía Madi, cousin Sofia and so-called friend LeeAnne looked positively gleeful at the turn of events.

Sure, for them, dinner just got more exciting. I, on the other hand, was dying to fly off on my broomstick. Actually, flying off on one of those *Game of Thrones* dragons would be even cooler, and who could blame me for taking a spin on a dragon?

I looked at my enchiladas again. They weren't going to do the trick tonight. I'd need to follow them up with serious sweets.

Mrs. Ruíz shoveled five enchiladas from her giant pan onto Julian's plate. They barely fit, and my grandmother did not own small plates.

Julian smiled his perfect smile at her, then at my grandmother, who told Mrs. Ruíz not to forget the rice and beans. Mrs. Ruíz managed to squeeze some of each at the top and bottom of the plate.

"Thanks!" Julian said. "This looks great!"

My grandmother, who was sitting across from me, and to Julian's left, beamed at him. "How has your work been since we saw you last?" she asked. "Has anything exciting happened?"

The questions were fine, but I couldn't get past the beaming. Lita was not a woman who beamed at men.

Clearly, I'd tripped and fallen into an alternate universe where I was a man-juggler and my grandmother was a beamer.

Hefty high school me would have thought this was awesome, but all I wanted to do now was go to my room, find anime to watch on my computer and eat everything I could find in the house.

No, not anime. This called for my Harry Potter collector's edition DVDs.

"Yeah, we had a crazy one," Julian said. "That's why I wasn't here earlier. It was a high-speed chase."

"Jesus Christ Superstar!" LeeAnne cried. "Was that the one where the guy stole the RV?"

"Yeah, did you see it?" Julian replied.

"You bet I did!" LeeAnne cried. "That means I saw you on TV! Or, at least your car." Always willing to poke the bear, she turned to Nick. "Did you see it, Nick? Julian, here, is a real hero."

"Yep," Nick replied. "Him and about a hundred other cops that were chasing the RV. When I saw the video clip on my news app, I was thinking it would have been a great time to knock off a liquor store. Cops seem to have a hive mentality, like bees or ants."

Julian's eyes met Nick's and I was sure it wasn't lost on him that ants and bees were tiny creatures with tiny brains. Nick returned Julian's stare as if he wanted to squash him with his big cowboy boot.

My grandmother fake-laughed and looked pointedly at Mrs. Ruíz who joined in the fake laughter. "*Neeek*," Mrs. Ruíz jumped in, "you're so funny, always making jokes."

"Yes," Lita agreed. "Such a joker." She followed this with more fake laughter and gave me a look that made me fake laugh along with them.

Okay, this was getting too weird. Lita and Mrs. Ruíz were normally women who said exactly what they thought and didn't fake their emotions.

They laughed when they thought something was funny. They cried when they thought something was sad. They yelled when they were mad, and, in my grandmother's case, threw heavy objects.

I couldn't remember ever hearing either of them fake laugh in my life.

Then an idea popped into my head. If I asked Julian about the crime scene, it might convince Nick he was here as something other than my date without having to have a one-on-one talk about it.

I turned to Julian. "Have you heard if they're done processing the conjoined twin crime scene?"

"Oh, man, that's a weird one," Julian said. "Everybody's talking about it. I mean Siamese twins...?"

Nick tilted his head at me expectantly. I knew he was asking, *Aren't you going to politically correct him?*

I ignored Nick. "I know!" I agreed. "I'll bet the scene's a nightmare to process. All those medical personnel had to go stomping around in there. Plus, they had to take the dead body with the live one."

"Yeah, it's a tough one," he said. "I heard they went back in today looking for something. Probably gonna be there all night."

*Crap.* That meant I couldn't get in there until at least tomorrow or the next day.

Nick stood. "I'm sorry, ladies, but I've got to go. Forgot to do something important."

"Go?" Mrs. Ruíz said. "You've only eaten one of my enchiladas. Do you not like them?"

"Love 'em," Nick said. "Save the rest for me and I'll eat them tomorrow."

"But where are you going?" Lita asked.

"If I don't get my clothes to hotel housekeeping tonight, I won't have any clean ones."

"We could do your laundry," Mrs. Ruíz volunteered.

"Yes, you should bring it here," Lita agreed.

Nick shook his head. "You ladies have been so kind, I wouldn't dream of it. See y'all later," he said to the table in general without making eye contact with me. Then he strode to the door.

I was overwhelmed by panic at the thought of Nick leaving and Julian staying. It was all backward.

What if Nick left and never came back? I had a history of

people I cared about not coming back to me, although they didn't leave me by choice.

I jumped up and sprinted to the door. "Nick?" I said from the front stoop as I closed the door behind me.

He was at the bottom of the steps, but he stopped and turned. "Yeah?" he said, his face blank.

My guts knotted. I was used to a lot of different expressions from Nick, but not blank. Anything but blank. "I know you don't need to get your laundry done," I said. "You mentioned leaving it for them this morning."

"Yeah?" he replied. It felt to me like this particular "yeah" actually meant "What's it to you?"

"Do you want to talk?" I asked.

His eyes focused on the steps. He seemed to be considering my offer. His chin dipped once in what I assumed was a nod, then he came up the steps to where I was standing.

He moved in close and propped a hand on either side of the door, making me feel kind of hemmed in. "Why don't you tell me what you're playing at," he said.

"I'm not playing at anything. I'm not that kind of person. Maybe, with a witness for a case, but not..." I didn't know how to describe the situation we were in.

"That's not how it looks from my end. It looks to me like you put out just enough signals to keep me here to finance your business. Then you invite poor, clueless Boy Band in there to dinner to keep him on the string so he'll keep feeding you inside information from the LAPD."

I gasped. How could he think I'd do either of those things? I genuinely liked Julian and Nick!

Well, Nick I lo—no, I couldn't let myself think the word right now. What if I suddenly blurted it out? We'd never been on an actual date and we certainly had never had sex.

"Are you a user, Rika?" he asked.

The air left my lungs and it took me a minute before I could speak. "How could you say that?" I asked. "How could you even think that?"

"It just occurred to me, sitting at that table with your family and the man you invited—who brought you flowers for the second time since I've been in town—that we haven't actually spent that much time together."

I'd thought we'd spent quite a bit of time together. I'd lived at his house for several weeks.

If Nick had been a geologist or archeologist, I could give him a pass because they dealt with time on a whole different level, but he was an attorney.

"I'm the same person who stayed at your house last summer," I said. "I thought we got to know each other pretty well."

He did another slow nod. "Yeah, I did too."

Was he saying he now felt like he didn't know me at all, just because of a dinner guest I had no idea was coming?

"Nick, I didn't invite Julian tonight. In fact, I was surprised when he showed up."

"He thanked you for inviting him."

"I know, but what was I supposed to say? I'm pretty sure it was my grandmother or Mrs. Ruíz who told him I wanted him to come." *Or maybe even my* Tía *Madi or LeeAnne just for kicks,* but I didn't say that part.

"So, you don't want him here." It sounded like more of a statement than a question, but Nick's level gaze said he was waiting for an answer.

"No." I shook my head, then felt kind of bad. "I mean, it's not that I don't want him here. He's a nice guy. And he's really cute, and in good shape..." Was I rambling? "Um, you know in a boy band, heartthrob kind of way..." Yes, I was rambling and in a very dangerous direction.

Nick's hands dropped from the door. He shook his head in exasperation and stared at me like he was on the verge of saying, "*Hasta la vista,* baby."

I closed my eyes and took in a deep breath for courage. "I'm saying, despite all that, I'm not attracted to Julian."

Nick's body relaxed slightly, but his stance said he wasn't done with this conversation.

"Plus, he keeps bringing me those fucking flowers." I flashed him a teasing smile. *Please smile back at me,* I begged silently. All my pride had melted away. I just wanted my smiling, smartass Nick back.

His eyes left mine, and he stared down at the cement between us as if deciding what his next words would be. His face hardened with what looked like determination and a sense of foreboding swept over me.

He cocked his head to the right. "Okay, then," he said. "What about you and me? Why have you been tensing up when I touch you?"

*Crap.* My pride came flooding back, even though I knew it could drown Nick and me before we became an "us."

But Nick still didn't know about my past as a Teletubby, and I didn't want to tell him. I didn't ever want him imagining me the way I was then.

It was bad enough that he pitied me because of what happened with my parents. What if I confessed everything to him and he asked to see pictures?

I shuddered.

I knew any of those women inside my grandmother's house would show him the old photos if he asked because none of them realized how scarred I still was from those years. They loved me the way I was back then, and, now, they seemed to think I was like them—another beautiful Delacruz woman.

I'd never talked to them about my issues because I didn't want them worrying about me any more than they already did. Not after everything we'd been through.

Nick was staring at me, waiting for an answer. And I couldn't think of one word to say in response.

But I didn't want to lose him.

*Do something!* a voice inside me screamed.

I lifted my hands, pressing them tentatively to his chest, feeling his heart thrumming almost as fast as mine. Shaking, inside and out, I forced my palms to move up until they slid around his neck.

I raised up on my tiptoes and tried to pull his head down toward me.

He resisted for a moment, his expression suspicious, or confused, or maybe annoyed that I hadn't answered his question.

His face remained hard, but his eyes darkened as he peered at me with what appeared to be distrust mixed with desire. I felt their pull, just before he reached out and dragged me against him.

One hot hand slid up my back and cradled my head as he pressed his lips, hard, on mine.

My heart lunged in my chest. His arms tightened and pulled me up until my toes were barely touching the ground. I opened to him and he swept his tongue over mine, exploring my mouth like he was looking for all the answers about our present and future in there. Or maybe that was wishful thinking.

Regardless, he felt so fabulous against me, my insides melted, and the surface of my skin hummed with a sensual joy I'd only experienced when Nick kissed me.

It was heaven and I never wanted it to end.

He released me suddenly and I wobbled backward like I was a toddler who hadn't fully learned to use my feet yet. Luckily, the door was there to keep me from going down.

Nick took a step back and looked at me assessingly. His eyes were dark and intense. I got the feeling the kiss wasn't just a kiss. It was like he needed to prove or maybe confirm something but I wasn't sure if he was proving it to me or himself.

"I'll see you tomorrow," he said abruptly. He turned, walked down the stairs, and got into his truck.

Knees weak, I pressed my palms against the door and watched him drive off, wishing I had the guts to follow him to his hotel.

I did a gut check.

Nope. No guts tonight.

~

### Rika

I missed Nick before his truck drove away.

He'd been sticking to me like glue, most days. I suspected it was because he thought he needed to protect me on the job.

*Annoying.*

Sure, in the time he knew me, I'd been arrested for murder, shot at, stuck in the trunk of a moving car, involved in a shootout on the freeway, and had a run-in with gangbangers...

What was my point?

Oh, yeah. Those were just odd one-off occurrences in two situations where I was personally involved. It wasn't like I was in danger all the time. Mostly, a private investigator just observed and investigated.

*Besides, a person can get abducted coming out of an exercise class.*

*Yes!* I didn't think the word "yoga" that time! I'd been trying to quit thinking of yoga in connection to my mom's abduction. There were yoga studios all over L.A. and you'd be surprised how often you notice people saying the word "yoga" in conversations after your mother's been abducted from the parking lot after yoga class.

Damn it! In congratulating myself for not thinking the word "yoga," I just thought the word, like, five more times. And now six.

Whatever. The important thing was that tall—clearly not from California—Nick made it harder for me to ask "casual" questions or to blend in and observe as a P.I.

Even in Los Angeles, a city with more than its fair share of attractive people, Nick was a standout. People's eyes tended to follow him. I wasn't sure if they were all as dazzled as I was or if they were convinced he was a movie or TV star and they were trying to place him.

*Hmm...* He was gone now and, if I remembered correctly, the circus had a show starting in an hour.

I put my hand on the front doorknob as I tried to decide what to tell all the people who were sitting at the dining table inside. I whipped my phone out of my back pocket and put it to my ear as I walked in.

"Sure. No problem. Thanks for seeing me," I said to no one. I pretended to hit the End button.

"Sorry, but I've got to go," I told the table at large. "A doctor I've been wanting to interview for the case is finally available." I'd mentioned wanting to talk to more of the doctors involved in the separation, and I figured my grandmother wouldn't be worried about me going to interview a doctor.

"But it's late to go out," Lita said, even though it wasn't. She glanced at Julian.

Damn. I'd totally forgotten about him. He thought I'd invited him to dinner and now I was bailing on him.

"I'm sorry." I glanced from Lita to Julian. I wasn't really that sorry, which made me feel even more guilty. "I can't miss this opportunity, plus it's only six-thirty."

Of course, the opportunity I was referring to was to be an old-school, lone-wolf P.I., but they didn't need to know that.

"I understand," Julian said. "I'm working toward being a detective on the force and I've heard how cases can get hold of you." He stood. "Thanks, everybody. The dinner was great. I'm going home to catch up on some sleep."

Lita and Mrs. Ruíz made vague objections about him leaving, but I could tell they were okay with it since he was supposed to be here for me.

Julian gave me a hug and a kiss on the cheek. "Take care," he said. "I'll see you soon."

*How soon? Does he think we're dating now?* I wondered but didn't ask.

Once he was gone, I headed to my room to get a zip-up hoodie. It was dusk and would be chilly outside and I figured the circus tent wasn't heated. When I turned back, LeeAnne was standing in my doorway watching me.

Her eyes flitted from my face to the hoodie in my hand then back to my face. "I want in," she said.

"In?" I repeated innocently.

"Yeah, you're up to something. I can see it in your shifty eyes."

Apparently, my eyes both flashed and shifted without my permission. I added "shifty eyes" to my mental list of things to work on to be a better P.I.

"It's nothing you'd be interested in," I said. "No breaking in or gunfire involved. I'm just going to watch a circus performance."

"I love the circus!" LeeAnne said. "Well, I've never been because they didn't come anywhere near Bolo, but I've always wanted to go, ever since I was a little girl."

*Damn it!* LeeAnne had been a small-town kid with crappy, mostly absentee parents and grandparents who were working to keep food on the table while trying to deal with her brother's situation on their own.

How could I deny her a trip to the circus?

Oh, well. I might not be going on my own, but at least I didn't have my big, Texas bodyguard with me. Besides, unlike the first two cases he and I worked on together, this one had nothing to do with me.

I wasn't accused of murder. My dad hadn't been kidnapped. I was just a hired hand. There was no danger involved.

"Okay, you can come with me," I said. "But I need to go soon." I knew how long it could take LeeAnne to get ready.

She threw her hands out in a *look at me* gesture. "I'm ready," she said.

I stared at her clothes. While, officially, she was wearing jeans and a shirt, the jeans had bling from waist to hem on both legs in the form of crisscross patterns that reminded me of DNA strands. The top could be described as a cowl-neck, sequin halter-top. Huge hoops hung from her earlobes, and, as usual, her hair was maxed out in height and width.

LeeAnne's style could best be described as "more is more."

"Let's go, then," I said.

"I'm driving!" she replied.

# CHAPTER TWELVE

**Rika**

I was glad to get to Cirque de Sorbet in one piece. LeeAnne was either the worst L.A. driver ever or the best, depending on how you looked at it.

On one hand, she always got us where we were going faster than the GPS claimed was possible. On the other, she did this by extremely aggressive driving, even by L.A. standards. And when she wasn't jerking the car into other lanes, cutting people off, she was opening her window, flirting her way to where she wanted to be.

This bugged me, but LeeAnne's feeling on the subject was that because men had kept us under their thumbs and beaten us down—she was referring to her ex-husband who literally beat her down—we had a right to use whatever methods available to even the score.

I saw her point but had mixed feelings when it came to her belief system.

As we walked up to the ticket booth, I looked at my phone. It was ten after seven. The show didn't start until seven-thirty.

A slim girl that looked like little more than a teenager sat inside the booth. As LeeAnne and I approached, I pulled out my business card and slipped it through the space under the glass.

"I'm Rika Martín," I said. "I'm investigating Grigore Vatamanu's murder."

Her eyes settled on my card. She expelled a sigh. "Sad," she said.

"Did you know them from Moldova?" I asked, trying to get her talking.

"From Moldova?" She pulled her shoulders back. "I am Ukrainian. Do I sound like I am Moldovan?"

Okay, in my defense, before I asked the question, I'd only heard her say the word "sad." She pronounced it "sahd," which could make her practically anything but a native English speaker since it seemed that we spoke one of the few languages in the world that used the short A sound.

I hadn't really thought about the fact that the circus had traveled around Europe for years. It made sense that they picked up employees from other countries along the way.

"Is there something wrong with being Moldovan?" LeeAnne asked genuinely. "I'm just wondering because I've never heard of it before this and wouldn't know where to find it on a map."

The young woman rolled her eyes and glanced over her shoulder at the tent. "There is plenty wrong with being Moldovan," she said derisively.

*Hm...* Did she really have something against a whole country full of people—because that was not okay with me—or could she be referring to that ass Anatolie? He wasn't exactly a goodwill ambassador for his country.

I heard voices and turned my head to see people getting out of cars as other vehicles arrived. I didn't have much time.

"Do you have any theories?" I asked. "About why Grigore was murdered?"

She shrugged and lifted one side of her upper lip before

saying, "I understand why someone would get angry with Teodor. Have you met his father?"

I nodded.

"Well, Teodor is most like him. Not as loud, but, kind of eh... pompous, jerk type. Too bossy with Grigore." She glanced over our shoulders at the customers walking up behind us and lowered her voice. "My theory is that someone wanted to kill Teodor and got confused. They looked more the same when they were sleeping." She snorted. "If I was told, 'You must kill one of these men or you will die,' it would be no contest. I would kill Teodor." She leaned in and whispered, "And I would feel no remorse."

*Uh. Okay...*

I could hear the voices directly behind us now. "Thanks for your time," I said. "I guess we need tickets. I wanted to—"

"Go 'head." She flicked her head toward the entrance. "If anyone asks to see tickets, tell them Aneta let you in."

"Thanks," I said. Although things like this would either be paid by the client or claimed on tax returns as business expenses, I preferred not to spend unnecessary money until more income —other than Nick's personal income—was coming in.

At least Erissa's partial payment was supposed to post to the business account tomorrow. That would make me feel a little better.

No one was inside the entrance when we got there, so we walked toward the backstage area.

LeeAnne looked back the way we'd come. "If that's how the ticket booth girl acts, I can't imagine what this Anatolie guy is like," she said. "I don't think I should have let you talk me into leaving my gun in the car."

We'd had a discussion on the way over about her gun. Yes, LeeAnne was a crack shot, but she was a little too quick to draw her weapon, evidenced by the shoot-out on the freeway when we were trying to find my dad and prove him innocent. Besides, I wasn't sure my recently acquired business insurance would cover something like that.

"It's going to be a tent full of parents and kids and babies in strollers," I said, gesturing to where audience members were trickling in. "Who do you think you're going to use a gun on?"

LeeAnne threw out her hands. "Well, you never know," she said. "Grigore probably didn't expect to go to bed and wake up dead."

We walked through the hallway of the building behind the tent and out the second door into the high-ceilinged area. I saw Constata come from the women's bathroom. Both bathrooms had wooden privacy screens that hid the doorway, like I'd seen in front of bathrooms at various zoos and entertainment venues. This one had a plaque with the word "Ladies" imprinted on it.

Constata didn't see me. Someone called out her name and she hurried back toward the wardrobe room.

"May I help you ladies?" an accented male voice asked.

LeeAnne and I turned toward the voice.

"Jesus Christ Superst...!" Her exclamation faded out on a breathy sigh as we took in the man in front of us. He was tall and slim but filled out his costume nicely. His tux jacket was red with tails, a gold vest underneath. His black pants tapered, the bottoms disappearing into tall black riding boots with a golden tassel on the front of each. But for me, the coolest part was his impressively tall top hat.

Once I got past the costume, I took in that he was a white guy, but tanned, as if he spent a lot of time in the sun. The hair that wasn't covered by the hat, was longish and curly brown with golden highlights. His eyes were green.

My eyes tried to move on but flicked back to his. Not because I'm into green eyes, but because I know green-eyed people are rare. I'm always suspicious as to whether green is the person's real eye color or they're wearing contacts.

Personally, I'm against colored contacts. In my experience, the eyes really are the windows to the soul. I tend to think people who try to disguise their eyes could be hiding something.

On the other hand, legit green-eyed people are much more common in Eastern Europe where the circus originated, so maybe this guy was okay.

As I tried to formulate a question that would tell me what I wanted to know, LeeAnne beat me to the punch. "If this is how they make 'em in Moldova, sign me up on the next cruise ship," she said. "Hell, I'll take a freighter!"

The man made a face like meat had just gone bad under his nose. "Moldova is landlocked," he replied. "And do *I* seem Moldovan to you?"

Hm... Now that he'd said two more sentences, I thought he sounded more like my dad than Anatolie. "Colombian?" I tried. "Mexican?" Those were the two Spanish-speaking ethnicities I always thought of first, having grown up a Colombian American in a Mexican American neighborhood.

His eyelids started blinking rapidly while his eyeballs rolled up in his head.

What was happening to him? He looked too young to be having a stroke.

His eyes rolled back to their normal position. "Do I look Colombian?" He appeared to be throwing up a little in his mouth. "Or Mexican?" Again, with the throw-up face. "This is like asking a British person if they are American." He made the face yet again! "I am of *España*—Spain. The motherland."

Okay, in the short time LeeAnne and I had been at the circus, I'd been offended on behalf of Moldovans, Colombians, Mexicans, and Americans. And maybe even British people since I'd met quite a few online and none of them were nasty about it.

I'd audited a marketing class when I'd started thinking I wanted my own business. The professor talked a lot about corporate personalities and how influenced they were by the person at the top.

Whoever owned this place had to be a huge jerk to have hired so many jerks. Regardless, I still needed to learn what I could from this particular jerk.

"Maybe we should start over," I said. "I'm Rika Martín. I'm investigating the death of Grigore Vatamanu."

"Martín?" he repeated. "So, you didn't drop the accent like—"

"Ricky." We both said together. I tried not to be judgmental, but it had always bothered me that Ricky Martín had turned himself into Ricky Martin. And at least this jerk and I had common ground now.

"I would never drop my accent mark," I said, making a mental note not to give him one of my cheap business cards. Who would have thought my attempt to save money would come back to bite me in the ass on my very first real case?

He nodded approvingly. "And I am Xavier Luna." He pronounced the "a" in his name like my dad would, with an "ah" sound and gave the "r" at the end a light flip. "I am the owner, ringmaster, and trainer of wild beasts."

"Wild beasts?" LeeAnne repeated. "I didn't even know they had wild beasts in Spain."

Xavier grasped the flaps of his tuxedo coat and pulled down as his body straightened. "*España* is where the greatest tamers of beasts are trained," he said. "The bulls were no match for me. Now I train tigers!"

At this point, my brain was torn. He was being so pompous, I had the urge to point out to him that bulls were not, technically, wild beasts. They were domesticated animals who got kind of pissed when you gouged them with spears, which was neither training nor taming them. But another part of me registered the fact that he was the owner of the circus—also known as Ground Zero Jerk—and might have valuable information.

"Oh," I said with exaggerated interest. "I guess I have the wrong information. I read that this circus started in Moldova."

"Yes." Xavier waved his hand as if he was sweeping my words

133

from the air. "It was started there, but I purchased it several years ago." He shook his head. "What Moldovan has ever made a success of anything?"

*Oh, my God!* Could someone give them a freaking break? What happened to the circus being the happiest place on Earth?

No, wait that was Disneyland. Or maybe Disney World.

*Whatever.* These people sucked.

"Did you know Grigore well?"

He shrugged and blew out a breath that said he had more important things to talk about. "He has been my employee since I purchased the circus about eight years ago. The Vatamanu family were already a part of it."

"Do you know of anyone who disliked Grigore or Teodor?"

His face went blank. Was he about to lie to me?

"I try to stay out of the personal lives of my employees."

He *had* just lied to me. I was sure of it. Was he covering for himself? Or someone else? Or just protecting his investment?

According to Anatolie, Teodor and Grigore were a big draw. If one of the other circus performers murdered Grigore, Xavier would be minus another act.

"But you've traveled around the world together," I pointed out.

"People talk," LeeAnne threw in. "Well actually, they get drunk, they talk, then they fight."

I wondered if she was thinking of her parents or her ex-husband.

After a slow blink, Xavier replied. "Yes, yes. They do all those things. But if they come in on cue and perform, I do not care about the rest."

He clearly had no intention of cooperating with me.

Okay, then. To paraphrase the fabulous Tina Turner, he'd gotten it nice and now he was about to get it rough. "*Señor* Luna," I said. "I'm getting the feeling that you don't want Grigore's killer found."

His chin jerked slightly to his left. It was almost like a tick. "What are you saying?"

"She's saying that any decent employer would want to see justice done for his employee, even if they hadn't traveled all over the world together. And if she's like me," LeeAnne continued, "she's starting to think maybe you had something to do with the murder!"

I cringed inwardly but tried to keep the emotion off my face. I was trying to imply what she'd said, hoping it would shake a little help out of him, not straight-out challenge a man who fancied himself the "tamer of wild beasts."

Xavier's face flushed. "Teodor and Grigore decided to get the separation and leave the circus," he said. "They were already dead to me."

LeeAnne put her hands on her hips and tilted her head in a taunting gesture. "So, you were pissed off at them. Sounds like a motive."

Xavier's body tensed threateningly, and both his hands fisted.

Was he going to hit LeeAnne? After all she'd done for me in Bolo and when my dad was missing, I felt it was only right that I take a punch or two for her.

I prepared to jump in, wondering if I was one of those people with a "glass jaw." I thought I could stand the pain as long as it didn't knock me unconscious. I had a fear of being unconscious.

LeeAnne eyeballed Xavier's fists. "You wouldn't be the first man to hit me, but I learned a lot since then and if you throw a punch, you'd better be ready to draw back a nub!"

Xavier's substantial eyebrows pressed in toward each other. "I do not understand what you are saying," he replied.

"Oh, LeeAnne!" I did an exaggerated eye roll and whacked her on the arm. "You're such a nut!" I turned to Xavier. "She thinks you're hot. She's got a weird way of flirting with men."

LeeAnne's mouth fell open. I gave her the *be cool* look.

Xavier relaxed, his expression changing to one of interest. He cast his eyes over LeeAnne from head to toe. She gave me a look that said, *Okay, but you owe me big for this one.*

"You are a very beautiful woman," he said. "You do not need to resort to such tactics."

LeeAnne blushed and I swear, if she had a fan handy, she would have been fanning herself and batting her eyelashes at the guy. "Thanks. That's sweet of you to say."

And suddenly, it was like we were on a very weird reality dating show.

"Oh!" Xavier glanced down to check his costume. "It's time." He pointed to a huge clock I hadn't even noticed, high on the wall.

I have trouble noticing things above my head. I blame it on never having grown to the full five foot seven I'd planned on.

"Petchoolie!" Xavier yelled.

A slim teenager came toward us. I gave him the once over. Sun-streaked hair, check. Board shorts, check. Weird name, check.

And when he joined our little circle, a thick cloud of weed smoke followed. Check.

White boy was definitely a local. Possibly still in high school.

"Yeah, boss?"

Xavier gestured grandly to us, like we were prizes Petchoolie might win in a game show. "These ladies are my guests. Please put them in my special seats."

~

**Rika**

The "special seats" turned out to be two rickety folding chairs placed in front of the bleacher-style seating directly in front of a row of paying customers.

I felt kind of guilty considering there was a mom with a toddler and a preschooler right behind us who probably thought she'd scored the best seats in the house. However, guilty or not, I had a murder case to solve and there was a chance someone here knew something, whether it was about a co-worker with a motive or information Teodor or Grigore might have shared about Erissa, who was still at the top of my suspect list until a more suspicious culprit came along.

Suddenly, the lights dimmed and prerecorded music poured through the tent.

"Whooo!" LeeAnne cried, clapping her hands. "It's starting!" She seemed as giddy as a four-year-old. My heart squeezed at the vision of little LeeAnne, more or less abandoned by her parents, dreaming of circuses and Disneyland—the first place she had me take her when she came to Los Angeles. How could her parents have chosen alcohol and drugs over their sparkly little girl?

The music rose to a crescendo as spotlights zoomed around the room, sweeping briefly over the faces of audience members.

*Is that Eli?*

The face was only lit for a split second before the light moved on.

The spotlights led my gaze back to the middle of the ring. As they converged into one bright, round light, Xavier was there in his top hat and tails, looking pretty yummy until I remembered how snooty he was towards us. I could take insecure, conceited, and occasionally selfish, if my two years with Brandtt was anything to go by. And I found Nick's confidence, smartassedness, and occasional cockiness kind of charming. But snooty was a total turn off.

"Ladies and gentlemen! Children of all ages! Welcome to Cirque de Sorbet, the most fun and exciting show on Earth!"

I noticed Xavier of "*España*" was now speaking in a standard American accent.

*Hmm... a chameleon.* I didn't like those much either.

"Tonight, we bring you the most excellent performers from all over the world for your viewing entertainment! Please stay in the designated audience area for the duration of the show and, for your own safety, never step into the ring. Now, guess what time it is..."

There was whooping and clapping from members of the audience who I assumed had been here before.

"That's right! Iiiiiiiiit's Showtime!" He lifted his top hat from his head and made a sweeping bow as the lights went off for several seconds.

The tent quieted, except for a few murmurs and whimpers from audience members.

The lights popped back on and the ring was filled with clowns. Some were driving little cars, others honking horns, a few of them were dwarf-sized while others were on stilts.

I heard a strangled sound next to me and turned to see LeeAnne's face devoid of color.

"Are you okay?" I asked.

"Th-that's a lot of clowns," she replied.

As one of them appeared to be coming our way, she leaned into me as if I was supposed to protect her from him.

*Holy mother of Zeus!* Was someone else inhabiting LeeAnne's body? This couldn't be the "let's drive like a maniac, break and enter on cult private property, get in a shootout on the freeway" LeeAnne Barr I'd grown to love and occasionally fear, mostly when I was in the passenger seat of her car.

Regardless, I was trying to get background for my very important—and also my only—case. I didn't need her freaking out on me.

"LeeAnne," I said. "Why would you come to the circus if you were afraid of clowns? The circus is where clowns come from." Okay, I didn't know for sure where clowns originated, but they certainly were associated with the circus.

"How would I know that?" LeeAnne replied, scooching harder against me. "I told you I'd never been to a circus."

"You don't have to have been—" I began, then changed my

approach. "Where did you think clowns came from?" I asked, hoping a conversation would calm her.

"McDonald's!" she replied. "When I was a little girl, they built a McDonalds in Digby, up the road from Bolo. My grandpa took me one time when he needed to go there to buy another gun—remember the collection?"

I nodded. No way could I forget the massive firearm collection that made up the bulk of the wall decor at LeeAnne's house.

"Well, when I saw Ronald McDonald sitting on the bench out front," she went on. "I went back and got the baseball bat my grandpa kept behind the seat of his truck and knocked Ronald's head clean off. But I still had nightmares about the son-of-a-bitch for years." As an orange-haired clown seemed to zero in on us, approaching with a pail of what I could only guess was confetti, LeeAnne grabbed for her handbag. "My gun..." she said as she stuck her hand inside.

*She'd better not have her gun!*

My eyes followed her movements as her hand searched around in the large—probably fake—designer bag. She turned and looked at me accusingly. "You made me leave it in the car," she wailed. "I never leave my gun in the car!"

Luckily, her words were drowned out by the honking, calliope music, and kids squealing with joy, plus a few babies who seemed to share her sentiment about clowns.

The clown swung his pail forward, dousing LeeAnne with its paper contents.

"Aaaaaaaaaack!" she screamed.

He leaned down, hands on thighs, his head tilted in fake concern. At least that's what it looked like to me. Who can tell what a clown's thinking?

LeeAnne was my best friend. She'd do anything for me, and it was my turn to stand up for her.

I stood and stepped on his huge clown shoes and got not quite eye-to-eye. I was tempted to pull his clown wig off but decided that it might upset the little kids in the audience, so I opted for grabbing him by the lapels. "Look, you need to move on. You can see she's not into this." I was proud of myself. I sounded calm and self-assured.

Maybe Nick was rubbing off on me.

"So, maybe I don't wanna move on," he replied. This clown may have been a former cast member of *The Sopranos,* if the Jersey wise guy accent was real.

"Well, you need to move on," I said. "There's a whole tent full of people here to terrorize." I stretched my arm out and swept it over the crowd.

"I just decided," he said. "I don't wanna move on." Then he grasped my waist and lifted me in the air.

I flailed around, looking for something to grab onto. Less than five seconds later, I was sitting on his shoulders.

Yes, his shoulders!

What the hell? Had I just been clown-napped?

I considered my options.

*Thumbs in his eyes.*

May not be small-child appropriate for the clown to be screaming in pain as I tried to blind him.

*Pull on his earlobes.*

Not sure that would do the trick.

"Stop!" LeeAnne said. "Let go of my friend!" I could see she was terrorized on my behalf, but afraid to get too close to the clown.

I glanced around, hoping for help from the ringmaster or at least a kinder, gentler clown. That's when I realized nearly every set of eyes in the tent was staring our way.

And they were laughing. They thought this was part of the show!

Okay, that was it. Watching people look at me and laugh brought back very unhappy memories.

I ran my fingers around the bottom of his scalp until I felt the edges of his wig. I grasped it from the back and pulled, forcing it forward until his clown hair was over his eyes.

"You can't do that!" he shrieked. "You can't unmask a clown!"

"I didn't," I said into his ear. "I un-*wigged* a clown, but the nose is next if you don't put me down and leave us alone!"

"Bitch!" he screeched as he clawed at my hands. But, lucky for me, he kept his nails cut short—I would've hated to explain the claw marks to Nick—so I just held the wig over his eyes as he screamed and the crowd roared with laughter. I guess with the ridiculousness of it all and with LeeAnne and I in "special" seating, I would have assumed this was part of the show, too.

But, suddenly, the clown curled his shoulders and ducked. I nearly flew off the top of his head but managed to hook my left arm around his neck in a headlock as my legs slipped down his body.

I was now a clown cape. I could have let go, slid to the ground and been done with it, but I was pretty pissed off. This jerk had terrified my best friend and manhandled me.

So, with my right hand, I reached around and plucked the big, red nose off his face. The crowd cheered, apparently on my side. I smiled widely at them and dropped to the ground.

As the clown struggled to right his wig, I punched my hand into the air, holding his nose up triumphantly. This time, the audience clapped and stomped and hooted so loudly, I felt it physically, like an earthquake. On impulse, I pulled my arm back and flung the clown nose as hard as I could into the crowd.

A Latino-looking dad caught it and handed it to his little girl, who looked a lot like the pictures of me when I was six or seven.

Holding the rubber nose tightly in her hand, she thrust her fist in the air and shouted. The crowd was still roaring, but I could have sworn I lip-read the words "Girl power!"

I returned her gesture, feeling like Wonder Woman and Super Girl and Hermione Granger rolled into one.

The crowd quieted as the ring cleared. The clown slunk to the back of the tent.

I sat next to LeeAnne. "Are you all right?" I asked.

She burst out laughing. "Am I all right? Hell, yes, I'm all right! I just saw you kick a clown's ass!"

"Well, I didn't exactly ki—"

"And he was the biggest one!" She pointed at his retreating back.

Wow. He *was* the biggest one. Or at least the biggest one who wasn't on stilts. Tall and broad-shouldered.

Then I realized the clowns had names on their backs, written in various ways, according to their personal style. His was done in orange glitter. "Happy," I read.

"Not anymore!" LeeAnne cried before she doubled over laughing. "Taken down by a petite, five-foot-two girl!"

"Five foot four and a half!" I replied automatically. Then I cracked up right along with her.

Suddenly, a spotlight appeared in the middle of the tent, again, Xavier in the center of it.

He was only a few yards from where we were sitting, and I could have sworn he gave us a dirty look before he announced the next act—Palba's Prancing Pups.

*Jerk,* I thought. My clown-taming act was clearly a hit. He should pay me for the performance!

I pulled up OneNote on my phone and added Xavier and Happy to my possible suspect list. Xavier, because he was clearly angry about the twins' decision to separate and leave his circus. Happy the Clown, officially because he seemed overly willing to engage with us physically, and had no empathy for my terrified friend, which meant he might be capable of murder without remorse. But truth be told, it was because I hated him and wanted him to be the killer.

The rest of the show was actually pretty cool. The acts alternated between light-hearted fun and gasp-worthy, "death-defying" performances. As I watched the pups, I wished I'd brought my cousin Sofia. She was a dog trainer herself and might have gotten a kick out of it.

Honestly, it rarely entered my mind to invite Sofia anywhere. We had one of those family relationships in which you always know you're there for each other, but you don't necessarily have a lot in common. Plus, I always felt she was holding something important back from me. Or maybe from all of us. Sometimes, I even felt like she was looking at me with resentment and it bugged me that I couldn't figure out why.

The show went on, and I had to admit, despite their asinine patriarch, the Vatamanus were amazing.

They contorted themselves into the most unlikely, yet beautiful, poses, whether on the floor or suspended in the air.

As much of an ass as Anatolie was, he was an artiste when it came to circus acts. When his round-bellied daughters ended their performance posed with fancy bows and arrows, dressed as pregnant warrior princesses, the crowd showed their approval with prolonged applause.

A magician came out to entertain the crowd while workers set up for the final act. They brought out pedestals of different heights, giant hoops, and a plank held up by two of the pedestals. Then the same stage crew came back out, pushing sections of gold-colored bars that, when assembled, looked like a version of Tweety Bird's cage, except this one was tiger-sized.

Xavier must have saved his "wild beast" act for the finale.

But as the workers were locking the sides together, I noticed the tops of the bars swaying. "That doesn't look like a very sturdy cage for a tiger," I said.

"Aw, it'll be fine. They do this every night," said the woman who'd been traumatized by a clown not an hour ago. I gave her a *Really?* look.

"What?" she said as if she'd already forgotten her Happy the Clown experience.

Xavier came out again, lifted his hat, and bowed to the excited crowd as a covered cage was wheeled up to the entrance of the gold one. A stagehand climbed on top and lifted a door and the tiger came out.

Not just any tiger. The biggest tiger I'd ever seen.

But, now that I thought about it, I hadn't seen a lot of tigers in real life. Maybe a couple at the zoo from a distance. But I'd never been in front of the front row at a circus, only a few yards away from one.

Palba, from the poodle act, appeared off to one side, holding a microphone. Her Russian accent took on an ominous tone as she introduced Egor, a male Siberian—the biggest kind of tiger—who weighed in at nearly seven hundred pounds.

The stagehands rolled the smaller cage away as Xavier entered the big one and closed the gate behind him.

During the next few minutes, I developed a grudging respect for him.

No way would I want to be in a cage with that beast. And you would never catch me cracking a whip in front of its nose and ordering it around.

Egor growled and swatted at the whip at times, which looked miniature in comparison to his big paws. But I guessed that was part of the act because, invariably, when Xavier cracked his whip and called out an order the second time—sometimes in Spanish, sometimes in a Slavic language—Egor would comply. He jumped from pedestal to pedestal, walked the plank, roared on command, and even lay on the ground and rolled over like a dog.

Then, the music became super dramatic with violins playing frantically. Xavier was handed a torch through the bars, which he used to set four elevated hoops, between the pedestals, on fire.

I was kind of hoping this was the end of his act. I glanced at LeeAnne and saw that she was totally mesmerized.

This wasn't the first time I'd noticed I didn't have the same attention span as other people. Not that I had more or less than others. It was just different.

Like, at this point, I was thinking, *Okay, we get it. The tiger is trained. Can this be over so I can try to talk to more of the troupe members?*

I scanned the audience. It seemed like I was the only person who wasn't awestruck. At times like this, I felt especially odd and alone in my own brain.

I heard gasps and focused on the show again. Egor was jumping from pedestal to pedestal through the fiery hoops.

When he finished, he was standing on the highest pedestal of them all. Xavier called out one more command and flicked his whip in our direction.

"Did he just say something about killing in Spanish?" LeeAnne asked.

I hadn't really been listening and Xavier wasn't miked for this part of the show, but when I reran what I thought I'd heard through the Spanish side of my brain...

*Mátalas... Kill them...*

No, I must have misheard the command.

Suddenly, Egor bounded off his platform, crashing through the bars of the cage, which now looked more like broken PVC pipe. Once free from his cage, such as it was, he stood, facing the audience, surveying the crowd like he had all the time in the world.

# CHAPTER THIRTEEN

**Rika**

The place exploded with sounds. I heard screams from the crowd, shouts from stagehands, and a gasp followed by a choking sound behind me.

I turned to find moms and nannies bailing off the bleachers with the kids they'd brought, but the auburn-haired mom directly behind LeeAnne seemed to be having a panic attack or worse.

"LeeAnne!" I cried, gesturing towards them. I checked Egor, who'd lifted his nose gently into the air as if he were on a field trip to the botanical gardens and wanted to stop and smell the roses.

Except, Egor was a carnivore and wouldn't be interested in floral scents. For him, this was probably the equivalent of looking at a restaurant menu. All he had to decide as his eyes scanned the crowd was whether he liked white meat, dark meat, or something in between—lucky for him there was plenty of diversity in L.A—and whether he wanted to sample some toddler appetizers or go straight for a mommy main course.

LeeAnne turned, grabbed the toddler from the woman and said, "Come on!" to the little girl sitting next to them.

I wrapped my fingers around their frozen mother's arm and half-dragged her along. I glanced at where we came in and saw the exit clogged with people, a dad trying to rip through the tent, moms pushing their children under the tent walls.

The adults were wild-eyed with terror. Most of the kids were screaming or crying, except for one little blonde boy on the far side of the tent who was standing on a bleacher, yelling, "Here, kitty-kitty!"

His dad, who had a baby strapped to his chest, threw an arm around his son's head, covering his mouth with his hand. I doubted that a tiger would respond to "Here, kitty-kitty," but better safe than sorry.

Meanwhile, Egor had started moving in our direction. I walked sideways, not wanting to incite his chase instinct.

I was relieved when one of the stagehands got his attention by waving a bandana around like a rodeo clown.

It was time to get out of here.

"This way," I said to the people near us. They followed as LeeAnne, our charges, and I ran around the side of what was left of the gilded cage toward the backstage area.

When we made it to the hallway, a quick survey told me we had acquired eight moms, each with one or more kids, plus two teenage girls who were bringing up the rear.

"Close the door!" I yelled. Then we'd all be safe.

LeeAnne took her phone out, I assumed to dial 9-1-1.

The girls were pulling and pulling on the door, but it was stuck open, maybe purposely to enable performers to get in and out of the tent quickly.

"Oh, my God! It doesn't close!" the skinny blonde girl said.

"How can a door not close?" her even skinnier, blonder friend cried.

"Come on!" I yelled. I took off down the hall, still towing the redheaded mom with my left hand as I tried doorknobs with my right.

I was shocked to find storeroom after storeroom locked. Didn't they need the stuff in here during performances? If not, this was a highly inefficient storage system.

Egor roared from just outside the hall and the echo shook the walls.

I grabbed the next doorknob. As I realized it was locked, I also saw several of the clowns inside, including the one I'd unwigged at the beginning of the show—Happy. He'd put himself back together, but I could see in his eyes that he recognized me.

"Let us in," I called. "The tiger's loose!"

"We know the tiger's loose!" he replied. "That's why we're in here!"

"Just let us in," I said, jiggling the locked doorknob. Why did they lock it? It's not like Egor had opposable thumbs and could be trained to turn doorknobs.

"I'm not opening that door," Happy said.

"We've got kids out here!" LeeAnne cried.

Happy shrugged.

"Kids!" LeeAnne screamed louder. "We've got kids and you're a clown!"

I wasn't sure if she'd gotten over her clown phobia, possibly replaced by a newfound tiger phobia, or if it only kicked in when she was in the same room as the clown.

"If I had my gun, you'd be saying howdy to St. Peter," she yelled at Happy. "Damn, I wish I had that gun." She looked at me accusingly.

"If wishes were horses, then beggars would ride," Happy yelled through the glass.

"Come on," I said to our crew. I tried the last couple of knobs, then we stepped out into the warehouse area.

I saw the privacy screen for the women's bathroom. Surely, the bathroom wouldn't be locked.

As I raced toward it, I checked back and saw that the whole group was still following me. We all ran around the privacy screen and into the bathroom.

"Get in! I'll close the door," I said. I sort of flung the woman I'd been dragging toward the back. The moms, babies, kids, LeeAnne and the two teenage girls hustled in.

I turned back to close the door and...

There was no door.

*Holy mother of Zeus!* It hadn't occurred to me there wouldn't be a door. I guess I'd been to places that were set up like this, with privacy screens and no doors, but, for whatever reason, the possibility hadn't entered my mind.

"There are no doors," the skinnier teen pointed out.

"Yeah," I stalled, not wanting everyone to panic.

Then, I remembered Constata. Surely the wardrobe room wouldn't be locked up during a performance.

If only I had run to the right instead of running straight across the warehouse. I mentally kicked myself. "I think I know where we can go," I said. "Just let me check..."

I left the bathroom and peeked around the privacy screen.

Egor was standing in the middle of the warehouse, glancing around, sniffing the air.

*Please tell me he isn't a bloodhound tiger.* I could have sworn Xavier gestured our way when he said *"Mátalas."* Could Egor possibly be looking for me and LeeAnne?

I stepped back into the bathroom where the women were chattering in freaked out tones. "Okay, I need you all to be quiet."

They fell silent immediately. I guess they'd accepted me as their leader.

"The tiger is walking around out there." I flicked my head toward the warehouse. Mouths dropped open, but I put my hands up to preempt any screaming they might be planning to do. I held my index finger to my lips to emphasize how quiet they needed to be.

Scanning the room for anything we could use as a weapon against a tiger, I realized everything was secured to the wall or the floor.

*Think, Paprika!* What did I know about big cats? I'd never studied them, specifically.

I mentally flipped through the facts I'd happened upon while reading articles on the Internet.

*They can swim.*

That didn't help.

*All kinds of big cats are attracted to Calvin Klein's Obsession for Men.*

I glanced around the bathroom. No men had gotten swept up in our net and it was unlikely the infant boys were wearing cologne.

*Siberian tigers can be patient and vengeful.*

I was recalling a story I'd read on the NPR website about a man who'd shot and injured a Siberian and stolen his prey. The tiger went to the man's cabin, tore up everything with his scent on it, then waited up to forty-eight hours for the man to return so he could kill him.

*Fuck.*

I could have heard a pin drop in the bathroom as I scanned the faces of the women and children. The women's eyes were crazy wide. A couple of them seemed to have stopped blinking altogether. One of the older babies, who had little blonde wisps of hair on her otherwise bald head had stopped sucking her pacifier and was also staring at me, wide-eyed and expectant.

How did I become the leader here?

Oh, yeah. I told them to follow me.

I stepped over and peeked out from behind the screen. Egor seemed to have homed in on us. He was padding toward the bathroom slowly, but with unmistakable confidence.

For the first time, I regretted not letting LeeAnne bring her gun, although I wasn't convinced the six-shooter she liked to keep handy could stop a seven-hundred-pound tiger. At least not before it did serious damage.

I stepped back into the bathroom. "Okay," I said in the calmest voice I could muster. "Mom's with babies go to the back stalls."

No one moved. It was like they were all carved from stone.

"Get the moms with babies to the back stalls," I said to LeeAnne.

She started herding moms, immediately.

One of the teenagers raised her hand. "Um...why?" she asked in a shaky voice.

"Because the tiger is coming this way." I tried to make my voice more authoritative. "Get into a stall and listen for my voice. Do whatever I tell you."

She and her friend nodded. Everyone stuffed themselves into stalls together.

They probably thought I had a plan.

Then I heard him. Egor was making huffing sounds just outside. Like he was the Big Bad Wolf and we were the little pigs.

After making sure everyone had hidden, I stepped alone into the first stall. As I closed the door, I noticed the locking mechanism had been removed, leaving a hole big enough to see through.

The huffing grew louder. He had to be inside the restroom with us.

I was missing something. Surely, sometime, in all those years alone with my computer, I learned a few facts that would help me now.

I peeked through the hole and Egor was standing there, inside the bathroom, maybe three yards away from me looking...hungry.

Then it came to me. The video I'd seen on YouTube of a tiger being frightened by a vacuum cleaner.

That was it! Tigers were afraid of loud or unnatural noises!

"Everyone flush your toilet on three," I yelled. Egor lifted his eyes to the sound of my voice.

"One...two...three!" I flushed my toilet—thank Zeus these were the super-loud kind. The others flushed theirs, too, and the startling sound echoed on the walls.

I peeped out in time to see Egor duck his head and take two steps back. I kept watching, willing him to go. But he stood there as the sounds died out.

That's when the bad news hit me. This tiger had been in captivity for years. Maybe forever. It must have heard toilets flushing before.

I was out of ideas that would protect all the occupants of the bathroom. And the way this circus was run, I wasn't holding my breath that someone would rush in with a tranquilizer gun at any second.

They might have had to call 9-1-1 or the zoo or something.

*Damn.* There was only one answer I could think of. I got these women and kids into this bathroom. It was up to me to make sure they got away safely.

I was going to have to sacrifice myself. Once Egor got my head between his jaws of death, he'd likely drag me away to feast on me somewhere else and LeeAnne, the moms, the kids, and the skinny girls would be safe.

The things that zip through your mind in the seconds before you're about to die are weird. I wondered if Nick would be sad about me for long or if he'd just find himself a blonde to marry. There were plenty of them in L.A.

LeeAnne would be okay. My family would watch out for her and she for them.

My family. Could my Lita and aunts and Papi survive another loss?

Tears burned behind my eyes at the thought. I tried to redirect onto something else.

Eli. Would he stalk my funeral? What was left of me after the tiger got finished with me would probably have to be cremated.

My thoughts circled back around to Nick and the regret flooded in.

I'd never gotten to experience Nick's gorgeous body on mine. In mine. I'd never told him I loved him or explained how vital he felt to me.

To my heart.

And now it was too late.

Egor's footfalls were so stealthy, I couldn't hear them, but the huffing got louder. I was sure I was about to die, but I decided I wasn't going down without a fight.

I reached into my pocket for my keys. Hopefully, if I faked with my left hand, I could poke Egor in the eye with the keys in my right hand.

I knew there wasn't a big chance that I could do any damage to a seven-hundred-pound cat who was out for my blood, but I pulled out my keys anyway...

And noticed my Space Invaders key chain.

# CHAPTER FOURTEEN

**Rika**

*Holy mother of Zeus!*

I'd been carrying the keychain for several months—ever since the online geek store sent it to me to review—so I hardly noticed it anymore. I had given it a less-than-stellar review because it had no screen. The invaders were on the buttons that you pushed as they lit up. It was more like a tiny Whac-a-Mole game, and I'd found it boring, although I liked the geekiness of having it as my key chain.

But now...

What was more unnatural sounding than Space Invaders music? I pushed the volume button until I was sure the sound would be at top level.

When I bent and looked through the peephole, Egor was standing a foot from the stall door, staring back at me like I was a top sirloin treat. And, this close, he was enormous!

My heart rate accelerated until I thought it might blow right out of my chest. For once, I didn't crave carbs. I just wanted to cover my eyes and pretend this wasn't happening.

But if I did, Egor could choose any stall, and chow down.

One of the toddlers whimpered. The sound was magnified by the bathroom acoustics.

Egor's head turned toward the back stalls. He lifted his nose and sniffed the air. The faces of the horrified mothers flashed before my eyes.

*Not today, kitty,* I thought defiantly.

I pressed the On button.

*Dun-pew-pew!* Space Invaders blared.

That's when—I swear to Thor—Egor, the seven-hundred-pound tiger, jumped straight up in the air, turned and ran out of the bathroom.

Had I just saved us all?

But I had no time to enjoy my success before the next thought hit me. *Will he go after someone else?*

I opened my stall door and raced out, planning to use my secret weapon to save other people, if necessary.

When I came around the privacy screen, I had to blink several times to be sure I was seeing what I thought I was seeing.

*Eli?*

Yes, Eli was on the tiger's back, his left arm hooked around Egor's throat, his right hand holding a now-empty syringe to the tiger's neck.

As Egor began to stumble, Eli slid off his back. Egor crashed to the ground and Eli handed the syringe off to a stagehand.

"Eli?" I said. That was all I could think to say. Was this a dream?

"It took these morons forever to find the tranquilizer," he replied. "Then they didn't know where the tranq gun was and nobody would get near the tiger to give it the shot." He rolled his eyes as if not wanting to jump onto a Siberian's back was the most ridiculous thing he'd ever heard. "I was headed this way with the syringe when I heard the Space Invaders. Nice work. He was so freaked out he didn't even notice me until I was on him."

I looked at Egor. He appeared even bigger spread out on his side than he had standing up, if that was possible.

I felt kind of woozy and wanted to regurgitate the huge ball of fear that filled my stomach. When I looked back toward the bathroom, LeeAnne was peeking around the corner.

"It's okay," I said. "He's down. You can bring everyone out."

She called back to the others, then came out from behind the screen with a baby asleep on her shoulder.

Gradually, each person emerged. The moms looked shocked and scared out of their minds as did a couple of the kids. Two of the babies had fallen asleep, including the one on LeeAnne.

*Oh, to be that innocent.*

I looked at Eli. "Where's Xavier?" I asked.

"Who?"

"The lion tamer. Tiger tamer. Whatever."

"I haven't seen him since I left the tent."

Did Xavier really sic his tiger on us? Was that even possible?

"Is it dead?" LeeAnne asked, poking Egor's paw with the toe of her shoe. Her average-sized foot looked child-sized next to his.

"No, it's just sleeping. Eli tranquilized him."

"Eli?" LeeAnne asked. "You mean your stalker Eli?"

"Yep," I said as I gestured toward Eli. Except he wasn't standing where he'd been a minute before. I scanned the area. He wasn't standing anywhere.

"You didn't see him standing right over here when you came out?" I asked LeeAnne.

"No, but, in my defense, I was pretty focused on Hell Hole Kitty over here."

I was surprised by the laugh that burst out of me, first, because I was still a bit hysterical after almost being eaten by this feline monster and, second, because the Hello-Hell Hole Kitty pun was kind of a stretch. The laugh made me realize I hadn't inhaled fully since we ran into the bathroom, afraid my breathing sounds would attract the tiger.

I took in a huge breath, then found myself laughing again. I tried to pull myself together, but the more I thought about what had just happened and how I'd fended off the beast, the more ridiculous it all seemed. I laughed so hard my stomach hurt but I couldn't stop.

The crowd from the bathroom gathered around me, except for the teenage girls who were taking selfies with Egor the Unconscious while handlers rolled the mobile cage over.

I was still laughing when LeeAnne reached out and touched my arm. My gaze met her extra-wide blue eyes and the expression on her face caused another round of uncontrollable giggles.

"Rika?" LeeAnne said. "Are you okay?"

I sucked in another deep breath. "Am I okay?" I said between bouts of laughter. "I just survived an attempted assassination by tiger!"

"You mean, you saved us all from the biggest freakin' tiger I've ever seen! You scared him off with your little geek key chain game, didn't you?"

"Yeah," I said. I stopped laughing and looked at the Space Invaders game still in my hand.

*Maybe I should go back and edit my review.*

As I said, it's weird what you think about at times like this. It also hit me that, even if I'd been eaten by the tiger, I still wouldn't have considered it the worst thing that had happened in my life. I'd be dead relatively fast, whereas losing my mother was a chronic condition that could never be cured.

However, lately, when I thought of it, I'd been switching my mind to Nick. I always felt better when he was in my presence or even in my head. He made me feel like maybe life wasn't all about losing people, but about gaining them, too.

*Oh, no! Nick!*

He was going to be pissed when he realized I came without him and almost became a feline's Fancy Feast.

But I didn't have time to worry about Nick right now.

Where was Xavier?

I rushed over to a burly Russian who was gesturing to other men about where to position the cage.

"Hi, I'm Rika," I said.

He turned, jerked his head back, a pleasantly surprised expression on his face. Then he smiled. "Hello, I am Rafael," he said with what sounded like a Spanish accent.

Apparently, just because a guy is blonde and big-chested and looks like he could take Sylvester Stallone in a *Rocky* movie doesn't mean he's Russian.

"*Dónde está Xavier?*" I asked in case Spanish would get me better answers.

He shrugged. "*No sé,*" he replied. Then he rattled off another sentence in Spanish I didn't quite catch.

"You don't know where he is?" I tried to clarify. How was it possible that asshole Xavier wasn't here, wrangling his "wild beast"?

"He is injured." He pronounced his J's like Lita and my father did, which was more of a Y sound. "He think is eh...how you say...dislocal..." He put his hand on my shoulder and kept it there, not that I minded. He was cute. And, though, I knew there were plenty of blonde Spanish-speakers in Europe, it was still kind of a novelty for me.

"Dislocated shoulder?" I finished for him. That must have been the part I missed. I knew the Spanish my grandmother and our neighborhood friends used and what I'd learned in Spanish classes in school, but I didn't know much medical Spanish.

"I don't remember the tiger attacking him," I said. In fact, I was sure the tiger didn't attack him because it was busy trying to attack me and maybe LeeAnne after he pointed at us and ordered it to.

LeeAnne handed the baby off to his mother, who seemed to have mostly recovered from the trauma. "The tiger didn't attack him," LeeAnne said. "It came straight for us."

"Where do people usually go when they're injured?" I asked.

"If they don't need the...eh...medics...?"

"Paramedics?"

"Yes. Eh...if don't need paramedic, go to Constata."

"Thanks," I said as I grabbed LeeAnne's arm. We headed for the wardrobe room, and I wondered how often the paramedics had to be called to Cirque de Sorbet. From the way the fancy tiger cage broke apart, it didn't look like safety came first in this circus. Those golden bars were more a suggestion than a restraint.

The overhead lights were on in the wardrobe room and the place was a mess. Clothes and costumes had been discarded all over the floor, I assumed from quick changes during the show.

Constata was holding an ice pack out to Xavier. He was looking at his shoulder, which was badly bruised, and testing it out by moving his arm in a circle.

"Ladies!" He spoke in the jovial tone of a man whose tiger had not just hunted us down like a couple of hedgehogs. He took the ice pack and set it on his shoulder. "How did you enjoy the show?"

"Are you fucking kiddin' me?" LeeAnne yelled.

That was not how I planned for this to go. I did a quick scan of Constata to make sure she didn't have any knives on her, then put my hand on LeeAnne's forearm, in a *be cool* signal. She got it and clamped her mouth shut.

"Is something wrong?" Xavier asked.

I decided to go along with his innocent act. "Well, maybe you didn't realize," I said calmly, as if a tiger tamer could be unaware his tiger had broken loose in the middle of an act. "But Egor came after us in the tent, then tracked us to the bathroom."

Constata got up, walked away and started picking clothes up from the aisle as if this was just a typical night at the circus and we were discussing the box office take.

"Oh, that!" Xavier made a sweeping gesture with his hands.

"Egor wouldn't hurt you. Sometimes kitties just take a liking to someone and want to play."

LeeAnne pulled her arm free from my grasp and yelled, "That tiger broke out of its cage after you told it to kill us!"

Xavier frowned, appearing perplexed. "What are you talking about?"

"You said, '*Mátalas*' and pointed toward us right before Egor broke free."

"*Mátalas*?" he repeated. "I never said '*mátalas*'."

"You did say it," LeeAnne cried. "We both heard you."

Xavier chuckled and shook his head. "Not '*mátalas*'," he said between chuckles. "'*Gata, más!*' It's what I say when I want Egor to roar louder, act more..." His eyes rolled to one side as he searched for the word. "Ferocious."

*Mátalas. Gata más.* They did sound kind of alike and there was a lot of noise happening at the time. But wait a minute...

"'*Gata*' is feminine. You would say '*gato*' when talking to Egor."

Xavier chuckled, again! His chuckling was becoming more irritating than his uppity behavior before the show. "Egor is female."

"But Egor is a male name." Or, at least, I thought it was.

"A male tiger sounds more exciting," he replied. "More frightening."

LeeAnne straightened her spine and stuck her chin out. *Uh-oh.* "Why, that's the most sexist thing I've ever heard." This was coming from a woman who taught me to use booty shorts, pushup bras, and shirts with suggestive messages on them to get more tips when I was working in her bar. But she always had my back, therefore, I decided not to point that out in front of Xavier.

In response, Xavier rolled his eyes and murmured, "Americans," under his breath.

LeeAnne looked like she was ready to throw down, so I jumped in. "But Egor is huge. Male tigers are the bigger ones."

"She's the largest Siberian female on record," Xavier said.

"They said her parents were both very large and she was raised in captivity, and she was well..." His eyes flicked to the side again. "Well-nursed?"

"Well-nourished?" I suggested.

"Yes, that is it. Well-nourished."

LeeAnne was staring intently at Xavier. She'd had some bad experiences with men. By the look in her eyes, she was not giving this one the benefit of the doubt. "How'd you hurt your shoulder?" she asked.

"When she broke the bars, I tried to stop her," he claimed. "I got my hands on her hind leg, but she threw me off like I was a fly." He sounded too much like a proud papa on the last sentence. "I landed on my shoulder."

I tried to replay Xavier's actions, but once Egor broke out, Xavier no longer appeared in my memory.

"*Mira, Xavier...*" I purposely pronounced his name with the most Spanish accent I could muster, "Sah-vee-er," the way his mother might have said it. I kept my tone even. "You gave a command, pointed at us, and your tiger hunted us —all the way to the bathroom—like a trained bloodhound." Instead of asking a question, I just waited to see what he would say.

"I've explained the command to you. The pointing was for what she is supposed to do at the end—bow to each side of the room. And—" He sucked in a big breath, then stepped closer to LeeAnne and sniffed her. "Tigers are attracted to certain perfumes. What is that scent you are wearing?"

"Oh," LeeAnne said. "Do you like it? The boutique I work in has it by the cash register. It's a fundraiser for an animal organization called HETOS-Humans for the Ethical Treatment of Other Species. They gave me a bottle in appreciation for selling it. This scent is called Catnip."

Xavier and I turned to look at her. "Catnip?" we both said.

"Yeah, they claim it's supposed to make you irresistible to your cat. Personally, I wouldn't want a pet that didn't like me for myself, but I do like the scent." She looked back and forth at our faces. "What?" Then a second later, her expression turned contrite as she said, "Ohhhh."

We kept staring. Me, because I didn't know what to say after this revelation. Xavier was probably tallying up all the money LeeAnne and her perfume cost him. I hope he wasn't planning to sue her or the non-profit for replacement costs—I looked at his bruised shoulder—plus pain and suffering.

"Well, we'd better get going," I said as I slid my hand in LeeAnne's and tugged. "Um, got to relieve the babysitters." As I hustled us away, I realized I'd picked the stupidest excuse I could have, considering most people went to the circus with their kids.

"Holy shit!" LeeAnne exclaimed. "Do you really think that tiger went crazy because of my perfume?"

I didn't want her to feel guilty, but I didn't want to lie to her either. "I don't know, LeeAnne. Xavier and this circus are super sketchy. Maybe you were right about what he said. Maybe it was the perfume. I honestly don't know."

"Hmm... I wonder if it would work on Justin Timberlake. I swear I saw him going into the fancy barber shop across the street from the boutique the other day."

I burst out laughing. "Good to see you still have your priorities in order, but J.T. isn't a tiger."

LeeAnne gave me a knowing look. "In my fantasies, he is."

～

## Nick

I paced back and forth on the sidewalk in front of Mrs. Delacruz's house, waiting for Rika and LeeAnne to return.

Like most people in the town we came from, LeeAnne loved to pass along a good story, and she'd been texting me the most bizarre one I'd ever heard. After the first text—*Rika and I were almost attacked by a tiger, but we're about to come home now*—I jumped in my truck and raced from my hotel to her grandmother's house.

Since they were stopped on a freeway behind an accident, LeeAnne had time to tell more of what had happened. At each stoplight, I checked my text messages and the story got more and more disturbing.

At first, I thought LeeAnne was punking me, but there were a lot of specific details, including the mention of the warehouse behind the circus tent. Rika would have to be in on it, too, and I just didn't think ridiculous practical jokes were her kind of thing.

But if LeeAnne wasn't exaggerating, that meant she and Rika almost died tonight.

I should have been with them. What if the tiger had attacked? He would have eaten Rika. *Eaten* her.

Working as a defense attorney in a large law firm in Austin, I'd heard of a lot of ways people were killed, even saw the pictures. But being eaten by a big cat was...

I had no words to describe it. Just a sick feeling in my gut.

I was supposed to be watching out for Rika, and I'd always sort of taken care of LeeAnne. Well, as much as LeeAnne would let me.

Why did Rika insist on going investigating without me? We were supposed to be a team.

Or maybe I had my "supposed to be's" wrong. Maybe I was just supposed to be the guy Rika had to put up with in order to fund her business.

Regardless, what was wrong with her? Hadn't there been enough tragedy in her family? I could keep her safe if she would just cooperate.

I heard a motor and turned to see LeeAnn's old Trans Am turn into the driveway.

When Rika got out, she didn't seem happy to see me.

"Hey, Nick!" LeeAnne called as she hopped out of the car. "What are you doing here?"

And that's all it took. I blew. "What am I doing here? You texted me and told me you and Rika were almost eaten by a tiger!" Saying it aloud made it sound ridiculous. It couldn't be true. "Were you punking me?"

"Would I lie to you?" LeeAnne asked.

Nothing came to mind immediately, but I was pretty sure LeeAnne had lied to me a few times in the past thirty years.

"Besides, we're fine." She flopped her hand back and forth, waving my concerns away. "I don't know why you're freaking out now. We're over it."

"You're *over* it?" I looked from her face to Rika's. They did appear over it. "But I just heard about it!" I turned to Rika, "What the hell? We're supposed to be partners!"

She sighed. At least she had the decency to look semi-apologetic. "All we did was go to the circus," she said. "I never thought I'd need a bodyguard there. It's full of little kids. How dangerous could it be?"

"Sounded pretty dangerous to me."

"Well, yeah," she replied. "We know that now."

LeeAnne stepped forward, putting herself between me and Rika in a move that appeared protective.

That just pissed me off more. If anyone should have been protecting Rika, it was me and, regardless of her past experiences with men, LeeAnne knew it wasn't in me to hurt a woman.

"Nick, you need to—" she began.

"LeeAnne!" I said in a tone she couldn't ignore. "Go inside. I wanna talk to Rika alone."

She stared into my eyes as if confirming it was safe to leave us out here together, then turned to look at Rika.

Rika gave her a nod and tilted her head toward the door like a crime boss in a mafia movie.

"Okay," LeeAnne said. "Play nice, kids." She went inside.

I turned to Rika and looked hard into her eyes. She looked hard right back at me.

"Why do you insist on investigating without me?"

"It's not a big deal, Nick. Most P.I.'s investigate alone. Besides, I just wanted to watch the circus to see if it gave me any more ideas about people we should interview. And LeeAnne had never even been to a circus, so it was more like a girls' night out." She gestured to me. "You know, like the boys' nights out guys like to take."

"Do you know the last time I had a boys' night out?" I asked.

She shook her head.

"When I was in college."

"Well, that's too bad," she replied. "Maybe we could find you friends to hang—"

"I don't need a boys' night out," I cut in. "I'm a grown man." I stepped into her space and wrapped my hands around her upper arms. "What I need is you... alive."

Her face softened as she stared up at me. I thought I saw moisture in her eyes, but she blinked a few times and it disappeared.

"I'm sorry," she said. "I thought it would be harmless fun with the slight possibility of a lead. And, really, there wasn't much you could have done against a seven-hundred-pound tiger."

I thought I'd already digested the information, but the reality of tiny Rika being mauled by a full-grown tiger hit me full force. A lump formed in my throat that I couldn't swallow. When had I reached the point where I couldn't imagine the world without her?

Didn't matter, I guess. I was there.

I couldn't resist touching a strand of hair at her temple, following it down with my finger until I reached her jaw. I cupped her chin.

"I—" My voice sounded croaky. I cleared my throat. "I, um..." Why was it this hard for me to tell her I didn't want to, couldn't, in fact, live without her?

Maybe because I'd never said those words to a woman in my life, not even my wives.

"I can't have anything happen to you," I finally finished. God, that sounded lame compared to what I wanted to say.

She took a deep breath and, when she spoke, her voice was mock-cheerful. "Well, LeeAnne always says that Gabe says you have a savior complex when it comes to women."

Is that what Rika believed? That our relationship was just part of my mental issue, diagnosed by a judge who liked to play psychiatrist on the side?

Damn Bolo! Nobody in that town could keep their mouths shut. Everyone was judged and pigeonholed, even by their best friends. How far did I have to go before I left my Bolo reputation behind?

And what the hell did I have to do before Rika understood it was all about her? Not my mom or my exes or Gabe's opinions or his—probably accurate—diagnosis of my savior complex.

Hell, there were plenty of women to save in Texas. I didn't have to come to Los Angeles, California to save one.

Rika must have noticed the frustration playing out on my face.

"Nick, I..." she started, then paused and let out a sigh. "Well, I hope you know I appreciate your concern for me...and everything you've done for me." She slid her arms around my torso and pressed her cheek to my ribs. But it felt like she'd stuck her hand in my chest and squeezed.

Not wanting the moment to end, I slid one hand around and pressed it into her spine while I caressed the back of her head with the other. Her hair felt like silk and smelled like flowers. Her breasts squeezed against me, causing my blood to rush south.

*Damn, if I died right now, like this, I'd die a happy man.*

Then I remembered that Rika was the one who'd almost died tonight. Was she manipulating me with a hug to make me forget?

Hugging her tighter against me, I bent over until my mouth

was next to her ear. "I'm taking you to the shooting range tomorrow."

She wrenched her head back to look up at me. "*What*?"

"The shooting range. You have a P.I. license now. You can get a concealed carry permit."

She shook her head adamantly. "I don't want to carry a gun, Nick."

"Do I need to list off all the things that have happened to you since I've known you? And tonight, a tiger tried to have you for dinner!"

"I doubt Egor could have been stopped by a pistol, not before he—I mean she—ripped my head off."

Was she joking about having her gorgeous head ripped off? I released her from the hug. "I'm not talking about LeeAnne's antique six-shooter," I said. "I'm talking about something that can fire off rounds quick enough to make an impression on anybody."

Her eyes flashed, sending hot sparks through my body. "Nick, listen to me." She spoke loudly and enunciated like she thought I'd lost my hearing. "I don't want a gun!"

"Then, you're in the wrong business!" I said even louder. This was one thing I couldn't give in about. She needed to be able to keep herself safe.

I heard a window slide open followed by the sound of unhappy Spanish.

"Uh-oh," Rika muttered.

"Paprika? Is that you?" Mrs. Delacruz called.

"Yes, Lita. I'm sorry if we woke you. It's just me and Nick."

"Well, it's late and I don't want you waking my neighbors. Nick, get your dog from the living room and go. Sofia can't take her tomorrow. She has an appointment. Rika, quit arguing in the street like a Jersey Shore."

"Does she know the Jersey Shore is a coastline and not a person?" I asked.

"She knows," Rika replied. "But ever since she watched that reality show a few years ago, it's become one of her sayings."

We both turned and walked toward the house. Sure, we'd face shooters and knife throwers and tigers, but neither of us wanted to tangle with her grandmother. She'd made quite an impression with her pot throwing.

She still probably had one of those clock radios from the eighties on her nightstand. And her aim with unwieldy objects was unbelievable. I imagined the corner of a clock radio hitting the top of my head and was pretty sure I wouldn't enjoy it.

So, I went inside, got my dog, and left, just like the tiny Colombian woman told me to.

# CHAPTER FIFTEEN

**Rika**

After Nick left, whatever remained of the adrenaline from the night's excitement drained from my body. I needed sleep. Or maybe I was asleep and the trip to the circus was a dream. I'd only been gone from the place for an hour and already the night's events seemed impossible.

When I got to my room, I found Sofia in my bed.

"What was going on out there?" she asked sleepily.

"Nothing. Move over," I said as I changed quickly into a pair of Ravenclaw pajamas.

She scooted to the other side of the bed and I climbed in.

"Were you out late with Nick?" she asked in a voice chock full of innuendo. "Is he super-hot in bed? He looks hot, but it's hard to imagine what—"

I suddenly realized I didn't want Sofia imagining my Nick as a lover. "Stop objectifying my partner!" I said.

She smiled mischievously. "Oooooh, somebody's jealous," she taunted.

"Grow up, Sofia."

She nudged my arm with her elbow and I flipped over on my side to face her. "What?"

"We're cousins," she pointed out unnecessarily. "And neither of us has a sister. We should share more."

"I don't remember you sharing any details of your relationship with Gustavo," I said.

Gustavo was Sofia's most recent boyfriend. She seemed to be a serial monogamist—always had a boyfriend, but the relationships never lasted more than a few months.

"You never asked," she said.

She was right. I never asked.

Should I have asked? Did she feel bad that I didn't ask?

I'd just always felt like our lives were sort of compartmentalized. We were cousins and we loved each other, but we were such different people with different friends. It usually didn't enter my mind to ask for details of her love life.

I suddenly realized how much time I'd spent in my own head.

Was I a narcissist?

"I'm sorry, Sofia. About not asking."

"No biggie," she said. And she sounded like she really meant it. "We've both had our issues we chose to handle in our own minds."

I wondered what issues she was referring to. Mine were obvious, but I always thought she was just living her life as a normal person. "And we don't have a lot of interests in common...but we do both like guys." The smile came back. Even in the dark, Sofia had a great smile.

We broke out in giggles like when we were little girls.

"So, what's it like, between you two?" she prompted.

Suddenly, I was overwhelmed by the need to talk about Nick and me. "We haven't, um, been together that way."

"Shut the fuck up!"

"Shhh," I said, covering her suddenly loud mouth with my hand. "Lita will hear you!"

She pried my fingers away. "You really haven't tapped that yet?" she whispered.

"No."

"Why not?"

I tried out the truth in my head: *Because I'm not comfortable in my own skin. Because I'm afraid Nick will see me naked and ask me to put my clothes back on. Because I'm not pageant material and I couldn't possibly stack up against the other women he's been with.*

But I couldn't make any of that come out of my mouth. Instead I ended up saying, "I'm not sure he's that into me."

She propped up on an elbow and, even in the dark room, I could see her wide eyes and raised brows. "After everything he's done for you?" she whisper-yelled. "Do you really think a man will represent a woman for free, let her stay in his house, race across the country when she calls, *and* start the business she always wanted with her if he's not into her?"

Well, when she laid it all out like that, I did sound nuts. However, I knew I wouldn't be enough for Nick in the long run and couldn't let myself get my hopes up. We'd been thrown in each other paths by a weird twist of fate at a time when we were both vulnerable. He'd barely gotten through with his last divorce when I was thrust upon him. "He didn't have any choice about representing me," I said. "The judge—"

Sofia shut me up with a frustrated sigh. "Holy Fruit of the Loom!" she cried.

I cracked up. We'd made the saying up as kids after Lita got after her for "using God's name in vain."

It reminded me that, no matter how different we were, we shared a past. And we were family.

I went from laughing to feeling tears prickling behind my eyes. "Sof, I'm afraid for Nick to see me with my clothes off," I blurted.

"What? Why?"

"Because of the... Because I'm... Because he's normally with gorgeous women who have zero body fat."

She lowered her chin and looked at me from under scrunched up eyebrows. "So?"

I let out an exasperated sigh. "I'm afraid he'll see the fat and be grossed out."

"Grossed out?" she repeated. Her face took on a knowing expression. "Nick is a man. The fat parts are the parts they like."

"Um...*what*?" If that were true, I should have been homecoming queen in high school. They probably would have needed to reinforce the throne, though.

In response, Sofia poked an index finger into the top of one of my breasts, then managed to pat one side of my rear before I slapped her hand away.

"That's what they like," she said. "You don't think Nick is attracted to you?"

My mind replayed the times Nick had kissed me. "He may be attracted to me," I replied. "But I'm not sure he's more attracted to me than he is any other woman. And I don't play in the same league as his type."

Sofia squinted at me, then asked, "Do you really not know how hot you are now?"

I'd wanted to be hot for so long, worked really hard toward it for several years, but, to me, "hot" was a very elusive state. Mostly, when I looked in the mirror, I still saw pudgy.

"I'm not hot, Sofia," I said. The rest was just too complicated to explain.

She whacked me on the side of my head with a force that fell somewhere between a tap and a slap—her way of knocking sense into me. "You are *so* hot!"

"I'm not, Sofia. Please, just drop it."

"I'm not dropping it because if you think you're not hot, then there's something wrong in your head, and you need to seek counseling."

*Oh, jeez.* That "seek counseling" line was from a lifetime of living with Tía Margo, the marriage counselor.

"Let's just agree to disagree."

She rolled her eyes. "Bullshit! When do we ever 'agree to disagree' in this family? We're Latinas. We yell until we straighten the *pendeja* out!"

This made me laugh, even as I remembered why Sofia always referred to us as "Latinas" instead of "Colombians." She'd been part of my life since I was two, and I often forgot she was adopted by my Tía Margo and Uncle Kurt under circumstances in which they didn't learn her exact ethnicity.

On her twenty-first birthday, I went out with her and her friends, even though we didn't normally socialize with the same people. Basically, I was the designated driver for the evening, but I didn't mind because it was Sofia's special night.

However, around two in the morning before I dropped her at her house, my very tipsy cousin confessed that it bothered her she probably wasn't of Colombian descent like the rest of us. Some butthead in school, years before, had pointed out that, considering this was Southern California, she was more likely to be Mexican or El Salvadorian than Colombian. She said it had bothered her ever since.

This was news to me. She almost never talked about the fact that she was adopted. To me, she was just part of the family.

"Look, dumbass..." She pulled out her cell phone, tapping and swiping until she found what she was looking for. Sofia was the artistic type who was always snapping pictures, so I wasn't surprised when she showed me one.

What did surprise me was the woman in the picture. She was a lovely brunette, outside, looking skyward as she smiled. It was a full body shot, and I was immediately jealous of how slender she was. But a second later, a weird feeling—one I'd experienced a few times before—came over me.

She was wearing my clothes.

She was also wearing the electrode cap that went with my mind-controlled toy helicopter, but it didn't detract from her beauty one bit.

I closed my eyes as the unsettling sensation enveloped me. This young woman couldn't be me, but she had to be.

This is why, while everyone else my age seemed to photograph every moment of their lives, I hadn't taken any more pictures since I dropped the weight than I did before. It was disturbing to have such a different view of myself in my head than photographic evidence showed to be true.

I was a woman of logic, damn it, not a head case!

"You can see it in the picture, can't you?" Sofia asked.

"Yeah, I guess," I admitted.

She stared hard at me as if she was working on a diagnosis for my mental state, and I thought she looked an awful lot like Tía Margo in that instant, adopted or not. Now, I just wanted her to remove the photo from my sight and leave me alone.

"So, you can see it in a picture, but not in your head?"

I shrugged and wobbled my head in half-hearted agreement.

"Or the mirror?" she said with even more disbelief in her voice.

This was going too far. I did not want to admit that I found mirrors as confusing as Gucci did. She barked at herself every time she saw her reflection in a mirror, a window, or even a stainless-steel refrigerator, thinking she was warding off a usurper.

I saw my reflection in the glass of a storefront and muttered "skinny bitch," in the back of my mind before realizing I was the only person standing there.

"Look, Sof, I don't want to talk about—"

She interrupted me with a snort. "Do you know how jealous I am whenever I look at the pictures I take of you? You look like a model!"

Okay, now she was being ridiculous. I was not tall enough to be a model. I had smallish breasts and too much butt, although the woman in Sofia's picture hadn't looked out of proportion. Her phone screen had gone dark, but now I wanted to ask to see it again so I could visually measure the ass to boob ratio.

Regardless, everyone agreed that Sofia had a knockout, bombshell body. "How can you be jealous of me?" I asked. "It's you who needs professional help! You're shaped like a Latina Marilyn Monroe. You're the one guys turn and look at when you walk into a room... plus you have the ringlets!"

I'd never admitted how much I lusted after those ringlets. When I was younger, I'd even tried to create them on my own head, but, no matter what products I used, the coils started going straight randomly here and there, leaving a mess of half-ringlet, half-straight hair, which was not a good look on anyone.

"The only reason guys notice me first is 'cause I dress it up, with heels and cleavage and jewelry. They whistle and yell at me, but then they look at you like they're ready to take you home to meet their mothers."

Did I say she was being ridiculous before? Now she was really being ridiculous! "You're crazy!" I said. "Guys have always said how hot you are! And it's not like they're falling at my feet proposing!"

"That's just because of the vibe you give off."

"What vibe?"

"There's a 'stand back' vibe you give off whenever a hot guy is talking to you."

Oh, my God! That was totally not true! "I am not stuck up!" I cried.

"No." Sofia gave a quick shake of her head. "Not stuck up. It's something else. I've seen it and a couple of my guy friends who think you're hot mentioned it. They called it giving them the 'Back off, Bud'."

I loved my cousin, but she was really starting to piss me off.

First, she showed me that confusing picture of myself and now... I didn't even know what to say about the vibe she claimed emanated from me. It wasn't like I'd ever been bitchy to one of her friends.

"I'm sleepy," I said, even though I was no longer sleepy at all. I just needed Sofia to stop talking. Then, I could decide whether to consider her words or lock them away in one of the many boxes in the back of my brain.

"Rika," Sofia tugged at a strand of my hair to make sure she had one hundred percent of my attention.

"What?" I said, the annoyance clear in my voice.

"Nick is a great guy. We all like him, even my mom and Lita. He clearly likes you and respects you. And, when you're not looking, *he* is. At you. The way every woman hopes a man will look at her someday." She paused to let her words sink in.

My mind tried to bat them away. That's when I realized what I was truly afraid of.

Hope.

As much as I hadn't wanted the awful things that happened in my childhood to define me, they were. Big time.

Even after losing the equivalent of another person in weight. Even after I'd dated a cast member from a TV show, although he wasn't one when I met him. Even after spending every day with the greatest guy I'd ever known, I was afraid to hope that my personal life would work out in the end.

Maybe that's why I'd stayed with that tool Brandtt for two years. Because I knew it wouldn't matter that much if we broke up. If you don't care too much, you don't get your hopes up.

Yeah. I had a problem. Would I ever be able to leave all the crap behind me and just be normal?

Okay, maybe normal was too much to ask for in my case.

"What I'm saying is..." Sofia continued. "If you want him, you need to show him. Not with hugs or kisses. You need to *really* show him or another woman will."

Then, as my body surged into fight or flight *What the hell am I going to do?* mode, Sofia rolled over and went to sleep.

**Rika**

As Nick drove us to Erissa's place, I held Gucci on my lap as best I could.

Unfortunately, all Gucci wanted was to be on Nick's lap, her back feet on his thigh, her front paws propped on the driver's side door so she could see out the window.

That meant we were locked in a battle of wills.

You'd think I'd be the clear winner, considering how much bigger and smarter I was. But Gucci was scrappy and determined, and I was afraid to hold her too tight for fear of snapping one of her tiny bones.

I picked her up, her legs flailing in the air, then re-sat her back in my lap.

I glanced up. "I thought we agreed we were going to drive by the crime scene to see if we can get in yet. You're going the wrong way."

Gucci escaped my clutches and hopped over the console. I plucked her from Nick's lap as she growled menacingly at me. Well, as menacingly as a Maltese wearing a pink sparkly collar can growl.

"I know where I'm going," Nick said in a tone of voice that let me know he wanted to end the sentence with the word "woman," as in "I know where I'm going, *woman*."

"Would you mind cluing me in?" I asked snarkily.

He turned into a parking lot. "Here."

I looked up at the sign. "Dead Eye Shooting Range," I read. "What the hell?"

"You got shot at in Bolo," Nick said.

I dipped my chin and looked up at him from under my lashes. "I thought that was just part of the Texas tour."

As he pulled into a parking spot, he ignored me and kept talking. "Then you got shot at when we were looking for your dad, here in California. In fact, here, there are cult members with guns, gang-bangers with guns and whoever that guy was that ended up driving you around in his trunk."

"That was just another cult member," I said. "And it was more of a misunderstanding than—"

"Anyway," he interrupted. "I've seen more guns in a few weeks here than I did the whole time I lived in Texas."

I knew that wasn't true. "Have you been inside LeeAnne's house?" I asked.

"Not since we were kids," he said. "Is the gun collection still all over the walls?"

"Yeah, and if you go inside with her, she starts offering to take them out to let you have a closer look."

"Okay," Nick said. "I'll amend my statement. I've seen more guns *used* since I've been in L.A. than I ever did in Texas."

"But what about hunt—"

Nick held his hand up, interrupting me again. "Pointed at humans," he hedged.

"So, you want to arm me and put another gun on the street?"

"You're a P.I. with a *stalker*," Nick said. "You need a gun."

"I don't like guns," I said. And I meant it. The idea of touching a gun gave me a queasy feeling while a voice from the back of my head told me I didn't want to know why.

"Yeah?" Nick sighed. "Well, no matter what your job is, there's going to be something about it you don't particularly like."

He got out of the truck, came around and opened the door for me. "C'mon," he said. "Humor me."

I was about to argue the point further, but I made the mistake of looking up into his eyes. Soulful eyes that said he really wanted me safe.

*Damn it!* I had no choice but to humor him because he'd already humored the hell out of me by becoming my partner in this venture.

I got out of the truck, handed him his dog, and followed him in.

# CHAPTER SIXTEEN

**Rika**

I stood inside the lobby of the shooting range while Nick talked to the guy behind the counter, a shaved-headed, burly, beige-skinned man named "Bart."

We signed waivers and picked our paper target—Nick pointed to a boring outline of a man. I rejected that one and chose a zombie that was much cooler than a bullseye but not as distasteful as shooting at an outline of what was supposed to be a live person. As Bart made copies of our ID's, I gave myself a tour of the guns, trying to imagine using one.

While this place was kind of scary, it wasn't nearly as shocking as LeeAnne's house. Of course, guns as home decor had been a new concept to me, whereas guns in a gun store-slash-shooting range made more sense.

Regardless, what was the chance a person would be ready with a gun when someone shot at them? Most criminals don't yell, "Hey, I'm coming up behind you right now and I'm going to pull a gun out of my pocket and blow a hole in your head." It was much more likely that someone would shoot you when you had your hands full or surprise you when you were sleeping.

*Or kidnap you after an exercise class while you're unlocking your car door and—*

*Stop.* I exhaled, blowing all the negative thoughts out through my nose, like my Jilly Crane weight-loss counselor had taught me.

We were here because it was important to my business partner and, since he'd agreed to switch to a career he'd never even considered before, I sort of owed him. I hated owing anyone, but I guess I liked having Nick around more than I disliked being in debt.

"Rika?"

I turned to find Nick holding a pair of safety goggles and what appeared to be earphones in one of his big hands. Gucci was still in the other.

"Cool, it'll be like when I work out," I said.

"What?"

"The earphones. I like to listen to music when I work out."

Nick looked at me like I was two aces shy of a full deck, as his people would probably say. "These don't play music. They're earmuffs. Protection for your ears."

*Oh, jeez.* I knew that. I'd seen people on TV wear them when they practiced shooting. I hated sounding dumb any time, but especially with Nick.

"I know," I replied. "I was just messing with you." He gave me a look that said he didn't believe me, so I pointed to the goggles and added, "Oh, and we're doing it underwater!" in a ditzy voice.

He snorted and shifted his gaze back to Bart.

Bart raised his eyebrows and nodded at Nick.

They were using that silent man language, but I was pretty sure Nick had said, *Women, right?* and the guy had replied, *Jeez, tell me about it.*

I wanted to object, but since they didn't make the sexist remarks aloud, all I could do was roll my eyes.

Nick set Gucci on the counter and leaned in. "Ever been divorced?" he asked.

Counter guy nodded and sighed deeply.

"My ex stuck me with this." Nick dipped his head toward Gucci. "And ran off to France with another man. Any place I can leave her while we shoot?"

Although I was pretty sure Nick was secretly glad Megan 'ran off', that was still a smart ploy to get free dog-sitting.

"No problem," Bart said. "I've got Elvis in my office. He loves other dogs."

"Thanks," Nick said, neglecting to inform Bart that Gucci did *not* love other dogs. He handed her off. As Bart baby-talked to her and carried her toward a door behind the counter, Nick took my elbow. "Let's get in there before Bart figures out what's what."

I cracked up. The memory of seeing Nick getting stuck with a frou-frou dog he didn't want was hilarious every time I replayed it.

I put my earmuffs on and headed to the other door. When we stepped into the shooting gallery, I was surprised to find most of the bays full. Before this, I didn't even know we had shooting ranges in L.A., much less the shooters to fill them.

Nick picked a bay for us and set up my zombie target. It went zooming toward the back wall. "You stand in the middle," he said.

"Wait, how am I hearing your voice through these earmuffs when the gunshots are muffled?" I asked.

"They're made by elves in the basement at Hogwarts," he replied.

*Ha. Ha.*

"Hogwarts only has house elves who work in the kitchens and clean at night," I said in an uppity tone. "You may be confusing them with Santa's Elves."

Nick ignored me, placed both hands on my hips and eased me to the left until I was centered. The warmth from his palms radiated right through my jeans, heating the skin underneath.

*Mmm...* I already liked shooting a lot more than I expected.

"I sprung for the good ones," he said. "They block anything over eighty-two decibels, but let you hear voices."

As I put my goggles on, Nick held the black plastic-looking gun up and shoved the clip—or whatever it's called—into the base of it. "This way, I can tell you what to do."

Nick was a natural leader. The kind of guy who'd be made the president of a club even if he wasn't running for office. However, he was not the president of me.

"You mean you'll *ask* me to do something...not tell me."

Nick gave me a smirk.

We'd only been in the gun range for a couple of minutes and I already felt annoyed. Maybe because of the way Nick kept throwing his money around on my behalf, like with the fancy earmuffs, and he didn't even ask for a receipt to use on our business taxes! Or maybe because of the superior smirk he just gave me.

Or maybe because of the mental picture my mind had created, years ago when—

*Stop. Breathe.*

Nick gave me a bunch of instructions and warned me about how powerful the weapon was and how it would feel when I shot it. Finally, he put the gun in my hands. "Pull your thumb up," he said. It should be resting along the barrel. "

I remembered how the *cholos* had held their guns when they were shooting.

"Why can't I hold it like this?" I let go with my left hand and turned the gun sideways in my right.

"Are you joining the Crips or the Bloods?" Nick asked.

"What?"

"It's a stupid way to hold a gun. You don't have much control and it's harder to aim."

"I'm not sure they'd let me into the Crips or the Bloods," I mused. "Maybe the *Sureños*."

"Rika, this isn't a joke. I want you to be safe." Nick peered at me with sincere eyes that had turned Bondi Blue—my favorite of all Nick's eye colors—in the fluorescent lighting.

*Those irresistible freaking eyes.* "Fine," I said. "Teach me how to properly gun down a person."

One side of his mouth turned up. Then he moved behind me, so close, I could feel the heat of his body on my back. Then, suddenly, he was wrapped completely around me, his strong arms against my scrawny ones, his warm hands on mine.

He crouched down until his face was even with mine. "Move the gun up a little bit more," he said as he guided it into the right position. I noticed the green laser light going from my gun to the target. That was kind of cool.

Nick exhaled, causing a strand of my hair to tickle my ear. My breathing went shallow. Had anything ever felt this good?

"Focus," Nick said.

"I am focused," I replied. It wasn't really a lie. I hadn't said what I was focused on.

"I can feel your mind wandering."

I hoped he couldn't feel exactly where my mind was wandering because, currently, it was wandering in the vicinity of his crotch.

Forcing myself to focus all my physical and mental energy on the target, I said, "Okay, I'm ready."

Slowly, Nick's hands released mine, being careful not to affect the position of the gun.

"Go ahead," he said.

I pulled the trigger. But in that same instant, my wrists sort of folded to the left and the shot went very wrong. However, that didn't bother me nearly as much as the power that had exploded from the relatively small object in my hand.

I didn't want to do this.

"Hey!" A man yelled and stepped out from two stalls away. "Who just shot my target?"

I opened my mouth to confess, but Nick shushed me. I hated being shushed. "Don't man-shush me," I said, figuring man-shushing would be a lot like mansplaining. He wouldn't shush his friend Gabe like that.

The man shrugged and disappeared into his bay.

"It's okay." Nick was breathing slowly, drawing on all his patience. "Let's try it again. Do you remember how I showed you to hold it?"

Of course, I remembered. It was, like, ten seconds ago. I was tempted to turn the gun upside-down and shoot it that way.

He was watching me expectantly. "Yes, I remember," I said in an exasperated tone. I put both hands on the gun and held it exactly like he'd told me, but he still felt the need to put his hands on mine and lift the gun about a half millimeter from where I had it.

*Control freak.*

He released my hands.

I fired.

Again, my wrists collapsed and the shot went way left—as in practically ninety degrees from where it was supposed to go.

"Fuck," Nick muttered as he leaned in a bit, trying to determine where the round had hit. "Why are you doing that?"

"I'm doing exactly what you told me to do!" I cried.

His brows leapt up his forehead and stayed there. "I didn't tell you to try to take out the people in the stalls next to us!"

Well, there was that.

"You also didn't tell me how *not* to shoot the people in the stall next to us. Clearly, it's a natural reaction you should have accounted for."

"It's not a natural reaction," Nick insisted. "I've never seen anyone that far off before, especially with both hands on the gun. I don't even know how you're doing it."

Just then, Bart came walking up. "I have a complaint about some crazy shooting," he said. "I know most of the people here.

Was it you two? 'Cause we don't tolerate that kind of nonsense here."

"She didn't do it on purpose," Nick said. I noticed he threw me under the bus immediately so the guy wouldn't think it was him who couldn't shoot straight. "Can you do me a favor and check her stance?" he asked. "Something's going wonky when she shoots."

*I'm not wonky! You're wonky!* the childish voice in my head chanted. Nick had practically dragged me to the shooting range, then ratted me out the first chance he got.

"Sure," Bart said. He, too, wrapped himself around me and put his hands on mine. This made me very uncomfortable. He smelled like gunpowder and cigarettes, not yummy like Nick.

Worse, as he adjusted the gun, his big belly pressed against my back. It was way bigger than the pregnant belly Anatolie's daughter was carrying around. I'm not proud that a man's big belly rubbing against my back bothered me. I was once a heavy-weight myself. But it did bother me and I wasn't sure if I should be ashamed of that. I mean, I suppose any guy I didn't know pressing against me would probably make me uncomfortable.

"Okay, you've got it," Bart said confidently. He removed his hands from mine even more gingerly than Nick had.

I pulled the trigger. My wrists folded again as the shot went off.

Someone to the right of us screamed. A gun went flying onto the floor of the range. From the left, I heard someone yell, "*Shit!*"

*Tell me I did not just put a hole in somebody.*

And why were people yelling from two different directions?

Bart ran toward the scream. Nick and I stared after him. Would Nick being here as a witness prevent him from representing me in court?

I realized all shooting had stopped. I pulled off my headphones and set them on the ledge. "What happened?" I asked.

"Best I can tell," Nick said, "there was a ricochet."

We stepped back and turned in the direction Bart had gone. He was standing with a petite blonde who looked a lot like Reese Witherspoon.

I'd seen Reese in person once after another actor friend got Brandtt tickets to a movie premiere. When I realized she was several inches shorter than I was, I was thrilled. I joked to Brandtt that I could totally take her in a fight.

Brandtt didn't have the best sense of humor. He gave me a puzzled look and asked, "Why would you want to fight Reese Witherspoon?"

I was jarred from that memory by the woman's voice, which got louder and shriller by the second. "I want to know who the hell shot at me!" Her high ponytail swished back and forth as she gestured with her hands.

"It was an accident," Bart replied. "I'll take care of it."

"It knocked the gun out of my hand!" she cried. "My hand almost got shot off! How does that even happen?"

She had a point. The walls of the bay went past the barrel of my gun. I'd assumed they were bulletproof. Had I somehow managed a triple, or maybe a quadruple, ricochet?

Nick was checking the sides of our bay, apparently thinking the same thing I was.

Bart had both hands up, palms out, in a *calm down* gesture. "I'll take care of it," he repeated.

"*I'll* take care of it!" Reese's twin said. Her body shifted and she noticed me. I must have looked guilty because she pointed at me and said, "It was you, wasn't it?"

I froze, not wanting to make a move that either confirmed or denied my guilt considering her gun was bigger than mine.

"It was her, wasn't it?" she yelled at Bart, who snatched the gun from her hand and stuffed it in the back of his pants.

He wobbled his head side to side, inadvertently confirming her suspicions. "I'll take care of it, Mitzi," he said again.

That was a cute name for a tiny pixie like her. She would have also made a great Tinkerbell. The thought brought a smile to my face.

"What are you laughing at, bitch?" she screamed.

*Uh-oh.* I wiped the smile off my face.

"I need something to drink," she said in an abrupt change of subject. She reached down and unzipped her duffel bag.

"Good idea," Bart replied. "Take a minute to cool off while I fix the problem."

Me being "the problem," of course. I felt my face heat and I really wanted to get the hell out before this became any more humiliating.

He came walking toward me. "Look—" he began.

But before he could get another word out, his body was jostled. Mitzi managed to push past him. My mind briefly registered that she had something in her hand she was shaking before she popped a top and started spraying me with cola.

I shrieked when the liquid hit me. It was ice cold, like it had come straight out of a cooler. "You bitch!" she screamed. "You could have killed me!"

I'd never thought of myself as a fighter. I was a victim of bullying through my school years. In the last few months, I'd had bits of success fighting off bad guys, at least until I could get help. However, those times had felt mostly like flukes.

But, in that moment, with ice cold cola hitting my chest and face, I didn't consider any of that stuff. I was way too pissed off. Sure, I'd scared Mitzi with my gun by accident, but she was purposely attacking my most beloved Wonder Woman t-shirt— the one where Wonder Woman looked 3-D, like she was coming straight at you, ready to kick ass. Unfortunately, it was on a white background and would likely be stained forever by this Mitzi and her spewing can.

Hot blood scorched through me, all the way to my fingers and toes. Nobody disrespected Wonder Woman! Not on my watch!

Stepping closer, straight into the spray, I grabbed for the can.

But Mitzi didn't let go. She hung on with the tenacity of...well, Gucci.

We wrestled for it, pulling the can and each other back and forth, until she slipped on her own soda, and we both fell to the floor. Lucky for me, I was on top which meant she mostly cushioned my fall to the concrete floor.

I gained control of the can, but it wasn't really spewing anymore, so I pushed the tab in the rest of the way and poured cola over her previously pretty hair.

She grabbed a chunk of my hair and pulled, probably thinking it would disable me. What she didn't know was that super tough scalps ran in my family. My Tía Madi and I pulled each other's hair for fun.

I reached out and grabbed Mitzi's ponytail, wound my hand in it and yanked.

"Ow!" she shrieked. "Owwwwwwwwwwwwch!"

She let go of my hair. I let go of hers, got up and stood over her. "Look, Tinkerbell, what I did was an accident." I tilted my head to one side and narrowed my eyes at her, trying to look as tough as possible. "And you don't fuck with Wonder Woman," I held out the bottom of my ruined shirt. "Ever."

She didn't try to get up. She just looked up at me like I was a crazy person.

Then I noticed the silence and glanced around. Not only was no one shooting anymore, but the entire gallery—mostly men— was at a standstill as people stared at me with various versions of shock and amusement on their faces. Nick and Bart were standing several yards away smiling.

Yes, *smiling*!

Worse, Nick's body was shaking like he was trying to stifle a laugh.

I stomped over to him, getting right in his space. I looked up at him. "Way to have my back!" I spat.

He pressed his lips together, but his eyes were clearly still laughing. "You weren't exactly out-matched," he replied. "And I figured you needed the hand-to-hand combat practice since this gun thing doesn't seem to be working for you."

I puffed out an angry snort, turned, and stomped past one patron after another, every one of them laughing.

~

## Nick

Bart and I followed Rika out of the shooting range as I tried to get my laughter under control. I didn't want to piss her off, but that was the cutest fight I'd ever seen.

It was also the closest thing I'd ever witnessed to the classic male fantasy that involved wet t-shirts and a catfight.

"Okay," I said to Bart when we were back in the shop. "I know this time didn't work out very well, but maybe if she wore a wrist guard while she works on strengthening her—"

"She's a head case."

Rika's eyes turned deadly. She thrust her head forward. "EXCUSE ME?" she said. *Damn.* Good thing she was no longer holding the gun. "And you got your degree in psychology from *where*?"

It was true that she'd been through a lot in her life, and there was probably permanent emotional damage, but she didn't deserve to be talked about like she was a raving lunatic.

"She's not a head case," I said firmly.

"I've been in this business long enough to know a head case when I see one." Bart pointed his index finger at Rika. "She doesn't want to shoot a gun."

"You don't know me," Rika replied, even though she'd made it clear to me she didn't want to shoot a gun seconds before we came in.

"She just needs practice," I said.

"I'm not a headcase," Rika murmured, as if to herself. Her

eyes were staring at a blank spot on the wall. I was pretty sure she was questioning herself, wondering if Bart could be right.

Bart ignored her and spoke to me. "I can't afford to have anyone injured in here. Do you know how much fucking lawyers cost?"

Since I was a 'fucking lawyer', I decided to treat this as a rhetorical question.

"Come over here." Bart gestured to a pegboard wall. "I've got other options for you."

I followed him to what turned out to be a display covered in various defensive gear. I ended up choosing long-range pepper spray and a stun gun for closer situations.

Rika stood several feet away with her arms folded, still dripping Coke. I noticed her nipples were now clearly visible through both the t-shirt and thin bra underneath.

A frog formed in my throat. I had to clear it out before saying, "I'll pay for any damage."

Rika came to life again. "*I'll* pay for any damage if I'm the one who caused it." Then she added, "Shooting damage, I mean. Any stains were caused by Tinkerbell in there."

I tried to repress the laughter, catching it deep in my throat, but Rika saw. And she wasn't finding this the least bit funny.

My breathing quickened, my groin tightening as if preparing to do something we couldn't possibly do in here. Why did she always seem extra sexy when she was angry? Maybe I was the one with the mental problem.

I peeled my eyes off her breasts to pay for the gear, but the wheels in my brain were turning, whispering innocent observations to me.

*Her shirt and hair are drenched with soda.*

*She needs to shower and change clothes.*

*Your hotel is only a few minutes from here.*

*She could be naked, in your hotel room within minutes.*

Okay, maybe the last two weren't so innocent, but I couldn't get the idea they spawned out of my head. She took off out the door and I turned to follow, still imagining her naked in my shower.

"Uh, hold on there," Bart said. He leaned over and picked Gucci up from behind the counter. "Had to move her out here," he said. "She was stressing out my pit bull."

I nodded slowly as I took her from him. "Can't blame him for that," I said. And we walked out the door.

# CHAPTER SEVENTEEN

**Nick**

Rika was standing by the truck, waiting. "Well, thanks for that humiliating experience," she said, re-crossing her arms on her chest. "At least you got your laugh for the day."

She seemed really bothered. "You know I wouldn't take you somewhere to intentionally embarrass you, don't you?" I replied. "I didn't even know what you did in there was possible."

Her eyes drifted to the pavement. "Do you think I'm a head case, too?"

Although she'd tried to sound bitchy, I knew she needed me to answer, but it wasn't something I wanted to throw out there willy-nilly.

Rika had been through a tragedy I couldn't even imagine. There had to be scars there, especially considering that she mostly lost her dad soon after.

But, unlike my friend Gabe, I did not think a degree allowing me to be legal counsel also meant I qualified to do other kinds of counseling.

"No more than most people," I finally said.

She stared at me, weighing out my answer. Then, she shivered.

Here was my chance. When we'd left her grandma's, it had been surprisingly warm out and she hadn't bothered to bring a sweater or jacket. Now, it had clouded over and cooled off a bit, and she was in wet clothes.

I hit the unlock button on my key fob. "You're shivering," I said as we got in. I put Gucci on the seat between us, but she scrambled onto my lap. "It'll take forever to get to your grandmother's house in this traffic." That might have been a slight exaggeration. I could see on my driving app traffic wasn't that bad right now. "And the heater in my truck isn't working." Now that was an out-and-out lie.

I hoped Rika didn't lean over to look at my phone screen or try turning the heater on herself.

Honestly, I'd never had to lie to a woman to get her to my place before. And, if you'd asked, I would have told you it was something I'd never do.

However, there had been almost non-stop sexual tension between the two of us since we met, as well as other feelings on my part I didn't want to delve too deeply into. Not yet, anyway.

I felt like we wouldn't know anything for sure until I got her to relax and quit tensing up half the time when I touched her. I wasn't sure what that was about, but I was certain I'd caught her looking at me with the same hunger in her eyes I likely had in mine.

"I can get you to my hotel in a few minutes and you can get out of those wet clothes," I said. Then I held my breath, waiting. The last time I'd felt this much stress over a female's response was when I'd asked KatyAnne Platt to the eighth-grade dance.

Rika tensed, apparently surprised at my suggestion. But she quickly reworked her expression into an impassive one. "That's alright, just take me home," she said. "I won't have clean clothes to put on unless I go home."

"Okay," I replied, but I wasn't giving up that easily. "Damn," I said a second later. "Multiple vehicle accident ahead. You're not getting to your grandma's anytime soon, but I've got a clean t-shirt at the hotel you can borrow."

I waited several seconds for her to object, then made the turn toward my hotel.

"I guess it wouldn't be the first time I borrowed your clothes." She smiled slightly and I could see she wasn't angry about the shooting range anymore. Damn, she was beautiful. Every expression that passed over her face was both cuter and more alluring than the last.

I tried to think of something else to talk about but was coming up blank. Finally, I said, "Good thing I didn't get the fabric upholstery." I flicked my eyes toward the spot where she was sitting.

Gucci's nose was working overtime. She climbed off my lap and started licking up the cola drops as they dripped from Rika's hair.

She looked down as if just realizing she was dripping onto the seat. "This will clean up, won't it?"

"Sure," I said. "It'll clean up great." Truth was, I had no idea whether the coke would stain my leather seats and didn't care. If re-upholstering the cab of my pickup was the cost of getting bedroom time with Rika, I'd gladly pay it.

When we pulled into the drive, I handed my keys to the valet and hustled her and Gucci through the lobby so she didn't have to put up with any more staring.

As I ushered her through the door of my suite, she looked surprised. "It's bigger than I imagined," she said.

Had she been imagining me in my hotel room at night? I liked the idea of that.

"The bathroom's over here through the bedroom," I said. I was glad to see the maids had come in and straightened up. "Go ahead and take a shower. There should be fresh towels in there."

"What am I going to put on afterward?"

"There's a bathrobe in there too," I said. "I never use it. It's all yours. I'll find clothes I can lend you while you're in there."

"Okay," she said. She didn't move, though. She just stood there, looking into the fancy bathroom like it might swallow her up.

When she didn't move, I asked, "Need any help in there?" I watched her face.

Her lips parted as her eyes stayed glued to mine for a good five seconds. I had the feeling she was going to say "yes," or, at least wanted to. Her gaze left mine and we both sucked in air.

"I've got this," she said with a half-smile. "You may be surprised to know I've been bathing myself for quite a few years now."

I chuckled as she walked into the bathroom and shut the door.

Her squirrely behavior since we partnered up had me disturbed, and I couldn't make rhyme or reason out of it. Her eyes said she wanted me, but when I touched her, no matter how casually, her response was unpredictable.

However, the handful of times we'd kissed, she'd seemed really into it. Maybe we just needed to be at the right place so we could follow through.

Of course, there was a difference between a kiss and something more.

For some reason, my brain felt the need to remind me that Rika didn't contact me once in the time between leaving Bolo and her dad disappearing. Six months and not a word. But I'd told her I was no good for her and sent her away which meant that could be on me.

Then the attorney in me really kicked in and offered up the other scenario. What if she really was giving me mixed messages in order to get me to finance her business?

It sure didn't feel that way with Rika, though.

In fact, she acted like it bugged her that I was footing the bill. But could that be an act? My wives pretended we had all kinds of things in common—at least the second two. The one when I was eighteen went the fake pregnancy route.

Regardless, I was sure my own mother wouldn't have married my dad if he wasn't already well-off. People would do practically anything for money.

*No.* Rika was nothing like my mom or my wives.

The evidence leaned more toward her wanting me but having some sort of issue that stopped her from taking things farther. Something about her? Or me?

It hit me that having multiple wives, a mother, and a sister hadn't given me any more insight into women than I would have had being raised by my dad alone. They'd always be a mystery.

Anyway, this was it. There was no telling when I'd have Rika alone and uninterrupted, again. I needed to sack up and go for it and hope it didn't totally ruin our friendship. I couldn't imagine living my life without seeing her every day. Not anymore.

Once I heard the water turn on, I grabbed the phone. I'd recently learned the hotel had hired a dog-walker.

The young brunette—who was supposed to be eighteen but looked about four years shy of it—showed up five minutes after I called.

"Look," I said. "I need this..." I held Gucci up on my palm, "...out of here for at least the next couple of hours." I didn't want to feel rushed. With Rika, I wanted to take my time and get it right. I dug the cash out of my pocket. It might have been a couple hundred dollars, but I didn't take time to count. "How much time will this buy me?"

She looked at the money in my hand. "Wow. That'll buy you the rest of the day, if you want."

"Done," I said. I stuck the money in her palm, then handed Gucci to her.

"Okay, I have food," she replied. "Unless she's on a special diet?"

"Nope. Stomach of steel." This was true. More than any of the dogs I'd had as a kid. Maybe because Maltese were bred to be companion animals and to constantly be fed people treats. Or maybe it was just a Gucci fluke, I didn't know.

"Great!" the walker said. "Just call me when you're ready for her to come back."

"Will do," I said as I wondered what would happen if I didn't call. My eyes met Gucci's. She was staring at me like I was the only person in the world. "Will do," I confirmed.

The pup had already been abandoned once by her designated human. That's when I'd become the center of her universe. I didn't have the heart to make her start over again.

"Okay. Have fun!" the walker said cheerfully.

"Yeah, okay," I replied. But it hit me that fun wasn't what I wanted with Rika. I mean, sure, I wanted it to be fun, but I wanted it to be a lot more than that.

I wanted it to be the beginning of a new phase in our relationship.

I heard the water shut off.

"Okay, Owen," I said to myself. "You've gotta get this right."

~

**Rika**

I stared at myself in the bathroom mirror, my hands shaking as I pulled the hotel robe tighter around me, then re-tied the belt over it.

Despite how big and fluffy the robe was, I felt exposed. I glanced at my pile of clothes on the floor. Thanks to Tinkerbell, even my underwear was no longer wearable. Soda had dribbled into the waistband of my jeans, soaking my bikinis.

Nick was out there, in the hotel suite, and the thought of his tall, masculine presence sent a hot shiver all the way down my torso, and I mean *all* the way.

I reached for the knob, then snatched my hand back as questions swirled in my head.

Was Nick thinking about the same thing I was thinking about or was this really just about me needing to dry off?

Did I want him to be thinking about, even planning for, how we were going to... going to...? I didn't even know what the appropriate term was in this situation. It wasn't exactly a booty call, but no one had made each other any promises either.

And maybe the biggest question of all was: *Should I be allowing another person to put his hands all over the skin I'm still not comfortable in?*

Brandtt had been a mistake. Was Nick another mistake? How was anyone ever sure?

Maybe I shouldn't have stopped after the Jilly Crane counselor. Maybe I needed another kind of counselor—a therapist, psychologist, psychiatrist...

I turned back to the mirror. If I opened the robe and looked at myself right now, would I see what was actually there?

Then maybe I could feel confident enough to jump Nick's bones. I snorted out a nervous laugh because that was one of Mrs. Ruíz's favorite sayings. In fact, I heard her telling Lita she should jump Mr. Garza's bones.

*Why am I thinking about my grandmother at a time like this?* I asked myself.

*Because you are a coward,* myself replied.

Sometimes inner voices aren't all they're cracked up to be.

I looked back at the mirror. I clasped my hands and held them under my chin, squeezing the palms together like I was pleading with myself.

My palms were sweaty.

I did a mental body sweep and noticed my skin felt damp under the robe.

Oh, my God! Was I sweating already? Or was I still damp from the shower?

I picked up my towel from the counter and slipped it under the robe, rubbing it over my body.

Then, I dropped it, steadied my breathing, and came up with a plan.

I'd flash myself—just a quick glance to convince me that things weren't that bad under this robe—and if I looked okay, I'd go through with it, assuming Nick wanted what I'd been dying for since I met him.

But what if this lighting was the kind that brought out all your flaws? I tilted my head back to check for fluorescent bulbs, but the decorative fixtures didn't allow me to see them. If they were fluorescent, I definitely didn't want to look at myself.

It was unfortunate that the lighting that brought out all my flaws was the same lighting that brought out the most beautiful color in Nick's eyes. I decided against taking it as a sign that we weren't meant for each other.

Climbing up onto the counter, I fiddled with a key-like screw on top of the light cover. It didn't budge, so I moved over to try to get a better angle.

My foot knocked the robe's hangar off the counter. It landed on the tile floor with a clatter.

"You okay in there?" Nick called.

"Sure," I said. "Everything's fine-good."

*WTF?* I had never used the term "fine-good" in my life. In fact, as far as I knew, no one on Earth had ever used the term "fine-good" because it wasn't a term!

My heartbeat escalated again and, this time, it didn't stop escalating. It just beat faster and faster and faster!

Was I going to have my first ever panic attack over the idea of sex with Nick? On the other hand, I'd be disappointed if he brought me here and didn't even have that in mind.

Okay, there it was. I had officially crossed over from quirky person with issues into full-blown crazy person.

I checked the mirror again and wished I could at least dry my hair. It looked drastically better dry.

Letting go of the idea of flashing myself—the chances of me thinking I looked good enough when I was this stressed were almost nil—I braced my palms on either side of the sink. "You can do this," I told myself. "You can walk out of this room, then whatever happens, happens."

I took a deep breath and opened the door. I expected to see Nick, but he wasn't in the bedroom. Maybe he did just bring me here to change my clothes.

I walked through to the living area.

On the couch were the sweats and t-shirt he'd promised, folded neatly. He was sitting next to them reading something on his phone.

He looked up from it, his gaze scanning me top to bottom. His eyes warmed and crinkled as the corners of his lips turned slightly upward.

I averted my eyes, feeling shy.

*Lame.* I wasn't a shrinking violet. Or, at least, I didn't want to be.

I forced myself to make eye contact. He was still staring at me with that same expression on his face and it was making me feel all melty inside.

"What are you smirking at?" I asked to break the tension.

"Not smirking. Reminiscing."

I hoped he wasn't recalling another time in a hotel with one of his wives. "Reminiscing?" I repeated.

"About our spa day. When you were learning how to give me a Microtologist massage."

*Ah, yes.* We were both in robes that day, although this one wasn't a mini robe, thank Zeus.

That was the day I'd gotten to see Nick's naked ass for the first and only time and it was...

I breathed out a sigh.

"Everything okay?" he asked.

*Get it together, goofball!* my inner voice scolded.

"How about a cup of coffee to warm you up?" He got up and walked to the mini coffee machine. "Or would you rather I order up hot chocolate?"

Hot chocolate sounded great, but it would probably cost him twenty dollars at a place like this and I was already uncomfortable enough with our financial situation, mentally tallying every penny he was spending because of me.

I scanned the room again. The hotel bill he must have incurred here in the last few weeks would probably induce nausea and vomiting if I ever saw it.

I shook off the guilt. "Coffee is fine. I guess you don't have a blow dryer?"

"The hotel has one in the drawer." He lifted his chin toward the bathroom. "Go ahead and use it, and I'll make you that coffee."

I ducked back into the bathroom and, with a still-shaky hand, picked up Nick's comb, slid it through my wet strands, then started the blow dryer.

The smells from Nick's shaving kit wafted up as I worked on my hair, sending strange shivery-warm sensations through my body.

In a way, it all felt right, standing a few yards from Nick wearing only a robe while I dried my hair.

But the way he'd looked at me in the living room was too intense. It meant his expectations were too high. If we did this, he'd know my body didn't match up to the ones he was used to. My boobs were too small for Nick. My legs weren't long enough. My hair wasn't blonde enough. And I was carrying around a ten-pound coating of extra fat.

Disappointment washed through me. I couldn't go through with it today, if that's what he had in mind. Not yet.

Maybe in a couple of weeks when I'd lost most of this extra weight—I could go on a chickpea and kale diet or something—so he wouldn't be pressing his fingers into flab.

*But, oh how I wish it could be today.*

Once my hair was mostly dry, I sucked it up again and walked into the living room.

Nick held up a mug of steaming coffee. "Perfect timing if I do say so myself." He smiled, clearly proud of himself.

"Lucky timing," I replied.

"No luck involved."

"How could you predict when I'd finish blow drying my hair?"

He shrugged. "We lived in the same house for weeks. How do you think breakfast was ready every morning just as you came out of your room?"

"How...? You *timed* me?"

"Yep."

I had thought Nick was just going about his usual routine, except for making extra food for me. It had never occurred to me that he was planning his morning around me. I wasn't even sure what to think of that.

"That's...creepy," I teased.

He chuckled. "I'm sure it's nothing Eli wouldn't do."

This made me laugh and, for a moment, I forgot to be uncomfortable.

I reached out and took the mug from him. The look he gave me as our fingers touched created giant moths in my tummy that flapped their massive wings so hard, I pressed my free hand to my abdomen to try and still them.

I didn't know for certain what Nick's look meant, but I knew it meant serious business.

Glancing into my coffee, I noticed it was black, the way I

always drank it. Unfortunately, I couldn't take a sip because I could no longer swallow.

As Nick turned away to get his cup, my hands started shaking again. My eyes were glued to the coffee. The cup was too full. At any time now the liquid would start sloshing out onto the carpet.

"Have a seat," Nick said.

I was relieved to sit on the sofa and set my mug on the coffee table.

But instead of sitting in one of the chairs opposite me, Nick came around and sat next to me. I noticed he also set his cup down without taking a sip.

So, neither of us wanted coffee. The coffee was an excuse for something. The somethings scrambled through my mind tripping and tumbling over one another.

What if this had nothing to do with sex?

*Shit!* He was going to tell me our business arrangement wasn't working out. Or that he just didn't like being a P.I. Or that he hated L.A.— which I knew he did—and couldn't stand it here anymore.

Maybe his mother had convinced him she needed him back in Bolo. Or maybe she really did need him. Maybe she was ill and Nick needed to go take care of her for the rest of her life.

*Oh, my God!* I couldn't lose him after thinking I'd found a way to keep him in my life.

*No. No. No. No!* My heart flipped over in my chest. And I knew.

Losing Nick forever would be as bad as losing my dad was when I was a kid. Maybe as bad as losing my mom. Not as confusing and terrifying, but the loss would be traumatic.

The fact was, the person who felt most vital in my life always left me.

That's not to say I didn't love and appreciate my Lita and my aunts and my cousin Sofia and even her brother, my cousin Max, who was often a butthead and a pain in the ass when we were growing up.

What was my point? Oh, yeah, that I appreciated and loved the people I had, but the people I needed most desperately tended to disappear from my life in the snap of a finger.

Nick hadn't even signed an apartment lease. It would be such a simple thing for him to pack his bags, check out of this hotel, and never return.

He rested his forearms on his knees and stared at the coffee table as if considering what he was about to say carefully. His lips parted, but he didn't speak right away. He kept looking at the cup, but not really looking at it.

He was about to give me bad news and he was choosing his words, trying to do it in the least offensive most lawyerly way possible.

That freaked me out even more. Nick was a kickass litigator who did *not* typically have problems choosing words.

My body shuddered and I thought I'd hiccupped, but then realized I'd been holding my breath for too long and my lungs were trying to make me aware of that fact.

Nick turned his face toward me. "Rika, breathe." The words sounded almost like a reprimand.

I forced myself to inhale as I wondered how he knew I wasn't breathing.

Was I a loud breather? Did I usually make weird whistling sounds when I exhaled like one of the boys in my fifth-grade class did? And why was I thinking of him right now?

I could feel my thumbnail digging into the pad of my index finger as it circled there. The fingers of my other hand followed suit.

Nick noticed, slanted his body toward me and took both my hands in his.

"Why are you so anxious?" he asked.

The question sent a new wave of panic through me. "Why are you so weird right now?" I blurted. I was going to leave it at that, but he looked like he didn't know what I was talking about.

"With your coffee-staring and this sit-down talk on the couch and..."

That didn't sound so bad. What else had he done? Jeez, now I just felt like an idiot.

"Are you sorry you asked me to stay in L.A.?" he asked. "Are you regretting the partnership?"

*What?* Why would I regret either of those things when all I wanted was to be with him? Okay, maybe I regretted the partnership a little because of the money he was spending, but I couldn't truly regret anything that kept Nick close to me.

Wait, what if he was hoping I regretted it because he regretted it? If I said it first, that would let him off the hook.

For all I knew, I could be seconds away from getting my heart broken. If I said I regretted having him stay instead of waiting for him to say it, maybe it wouldn't be as humiliating.

But I couldn't make my lips form the words I'd need to tell that lie. "No." I cleared my throat. "I don't regret it."

"Then why have you been acting so squirrelly?"

"Squirrelly?"

"Loopy."

"Loopy?"

"Batty. Loony. Screwy. Irrational. *Loco*?"

"I'm female so '*loca*' would be the correct usage."

He threw his head back and looked at the ceiling as if requesting divine intervention, although, I didn't see how he could expect any considering he only went to church to get married.

He sucked in a breath, made eye contact and tried again. "There's been a... *strain* between us since we became partners, and I'm pretty sure I'm not the one causing it."

"I don't know what you're talking about," I lied.

I totally knew what he was talking about, but I didn't want him to know why I'd been acting so "squirrelly." Then I'd have to explain about my weight issues and how I didn't want to give him the green light until I was as perfect as I could be, which probably still wouldn't be perfect enough for him to want to look at me on a regular basis.

Why did he have to ask me about this now? If he'd just waited a few weeks, I could have gotten the extra weight off and this wouldn't be an issue.

Maybe.

Or maybe there would always be an issue with Nick because I didn't think I was hot enough to be with him. My body would never be described as "willowy" or "elegant." Hell, I'd kill to be referred to as a "bean pole."

Nick patted the space between us.

"Come 'ere."

I wouldn't have thought I'd go to a man just because he told me too, without at least a "please" attached, to make it clear I wasn't expected to answer to his commands.

But his eyes had turned this alluring dusky blue and he was drawing me in like a fish to a worm.

I scooted to where he'd indicated, which was just about as close as I could be without sitting on his lap. I looked up at him questioningly.

He lifted a hand and traced my jaw, then cradled the back of my head with his fingers. His lips parted and his head dipped. My eyes fell closed. My lips parted, clearly ready whether my mind was or not.

He paused centimeters from me, so close we were breathing the same air.

# CHAPTER EIGHTEEN

**Rika**

When Nick didn't seal the deal, I opened my eyes, my gaze resting on his lips. I remembered the way those lips had felt on mine. I needed to kiss him but I was immobile—stiff as a statue.

Had my heart stopped beating?

Nick hovered there for a moment, his chest rising and falling like when he was fresh off the treadmill at his house. He pulled back a bit but didn't release me. "I'm going to need some consent, here."

I blinked hard. What the hell was he talking about? And why wasn't his tongue in my mouth already? "Consent?" I choked out.

"Okay..." He took a deep breath. "Let me be clear. I plan to get you out of this robe and anything you have on underneath, if applicable. Then I'm going to remove my own clothing and—"

Nick stopped talking because I'd inhaled two jerky breaths as the mental image of him getting naked right here, right now, while I was also naked, tore through my brain.

Heat spread across my shoulders before radiating down the rest of my body. Too much heat. For a second, I thought I might faint like a southern belle in a too-tight corset.

"That was pretty specific," I said as casually as I could manage. "I guess since you're a lawyer, you have a boilerplate contract you want me to sign?"

Nick's lips quirked up for a split second, then all humor left his face and his expression was deadly serious. His eyes turned a deep, deep blue, and the intensity kind of scared me.

He shook his head. "In the past, I never needed one. Women have made it pretty clear what they wanted, but with you..."

My cheeks burned and I couldn't stare into his face anymore. He was basically telling me what a lame, geeky dork I was. Too cowardly to let a man know what I wanted.

My eyes flicked to his collar bone, then his chest. His body was taut, one hand still cupping the back of my neck. The other hand settled on my knee, then started sliding up very slowly as he watched for my reaction...

A tingle began where his hand met the flesh above my knee. The sensation wiggled its way up until it settled firmly in between my thighs, even though his hand hadn't gotten close to the spot yet.

*Holy mother of Zeus!*

"Rika?"

I swallowed hard. "Huh?"

He threw back his head again. "Fuck," he said to the ceiling.

What I needed was Nick's arms around me. Nick's body against mine. Better yet, Nick's body on top of mine.

But it was still broad daylight, I was extremely self-conscious, and I didn't know what to say.

"I don't know what to say!" I blurted out, surprising myself.

Nick's hands moved to my shoulders. His expression changed slightly and I thought I saw a hint of naughty in there.

He cleared his throat and spoke in a quieter version of his courtroom voice. "If you want this to happen, repeat after me," he said. "I, Paprika An-eees Mar-teeen..."

The overemphasis of my names nearly set off a case of the

nervous giggles, but I held it together. I had trouble looking him in the eye, but he pressed my jaw up with his thumb, lifting my gaze to his. I cleared my throat. "I, Paprika Anise Martín..."

"Do hereby agree to allow Nick Owen to pleasure my body in any way he sees fit for the next twenty-four hours."

"Twenty-four hours?" I said, trying not to pass out at the idea of Nick Owen "pleasuring" my body. "Are you kidding? We have a case to solve!"

He didn't look disappointed. In fact, his eyes sparked as if he expected that response and was prepared for it. "Sixteen hours," he said.

Oh, yeah. He was a trial lawyer, used to bargaining over time. Usually, it was the time someone was going to spend in jail, but I guessed the strategy was the same.

"But if I don't show up at Lita's—" I stalled.

"Is that the only issue?" he asked so quickly, I knew he'd anticipated my objection.

I nodded, feeling like I'd walked into his trap.

He lifted my cell from where it was lying on the coffee table, stuck it in front of my face to unlock it with the facial recognition feature, and began tapping around on it.

I grappled for the phone. "What are you doing?"

He stood. I stood, too, but he held it too high for me to reach while he continued typing.

God, I hated tall people.

One final tap and I heard the swooping sound that meant a text had been sent from *my* phone. Nick handed it to me.

It was to Tía Madi. *On stakeout that may go all night. Tell everyone not to call my phone until after 8 a.m.*

After giving me a second to read, he took the phone and set it on the coffee table.

Weaving his fingers into mine, he took a step toward the bedroom. When I didn't move, he gave it a little tug.

But instead of following him, the scaredy cat in my head I'd been trying to silence blurted, "I don't think I actually agreed to anything."

Nick turned to me and took my face in his hands. "You know," he said. "I used to be a pretty confident guy."

"Be careful," I replied. "There's a fine line between confidence and arrogance."

He smiled his unbelievably sexy smile at me. It was a smile that said he had reason to be arrogant about this kind of thing. A blazing hot shiver shimmied down my back.

Lacing his fingers through mine, again, he led me into his bedroom...

...and I was shocked at how bright it was.

During the time we were in the living room, the sun had dipped just low enough to shine directly in through the huge bedroom window, streaking right across the bed.

I'd be having sex in a spotlight! Every stretch mark, every extra pound I wore on my body would be on display.

"Um, this is, um, bright for me," I said.

"Yeah, it's blinding at this time of day," he replied. He walked to the window and began pulling the drapes closed. "Tell me when," he said. After he'd pulled them almost closed and I hadn't said anything, he turned toward me. "Rika?"

"Um, that streak of light is still kind of bright."

"All right..." He closed the drapes, which meant most of the light coming in now was from the living room.

I shut the door, making the room almost completely dark.

That was more like it. I could totally get my groove on with Nick in this lighting!

Nick turned on the floor lamp next to the drapes.

*Damn it!*

"Could we just leave it dark for now?" I asked.

"Why?"

"It's, um, a turn on for me." It wasn't a lie, exactly. I certainly could be more amorous if I didn't have to worry about super-hot Nick noticing my imperfections.

"But I'm a very visual person," he argued.

*Not to self: No more sex with lawyers. They'll argue about anything.*

I pulled the ends of the robe's belt, tightening the knot even more. It had been an unconscious movement, but Nick noticed.

"Okay, we'll do it your way," he said. "This time."

*This time.*

*Oh, God, that means he plans for there to be more times!* I mentally fanned myself.

As he walked toward me, the only light left in the room was a glow coming from each end of the drapes, just enough to keep the room from being pitch black.

Would he feel my heart going kaboom kaboom kaboom in my chest?

Oddly, when he got to me, he didn't kiss me right away or even try to take my robe off. He wrapped his arms around me tightly and held me. My arms were trapped awkwardly against my body, but, after several seconds, my muscles started to warm and relax. Then, surprisingly, my doubts melted away.

He'd just proven his case. No question. This was where I belonged, in Nick's arms.

Once the tension was gone from my body, I felt his lips on my ear. "Are we good?" he murmured.

I pulled my head back and looked up at him.

It was a question I was finally ready to answer. Lifting myself onto tiptoes, I slid my hands over his shoulders. He met me halfway as I pressed my parted lips to his.

After giving the nape of my neck a squeeze, he ran his fingers up to caress the base of my scalp.

I moaned, shocked at how good it felt.

Nick's other arm circled around me. Pulling me closer, he

tightened his grip on my head, holding it still as he slid his tongue along my bottom lip.

Then suddenly, he slipped inside, and we were locked in a full-on tongue battle—him pressing deep as I wound around him.

*This is good. This is good. This is so, so good,* my mind whispered.

God, I could kiss Nick forever if I didn't have a million other things I wanted to do with him.

I pressed my body harder into his as I thrust my tongue into his mouth, trying to take control of the kiss.

A growl came from the base of his throat, which only made me want more.

I don't know what got into me, but one of my hands slipped under his shirt, sliding up the expanse of skin on his back. My other hand went really rogue, moving down to cup his ass.

I may have squeezed, just a little.

Nick broke off the kiss with a groan. "Slow down, Paprika," he murmured against my ear. "We don't want this to be over before it starts."

If he wanted me to go slower, the last thing he should have done was make that growly sound because it was hot, let me tell you.

"Slow down?" I blurted. "It seems like I've been waiting for this forever."

"Yeah," he murmured as he ran his tongue along the curve of my ear. "But we'll only have this first time together once. I want us to have plenty to remember."

That was so damn sweet, tears tried to burst from behind my eyes. I blinked them back and kissed him even harder. Ignoring his command, I grabbed the hem of his shirt, wrestling it up until he helped me by whipping it off.

*Holy. Mother. Of. Zeus.* His torso was even better than I remembered—muscles from top to bottom.

Hm... he hadn't gained weight pining over me like I had pining over him. Maybe he wasn't pining at all.

But what did that matter now? I was getting me some Nick Owen, right here, right now, or I'd die trying. I could worry about the rest later.

His kisses moved to my jaw, then my neck as I slid my fingers over his ab muscles—Yum, yum, yum, yum, yum—until I reached the waistband of his jeans.

He was working on the knot I'd made on the belt of my robe. "Damn," he said when it wouldn't budge. My pre-make-out anxiety had caused me to yank it crazy tight.

That's when he reached into his jeans and whipped out a pocketknife.

"They'll make you pay, like, a million dollars if you ruin this thing," I said.

He chuckled as his knife sliced cleanly through the fabric. "Totally worth it."

I experienced a fresh wave of anxiety. "You don't know that, yet," I pointed out, only half joking.

Did I have what it took to satisfy a guy like Nick? What was he expecting?

I didn't know any special tricks, if there were any. Brandtt hadn't been adventurous in bed and I'd let him lead the way. I'd had zero sexual experiences when I met him unless you counted the weird porn I'd happened upon when binging Sailor Moon.

I looked past Nick to the bed. The feeling of inadequacy threatened to overtake my confidence again.

He cradled my jaw in his hand and forced me to stare into his eyes again. "Stay with me, babe."

*Babe.*

The word reverberated in my chest. It sounded so intimate I felt tears behind my eyes again. I had expected sex with Nick to be hot. I hadn't expected this many complicated emotions to be involved.

I blinked a few times and swallowed hard. "I'm with you," I whispered.

And I meant it. If ever I wanted to be fully present for something, it was this.

Nick's face broke into a smile. All his smiles were gorgeous, but I could have sworn this one was different than any of the ones I'd seen before. Nick Owen's private, bedroom smile.

His thumbs caressed my collarbone as he slid the robe off my shoulders. He kissed his way down my neck to my newly exposed shoulder.

I'd never realized how neglected those areas were until Nick put his lips on them. As my skin cried out for more Nick lip touches, I felt his mouth move back to the spot where my neck curved into my shoulder. His teeth grazed my skin.

My shoulders gave a little shake, but, in the same instant, the nerves there communicated with the nerves in my legs and my knees sort of buckled.

*Holy mother of Zeus!* Nick knew some sort of Vulcan nerve pinch! But instead of making men go unconscious, it made women's knees go weak, an impressive superpower.

Luckily, his arms were around me, so I didn't hit the floor.

With an "Mmm..." he slid a hand up my side and captured a breast, teasing over the nipple with his thumb.

I sucked in three quick breaths and my knee jerked involuntarily, jabbing him in his inner thigh.

He jumped back reflexively to protect his crotch. We both looked down and I realized the fly of his jeans was straining over his erection.

He chuckled. "This might be safer on the bed," he said. And, without another word, he swept my feet out from under me, yanked the bedspread and top sheet to the bottom of the bed and laid me down.

The sheet was cool, but I felt exposed, even in the dimly lit room. Truth be told, the only time I ever got naked was in the shower. Otherwise, I had a habit of covering up that was established many years ago.

As Nick divested himself of his remaining clothes, I experienced a pang of regret about the lack of light. I'd seen various bits and pieces of Nick, but I'd never gotten to examine the whole package at once.

He was standing with his back to the window, making his body look like a shadow more than anything else. That's when I made a pact with myself that I would cut all carbs from my life until I felt confident enough to have sex with the drapes open.

Nick got on the bed with me and pulled me close. His mouth trailed down my chest, teasing my nipples with his lips, then his tongue.

I threaded my hands through his hair. "Nick..." I whispered, not sure what else I wanted to say after that.

It didn't matter. He wasn't in the mood to talk anymore, except to murmur "Damn, you taste good," against my breast.

A part of me still couldn't believe this was happening. I'd thought about him every single night for the past seven months. I'd touched myself while I fantasized about him, but it was a poor substitute for the real thing.

His lips brushed the ribs just below my breasts. He was headed south, sucking bits of flesh into his mouth as he went.

Panic tried to rise up in me again. If he stayed on his current trajectory, he would be kissing my stomach in a matter of seconds. Would it feel too squishy under his lips?

Besides, I'd been dreaming of Nick every day and every night for months. I didn't have the patience for the works. Not this time.

"Nick?" I said.

He responded by rolling his thumb over my nipple. It sent a zing through me that bounced around until it landed *down there* and turned into a needy throb.

I sighed, nearly forgetting what I was trying to do.

"Nick," I said louder, in case arousal made him hard of hearing.

Again, he ignored me, this time pressing a kiss in the vicinity of my last rib. The throbbing swelled and deepened until I thought I would go crazy if Nick didn't get to the main event, and fast.

His teeth scraped the spot where he'd just kissed me.

I raised up on my elbows just in time to, not only feel, but see Nick sliding his tongue toward my belly button.

"Nick!"

He lifted his head, and I couldn't miss his sexy gaze as he traced a circle around my belly button with his tongue.

Seriously, this was too damn hot. I was sure I couldn't take another second without losing my mind.

"Oh, my God, Nick!" I blurted. "Fuck me, already!"

Nick stilled. Then I felt his body shaking with laughter. How dare he laugh at me in my time of extreme need! I decided if he didn't get down to business immediately, I would have to kill him.

He was still smiling as he moved over me. He leaned in until we were nearly nose to nose. "Do you kiss your partner with that dirty mouth?" he asked, but it sounded more like a dare.

I took that dare. I grabbed his head with both hands, lifted mine off the pillow, and kissed him with all the passion I'd saved up the past seven months. Then, I dragged my fingernails down his back, all the way to his perfect ass.

I felt the ragged groan from the base of his throat more than I heard it.

I'd never heard Nick make that specific sound before, and it brought out something feral in me.

As I dug my fingertips into his ass, I nipped his bottom lip.

He retaliated by sliding his teeth along the curve of my ear and biting my earlobe as he pressed himself, thick and hard against my lower abdomen.

*Oh. Yes.*

He slid his hand down my side, over my ass, lifting my thigh until my calf rested on his lower back.

"You feel so damn good," he said as he buried his face in my neck.

I breathed out a sigh of relief because, in the middle of that sentence, I was afraid he was going to comment on my extra flab. Like, "You feel so squishy." Or "You feel like you've eaten a thousand Double Stuf Oreos," which I had in the months we were apart.

I squirmed underneath him, trying to get in position so he could do what I'd so crassly ordered him to do already.

But Nick was clearly the one in charge in this bedroom. "It's okay," he murmured soothingly into my ear. "Let me handle this."

He lifted his head. I looked up at his face and, even in the shadows, it was beautiful. That's when the knowledge hit me that Nick's face would always be beautiful to me. Even if it was scarred. Or wrinkled. Or even burned.

Because he was Nick.

He cupped my cheek, his thumb sliding back and forth across my bottom lip. The other hand moved from my thigh to between my legs.

"Wow," he said, and I was pretty sure he was referring to the evidence of my arousal. "Definitely a good sign."

Embarrassment washed through me, causing my eyes to shut and my chin to turn toward my shoulder. I didn't know why. It's not like I was a virgin. But being with Nick made me feel like I wasn't *not* a virgin either, if that made any sense.

Nick's fingertip touched the side of my face. "Rika, look at me," he said.

I forced myself to look into his intense gaze.

"Since the day I brought you home with me, it's only been you."

Did he mean he'd been with no one at all in the past seven

months? That seemed like an incredibly long time for a guy like Nick.

*Say something!* My mind yelled. *Tell him how you feel!*

I opened my mouth to reply, but all I managed was a breathy "I..." that turned into a sigh as he moved between my thighs and I felt his tip make contact.

He slid his hand up a thigh again. This time, I wrapped my legs around him as tightly as I could. He captured my lips and two different parts of him thrust into me at the same time.

And I thought I'd die.

From the kiss. From the feel of him inside me where I'd wanted him to be since I met him.

I never knew friction could be so sweet.

A shock of tears burst through from behind my eyes. One thing had never been clearer—I wanted all of Nick. Regardless of our silly disagreements, I wanted to spend my daylight hours with him and go home with him every night. I'd missed him enough in the months we were apart and every evening when he left. I didn't want to ever have to feel like that again.

As he kissed me, he threaded his fingers through my hair, stroking my face, my side, my thigh.

I kissed him back with the same intensity and met him stroke for stroke. A growl came from deep inside him, his muscles tightened, and the thrusting turned to pounding.

The change in force was like a bolt of lightning inside me. I climaxed, hard. So hard, I wasn't sure I'd live through it and didn't care.

Once I'd stopped shuddering under him, Nick kissed my forehead, my nose, my eyes, my lips.

And I felt cherished in a way I never had before.

"Mmmm, Paprika," he murmured just before he found his release.

And it hit me that, for the first time ever, I'd experienced something more satisfying than a bag of Double Stufs.

# CHAPTER NINETEEN

**Rika**

I awakened, confused.

Bright light was shining in. Was it morning?

*Ho-o-ly—*

That was as far as my brain got because the drapes were open and Nick was walking back to the bed, naked and gorgeous.

I swallowed hard and cleared my throat, searching for suitable post-coital conversation. "How long was I asleep?" I asked.

"Only twenty minutes or so."

It was good sleep, though. I'd never been into power naps, but maybe there was something to them. I felt like I could leap over buildings and stop runaway trains with my bare hands.

The air conditioning kicked on and the cool air hit my skin.

I checked and found I was completely uncovered.

"Oh, my God!" I grabbed the sheet and pulled it over me. "How did that happen?" I remembered tugging the sheet over me, then relaxing into Nick's shoulder before I conked out.

"It mostly slipped off of its own accord when I got out of bed."

"Mostly?"

"Yep." He walked back to the bed.

"And why didn't you cover me back up? You knew I..." I wasn't sure how to word the rest. I hadn't confessed the true reason I wanted the drapes closed.

"I wanted to see you."

My mind raced. How long had the drapes been open? Did he have time to examine me for imperfections?

*Ugh!* The thought of it made me queasy. "Kind of pervy, considering I was asleep."

He climbed into bed, stuffed an extra pillow under his head, then turned on his side. This meant I had to look up at him, just like when we were standing.

*Annoying.*

I stuffed the fourth bed pillow under the one I'd been using, putting us at the same level.

"Tell me," he said, "how's it perverted to want to look at the woman I just made love to?"

His choice of words caused the thoughts to go all floopy in my head. But it was true. He really had made love to me.

It was a lot to process. I let my eyes drift to his collar bone.

He slid his hand up my jaw then lifted my chin with his thumb until my gaze met his.

I couldn't decide if his constant insistence on eye contact in the bedroom was endearing or irritating.

He took in a long slow breath, then exhaled just as slowly. "Rika, what's wrong?" He seemed really, truly concerned about me. "Did something happen to you? Before?" He swallowed hard. "Did somebody do something to—?"

"No!" I said firmly. "Nothing like that ever happened. Does something have to have happened just because I don't want to flaunt myself in front of you?"

Nick kept his gaze steady on me but seemed to be considering my question. "Yes," he finally said. "When someone as beautiful as you are doesn't want the man she's sleeping with to see her, something has to have happened."

*Damn it.* If I didn't give up something, Nick was going to keep thinking I had an awful abuse story from my past. He didn't deserve to carry that concern around.

But I didn't want to tell him the pitiful tale of my life as a blimp. Not today, anyway. Maybe not ever.

I decided to split the difference. "Look, Nick, I'm just self-conscious about the weight I gained. That's all."

Nick peered hard into my eyes as if he was trying to determine whether I was telling him the truth. "You can't possibly think you're too heavy."

*Jeez!* Couldn't he see how hard this was for me to talk about? "I've gained a few pounds and I'm heavier than I'm comfortable with," I said.

*There, that should shut him up.*

"Rika, when I met you, you were really thin," he said, the memory of his concern clear on his face. "That's why I made sure you got plenty to eat."

"You were trying to make me fatter on purpose?" I cried.

*What a jerk!*

"'Fatter' implies you were fat in the first place. I was just trying to make sure you didn't disappear completely."

Anger welled up inside me. I didn't need his lies, even if he just thought of it as post-sex sweet talk.

"Don't mess with my head, Nick."

"I don't even know what that means," he said. "Your body is perfect."

"Nobody's body is perfect," I said, even though I didn't believe that myself. When you spend years imprisoned in a fat suit, you notice the perfect bodies all around you.

"Yours is," he insisted.

I suddenly had the urge to flee. I'd always thought if I got into Nick's bed I'd never want to leave, but I didn't expect him to insist on a post-sex conversation that pushed my most sensitive buttons.

I glanced around, trying to remember where my clothes were. Oh, yeah, my clothes were a mess. I was supposed to put on Nick's clothes, and they were still in the other room.

Nick's hand slid around my back and he scooted me closer to him. His legs captured one of mine between them. "I'm not going to let you go."

My heart stopped. I mean, he probably only meant it for the time being, but the way he said it sounded so permanent.

Suddenly, a fear welled up inside me, so strong, a giant lump formed in my throat. The emotion that came with it took me by surprise and, for a moment, I couldn't assemble an explanation in my brain. At least, not in a way that made sense.

Then, one by one, the words lined up next to each other.

I could lose Nick.

If I let this thing we had grow, I was certain I'd end up devastated.

Not just because he was too handsome for me or I was too geeky for him. But because that's what happened to me. I lost the person who was the center of my universe. It happened with my mother, then my father. After that, I'd made food the center of my universe.

When the weight loss allowed me to believe I'd pulled myself together, I'd convinced myself I cared for Brandtt. I didn't *need* Brandtt, though.

But, at some point, Nick had become as essential as air.

I tried to logic my way out of the fear. Nick was a big guy who was unlikely to meet the same fate as my mother. He couldn't be barred from the country like my father. But he was human and could die at any time from any number of things.

Statistically, men died before women, sometimes way before. Plus, he was ten years older than I was. If this worked out permanently, I'd still have to go through losing him, sooner or later, unless I managed to beat the statistics and die before him.

What was it his father died from? An aneurysm or something? Was it genetic?

"Paprika..." Nick murmured as his finger traced a lock of my hair from temple to jaw. God, I loved it when he did that. "I wish you would talk to me. Whatever it is, I want to fix it."

I blinked hard to keep the tears at bay, then gave him a half-smile. "This isn't in your jurisdiction," I said.

To most people, this would have been a strange remark, but Nick nodded as if the answer made sense to him.

"Okay, if I can't fix it, I'm going to have to do what I can to make you feel better."

"And what's that?"

He pulled my body tight against his and I could feel what he had in mind because it was digging into my abdomen.

"I'll give you three guesses." He tugged the sheet until my breasts were exposed, then his hand disappeared under the sheet, sliding down my body until it found my ass.

A giddy feeling bubbled through me. Nick Owen wanted seconds from me!

"On second thought," he said. You've inspired me to invent a game. His expression was mischievous. "Point to any spot on your body and I'll either lick, suck or bite it. My choice."

Ha! He wasn't the only one who could be mischievous. "Mmm... I'll agree to that game with one modification."

His eyes sparked. "Okay, what's your proposal?"

"In my version of the game, you point to places on your body. I lick, suck, or bite. My choice." I was proud of myself for managing to say that aloud.

"Oh, I can stipulate to that," he said with a smile. "I can stipulate to that all day long."

**Nick**

I was a happy man.

Paprika Anise Martín was finally mine. She was in my hotel room. In my bed. Her head was on my shoulder, her hand on my chest. One of my arms was around her. The fingers of my other hand couldn't stop skimming the side of her breast.

I wondered if she knew I was smelling her hair. Inhaling as much of its fragrance as possible. Then I could recall it whenever we were apart.

Wait, why did we need to be apart? Now that we'd gotten over this hurdle, there was no reason to have to miss her anymore. At the end of a day's work, we could come home together.

I scanned the room. Fancy as this place was, it didn't qualify as a home. I'd need to buy one so Rika and I could live comfortably. It hit me that I had no idea what type of house Rika would want to live in.

Maybe GracieAnne would know someone who sold residential real estate.

I'd keep the house in Bolo. That way, we could visit my mom without having to stay with her.

Should I ask Rika to move in with me now? I didn't want her to feel pressured, but I also wanted to erase any ambiguity from our relationship. She still seemed to have a lot of warring emotions happening in her head that I didn't understand.

But one thing was crystal clear to me. She and I were supposed to be together, and I needed to cement the relationship somehow.

Truth be told, I'd never officially asked a woman to move in with me before. And I had no recollection of ever proposing to anyone, either.

Seems impossible for a man to have been married three times without ever having proposed, but it was true.

The first marriage—which I didn't think should count, considering we were barely eighteen—was because of a baby. Kelli came from the exotic—by Bolo standards—land of Florida.

She looked like my sister's Malibu Barbie, which had been handed down from my mom, who had quite the extensive Barbie collection.

I'm pretty sure my mom thought of Barbie dolls as aspirational gifts, as in "this is what you're supposed to look like when you grow up." And I was pretty sure my sister still—to this day—considered it child abuse.

Anyway, Kelli was a prize every male senior in our class was after. I had a genuine crush on her myself and was happy I'd won her, initially.

But as it goes with teenagers, two months later, I'd kind of soured on her constant jealousy and unreasonable demands. That's when she played the pregnancy card and I said something like, "Well... I guess maybe we should get married, then."

That was the closest I'd ever come to a proposal.

A few months later when Kelli had no baby bump and I found out she'd been drinking margaritas with her friends in the next town, she'd had to admit there was no baby. And I had to listen to my mom's "I told you so's," in the form of "I knew she was white trash as soon as I laid eyes on her and when that 'baby' came along right after she found out we had oil wells..."

The other two wives somehow managed to move in and usurp my life without me ever expressing a desire to live with or marry them. I guess I must have wanted the company in the beginning.

Damn, my brain was hopping from one thought to the next like a jumping bean. And why was my romantic life flashing through my mind now?

Because all that old craziness was over. I was up for new craziness. A craziness of my own choosing. For the first time in my life, I wanted to propose.

*Whoa! Hold up there!* the sensible part of my brain cried. *Are you seriously ready for wife number four after spending less than two months of your life with her?*

*Point taken.* Besides, Rika had a good head on her shoulders and would probably decide I was a crazy marriage addict if I brought it up now.

Still, I had the urge to nail this relationship down in a way that would make her off limits to the hyenas at the door—Julian, Dr. Choi and any future suitors.

Julian, I didn't think was much of a problem. Rika's grandmother may have set her sights on him as a grandson-in-law, but he wasn't smart enough for Rika, in my opinion.

*Choi.* He was the one I needed to watch out for. Not only was he smart, but he could lure her in with his geek crap like a crack whore to, well, crack. They had way too much in common to rule him out as a threat.

My arm tightened around her involuntarily.

When had I started thinking like a general planning to outmaneuver his enemies? I'd never put this much thought into a relationship before.

But the more Rika roved around the city, working on cases, the more men there would be, lining up to try to take her from me.

When I got here, there was Eli. Within a day or two of starting the search for her father, she'd been reunited with her old classmate Julian. And now there was a doctor after her. If she gained one admirer per month—

"Nick?"

Rika's head was cocked back, her eyes rolled up to look into mine. "Yeah?"

"Are you okay? You went all tense."

I wasn't about to confess my concerns about losing her. I was the guy who got the girl. And this one I was going to keep.

"I was just thinking about that tiger. And how glad I was it didn't eat you, at least before this happened."

She burst out laughing.

Damn, I loved to make her laugh. I loved to tease her and make her eyes flash.

And this part—being in bed with her—I slid my hand over her rear end and squeezed. I loved this most of all.

But other men were falling for her, too, and there were a number of steps a guy had to go through to lock a woman down. I didn't want to waste any more time. Was it too soon to tell her I loved her?

I felt her fingers on my stomach and realized she'd switched her focus to that part of my body.

"Whatcha doin'?" I asked.

"Counting," she said. "This is a lot of abs. You may be deformed."

Now, I was the one laughing, my abdomen shaking as her palm pressed against it.

This was the time. I had to say it. "Rika, I—"

My phone went off. Billy Ray Cyrus's "Achy Breaky Heart," the song my sister had gone around singing, non-stop, when she was five. My dad would sing it around the house, on occasion, and anything he sang, DeeAnne sang.

Of course, this just frustrated our mom more. She didn't understand why DeeAnne wouldn't sing it full out on pageant stages, instead giving a passable, but lackluster performance. Mom tortured DeeAnne with those pageants until sometime in high school, when she flat-out refused to get in the car anymore.

"I need to take this," I said as I slid away from Rika and grabbed the phone. "Yeah?" I said after I hit the answer button, already concerned. My little sister—who preferred to be called "Dee" in her Seattle life—mostly texted me. I'd gotten into the habit of calling her on Sundays to catch up, but she didn't initiate a call unless it was important.

There was no sound on the other end, then I thought I heard deep breathing.

"Hello?" I said. "Are you there?" Maybe it was a butt dial.

"I'm here," she said. Her voice was thin and raspy, like it was when she had a sore throat as a kid.

My heart pounded hard in my chest, and not in the good way it had a few minutes ago. I needed her to cut to the chase so I could help her. "What's wrong, honey?" *Please let this be something I can fix.*

"It's... It's just..."

I jumped up from the bed and paced into the bathroom. "What happened?" If this had to do with that creep she used to be married to, I was going to fly to Seattle, track him down at Amazon or Google or whichever company he was working for this year and beat the crap out of him. When DeeAnne divorced him, he did all kinds of nasty cyber shit to her.

His position was that, because she was leaving him, he should get to keep everything. After their mediation session, he realized that wasn't going to happen. Since he was a techie, he'd set up everything on her computer for her and, within a few hours after mediation, he'd purposely screwed up everything—changed passwords and other information on her various online accounts, moved money from all their bank accounts to who knew where, and erased a lot of her files just for spite.

"No, nothing happened, really," she said unconvincingly. "I just wanted to call and see how you were. Mom said you were still in L.A., and she's not happy about it." By the end of that statement, she'd managed to pull her voice up to a teasing tone and was trying to redirect the conversation onto me.

She didn't fool me one bit. I'd known her since before she was born.

And the tears I'd heard in her voice when I answered still ripped at my guts. I'd considered my little sister my responsibility after our dad died.

I was ten and she was six.

Sure, officially, my mom was in charge, but she tended to be distracted and a little on the narcissistic side. It was up to me to make sure my baby sister felt cared for enough that she didn't end up a teenage mom or workin' a pole.

She'd grown up to be a smart, compassionate person, employed by a non-profit that helped low-income kids.

Kyle had seemed smitten with her when they got married. I felt like I'd done my job—or, I guess, my dad's job—warding off the daddy issues that seemed to throw women's lives out of whack.

But Kyle had turned out to be an ass and my sister had to divorce him, so maybe I hadn't done such a good job, after all.

Now, I was sure she needed me and I wasn't going to let her throw the conversation off track with mom talk. If I couldn't prevent her heart from getting broken, the least I could do was pick up the pieces. "Baby girl, you've got to tell me what's going on."

"It's silly," she said. "It's just this stupid PMS."

I'd had a mom, a sister, and three wives, but had never come up with a cure for that malady. Of course, DeeAnne knew that about me and could be using it to shut this down. Maybe a more circuitous tactic was in order.

"Are you still living with the same roommate?"

"Raine? Yeah, she asked if I wanted to stay. I'm paying rent now. I'm planning to be here for a while."

I didn't know much about Raine, but I was glad my sister wasn't alone. "You know I can take care of you. You don't have to stay—" I began.

"I like it here," she said. "I'm not letting him run me out of town."

I sucked in a full breath for the first time since she called. It was a relief to hear the fight hadn't left her. But I still worried.

Could she need money? As a software developer, Kyle made a lot of money. DeeAnne did not and, thus far, had refused to take any of the oil money on principle. "Let me wire you money to help with—"

"I'm fine," she said, but I knew her pride might keep her from asking for help.

"Honey—" I tried again. "You know if you need anything..."

"I'm fine Nick. I'll talk to you later, okay?"

I heard the tears in her voice again and I could hardly stand it.

"Okay. Call me if... Well, if anything."

"I will. Bye," she said.

As I hung up, I was glad Rika was here. I'd wanted my baby sister's life to be perfect—as perfect as a life could be—anyway. I felt like I'd failed her and needed someone to share that feeling with.

I walked back into the bedroom but Rika wasn't in the bed anymore. The robe was still on the floor where we'd left it.

Maybe she was getting more coffee?

I strode to the living room.

Still no Rika, and there was nowhere else to look.

I rewound to just before the phone call. I thought things were going well, but maybe I was wrong.

I had to be wrong, didn't I? The first chance she got, she took off.

My mood sunk even lower than it had with my sister's call.

*What the hell?*

# CHAPTER TWENTY

**Rika**

I watched the map on the Thumbin' It app, the latest ride-sharing startup in town.

*Please, come faster,* I thought as I stood on the curb outside the hotel.

I became aware of my right palm pressing against my chest, where the pangs hit every time I replayed Nick's phone call.

In my fantasies, after sex, there was lots of pillow talk. I'd finally feel comfortable in my own skin. We'd tell each other how we felt.

In those fantasies Nick was one hundred percent in love with me.

That phone call had thrown me for a loop. First the custom ring tone was "Achy Breaky Heart," sung by Miley Cyrus's dad. Any detective worth her salt would know that, if you chose a ring tone like that for a person, that person had a piece of your heart.

Worse, he had a special voice for the person who called, which meant whoever that caller was, she had history with Nick.

He'd never used that voice with me.

When he called her "honey," I slipped out of bed and started getting dressed. I felt most vulnerable when I was naked. That phone call made me feel like I needed a full suit of armor. Unfortunately, all I had were Nick's very oversized sweat clothes to put on.

Seconds after he called her "baby girl," I was on my way out.

It was BreeAnne, Nick's second wife, I was sure of it. When I was staying with Nick, she'd shown up, acted like a helpless female, and gotten him to go over to her house and check her electrical problem. Her husband had been out of town then, but what if they'd broken up and she wanted Nick back?

Of course, the caller could just as well be Megan, Nick's most recent ex-wife. Last I saw her, she was dumping Gucci on Nick and taking off to France with her new boyfriend. But what are the chances that lasted? And if she were stuck in France, needing to be saved...

The thing is, I wouldn't have minded him sending either of his exes money or helping them out in some way. I knew the kind of guy Nick was. I liked that it wasn't in him to leave a woman on the streets with no place to go or to help an ex who's living in hundred-degree Bolo, Texas get her air conditioning working.

I was truly okay with all of that.

What got me was the voice.

I loved the various versions of Nick's voice, especially when he'd murmured, hot and sweet, in my ear in his bed a few minutes ago.

But he'd never used *that* version of his voice with me. It was a special voice reserved for a special person.

And it didn't bother him, at all, to use pet names with another woman while I was in the room? Did he forget about me as soon as she called?

Maybe what he told me back in Bolo was right. Maybe he did have too much of a past if he could get a call from it and forget about me completely, minutes after we'd gone to bed together for the first time.

A white Hyundai Sonata pulled up. I checked for the sticker with a bright red thumb on the back windshield, then got in the car.

~

## Nick

I woke up from an unplanned nap with Rika on my mind. Maybe because my bed smelled like her freshly washed hair and us, together.

Nothing in my life had felt as right as Rika underneath me, in my bed. But I had a feeling Rika on top of me—cowgirl style—would feel every bit as right.

*Next time. Maybe tonight, even.*

I was a little freaked out when she took off after our first time. But while I was standing in the living room of my suite wondering where she was, I'd gotten a text from her.

Something about one of her grandmother's friends being taken to the hospital. Mrs. Delacruz was getting a colonoscopy today and Mrs. Ruíz was supposed to bring her home from the procedure. Rika explained in her text that her cousin and aunts were stuck at work and her grandmother's friend didn't have any family.

I would've loved to have kept Rika here all night, but I wasn't going to quibble. After many months of missing her, and several more weeks of crossed signals, we'd finally made undeniable progress in our relationship.

She felt like mine, now, and my chest expanded with the emotion of it. Elation, like I'd expect to feel if I'd scaled Mt. Everest. Pride, because she was brilliant and gorgeous.

There was also an odd sense of relief which I attributed to learning that I didn't have to grow old with the type of woman I'd spent time with in the past. Rika would always be beautiful to me, I knew it like I knew my own name.

And, now...?

First, I wanted her out of the P.I. business. I hadn't been thrilled about it before, but now that we were together, I was responsible for keeping her safe. Skip tracing online was one thing but investigating murders in the field was a completely different animal.

If a murderer thinks you're getting too close to the truth, there's a good chance he or she would be willing to kill you to shut you up.

Rika was smart, but, physically, she didn't have much going for her if someone attacked her—small shoulders, small hands, and no weight to throw behind her impressive determination.

The memory of Detective Hertz getting cactus needles extricated from her ass made me chuckle. Okay, maybe Rika had a *little* weight to throw around.

As the excitement of this new version of our relationship calmed, reality set in. I wasn't going to be able to stop Rika from being a private investigator. Not yet, anyway.

I'd need to bide my time. Maybe it wouldn't turn out to be what she expected. Plus, she was business-minded and practical. If it wasn't profitable—and it had to be hard to get established in the business—she would eventually let it go. She had a lot of college hours under her belt and was smart enough to be successful at anything she chose. Hell, she didn't have to do anything if she didn't want to, but it might be hard to convince her of that.

We could travel the world. Go for long visits to her dad in Colombia. I wasn't sure if he approved of me or not, but if Rika wanted to make up for lost time with him, I'd learn Spanish *and* soccer for her.

Even so, getting her onboard with dropping the P.I. thing would take time.

Meanwhile, she needed to be able to protect herself.

I considered what Bart said. I didn't appreciate him calling her a headcase, but maybe he was onto something. Maybe Rika's mother had been shot by her killer.

But Rika was so young when all this happened. Would she know the details?

She searched online for the answer to pretty much any question that crossed her mind. Would she have googled her mother's murder?

As I sat up, I grabbed my phone from the nightstand.

I googled "Martín murder Los Angeles" and scrolled around until I found an article with "Coroner's Report Released" in the headline. Mariana Martín was kidnapped from the parking lot of a retail strip center while leaving her yoga class.

Then came the part about the coroner's report. Defensive wounds. Struggle. Strangled.

*Strangled.*

My eyes flicked from the words that were jumping out at me on the screen to the photo of Rika's mother when she was still alive. She looked just like Rika. Maybe I should have expected that, but I hadn't and nausea filled my gut as I tried not to let myself picture Rika being strangled by a psychopath.

I breathed in slowly, trying to get control over my innards.

I reminded myself that, although the information about Rika's mother was new to me, the crime had happened many years ago. She was at peace now and had been for more than fifteen years.

I walked over to sit on my bed. The screen on my phone had gone dark, thank God, but I could still see Mariana's lovely face in my mind's eye.

She was just a few years older than Rika when she died. She didn't even get to see her daughter grow up. "I'm sorry," I said to her as I touched the top edge of my phone to my forehead.

So, Rika's mother hadn't been shot. But did Rika know that?

When you're a little kid and nobody tells you the facts, you tend to fill them in with your imagination.

Hell, I'd done it, and I was older than she was when my dad

died. My mom was a wreck and couldn't talk about it. For the first day or so, I assumed he'd died in a car accident because the only person I'd known who died suddenly was a friend's dad who'd been taken out by an eighteen-wheeler.

Maybe Rika assumed her mother was shot. Who would want to tell an eight-year-old exactly how her mother was killed?

*Strangled... Holy hell.*

But it was possible Rika believed her mother had been shot and couldn't stand holding a gun in her hand and firing it, even if it was at a paper target.

Yet another bad feeling rolled through me, this one from the guilt of making her go to the range.

Then I remembered why I'd done it. In the few weeks of her life I'd spent with her, Rika had people following her, throwing knives at her and shooting at her.

Maybe it would never happen again, but with the line of work she was now in, chances were better than average that someone could get pissed off about her snooping.

I was back to wanting to forbid her from doing any more investigating, even though I knew how that would go over. That receptionist job she had before didn't sound so bad. And what was that job she had just before I met her?

An E. coli tester in a meatpacking company?

I guess there was the chance of getting E. coli there, but many people lived through E. coli. More than lived through a bullet to the brain, I assumed.

However, Rika was too strong-willed and determined to stop just because I wanted her to. And I had too much respect for her to suggest she should settle for a job that didn't make use of her impressive mind.

*Hold up...*

Could her mother's murder be the reason she wanted to be a private investigator in the first place? To right wrongs? To somehow balance out the tragedy of her mother's death by stopping other killers?

If that was the case, maybe Rika could see a therapist, get past her obsession, and take a nice, safe job.

Did I have the right to suggest the therapy thing?

Probably not. Not yet, anyway.

I checked the time and headed for the shower. I was supposed to meet Rika at the crime scene in a couple of hours.

When I shut off the water, someone was knocking on my door. Probably the dinner I ordered.

I wrapped a towel around my waist, went to the door and opened it.

The dog walker, whose name I hadn't bothered to learn in my rush to consummate my relationship with Rika, was standing at the door. Her eyes expanded to the size of plums as they drifted down my body.

I cringed inwardly. She looked like a kid to me and my current attire wasn't kid appropriate.

A quick glance verified that, at least, the towel wasn't hanging open in the front.

She managed to stop staring, but her eyes darted around unnaturally.

"I've got your..." She held up Gucci, who was now wearing a tiny pink ball cap with slits in the sides that showed off her long, silky ears and a matching shirt that read "Diva."

Why did every woman who got hold of this dog want to put clothes on her?

The walker was stammering, "...your...your...*thing*."

Once more, I checked to make sure my *thing* was under wraps.

"I mean your dog!" she said with a head shake. She laughed nervously. "Weird for a dog walker to forget the word 'dog,' I guess." Her eyes landed on my abs and stuck there. "I mean of all the words to, um...um..."

"Forget?" I offered.

"Yeah, ha-ha. Guess I'm just really forgetful today."

Gucci was paddling her feet as if she thought she could swim through the air to get to me. I took her from the walker's shaky hands.

This was one of the reasons I wasn't convinced I wanted kids.

They could be girls.

That might sound sexist, but I'd seen what having a girl did to a man. She'd act cute and sweet and adorable and make her daddy love her to the point that he'd die to protect her without a moment's thought. Then she'd turn into a teenager, get boy crazy and dump poor old dad out of the loop so completely, he could only guess what was happening with her and didn't have a clue how to protect her.

I knew myself well enough to understand how that would eat me up on the inside. Having a younger sister with no dad around was hard enough.

"I'm eighteen," the walker announced suddenly.

I rewound the conversation, trying to remember asking about her age.

She pulled a chunk of hair forward to cover a pimple on the left side of her forehead. "I mean, if you get lonely..."

*Oh, hell no!*

"I think that's my phone," I said, taking the coward's way out. But the alternative was to engage in conversation about sex with this girl who looked more like thirteen than eighteen to me. I turned to the suite's entry table and pulled the drawer open. I kept cash there for tips. Forgetting I'd already overpaid her, I grabbed all the money that was in there and held it out to her. "Thanks for your help!" I said.

She took it, then looked at the wad of ones, fives, and tens. "Are you sure you meant to give me this much tip?" she asked. "You already—"

"Sure," I said. "You got her clothes and everything!" I smiled as if I heartily approved of dogs in diva shirts. "Thanks again!"

Then, I shut the door before she could say—or do—anything more.

~

## Rika

When I got back to Lita's house, I found Sofia there, pulling leftovers out of the fridge.

She looked cool, as usual, in a form-fitting V-neck t-shirt that featured a beautiful watercolor butterfly. With it, she wore snug jeans and the hoop earrings she was always trying to get me to wear.

I didn't refuse because they weren't my style, which they weren't. I refused because I had a fear that I'd spazz out, get something caught in one of them and pull my earlobe off.

How did Sofia always look all stylish and cool? Not to mention that most days we were wearing essentially the same clothes—jeans and t-shirts—but she always looked unmistakably sexy, while I just looked like I was wearing jeans and a t-shirt.

"I thought you were busy today," I said.

"I had a dentist appointment and I've been waiting for an hour to get to eat something." She pulled the foil off a bowl, then set it on the counter and went back to the fridge. "My tongue is still a little numb. I hope I don't bite it off like you did yours that time. Remember?"

Remember? How could I forget?

Sofia had no idea how mortified I'd been by that incident.

I was a high school freshman, as self-conscious as a kid could be. While in the dental chair, I'd gotten curious—of course—and tried to turn to see what the dental hygienist was doing behind me.

However, as I turned, I put too much of my considerable

weight on the arm of the chair and it broke off. I then had to sit through the filling with the dentist and hygienist knowing what I did, and all three of us knowing why it happened.

All I could think about was getting home and stuffing myself full of Double Stufs. But, when I got home, I didn't wait until the numbness was gone. I ended up biting my tongue, causing blood to dribble out of my mouth.

Worse, it dripped onto the plastic tray of cookies, causing Tía Margo to throw away four of the precious Oreos.

I was not in the mood to talk about that humiliation, especially on the heels of my latest humiliation with Nick and his special phone caller.

I mumbled a reply and headed for the shower. When I finished, I pulled on a clean pair of jeans, topping it with my black "Trust me. I'm a Jedi" shirt that had sleeves long enough to cover my wristband.

I picked up the sweatpants and shirt I'd borrowed from Nick. When I came out of the bathroom, I found Sofia sitting on my bed, a plate of leftovers in one hand, a fork in the other.

"So... I noticed you were wearing different clothes when you came in." Her gaze shifted to the clothes I was holding.

I opened the hamper in my closet and tossed them in. "Yeah, I try to wear different clothes every time I take a shower," I replied.

She chuckled. "I meant that you were wearing clothes that clearly weren't your style."

I really needed to talk to someone about what happened with Nick. And, again, Sofia seemed to be the safest person to confide in. It was weird how family worked sometimes.

I sat next to her on the bed. "I... Nick and I, um, did the...um, did it... today."

"Really? Oh my God!" She took a beat to swallow the food in her mouth and digest my information. She stretched toward my desk and set her plate on it, giving me her full attention. "So, how was it?"

"It was..." How did I explain what it was like to be with Nick? "Amazing," I finally said. "Better than I ever imagined... at least... during. But after..."

"Did he kick you to the curb?" Sofia said, like she was ready to kick some hot guy ass on my behalf. "Is that why you're home?"

"No, like I said, it was great...twice." I felt a blush crawl up my neck.

Sofia leaned in. "Twice is good! And then?"

"We were lying there talking. Everything felt right, almost normal, in a way. You know, like we should always have been lying around in bed talking."

She nodded. "So, what happened?"

"He got a phone call. I'm not sure who it was, but I know she was female. He jumped out of bed and walked away like he wanted privacy. He seemed completely absorbed in whatever she was saying."

Sofia rolled her eyes. "Maybe it was his mom?"

"He doesn't call his mom 'honey' or 'baby girl'. It was some-body else." Humiliation washed over me at the idea that Nick valued our first time together so little he answered his phone right after, then seemed to forget about me. "I keep thinking about his ex-wives," I confessed. "It could have been one of them. Whoever it was, it sounded to me like they'd had a breakup and called Nick to console them."

"Ohhhh..." Sofia nodded sagely. "I get it. You're freaking out without having any idea what's going on." She knocked her shoulder into mine, jostling me. I leaned against her, pushing her back into her own space. "And you call yourself a detective!"

"Well, it's not like I have what it takes to *be* with Nick, long-term, Sof."

She jerked her head back. "So, you're back to thinking he doesn't have feelings for you?"

"Yeah, maybe," I replied. "I guess he has feelings for me, but he's had feelings for lots of women." I felt my nails dig into my palms. My Tía Margo referred to them as "anxiety fists." "I told you I wasn't enough to keep his interest."

She looked at me straight on. "You're nuts."

"I know you're trying to make me feel better, but we both know I'm just a chubby geek girl and he's..." I sighed not knowing how to sum up the awesomeness that was Nick. And the craziest part was that I wasn't even sure if, when I called myself a 'chubby geek girl', I was talking physically, mentally, or both.

Her mouth dropped open. "Uh... wow." She stared at me like she was looking at me through fresh eyes.

"That's it! I'm calling it. I was going to wait for a professional to do it, since it's not really my job, but..." Her dramatic pause lasted at least three seconds before she pointed her index finger at me. "You... have body dysmorphic disorder."

*Boom.* She'd dropped the sentence on me like a bomb.

I knew what body dysmorphic disorder was. I'd seen it on a talk show, years ago, then googled it because it was interesting. I remember being shocked at how attractive some of those people were, considering how hideous they thought their faces or bodies looked.

However, it never entered my mind that I was one of those kooks who had it!

"I'm not crazy!" I yelled at Sofia. "And you're a dog trainer, not a psychologist!"

"It doesn't mean you're crazy," Sofia said. "Like, one in fifty people have it." She reached out, took my hand in hers, and peered into my eyes. "And I'm not trying to insult you. It's just that you're one of the most beautiful people I've ever seen and you think there's something wrong with you. There's nothing wrong with you, Rika," she said. "Aesthetically speaking, anyway."

Anger screamed through my body. I yanked my hand away. "Don't say that to me, Sofia."

"Why?"

"It's cruel to try to convince me I'm all that, and you know it."

"You see..." Her hands turned palm up. "That's what I mean. You're convinced there's something wrong with you physically, but there's really something wrong with you mentally."

*Shit.* I did not want to go there. Not with Sofia. Not with anyone. I just sat, staring at the floor, fuming.

"Rika, this is the second time, *this week*, that we've talked about this. I showed you photographic proof of how beautiful you are, and you already seem to have blocked it out!"

"I haven't blocked it out!" I replied, thinking that blocking things out sounded like something a crazy person would do.

"Okay..." Sofia tried again. "Could you see yourself getting thinner in the mirror when you were losing weight?"

For several seconds, a battle raged inside me. Half of me wanted to shut Sofia up, push all my emotions down and bury them under a gallon of ice cream. The other half knew I probably needed help.

"Yes...and no," I replied honestly. "Every time I dropped another five or ten pounds, I could see it and feel it for a little while. I might even buy new clothes and feel really good the first time I wore them."

"And then?"

"I'd wake up a day or two later, look in the mirror, and my eyes would go straight to the fat that was still there."

"And now?"

"Same thing. Plus, I gained nine or ten pounds—about half of it in Bolo and the rest after I got home."

"And where do you *think* you stand as far as your 'perfect weight' goes?" She'd emphasized the word "think" like she assumed whatever I thought wasn't going to mesh with reality. And she'd made air quotes when she said "perfect weight" because, according to her mom, Tía Margo, we were supposed to eat healthy and exercise, then appreciate our bodies whatever their shape.

I decided I didn't want to talk about this after all. "Is this a counseling session?" I asked. "You know being born to a therapist mom doesn't make you qualified to take on patients, right?"

"Maybe not, but I learned a few things in the two decades I lived with her."

Truth be told, Sofia wasn't the first to bring up the possibility that I wasn't quite right in my thinking. When I reached my goal weight, but still felt the need to keep losing, my Jilly Crane counselor warned me that if I kept having those feelings, I might need to seek therapy.

I ignored her because I saw what I saw. I mean, what kind of idiot believed what someone else told them over what they saw with their own eyes? "I can see the fat, Sofia. It's not like it's a figment of my imagination."

"Oh, my God, Rika! Everyone has fat on them. It's normal to have body fat. If you had zero body fat, you'd be dead." She paused as if trying to decide if what she'd just said was factually correct or not. She sighed. "When you look at me, do you think I'm too fat?"

"Of course not," I replied. "You're gorgeous! Everyone says you're a bombshell!"

"But I outweigh you by twenty-five pounds. Maybe more."

"But you're four inches taller and yours is all in the right place."

"Rika..." She squeezed my arm. "I think you should talk to my mom about this and maybe get a referral for someone who specializes in—"

"I heard you the other times!" I yelled at her. "I didn't block anything out! I'm an adult. If I decide I have a problem, I'll decide to see someone. Case closed."

Sofia lowered her voice. She knew she wouldn't get anywhere if we were yelling at each other. "Okay..." she said. "You're right. You're an adult. But, as far as Nick goes, why don't you mention that the phone call sounded serious and ask him if everything is okay?"

Maybe she was right.

But what if it was the opening Nick needed to tell me he was going back to BreeAnne in Bolo? Or Megan, wherever Megan was right now? And I knew next to nothing about his first wife or any other women he'd dated. Maybe there was a special one who got away.

Wait, what if that Grace person had invented a problem Nick needed to "help" her with?

*You should never have called Nick to come out to L.A.,* a voice whispered in my head.

Like I'd had a choice. I'd missed him every single day, and when my dad disappeared, Nick was the only person I wanted by my side.

"Thanks for the talk, Sof, but I need to get going," I said. And without another word, I grabbed my keys and headed for my car.

# CHAPTER TWENTY-ONE

**Rika**

I drove toward the crime scene before sundown, planning to be there an hour before Nick thought I'd arrive. Despite having the key and Erissa's permission to be in the duplex, I preferred to do this without him.

The house was still a crime scene and I didn't want him to get in trouble. I was sure Nick had never in his life been arrested, and I didn't want to be the reason he got cuffed and stuffed into the back of a cop car.

As I waited at a light just a few blocks from my destination, my window open, due to the beautiful seventy-three-degree weather, I heard someone say, "Hey, *mami*. Don't I know you?"

My first impulse was to ignore it. There were cars in three lanes waiting at the light and the words weren't necessarily directed at me.

But I could feel the goosebumps swelling on my arms. My brain whirred as it rewound the two sentences and replayed them.

*Hey, mami. Don't I know you?*

Hm...it was the voice more than the words.

I'd heard that voice before.

I turned and discovered, less than four feet away from me, in the passenger seat of the car in the very next lane, a man so distinctive looking, I could never, ever forget him. Shaved head, moustache, a weirdly long, thin goatee that grew in a small vertical strip under the middle of his bottom lip down almost to his chest, and the Jesus neck tattoo of the quality one would get, say, in prison.

*Holy mother of Zeus!* He was the head *cholo* from the gang I'd encountered while evading the cops and running from the Microtologists just a couple of weeks ago!

His ride was an old refurbished Chevy with custom hubcaps that shimmered like LeeAnne had taken her Bedazzler to them. Two of his boys were in the car with him. One driving. One in the back.

What the hell were they doing here?

Sure, I was only five miles from the neighborhood we sort of shared, and he clearly had transportation. But I'd never imagined running into him, as long as I avoided those blocks my grandmother had always warned me about.

"Hey, *mami!*" he repeated louder. "Don't I know you?"

I shook my head and looked straight through my windshield while I tried to figure out my options. I didn't want him to follow me to my destination. I needed to change my route.

That shouldn't be hard since I was in the right lane already. I could just turn when I got up to the light. And if they managed to cut someone off and follow me?

I glanced around my car. The only thing I had that resembled a weapon was the plastic blade on my Assassin's Creed Origin wrist guard.

If only it was made of real metal.

My only choice was to ignore these guys, then lose them.

"What's the matter, *mami?*" His voice had turned gravelly,

which, in his case, made it sound more threatening. "We're not good enough to talk to you?"

*Damn it! Could this light be any longer?*

"Hey!" he called louder. "Are you deaf?" He waved his hands at me while his boys broke into fits of laughter.

That was it!

I pretended his waving had gotten my attention and turned toward him. I pantomimed rubbing my chest, passed one open hand in front of the other, then rolled my fists around each other.

If he knew sign language, I was screwed because I was pretty sure I'd wished him a happy new year. I'd taught myself quite a bit of sign language from the internet when I was in junior high, but, as with any language, if you don't use it, you lose it.

"So, you're deaf, now?" He snorted. "But not dumb 'cause you're the girl who ran up to me screaming the other day. Who were we shooting at, *mami*?"

I assembled my features into what I hoped was a puzzled expression, then shrugged apologetically.

"Yeah..." he continued anyway. "I think you owe us for protecting you."

*Uh-oh.* Those words spoken in that tone of voice sent a ripple of fear and disgust down my spine. I was pretty sure I knew his preferred method of payment and there was no U.S. Treasury or pictures of dead presidents involved.

The light turned green and traffic started moving. I held my breath until I made it to the intersection, then I turned right. Two blocks later, I turned left.

I pulled up to a stop sign and breathed a sigh of relief.

I'd lost them!

I heard a loud car and looked left to find my friendly neighborhood cholos at the same intersection.

*Shit!*

I moved my foot from the brake, planning to mash the accelerator and get the hell away. But as soon as I started moving, the gangbangers' tires squealed. It pulled forward into the intersection as I slammed my brake on.

They had blocked my way.

I checked my rearview mirror. This was a residential street, quiet this time of day. No one behind me.

I crossed myself automatically, put the car in reverse and backed up as fast as I could. I saw a car coming, but kept backing, hoping the driver was paying attention.

It worked! The car went around me, cutting off the gangbangers who had turned and were trying to follow me. As soon as I hit the next street, I slammed the gear shift into Drive and took off.

I turned at one corner, then the next as I tried to formulate a plan. The cholos were committed to chasing me. By man rules, they couldn't just give up.

*Think, Paprika! Think!*

My driving was okay. I'd never gotten a ticket. But I was no Danica Patrick, either. My brain scanned through data—street maps as I remembered them, traffic patterns, businesses...

That was it! The dealership where I'd bought my Honda Fit was a few blocks away!

Now that I knew where I was going, I headed for the car lot in as direct a route as I could. I made it to the freeway.

The light was changing from yellow to red as I turned on the road that ran next to it.

I checked my rearview. The gangbangers were behind me, two cars back.

I moved to the left lane, swung around the cars that had been in front of me and forced my way back into the right lane just in time to make the turn.

From the tiny street that ran next to it, I slipped into the car lot.

I passed row after row, looking for the Honda Fits. But, when I found one, I realized my car was several years old and not nearly as pristine as the new versions.

Glancing around, I saw the "Pre-Owned Cars" sign and weaved my way toward it.

As soon as I made it to the used car side, I found a row of Fits from various years with an empty slot right in the middle.

Finally, I'd caught a break!

Sliding into the parking spot, I put the car in Park, and turned off the ignition.

I looked around to see if I was safe.

*No!*

The cholos' car turned into the lot on the new car side. I'd hoped they'd assume I was on the freeway and either get on it to chase me or concede defeat, but they were craftier than I gave them credit for.

I'd heard cops on TV say most criminals weren't that smart, but clearly, I was the lucky girl who hit the gangbanger I.Q. jackpot.

*Great.*

Had they memorized my plate? I tried to remember any other distinguishing characteristics my car had.

The House of Ravenclaw sticker on my back window.

*Crap!* They may have noticed it when we were stuck in traffic.

The cholos were driving methodically between each row of new cars. It wouldn't be long until they made it over to where I was parked.

Another movement caught my attention and I realized Peter, the Cambodian immigrant car salesman who sold me my Fit was coming my way, smiling. He probably thought I was here to trade it in for a new model.

The gangbangers were being very methodical in their search. They only had a couple more rows to go before they'd cross into this lot and find me.

I rolled down my window as Peter approached.

"Miss Rika Martín!" he said warmly. "I'm happy to see you again!"

"Look, Peter," I replied as I automatically shook his outthrust hand. "I'm sorry to ask you this, but I need to hide—with my car —somewhere. Those guys in the low rider car are after me."

Peter's face went serious and he squeezed my hand tightly as he followed my line of sight to the cholos.

"It's okay," he said. "You drive to the back, into one of the bays in the repair shop. Tell the big lesbian—Karla—that I sent you there to have your tread measured on your tires."

Due to my current time constraints, I controlled the urge to explain to him why describing someone as a "big lesbian" seemed wrong.

Regardless, I'd feel terrible if something happened to Peter because of me. "But—" I began.

"I know how to stall the bad guys," Peter interrupted. He gave me a comforting pat on the shoulder.

"Don't approach them," I said. "They probably have guns." I didn't mention that even if they didn't have guns, he was smaller than they were. He was shorter than I was, in fact.

"The bad people in my country had guns, too," he said. "They were much worse than your Los Angeles criminals."

How could he know what cholos might do? He was a car salesman, for Zeus' sake!

"No, Peter..." I began. I really couldn't let him get hurt. When I bought my Fit from him, he'd thrown in free floor mats and a bunch of free oil change coupons, even though we'd already come to an agreement about the purchase, and the coupons were supposed to be one per customer.

"Just do as I say," he replied confidently as he walked away. I watched as he got the attention of the other salesmen who were standing outside the dealership and flashed a backward peace sign.

The middle eastern-looking salesman nodded and slipped his

phone from his pocket. Then, Peter headed toward the cholos, waving and smiling widely as if he thought they were here to buy a car.

Maybe he could pull this off.

I backed out of my space and headed to the repair shop. When I pulled in, a broad-shouldered white woman with short gray hair was typing on a computer.

I gave her a nervous wave as she turned to look at me. "Hi, I'm looking for Karla," I called. "Peter sent me to get the tread on my tires checked."

Her demeanor changed from friendly to concerned in a split second. "Okay, pull your car the rest of the way in and turn off your motor," she ordered.

I followed her instructions. The second my back bumper was inside, the huge garage doors started closing.

Okay, then. They really did seem to have a plan in place for this type of situation. Why would they need a plan?

"Luckily, this is the slow time of day," she said. "Come on in my office and have a cup of coffee."

I figured I was stuck in here for the time being and grateful to be. I got out of my car and followed her.

After she had me seated in a simple black office chair, she ground beans in a small coffee grinder she kept on the credenza behind her desk.

"So, what's up?" she asked as she waited for the water boiler to do its job. "I mean the obvious guess is a pissed off ex. You've got that sexy geek thing going on."

Sexy geek thing? I'd showered and put on a new shirt that wasn't covered in cola and didn't belong to a man twice my size, but I'd never imagined my plain jeans and "Trust me I'm a Jedi" t-shirt qualifying as sexy.

"No, my ex is in New York," I replied.

"Stalker?"

"No, my stalker's a really nice guy."

She burst out laughing, clearly believing I was joking. She looked at me expectantly.

I figured if she was saving my life, I owed her the story. "I pissed off a pack of cholos and now they're after me," I said.

"You don't look like you hang with bangers," she mused. "Got a drug problem?"

I shook my head. "Nothing like that. It's just that my dad was suspected of murder. The cops got a warrant for the house, but I snuck out with my computer gear so they wouldn't take it away. I was on foot and I ended up on the cholos' turf and I sort of tricked them into shooting at the cult members who were trying to kidnap me."

Karla handed me a brown and white cow mug full of coffee, then stared at me assessingly. I replayed the words I'd just said and realized it was my sanity she was assessing.

"I know it sounds nuts..."

She waved her hand dismissively. "No, I get it. A lot of weird shit has happened to me, too."

I took a sip, grateful for the camaraderie and the coffee.

"Oh, let's see what's going on." She picked up a remote, aimed it at the corner of the ceiling and hit a button.

I tilted my head back and realized I was looking at the exterior of the car lot on a TV screen. Karla flipped to different cameras until she saw the cholos, then zoomed in.

"That's awesome picture quality," I said. I always found it frustrating that in a time when nearly everyone had a good quality digital camera on his or her phone, the security footage from robbed convenience stores always looked like the robbery had happened in the 1960s.

"Yep," Karla agreed, her eyes on the monitor.

I checked it again. The salesmen and cholos were interacting. "What are they doing?" I asked. "The head cholo looks pissed."

"My guys have 'accidentally' blocked him in," she replied.

She zoomed out and I saw that several cars had been moved and the narrow aisles were blocked.

Peter was smiling, as always, seemingly trying to sell the cholos a car while they looked at him murderously and told him to "get the fuck" out of their way. There was no sound, but it didn't take a master lip-reader to catch that phrase.

"Man, those dudes are hot under the collar." Karla chuckled. "If they wore collars, I mean."

"Yeah," I agreed. "I think Peter better—"

Just then, the head cholo lifted his gun threateningly, not quite pointing it at Peter...yet.

"No!" I said.

"Don't worry," Karla replied.

Peter pointed right at us. I ducked reflexively. Then I realized he was gesturing at the camera, not us.

"You see," Karla said. "Right now, Peter is showing him the security cameras, but he's saying something about how secure the parking lot is, so the dude can leave his car safely in the lot while they go for a test drive."

"Huh?"

"He says it that way because if he phrased it as a threat, the dude would be forced to act all badass and maybe shoot someone. Peter had to deal with a lot of bad guys in the past. He knows the mentality."

The gun had disappeared. Now, it looked like the cholo was practically begging Peter to stop selling him a car and leave him alone.

I chuckled along with Karla. She and Peter and the other dealership people were pretty cool. I kind of wanted her to be my friend, although I didn't know when I'd see her again.

Plus, she and LeeAnne could be a disaster. LeeAnne wouldn't take no for an answer when she determined someone needed a makeover. I'd had one of her makeovers in the past and was pretty sure Karla would not want LeeAnne to make her over.

"How is it that you guys had a plan in place for...well, this type of eventuality?"

Karla took a sip of her coffee from a mug adorned with Snoopy lounging on top of his doghouse, which was flying a rainbow flag. "I drove in here a few years ago, trying to escape my abusive ex-husband—yes, I married a man, but I was from a small town and I thought it would cure me from being gay. Obviously, it didn't work. Just grossed me out a lot." She took another sip. "Anyway, the guys here helped me. Peter diffused the situation. Then, they got me a job here so I could afford to live on my own and came up with code words to make me feel safe. So, if my ex came back, one of them could pick up the phone right in front of him and tell me a customer needed her tread measured, I could close the bay door, and he'd never know I was here." She shrugged. "You know, some of them are from countries where it's illegal to be gay, but they still have my back. I love these guys."

Wow. I'd never worked at a place where I felt that way about my co-workers. Maybe I wanted to come work here.

I tried to imagine selling cars or changing oil.

*Okay. Bad idea.*

On the monitor, Peter was motioning to another salesman to move a car. He turned back to the cholos and patted—yes, patted —the head cholo on the shoulder. Then he stuck his hand inside the car and the head cholo shook it.

As soon as the path was clear, the Chevy sped out of the lot.

Karla's cell rang and she put it on speaker. "Hey, Peter," she said.

"Were you watching?" he asked. "The coat is clear!" I was pretty sure he meant the *coast* was clear, but English was, like, his third or fourth language and he spoke it a lot better than I spoke Spanish.

"You were awesome!" Karla cried. "First round's on me after work." She clicked the phone off.

I wasn't sure why she was rewarding these guys on my behalf. "Let me get money from my car for those drinks," I said.

"No way. This was fun!" she replied. "I've never gotten to be the rescuer before."

I understood what she meant. She was paying it forward and the thought made me feel warm and fuzzy all over.

"You're interesting," she added. "Are you on Con-akopia?

Oh, my God. Con-akopia was a social media site for people who enjoyed going to cons.

"Sure!" I replied. "Are you a cosplayer?"

"Yep. Friend me. My handle is BigLesbian."

I raised my eyebrows in surprise.

She smiled, clearly understanding why. "So, my ex can't find me if he searches," she explained. "Plus, I kind of enjoy shocking people."

As good a reason as any, I figured, and she certainly had the right to call herself anything she wanted.

Hm... I wondered if I should just accept that I was never going to grow to be five-foot-seven and become "LilLatina" on social media.

Not until after I found out if it was too late for me to try human growth hormones, though.

I tapped my phone screen until I found Karla on Con-akopia. "Friend request submitted," I said. "Thanks for everything. You guys are awesome."

# CHAPTER TWENTY-TWO

**Nick**

I decided to head over to the duplex about an hour before the scheduled time. When Rika said to meet her at nine, she had a look in her eye I didn't quite like. I had a feeling she was planning to do this without me.

I hoped she didn't bring LeeAnne this time. I'd noticed a pattern developing when the two of them went investigating together. Despite my concerns about her running around without me, I knew that, alone, Rika had a good head on her shoulders.

LeeAnne always had a streak of wild child in her, but her marriage to an abusive ass aside, she hadn't had a lot of opportunities to get into trouble on her own in Bolo. As soon as she was old enough, her grandparents had her working with them at their restaurant-bar.

However, when LeeAnne's wild child intersected with Rika's murder investigations, anything could happen, from their little plan to get the goods on JimBob in Bolo to the freeway shootout, and now the tiger.

Sure, the most recent incident may have been a freak accident

I couldn't have predicted, but, at this point, I felt certain the two of them shouldn't be running down a case together.

I pulled up in front of the duplex, not the least bit surprised to see Rika's Honda already in the driveway. I was, however, surprised to see a customized Chevy Impala, circa 1960 or so— the car I'd smashed up pretty good only a few weeks ago.

I'd felt kind of bad when I wrecked it. Someone had put a lot of time into that beauty. As I walked by it, I looked for the damage.

If this was the same car, the owner had an excellent body shop.

Or maybe it wasn't the same car. How would the gangbangers know to find her here?

I moved up the steps quietly, sidled up to the door, and peeked in.

Three men were standing, facing Rika and, even from the back, I knew who she was dealing with. These were definitely three of the gang members we'd encountered previously.

Out of necessity, she'd used them and made them look foolish that day when she was running from the Microtologists.

At least they weren't holding guns on her, but why the hell were they here?

Since they didn't know I was on the scene, I decided to gather more intel before acting. On one hand, as far as I knew, they were used to using guns, not fists, and they weren't holding guns now.

But there were three of them and my knuckles had barely healed up from the run-ins with the Microtologists.

When I was going to college, then law school, I didn't expect my future to involve a lot of manual labor, much less fist-fighting. Yet, my degrees never stopped my mom from thinking I should be her personal carpenter and landscaper. And, thanks to Rika, I'd been using my fists more than I ever imagined.

I'd never regretted one thing I'd done for Rika, though, no

matter what it cost me or how much it hurt. If I had to take on all three of these "cholos," as she called them, that's what I'd do.

Rika smiled at the chief banger, a smile so alluring, it would make any man tight under the fly. "Wow, I haven't seen you guys in weeks!" She was trying to sound casual, but I could tell how nervous she was by the pitch of her voice.

"That's funny," the one in the middle said. "We saw you a half hour ago. That's some wild driving you do, *chica*. You lost us for a while, but we're...persistent." He nodded as if satisfied with his choice of words. Then he tilted his head way over to one side. "How come you didn't want to talk to me, *mami*?"

He stepped a little closer to Rika. My hands tightened into fists. If he touched her...

"Was that you?" she said almost convincingly. "I didn't recognize you. You changed your sideburns, right?"

The dude looked surprised at her response. He untilted his head then tilted it slightly in the other direction, kind of like Gucci when she was trying to figure out what was going on, which was pretty much all the time.

"Hey, Chino!" The guy next to him said. His head was shaved except for a mohawk that continued down his back in the form of a braid. "You did change your sideburns, dude. She remembers you!"

Chino cut his eyes toward him. "Shut the fuck up, Pepe."

The third one, whose hair was short on the sides with the middle long and slicked back, chimed in. "Pepe's right. I think that means she loves you, Chino. Maybe you should take her out on a date."

Both men cracked up. Chino gave them a sly smile, then refocused on Rika. "Is that right, *chula*? I bet you clean up real nice. A short dress. High-heels?"

I knew it was in the best interest of mankind for Rika not to wear short dresses with high heels. When I saw her in LeeAnne's clothes—the hoochie ones for the bar and the snug skirt and blazer for court—I almost swallowed my tongue. And the day we had to go to church, she looked like a million bucks in a never-worn designer dress my ex had left behind. The memory always caused me to suck in a huge, involuntary breath.

But I didn't like this guy imagining Rika scantily dressed one bit.

"Sorry." Rika managed to look disappointed. "I'm not the right girl for the job. I don't own any clothes like that."

That's when Chino got right up in her space and said, "It don't matter, *bonita*. The clothes won't be on for long, anyway."

Shock registered for only a split-second on her face. In fact, if I hadn't studied her every minute I could from the time we met, I wouldn't have known. She appeared calm and steady, but her eyes flicked to the doorway, like she was trying to determine her chances of escape.

That's when she spotted me.

"Look guys," she said. "This has been fun, but my partner over there and I have work to do."

All three of their heads swiveled to look at me. Chino assessed me—head to toe—with narrowed eyes. He didn't seem to recognize me from the day I rammed a truck into several of his friends' cars. That was probably for the best. Also, in my favor was the fact that I was noticeably taller than all of them.

Downside? There was still only one of me.

Chino turned back to Rika. "Yeah? What kind of work?"

"State Department," she replied.

"State Department?" Chino repeated. He turned to the guy with the slicked-back hair. "*Cerebro*?"

I knew a few Spanish words, but that wasn't one of them.

"Yeah, Cerebro," Pepe said. "What the fuck is the State Department?"

"Government. Could be CIA," Cerebro replied. "The agents don't actually say they're CIA."

"Guys," Rika said. "We need you to clear out. Something's

about to happen, and you can't be here when it does or you'll have to disappear."

Pepe and Cerebro looked a little nervous. Chino did not.

"She's a tiny little thing. What do you call it, again, Cerebro?"

"Petite," Cerebro supplied.

"Yeah..." Chino nodded. "She's too petite to be some badass spy or whatever. I think she's full of shit. Are you full of shit, *mami*?"

Rika flipped her arm over.

Holy hell. She was pulling up her sleeve, exposing her ridiculous cosplay wrist band. Once they saw her wearing a toy, our State Department charade would be over.

She pressed a button and the blade popped forward. Chino jerked back, then looked at his boys. "Where are your guns, *pendejos*?"

"You left yours in the car, so we left ours, too."

"Fuck!" Chino put his hands on his hips and shook his head in frustration. "You're supposed to watch my back at all times. I'm not going to carry if I'm here to talk to a chick! That would be disrespectful! But you two are supposed to be prepared...like Boy Scouts or something." He shook his head again, clearly feeling good help was hard to find.

Cerebro straightened to his full five-foot-six. "It's not like we got any training," he pointed out. "The 5-0 just picked *Ratón* and Joker up a few days ago." He lifted his hands, palms up. "It's our first week operating in this capacity."

No doubt, this Cerebro person had the best vocabulary of the three.

Regardless, I'd had enough. I stepped fully into the room. "Sorry we don't have time to help you train your colleagues. We have serious shit going on and we have to get you out of here in..." I looked at my phone. "...the next three minutes, one way or the other."

"Colleagues," Chino repeated as he turned to face me. "I like that. But what if we don't care about your shit?"

"You need to start caring because *I* didn't forget my gun," I lied. I flicked my head toward Rika. "And she can carve you up faster than you can say 'Edward Scissorhands'."

Chino glanced back at Rika before his eyes returned to me. I reached behind me as if about to pull a gun out of the back of my waistband.

"*Tus madres no tendrán cuerpos que enterrar*," Rika said.

Damn. I hated not knowing what was going on. Sounded like she said something about their mothers, which I hoped didn't piss them off more. But Chino's body language was less certain than before.

He shrugged. "Hey, it was no big deal, *mami*. I just wanted to get to know you a little better."

Rika's expression went cold. When she spoke, it was in a deep, husky voice I'd never heard. "I'm not a person you want to get to know," she said.

I'd always wondered about women who were attracted to violent criminals, yet hearing Rika talk like a mafioso both disturbed and aroused me.

Maybe I'd been too hard on those women.

Pepe murmured something in Chino's ear. I heard the word "*loca*" and almost chuckled.

*Loca* like a fox.

"Okay, whatever, we've got shit to do, too," Chino said. He took a couple of steps back as if he was concerned about turning his back on Rika.

She raised her wrist blade a bit more, aiming right between his eyes. "Now," she said.

Chino nearly stumbled on his third step back. He recovered, and, without using his hands, threw an audible kiss her way. "Okay, see you around, *chula*."

He turned and exited the house, giving me a half-hearted

chin lift. His boys hustled out behind him with a few more glances back at her, then me.

I turned as they walked by so they wouldn't see that I didn't have a gun.

Seconds later, we heard their car doors slam. Rika's lips turned up in a slow smile. Her body started shaking with laughter as her "killing" arm dropped and held onto her stomach. When she breathed in, she made the most adorable snorting sound.

Closing the distance, I wrapped my arms around her, relieved she was okay.

"Admit it," she said.

"Admit what?" I asked.

"Admit that my 'toys' are pretty awesome."

Oh. She was thinking about her fake wrist knife while I was imagining her snort-giggling in my bed, just before I slid into her and turned it into a pleasure sigh.

I loosened my grip on her. "You got lucky," I replied, genuinely annoyed.

The plastic blade pressed into my back, feeling sharper than I expected. "Admit it," she said again.

My annoyance melted away and I smiled down at her, loving this relaxed, playful side of her I hadn't gotten to see enough of. I let my hand slide south, applying enough pressure to her backside to press her hips into mine.

Her breathing quickened. I leaned over and touched my lips to hers. Having her in my bed had only made the craving for her worse. I hoped she'd follow me to my hotel after this.

I wrapped my tongue around hers as my hand slid under her shirt.

*Tap, tap, tap.*

We both jerked and turned toward the door.

*What the hell?*

Eli was standing there, watching us.

I was shocked to realize that with everything else going on, I'd practically forgotten the little creep existed. But he hadn't forgotten Rika and he didn't look happy. "Are you two really making out in the middle of a crime scene?" he asked.

Rika's hand darted up to wipe her mouth. "What are you doing here, Eli?"

"My job. Duh. I'm your stalker. Remember me?" He sounded as peeved as he looked.

"We have reason to be here," I said. "We're here on business. You need to get the hell out and find someone else to stalk."

"Rika?" he looked at her with puppy dog eyes. "Are you going to let this guy talk to me like that?"

She sighed. "Nick, Eli and I..."

Tell me she wasn't about to defend him.

"...well, we go way back. He's sort of a friend."

I let go of her completely so I wouldn't be tempted to shake her. "Really? Because he doesn't even introduce himself as a friend. He's made it clear he's stalking you. It's pretty damn stupid to treat him like anything but a stalker."

Clearly, that was the wrong thing to say. Rika's eyes turned murderous. "Did you..." she began.

"...just call her stupid?" Eli said as he took a step inside the room.

Great, now they were finishing each other's sentences. "If you don't respect her intelligence, maybe you're the one who needs to leave," he added.

The fireball of anger that had been rotating slowly in my gut burst open, the flames racing to my extremities.

Then, I did something a well-bred Texas boy never did. I got in his space, glared down at him, and stuck my finger in his face, close enough to make him go cross-eyed if he'd looked at it.

Instead, he was staring me straight in the eye. His irises were light brown, but his gaze was strangely menacing for a guy his size.

"You," I began.

Then, quick as lightning, he grabbed my extended arm, turned his back to me and managed to flip me over him onto the floor.

In the second I was on my back, several thoughts went through my mind, like, *How the hell did that tiny bastard take me down?* and *Damn! Rika is in a lot more danger than she thought she was,* followed by, *I'm gonna fucking kill him!"*

As I sat up, I saw the smug grin on his face. He reached out a hand to help, but, if I were religious, I would have sworn I saw the devil dancing in his eyes.

I grasped his forearm, and as I stood, I sucker-punched him with a left to the jaw.

Normally, I'm not a fan of the sucker punch. If it had just been me involved, I wouldn't have done it. But this guy had Rika convinced he was a mild-mannered admirer, instead of the crazy, dangerous weirdo he was.

By the time I was all the way up, he'd recovered. His leg came up, fast as lightning. I was barely able to tighten my abs before his foot caught me in the gut and knocked me back a few steps.

So, he was a lot stronger than he looked and possibly trained in martial arts. Who the hell was this guy?

His next move was a windmill kick and his foot came flying fast toward my head.

I didn't have martial arts training. Hell, we didn't even have soccer teams in Bolo when I was growing up, much less Tai Kwan Do.

I jerked back, which meant Eli's foot only connected with my nose instead of my jaw, and grabbed him by the heel, pulling up. His other foot left the floor and he landed on his face.

I fell onto him, my knee in his back, and grabbed his wrists, holding them tight. "Look, you little perv," I said through my teeth. "I don't care what kind of sick arrangement you think you have with Rika. It stops now."

Eli twisted his head back as far as he could. "Not your call," he said defiantly.

We both looked at Rika. I hadn't been aware of her while Eli and I were fighting, but her expression was more shocked than I'd ever seen it, which was weird considering the bizarre situations we'd been through together.

"Rika?" I said as she stared at me with what appeared to be concern. I felt warmth ooze over my upper lip and realized my nose must be bleeding. "Rika!" I tried again.

"I...um..." She seemed shaken. "Eli...we're working. You need to go."

Eli shrugged as best he could under the circumstances. "Okay, that's all I needed to hear. I'm out of here, if you can get the farm boy off my back." His voice was cool as a cucumber.

I let go of him and stood, half expecting him to start things up again, but he just straightened his khakis, tugged on the hem of his long-sleeved t-shirt and brushed himself off. "See you later, Rika."

"Yeah, okay," she said quietly as Eli sauntered out.

"Oh, my God! Is your nose broken?" Rika asked as she ran into the kitchen and came back with wet paper towels.

After seeing Eli turn into Bruce Lee before our eyes, she was worried about my nose?

I took the paper towels from her and tilted my head back to try to stop the bleeding. "It doesn't feel broken," I said. "But what about Eli?"

She still seemed dazed. "Um, he looked fine. Well, I think there was a bruise on his cheek from—"

I lowered my chin to look at her, the blood on the paper towels barely registering. "Rika!" I yelled. "I'm asking if you still believe Eli is as harmless as you thought he was."

"I..." She shrugged, but her eyes gave away her concern. "We're here to do a job now," she said. "We'll talk about it later."

"You can't avoid this forever," I said angrily. "There's a lot more crazy going on there than you want to believe. How did he know this address or that he'd find you here?" I rubbed the stinging sensation on the back of my neck. "Hell, maybe he found out about your first P.I. job and killed Grigore to make it more interesting for you!"

"That's ridiculous!"

"Is it?" I asked. "If you hadn't been here to see it, would you have believed he could take me down even once?"

She shook her head but didn't say anything.

"I'm telling you, Rika, when a guy that small can do what he just did, he's got a story to tell. Has he told you any of it?"

"I think he mentioned a trust fund, once. I just figured he was a rich nerd with nothing to do."

"Trust funds let you hire people to do things for you," I said. "But they don't turn you into Bruce Lee. What's this guy's hold on you?"

Her gaze shifted away from mine, then back, then away again. "Eli..." She seemed to be searching for words. After everything we'd been through together, everything we'd done together in my hotel room, everything I thought we felt for each other, why couldn't she just talk to me? "Eli was there before..." she began again, but her voice just drifted off to nothing.

She glanced around. "We don't have time for all that," she said.

"All what?"

"It's complicated. We'll talk about it later."

She turned around and headed for the bedroom.

# CHAPTER TWENTY-THREE

**Rika**

Okay, waaaay too much stuff had happened in the last few minutes and my brain was jumping all over the place. The Cholos had shown up right before Nick arrived despite my best efforts. Somebody really needed to invent cloaking devices for cars. We got rid of them, then, Eli and Nick got into a fight over me.

A fight!

Over *me*!

I'm not sure if there are women who dream of two men fighting over them. I'd never imagined it could happen to me. Regardless, there was nothing cool about it.

It was scary. I felt guilty. And confused, because I felt like I needed to defend both of them, but for different reasons.

Nick was, well, Nick. I never wanted to see his beautiful face bloodied, certainly not over me.

But Eli had started stalking me well before I reached my goal weight, at a time I constantly felt either invisible or overly visible to men. There was no in between back then. No man gave me the time of day.

Except Eli. I still don't know what he saw in me, but he stuck with me through thick and thin, literally.

Seeing his impressive fighting skills was a shock, but it didn't change what he'd done to buoy a chubby girl's fragile ego. His support had helped me stay on track.

He'd given me hope.

As I walked toward the twins' bedroom, my mind rewound to when Eli had first come in. Nick and I had been kissing. At the time, I got lost in the moment, but now I felt weird about the kiss.

I'd been humiliated that Nick seemed to forget me when the other woman called. Leaving his room, I'd finally understood the term "walk of shame."

And now what? He'd gotten what he wanted, then ignored me. I didn't really expect him to kiss me again. Now that he had, I was confused as to whether he wanted me for a relationship or only for friends-with-benefits booty calls.

"So, how did the gang-bangers end up over here?" Nick asked.

Oh, yeah. The cholos. I stopped next to the kitchen to answer him. "They pulled up next to me at a light. I drove around and lost them, but they must have found my car."

"And, since you came earlier than we planned, I wasn't here to protect you."

*Protect me.* The phrase sounded sexist to me. But did the fact that he kissed me a few minutes ago and still wanted to protect me mean what I wanted it to mean?

It hit me that, aside from Brandtt—who probably shouldn't count—I hadn't had a ton of exposure to men. I'd grown up with mostly women around me, especially after my dad was kept from me and Tía Margo divorced Uncle Kurt. Then, the only male around was their son Max, who was younger than his sister Sofia and I were.

Nick was looking at me like he expected a response.

"I was fine," I replied. "He didn't even bring his gun in."

In truth, I was not fine. Chino seemed to want to date me and that was every bit as scary to me as Chino wanting to kill me. For all I knew, he killed women who left him because they knew too much.

That's what mafiosos did on TV, but no one I knew associated with gangbangers. I had no way to predict their post-relationship demeanor.

"Rika..." Nick's voice, now soft and concerned, pulled me back to the conversation at hand. I looked into his eyes as he lifted my arm by the wrist. "They don't need guns. You're a tiny person."

Did he just call me a tiny person, again, after I asked him not to?

"Well, maybe I'm not as big as you are, but I've used my head and held my own with people twice my size. Your homeboy JimBob McGwire, for one."

"Rika..."

"And when my dad was missing—" I was mentally trying to arrange all the times I'd had unexpected success dealing with thugs and creeps. Nick had saved my ass a few times, but I'd saved his, too, whether he wanted to admit it or not.

"I know, Rika. No one has more respect for what you're able to do with that brain of yours, and sometimes this little body..." He put his hands on my hips. "But you can't deny that you're a tiny person."

*Grrrrrr!* There was that word again! And as he said it, he squeezed my waist in with both hands until his thumbs and fingers touched each other. No one had done this to me before, and it was confusing to be ten pounds over my ideal weight and still be thin enough for Nick to play ring-around-my-tummy.

Hm... he did have really large hands, though.

Regardless, I didn't want to think of myself as a tiny person. Terrible things could happen to people who weren't strong enough to defend themselves.

I turned back toward the bedroom as a photo of my mom flashed in my head. That's how I remembered her face, now, from family photos. Sometimes it felt like that was the worst part of it —no longer being able to see her face in my own memories of her.

People had described my mother as "petite." My father even called her the Tiny Tornado because she was small but lively.

What I remembered most, though, was her calm patience with me. My earliest memories are of being snuggled up in my mom's lap or in her bed. I didn't want to be next to her. I wanted to be on her.

She was my happy place. She didn't seem tiny to me then. She seemed warm and safe.

God, I missed her. There were so many times I wanted advice. My mother's advice.

I appreciated the advice from my Tía Margo, Tía Madi, and my grandmother, but my mother was her own person and I always wondered if her advice would be different.

I don't know, maybe if she'd lived, I would have taken her for granted like most kids did with their moms. Maybe I would have even kept things from her and gone to Tía Madi for advice as Sofia often did.

I would've liked to have had the option, though.

Before tears could form in my eyes, I turned my sadness into anger. At Nick. What right did he have to tell me what to do?

"Rika—" he prodded.

I whirled and he almost ran into me. "Look, Nick," I said. "I'm trying to conduct business here. We have a paying client. If you have other matters you want to discuss as my business partner, set up a meeting and I'll be there."

Nick's eyebrows flipped up in surprise, then down again. Damn it! Why wasn't he ugly when he scowled?

"Did you just tell me to make an appointment?" he asked.

"I think my exact words were 'set up a meeting'." I spun back around and strode into the bedroom as Nick gave an angry snort.

I made a mental note to learn not to let Nick derail me while I was working. I pushed the drama into a corner of my mind and focused on the bedroom.

The first thing I noticed was how much of the clutter was now missing. Tools, phones, a turntable I remembered on the floor, computer towers—maybe the cops thought they'd find something on those, but I was pretty sure they were just here to be fixed like most other things in the house.

When I glanced over to check on Nick, he was bent over, scanning the windowsills, probably looking for signs of forced entry.

I was pretty sure the cops were done collecting prints, but just in case, I took the two latex gloves I'd brought with me out of my jeans pocket and put them on. I pulled Grigore's nightstand drawer open, hoping to find one of those, "If something happens to me, so-and-so did it," notes. Sure, that would be a little too easy, but I was eager to close a case and have legit money in the account that wasn't from Nick. Until that happened, I couldn't relax about our business relationship, much less our personal one.

The drawer was empty. If there had been anything here, the cops already took it.

I scanned what was left of the bed. The sheets were gone and I could see various places where samples had been clipped from the mattress. It was an old one. I wondered if the forensics lab was having to meticulously sort out the old stains from the new.

The elderly lamp that had been on Grigore's side of the bed was gone. The one on Teodor's side was still there.

I grabbed the stem of the lamp and turned it over.

*Aha!* Just as I suspected. Whoever had searched this room hadn't done a perfect job.

Cops, crime scene investigators, and crime labs were usually slammed with work in a city the size of Los Angeles.

I peeled the folded scrap of thin paper from the bottom of the lamp.

"Got anything?" Nick asked. He was kneeling on the floor looking at a spot on the baseboard.

I slipped my nail in and opened the scrap, realizing it was just one of those tiny receipts you get from a convenience store. Old and unreadable.

It wasn't a hidden, overlooked clue. It had probably slid underneath the lamp on its own.

I sighed. "Not so far," I said. "You?"

"No. I thought these spatters..." He pointed at some tiny dots on the wall, "...might be dried blood. But they smell more like chocolate."

"Why would there be chocolate spatter in the bedroom?" I asked.

Nick shrugged. "We don't know what kind of stuff Teodor and Erissa were into."

"But don't people do that kind of thing because they want to feel like they're being kinky?" I asked. "She was already doing the nasty with a man who had another man attached to him! That's got to feel kinkier than covering a guy in chocolate."

"Maybe it wasn't about being kinky," Nick said. "Sometimes you just do things 'cause they're fun."

Suddenly, I was imagining Nick, lying naked on his hotel sheets as I drizzled chocolate syrup down his chest and over his— "

Our eyes met and I saw him looking at me the way I was probably looking at him, his eyes scanning my torso, then pausing. Was he imagining sucking chocolate syrup from my belly button?

Or lower? *Holy mother of Zeus!*

Turning away from Nick, I went around the foot of the bed to get to Grigore's side.

I hoisted up the mattress. If anything had been there, it wasn't anymore. I checked under the bed, but there was nothing.

Hm, where might the cops have overlooked?

I checked the space between the mattress and the old wood

headboard and noticed the box spring underneath was crammed tightly against it. "Nick, could you give me a hand?" I asked. "I'm trying to pull the bottom mattress away from the headboard."

"Sure," Nick said. It only took him a couple of tugs to move the entire mattress set.

"Thanks," I forced myself to say. I hated not being strong enough to do for myself and kind of hated that he could move them that easily.

Nick caught the look and smirked. "You're the brains and I'm the brawn, remember?"

I ignored him and stuck my head in the space he'd made.

*Aha!* Just as I'd hoped, there was a little space between the top end of the box spring mattress and the iron bed frame. And caught in that space was a torn scrap of light blue paper. I pulled it out and examined it. It wasn't any sort of writing paper or wrapping paper. But there was something vaguely familiar about it.

Nick was kneeling on the floor. "A few things fell out when we moved the mattresses," he said.

I perked up and looked to see what he was holding.

Two triple A batteries. One tiny screwdriver. One small tube of glue that claimed it was good for plastics and metal and guaranteed to be waterproof.

Nothing out of the ordinary for the twins.

Then, I realized Nick was holding them all in gloved hands.

"Where'd you get the gloves?" I asked.

"I passed a medical supply store the other day and figured I should stock up, now that I'm a private investigator."

The words swung through my heart like a trapeze artist, ending with a little flip.

No matter how much he annoyed me at times, I was worried every day that Nick would decide none of this was for him and take off. Him taking the initiative to buy the gloves specifically for our work made me feel a smidge better.

I pulled a folded Ziploc bag out of my back pocket and

dropped the paper scrap in there with the other stuff. After they were in plastic, we stared at them for several seconds.

A screwdriver too big to use on glasses, but too small for most other things. Two triple A "bunny" batteries, as Sofia used to call Energizers. A tube of Sea-ment brand multi-purpose glue. And the paper that wasn't quite paper, which was torn all the way around, as if ripped from the middle of something.

"I don't think we've got much of anything," Nick said. "It's all the kind of stuff you'd find around anyone's house or in a tool chest. These guys treated the whole house like it was a tool chest."

"You don't think that piece of paper means anything?" I asked.

He shook his head. "Like what? Everybody has little scraps of paper around their house."

"I know but..." I had to let the sentence taper off. I didn't have anything but a feeling.

"Rika..." Nick said. I met his gaze. "Just because the answer to Avery Cook's murder was on a scrap of paper doesn't mean that's how all your cases will be solved."

*Really?* Did he really just say something that insulting to me? Of course, I knew not all my cases would be solved the same way. I wasn't an idiot! Sheesh!

I was trying to come up with an equally rude response when I looked down the hall and saw Erissa in the living room.

This was as good a time as any to have another conversation with her. "Erissa," I said as I strode toward her.

"Oh, hi, Rika." She glanced around. "This place actually looks better than it did before cops came. My side is trashed."

"They searched your house?" Nick asked.

"Yeah. They took my computer, too," she said with mild annoyance. "They couldn't tell me when I'd get it back and I can't live without a laptop, so I had to buy a new one."

If she was involved in the murder, it certainly didn't show.

Even if she wasn't guilty, though, she could still end up in jail if only because there was no other viable suspect, except maybe Teodor, and if he was arrested, she might still be, as an accessory.

"Did they question you?" I asked, knowing they must have.

"Yeah, for like three hours before I told them if I wasn't under arrest, I was leaving and they could talk to my attorney from now on." She shrugged. "I know Teodor wants me to help find his brother's killer, but I'm not getting railroaded to prison for something I didn't do."

I could relate to that. I'd be in prison somewhere in Texas if I hadn't taken matters into my own hands.

"We were told they fixed things," Nick said. "Did they have a lot of customers?"

"They did make extra money repairing things," she replied. "They were pretty good at fixing just about anything. I had them doing work around the duplex. Fixed the pipes under the sink in the bathroom and installed new doorknobs, but they could even repair computers. For that, they ran an ad online somewhere. I know they had a few customers, but, honestly, it wasn't something I was interested in, so I don't know how many different customers they had. Occasionally, I saw someone dropping stuff off or picking it up, but I didn't pay much attention."

Nick glanced around. His eye caught on something and held, but, when I followed his line of sight, all I saw was Grigore's empty nightstand. "There was a woman's hair doodad here the first time we came in," he said. "I noticed it coming through the door, before we realized the place wasn't empty." This was news to me. Maybe it just came to him, now that we were in the room again. "One of those claw things. Do you think it belonged to the person Teodor was having the affair with?"

"No. If you mean the black one, that was mine. Besides, I never thought it was any particular woman. Teodor was just acting strange towards me. I guess I got paranoid. Anyway, it was Grigore who always tried to turn him against me, so I'm not worried about that anymore."

Strange that she was worried enough about Teodor's faithfulness to hire a private investigator, but now she was blowing it off like it was nothing. One might say "suspicious," even.

I looked her in the eye, with what I hoped was a serious businessperson expression. "Erissa, if you want us to continue working this case, we're going to need the rest of that retainer."

# CHAPTER TWENTY-FOUR

**Rika**

"I have a bad feeling about getting paid for this job," I said as we walked out the door. I'd said it before, but I felt it was worth repeating.

We'd spent more time searching after Erissa left but didn't find anything else that looked like a clue.

The client was supposed to pay for my time, regardless of the result. However, even though Erissa appeared to have the money, something about her just felt sketchy. I didn't blame the cops for thinking she was a murderer.

"Don't worry about it," Nick replied as he shut the front door. "We'll chalk it up to on-the-job training."

I hated it when he was so cavalier about money! "It's a business," I said. "We're supposed to get paid."

Nick shrugged as if it was no skin off his nose either way, which only served to annoy me more. "Do you still think she might be involved in the murder?" he asked.

We were only standing a few feet apart, close enough that I had to look up into his face. His eyes appeared black on the duplex's dark porch, but I could still make out his expression.

The one that said he was genuinely interested in what I had to say, which was one level away from the warm, appreciative look he gave me when I surprised him with my knowledge of random things.

Oh, my God! That's how he'd gotten me to fall for him! He'd given me that same look at the police station in Bolo and at least a couple of times a day, every day that I stayed with him. It always felt like something special, just for me.

But what if it wasn't just for me? What if he'd learned in high school—no this was Nick we were talking about. Okay, what if he learned in elementary school that gazing into a girl's eyes with interest got him wherever he wanted to go with said girl?

As for me falling for a guy based on a look...

I sighed, not wanting to acknowledge the voice in the back of my mind.

*What if you're more damaged than you thought? What if losing your dad from your life that young made you desperate for validation from men?*

I'd focused so much on the weight issues I associated with my mom's death that it hadn't occurred to me to consider what the absence of my male parent might have done to my psyche. Just because you don't think you've been scarred in a certain way doesn't mean you haven't. There were thousands of people all over the country making a living off the fact that people didn't always understand their own motivations, my Tía Margo being one of them.

"Rika?"

How long had I been staring up into Nick's eyes?

"What are you thinking about?" he asked.

"I was thinking about the question you asked me," I lied. "And the answer is, 'I don't know'. Erissa's weird in a way I can't put my finger on. She feels sketchy. But a lot of people are weird and seem sketchy until you get to know them. Regardless, it's unusual for a person who's, like, thirty years old to have been this close to two murders."

"You're younger than that and have been close to three," Nick said, being the devil's advocate, as usual. "Three that I know of, that is."

"Ha...ha," I replied sarcastically. I didn't correct him, though I was painfully aware that I'd been close to four murders if we were counting from birth.

I glanced at my car. I always hated to leave Nick, even when he was annoying me, but we probably shouldn't be hanging around outside the crime scene.

I thought I'd felt awkward around Nick before, but now that we'd been to bed together, it was worse. At least for me. "Well, I'd better—" I began.

Nick interrupted. "You seem tense," he said. "Why don't you follow me to my hotel and let me take care of that?"

A warm thrill wiggled through me at his indecent proposal, but a second later it turned cold and not so thrilling as my mind replayed his words.

There was nothing romantic in them. I needed to hear something from Nick that would convince me I could be enough for him, long-term.

"I love you," would have been nice, especially after the deed was done. But almost anything would have been better than, "I need to take this," followed by him getting on a call from a female he obviously had a very special relationship with.

And now, all he was offering was stress relief, which would be great if I were a person who could just do it and not get more emotionally attached. But I wasn't that person, at least not where Nick was concerned.

"Rika?"

My eyes had drifted to the middle of his chest. I lifted them to meet his gaze. He was so fucking beautiful, I wanted to go back to his room and make love to him until I died from exhaustion.

The problem was that I likely wouldn't die from it. I'd have to live on to watch Nick get over the novelty of me and fall back into his normal routine of sleeping with, then marrying, tall blonde pageant girls.

My heart sunk at the thought.

If Nick would just say *something* to make me believe that he believed our relationship could go somewhere, I'd risk it. I'd still probably end up hurt, but there's no way I could resist Nick telling me he loved me.

He reached out, running a finger down a strand of my hair, sliding over my temple, my cheek, my jaw... "It was fun last time." One side of his lips lifted in a sexy half-smirk. "I think we could do better though."

I sighed. As hot as he was, all he was offering me was stress relief and fun. And, yeah, it would be great, but what would happen afterward? Would he get another "phone call" to let me know it was time to leave?

That walk—and ride—of shame I did last time was as humiliating as it was disappointing.

Not heart*breaking*, exactly. That was too melodramatic. But I was sure my heart had cracked a little.

Maybe the truth was that I needed more from a man than Nick was willing to give. I needed someone that made me feel more confident and secure. There were times when Nick did that for me, but after our first time together, when I needed it the most, I got zilch.

Appreciative looks only took a girl so far.

"I can't," I said.

Nick's head tilted slightly, his expression hardening. "Do you have other plans?" he asked in an oddly formal voice.

Was he jealous? Or just pissed that he couldn't get easy sex from the woman at hand?

That was pure laziness. There were plenty of dating apps, and I was sure no one would ever swipe left on Nick Owen.

Then I remembered he didn't have to bother swiping. Grace had made it crystal clear she was more than interested. Nick wouldn't even need to take her to dinner.

The mental picture incited panic. My heart started beating so fast, I thought it would burst through my chest cavity.

A part of me wanted to go with him just so another woman couldn't have him tonight. But that was no reason to go home with a guy, especially a guy who could break your heart.

Nick was *so* confusing!

The burly moving men, who'd lived inside me for years, got to work as they always had, pushing my feelings down, reminding me that the best cure for stress-nausea was chocolate.

Seriously. It worked for me every time. I wasn't sure why doctors didn't prescribe it.

"I promised I'd help Lita," I blurted out. I figured nobody could challenge a girl needing to help her grandmother.

"Really?" Nick sounded surprised. "Help her with what?"

Correction: Nobody but a lawyer could challenge a girl needing to help her grandmother.

I racked my brain, trying to think of something I could help Lita with. She was always cooking, but there's no way Nick would believe she needed my help with that. I started to say I had to help her take her folding chairs to the church, but Nick might offer his truck for the non-existent errand. Besides, it would be nearly ten o'clock when I got home. Who would need to take chairs to a church that late at night?

Then, it came to me, "Her computer!" I said, a wee bit too excited about my lie. "I need to get home and get her computer from her room before she goes to sleep. It's been acting glitchy. I promised I'd rebuild it for her."

"Rebuild it?"

"Back everything up, install a new operating system, re-install her programs," I explained. "Clean it up, so she can start fresh."

Nick didn't say anything right away. He watched my face, no doubt looking for some sort of tell that I was making this up.

No more than five seconds into it, I wanted to blurt out the truth. That my grandmother's laptop was fine. That I wanted to be with him, but I was afraid because I didn't think I could stand to lose one more person from my life. That I loved him and could he please state his intentions so I could breathe again?

I wanted to, but I didn't say any of it.

"Okay," Nick said. "I'll see you tomorrow." He kissed my forehead, which was kind of a disappointment, even though I'd just turned him down for more. He watched me walk to my car and didn't get into his truck until I was inside with the doors locked and the motor running.

I sucked in a shaky breath and let out a long slow sigh.

And, I swear, I wasn't sure if it was from relief or disappointment.

*If only I could just live one day as a normal person, maybe I'd see everything more clearly...*

*If only...*

～

**Nick**

The next morning, I picked Rika up and we headed to the medical examiner's office where her friend was working.

I turned to check out the t-shirt she was wearing as had become my habit since I'd come to L.A. This one was bright red and depicted all the Marvel superheroes as toddlers. The images rested on her breasts and I had a hard time prying my eyes off them.

Rika, however, was already staring into her phone like I didn't exist.

I'd texted to let her know I was outside her grandmother's. She'd said she'd be right out, and now, nothing. She hadn't even said anything when she opened the door. She just climbed into my truck and now seemed engrossed in whatever she was reading on the screen.

I'd honestly thought that once we'd made love, that would be it. We'd work together during the day and go home together at night.

Instead, she'd taken off from the hotel before I could get off the phone. And after that, her weirdness with me had gotten even weirder. When I kissed her at the crime scene, she'd kissed me back. But when we left, she wouldn't come home with me.

I'd accepted her excuse at the time, but the more I thought about it, the more it seemed like a lie.

I pulled into the lot and parked. *Do you know for sure she didn't promise to help her grandma?* the hopeful part of my mind asked. Sometimes people have obligations. It was unreasonable to expect her to jump in bed with me at a moment's notice, even if that's what all the others had done.

Rika was special, therefore worth the extra trouble.

To test the temperature of the water today, I reached over, caressing her cheek with my knuckles. She shivered with pleasure. I know she did. I felt it.

But instead of turning to me for a kiss, she unbuckled her seatbelt and opened her door without making eye contact. My offending hand closed into a fist, embarrassed it had made an unwanted advance.

Trying to date Rika Martín was quite the humbling experience.

When we got out of the truck, she seemed to know where she was going. I followed her, both of us as silent as I expected the corpses inside to be.

I followed her past the front of the building. We were about to go around the side when I thought I saw movement out of the corner of my eye. My brain wrote it off as an optical illusion.

Rika stopped walking. "Hi, Eli," she said. "Good job with the camo."

I stopped and looked where she was looking, but it took a beat for my mind to process what I was seeing.

Eli's entire body was painted to look like an exterior wall.

I glanced at the one behind him.

Not just any wall. He'd painted himself to look exactly like the piece of wall he was standing in front of—exact color of reddish bricks on the top, exact color of concrete on the bottom. He'd even included the tiny cracks in the clay.

"You like it?" he asked Rika, clearly eager to impress her. When he blinked, I noticed he'd painted his eyelids.

And she thought Erissa was sketchy? This guy was sketchy as hell! Why was Rika okay with this?

*Pot meet kettle.*

Okay, when I met Rika, I also had too much time on my hands, but I didn't follow her around like a demented puppy. I came to L.A. half a year later because she called and asked for help. I stayed in L.A. because she asked me to be her partner.

"It's super cool," Rika said to Eli. "And it will go great with that superpower you're hoping for."

She was encouraging him again! What the hell was wrong with her?

Rika had turned to face Eli. I moved in next to her. Call me crazy, but I wasn't comfortable with her standing three feet away from her self-described stalker.

"What superpower is that?" I asked, attempting to gain more insight into the creep.

"We've been calling it 'the power of self-inanimation'," Rika said with a chuckle.

She and Eli smiled at each other like besties with an inside joke.

A surge of acid jealousy burned through me at the idea that this weirdo probably knew Rika better than I did. My time with her could be measured in weeks, months at the most. Eli had apparently known her for years.

"Self-inanimation?" I repeated.

Eli's attention shifted to me reluctantly. "Like in movies where characters can jump and freeze in mid-air." His gaze went right back to Rika. "It's just our word for it." He'd emphasized the word "our."

"Doesn't seem like much of a superpower to me." I hated the petulant tone in my voice. Like a jealous teenager.

*Get your shit together, Owen.*

Rika and Eli were laughing together, at me, I guess, while her eyes sparkled at him.

I took in a deep breath, trying to ease the pain of the invisible blade she'd plunged into my chest.

"That's what we were saying," Rika replied. "But if you combine it with his new ability to blend into his surroundings, it could be awesome."

"That's exactly what I was thinking!" Eli said. He lifted his hand and Rika gave him a high five.

Was this new? Them touching each other? Was Eli finding ways to get closer to her, inch by inch?

Regardless, I'd had enough. "As intriguing as all this is..." I swept my eyes over Eli dismissively, "we have to get going."

I took Rika's elbow and nudged it forward. She resisted for long enough to say, "See you later, Eli," then started walking.

Her lack of concern about this nut was exasperating. "'See you later, Eli'?" I repeated. "You basically invited him to keep this up. That's got to be the dumbest thing a woman's ever said to her stalker!"

Rika's gaze lifted to meet mine, then jerked away. In the brief time our eyes met, I'd seen the hurt in hers.

*Damn.* I usually loved her mind and all its brilliant and quirky ideas. I'd told her she was smart more than once. I guess my exact words were "pretty smart for a hot chick."

Those words had come out of my mouth during our first real conversation because, for an instant, I, Nick Owen, had felt intimidated. It was the first time I'd ever worried that a woman might be out of my league in some way.

Then, I'd remembered she was my client and out of bounds in every way.

And now that she wasn't out of bounds and we'd finally made progress in our relationship, I'd called her stupid. But damn it, it was stupid to let your stalker think he had a chance with you!

She hadn't replied to my comment, but I didn't think I'd been doing her any favors by letting this go the other times. "Why do you do that with him?" I asked.

"What?" She still wasn't looking at me. Regret washed over me. I didn't want Rika angry with me. But I needed her safe.

"Why do you encourage him? That's a dangerous game to play."

She rolled her eyes in my direction. "Eli is, like, my size," she said. "He's harmless."

"Harmless?" I threw my hands out and shook my head in disbelief. "Have you forgotten about last night? Not to mention the peeping Tom he captured when we were dealing with the Microtologists. The guy was twice his size."

"Look," Rika said as she made a slicing gesture in the air with one hand as if by "look" she meant, "cut it out." "I've known Eli for years. He's been nothing but nice to me. He's the only one who liked me, even before—" She pressed her lips shut as if she was about to reveal a carefully guarded secret.

"Before...?" I prompted. She'd said almost exactly the same thing previously. Why did she always stop herself from coming clean with me?

Instead of answering, she looked behind us, then said, "Come on, we have to go this way." She slipped around the next corner to the back of the building and I followed her.

"This isn't the entrance," I pointed out.

"We're not going to the main entrance," she replied. "And this is *an* entrance."

What it was, was a solid metal door next to a pile of discarded boxes.

Rika pulled her phone from her pocket and typed into it.

So, we weren't going to be logged in anywhere as visitors.

I wasn't a person who like the idea of sneaking around. Made me feel too much like an Eli.

*Wait a minute...* "Rika, how did Eli know we'd be here today?"

"What?" she said as she looked up from her phone.

"You only found out last night that we could come to the M.E.'s office today. How did Eli know where to show up this morning...and last night, for that matter?"

That got her attention. Her eyes were unfocused, but I could practically see the wheels turning in her head. "He could have a tracking device on my—" She stopped herself, realizing that wasn't a viable explanation.

"Yesterday you were in your car, but today we're in my truck," I began. "Even if he had tracking devices on both and followed us, that wouldn't explain how he had enough time to paint himself to match the building."

Rika frowned. "He would have to have known ahead of time, around the same time we found out, so he could go over, take photos of the wall, and paint hims—"

The door was pushed open by a lovely young woman with soft brown skin and brown eyes that twinkled mischievously. She wore a sea green hijab over her hair, a long black skirt and a bright pink t-shirt that read "Geek is the New Chic."

"Rika!" She gave her an enthusiastic hug. "Hi Nick," she said as if she knew me. "I'm Najila."

I lifted my chin at her, a little disappointed that all I'd gotten was a wave.

She led us through a hall into a room full of metal drawers, a couple of desks, and a bunch of file cabinets. We've only got twenty minutes or so," she said. "My boss prefers to pick up lunch and bring it back here to eat with his friends." She gestured toward the drawers.

"That's not creepy at all," Rika said sarcastically.

"I know," Najila said. "He wanted me to do the same thing, but I told him I'll assist him on any case, but I want to have my meals—and my social life—with the living."

"Seems reasonable," I replied.

She smiled at me and made me wonder why I was exclusively into blue-eyed blondes for so long. She led us over to the wall of drawers.

"I'm glad I took the internship. It's made me realize I don't want to do this for a living."

"Too gross for you?" Rika asked.

"No, I don't mind the bodies or the autopsies. It just gets so freaking quiet sometimes. I'm an extrovert. I need a job with livelier clientele." She pulled out a drawer. "Here he is," she said. "Grigore Vatamanu...or what's left of him."

# CHAPTER TWENTY-FIVE

**Nick**

Grigore had developed a grayish pallor since we saw him last. He had Frankenstein seams zigzagging down one side from the rushed separation. The screwdriver was gone and only a hole in his eyelid was left to tell the tale.

"I didn't see him up close like this before," Rika said solemnly.

"Oh, and I guess he still had the screwdriver in his eye when you found him," Najila added. "The eyeball was destroyed. That thing went straight through to his brain."

It made sense that, if the wound was fatal, the screwdriver had gone all the way through, but hearing it stated outright while staring at Grigore this close was jarring.

"Do you know the angle of trajectory?" Rika asked.

Damn, she was impressive. I thought I was the more seasoned of the two of us from the murder trials I'd been involved in. As it turned out, graphic pictures didn't bother me that much, but looking at Grigore's chopped off body made all the questions I had in mind disintegrate. Not that I'd ever tell Rika that. She seemed to be completely focused on the investigation.

Najila walked over to the file cabinet and plucked the file

from the top. The three of us met at the desk. She opened it and we all peered down at it.

"Looks like it went straight in," she said.

Rika and I looked at each other. I knew she was wondering, like I was, if it was possible for Teodor to lift his arm high enough to plunge a screwdriver straight into his brother's eye.

If this were a crime of passion while they were in the middle of an argument, one would expect the screwdriver trajectory to be at an angle, considering that Teodor would have been lying next to the brother he was attached to.

"Have you heard if there are fingerprints?" Najila asked.

"No fingerprints," Rika said. "According to Juli—" She stopped herself, likely realizing she was about to give her informant's name away. "According to my source, it was wiped."

"Oh my God! Is Julian Suriano your source?" Najila gushed. "I saw him talking to you before I knew who you were, when I was taking a course at the community college. I had a major crush on him that semester. Are you seeing him?"

Was she *seeing* him? Why would Najila ask such a thing when I was the one standing here with Rika?

I tried to keep my face impassive as I processed what this meant. Najila knew my name which means Rika had mentioned me, but Najila's question meant Rika had not mentioned that we were seeing each other. She didn't even hint to her girl buddy that she was interested in me that way?

Maybe that's why people kept coming on to us in front of each other. Rika was giving off no *I'm with him* vibes whatsoever.

Meanwhile, I was finding her behavior more and more insulting.

*Is she ashamed of you?*

Where did that come from? I'd never in my life considered such an idea. I'd been popular with girls since I could remember. I was well-educated and could hold conversations on a myriad of topics.

I looked at Najila's shirt again. Was Rika embarrassed that I wasn't smart in the *read Wikipedia for fun* way she, and, probably, Najila were?

Or maybe it was something else. Rika's ex-boyfriend was an actor and this was Los Angeles. A working actor was probably at the top of the dating heap here. Maybe she was embarrassed because dating me would be a comedown after flouncing around L.A. and New York with—what was his name?

*Brandtt. With two T's.*

"Nope." Rika said casually. "Julian's just a friend. Anything else of interest?"

"Indeed!" Najila gestured toward a manila folder as if it were a game show prize. "Check these out." She pulled pictures from the file and laid them out on the desk. "They look like defensive wounds. This one at the base of the index finger matches up perfectly with the shape of the business end of the screwdriver."

"So, Grigore was awake," Rika seemed to be thinking aloud. "Or he woke up right before the attacker struck."

"That's what I would guess," Najila replied. "Looks to me as if, the first time, the killer got the hand instead of the eye. Then, on the next try..." She pulled out another picture with a closeup of Grigore's left palm.

"Oh, my God!" Rika cried.

I stared at the photo, trying to figure out what I was seeing. There were straight lines going one way and other straight lines perpendicular to them. Much of the palm was bruised.

"Do you know what it is?" Rika asked.

"The M.E. won't say in his report, of course, because he doesn't speculate. Plus, we can't be sure about what the rest of it looks like. The design seems to continue off the hand. But with the way the indentions are positioned, the only thing I've come up with so far is that it's a—"

"Crucifix," Rika finished.

"Hey, great minds!" Najila cried. "Look at the more organic-shaped depressions. They're deeper, which means the object had a 3-D effect happening."

Rika stared at the photo for several seconds. "Like Jesus on the cross... maybe."

"And check this out." Najila quickly cleared the top of the desk and lay down on it, face up. "Come at me," she said to Rika.

Without hesitation, Rika lifted her fist in the air as if holding the weapon and lowered it to directly over Najila's eye.

Meanwhile, Najila threw her palm up in defense and it landed on Rika's chest.

I tried to reconstruct the crime in my mind. "So, you think Grigore fended off the first attempt—probably from someone standing to his left since they wouldn't have been able to reach across the bed over his brother—and got the hand injury, then tried to defend against the second attempt by shoving his palm against the perpetrator's chest, which had this cross-like thing on it, causing an imprint." I summed up.

Najila got up shaking her head. "We can't be sure how many attempts were made," she pointed out. "But it looks like there were at least two."

"What's the actual size of this imprint?" I asked.

"Come see for yourself. It's not as clear as it was right after he came in, but you can still see the outline."

We went back to the body and studied the imprint. It was about an inch and a half wide across his palm, and the bottom of the "cross" went down for about an inch from the crossbar. We had no way of knowing what was at the top of the item.

"Could he have gotten that imprint in some other way that had nothing to do with the murder?" I asked.

"Anything's possible," Najila said. "But it took a lot of force to make this impression. Otherwise, the skin would have plumped back out immediately."

My gut did a slow roll at the idea that Grigore, incapacitated by his sleeping brother, awoke just before the murder and tried to fight for his life.

I kept staring at the imprint but couldn't be sure what it was. The lines and impressions weren't that clear, on Grigore or the photo. "If there was that much force involved, was there any transfer from the object to Grigore's hand?"

"No DNA. No particles of metal or wood. No paint, even though there had to have been force involved in the victim's struggle to stay alive." Najila replied. "But sometimes there's just no transfer detectable."

Rika was examining the body, adjusting the angle of hers in relation to it. "Do you mind if I..." She gestured toward Grigore's hand.

Najila pulled gloves from a dispenser and handed them to Rika. "Knock yourself out."

"Nick, would you say he's lying at about the same height he was on his bed?"

I stepped back and assessed the distance from the floor to Grigore's drawer. "Yeah, I think that's about right."

Rika planted her feet solidly next to Grigore's torso, facing him. "Okay, assuming I had a few seconds before he woke up and could choose, this is where I'd stand."

Should it bother me that the woman I wanted to be with twenty-four-seven could put herself in the mind of a murderer this easily?

She lifted Grigore's left hand, pulling up his very stiff arm, positioning it as it would have been if he was thrusting it up, trying to hold someone away from him. His hand hit her at the neck.

A creepy crawler moved down my spine at seeing that pale, lifeless hand at her throat. If anything could make me start having zombie nightmares, this was it.

She tried positioning herself differently, but any way that made sense turned out the same.

"Nick, could you come over here?"

*Who me?* I wanted to say. But I wasn't about to beg off. It was like when Megan or BreeAnne saw a spider and wanted me to kill it.

Did I like to get near spiders?

No. They creeped me the hell out. When I saw a spider walking along the floor, it might as well have been crawling on my back. That's how much I hated spiders.

Would I say that to a woman?

Not in a million years.

Men were supposed to be the hunters, even if we'd been reduced to hunting down the occasional bug that crawled under the bed.

More than once, my drama queen ex, BreeAnne, ended up standing on furniture that wasn't meant to be stood on while she screamed like she was the victim in a horror movie. In between screams, she yelled, "Kill it! Kill it! Kill it!"

One day in the living room, the spider was crawling fast and I didn't have anything to hit it with. I ended up smashing it with my bare palm. For two weeks, I had nightmares about that spider —except, in the nightmare, it was bigger than I was—but I didn't tell anyone about it, not even my then-wife.

So, just as I'd sucked it up for my wives, and before that, my mom, I sucked it up for Rika.

I moved around the table and stood where she'd been standing. She lifted Grigore's hand and stretched his arm out toward me as if the corpse was trying to protect itself a few days too late. His hand landed on my upper abs.

"Hm..." Najila said. "Is there such a thing as a crucifix belt buckle?" That was an exaggeration. Grigore's hand hadn't hit me that low, but I could see where she was going with this.

Rika set Grigore's hand down gently, then said, "It doesn't matter. No one trying to defend themselves against a screwdriver to the eye is going to reach out toward their potential killer's waist. You'd put your hand up and brace on their chest." She thought for a moment. "If it were me, and the killer was on the left, I'd try to get my right arm around to help hold him back, then grab his screwdriver arm with my left."

"Sure, but, by the look of the stitches, this guy wouldn't have been able to turn enough to get his right arm around because his brother was attached along his right side," Najila said. "Plus, when we examined him, we realized he had limited range of motion with his right arm. He had old stress fractures as well as more recent injuries I wouldn't have expected from a conjoined twin."

"He and his twin were acrobats...or contortionists or something," I said. "Circus performers."

"That would explain them," she replied.

"So, he only had one hand to defend himself with," Rika recapped. "And assuming he tried to lock his elbow and brace against his assailant's chest, and the object was hanging around the assailant's neck, the killer is probably taller than me, but shorter than Nick."

Najila shrugged and wobbled her head back and forth. "It was a pretty unscientific experiment, but probably..."

"That's most people," I said.

Rika's mind seemed to be busy elsewhere. She looked up from the corpse. "What?"

"Most people are taller than you but shorter than me."

Her gaze shot up to mine, her eyebrows pressed together like she was angry. She sucked in her cheeks, then inhaled a slow breath as if trying to exercise patience. "Good point, Nick," she said in a patronizing tone. "But, more importantly, what the evidence here shows us is that it's even more unlikely that Teodor could have done this to his brother in the heat of passion." She pulled off her gloves and threw them in the trash.

"Yeah, that's pretty much impossible," Najila said. "Even if

Grigore's twin were wearing a crucifix, the angles would be all wrong for the defensive wound and the screwdriver."

"It means he probably didn't wield the screwdriver," I pointed out. "It doesn't mean he wasn't involved." A new question occurred to me. "If Grigore was awake during the attack, why would his eye be closed when the screwdriver went through it?" I asked Najila.

Rika swung her arm up, thrusting her index finger through the air toward my left eye. My eyes shut automatically before I felt the touch on my eyelid. "Normal human reflexes," she said in a superior tone.

This both embarrassed me, because I didn't think of it, and turned me on.

On impulse, I grabbed her retreating finger and put the tip between my teeth.

Rika's eyes flashed angrily at me, which only made her sexier. Damn, I needed to get her back to my hotel.

Najila laughed, then glanced at the clock on the wall, reminding us our time here was limited.

"We'll get going," Rika said. "Thanks, Naji." The two women hugged. The idea flew through my head that I wouldn't mind being the meat in that sandwich, but I squelched it fast, not wanting Rika to see any hint of filthy-minded man on my face.

She was all the woman I needed, anyway, if I could just get her nailed down. Then, without a glance at me, she turned and walked out the door.

*Definitely not nailed down.*

A song from *The Sound of Music* came to mind. I knew them from when my baby sister DeeAnne insisted on watching the movie over and over when we were kids. More than twenty years later, those songs still popped into my head. This time, it was the one the nuns sang when they were trying to figure out how to get Maria to act like a normal nun, something about not being able to catch a moonbeam in your hand.

Maybe that was Rika. As much as I was attracted to her and as much as we seemed to have a connection, I still wasn't sure I could "catch" her.

As we walked around the corner of the building, her two steps in front of me, I scanned the parking lot, looking for Eli. I didn't trust that weirdo one bit.

Suddenly, she stopped and spun around. "Don't ever do that again!"

I rewound the last half hour in my mind scanning it for misbehavior on my part. I'd had thoughts, but how would she know about those?

"Do what?" I asked.

Her eyes flashed like a neon sign as she puffed out an angry breath. Then, she turned away and strode determinedly toward the truck. My legs were longer than hers, which meant I caught up to her in two strides.

"Rika!" I said, once I was walking beside her.

She checked over each shoulder, confirming no one else was in earshot. "Don't nibble my finger while we're interviewing witnesses!" she whisper-yelled.

"We weren't interviewing witnesses," I replied, realizing I was splitting hairs. "The only person in there was your friend Najila. Is there some reason you don't want your friends to know we've done the deed?" The euphemism was lame, but our relationship seemed so convoluted right now, I didn't know whether "made love," "screwed," or "bumped uglies," was the appropriate term.

We were nearing the truck. I followed her to the passenger side.

"We're partners," she said. "When we're in front of people involved in our cases, I expect you to act like a professional and not demean me and treat me like a sex object."

*Demean* her? Every muscle in my body tightened at the accusation. I put my hand on her forearm, just wanting her to face me, but her momentum caused her to spin around, lose her balance, and land with her back against the passenger door.

A split second later, I had my hands braced on the truck on either side of her. "Since we're not interviewing anyone now, maybe you should give me a rundown on what you consider demeaning."

~

**Rika**

As soon as my back hit the door, Nick's arms moved to either side of me, his hands bracing on the truck, making me feel trapped, even though I was pretty sure he wouldn't physically detain me.

I met his gaze. I didn't trust where he was going with this but couldn't bring myself to break away. Not with his biceps bulging from what was basically a standing push-up.

I kind of liked being in the middle of a Nick push-up, not that I'd share that with him.

"For instance," he continued, "is it demeaning when I touch your arm?" He let his fingers slide up my arm. My shoulders wiggled involuntarily.

Half of me—maybe two-thirds—wanted to beg him to take me, right now, in the cab of his truck in the medical examiner's parking lot. But my job wasn't a game to me and I wasn't some bimbo, here solely for Nick's amusement.

I slapped his hand away. "It's demeaning when we're working as professional private investigators and you can't act like a professional."

He lifted his chin and pulled his head back. "You're saying I can't act like a professional?"

"Oh, I know you *can* act like one if you want to. But would you nibble a colleague's finger while you're sitting at the defense table in the middle of a trial?"

"Of course not."

"The defendant's finger?"

"No, but Rika we have a personal relationship that—"

"You and Gabe have a personal relationship. Ever ask to approach the bench, then nibble his finger?"

Nick sucked in a breath then blew out an annoyed huff. His jaw went tight.

Did I just win an argument with Nick using his own profession against him?

Did that mean I could beat him in court? It was almost worth going to law school for three years to find out.

I felt my phone vibrating in my jeans. Nick's hands dropped from the door. He walked around to his side of the truck. I pulled the phone out and climbed in.

"Teodor can have visitors now," I read aloud off the screen. "It's from Dr. Washington." I was surprised it was she who texted me instead of Dr. Choi considering he was the lead doctor on the case. "I wonder if she contacted me because Teodor is wanting to help us find his brother's killer. That could mean he had nothing to do with the murder."

"Or that he's smart enough to act like he wants the killer apprehended," Nick said.

He was right. How many times had I seen parents or husbands or wives of victims go on TV, making pleas to the public, just to find out later the spouse was the perpetrator? Those people should get extra time tacked on to their sentences just for the added expense to taxpayers and stress on the rest of the other members of the family who end up double traumatized.

I'd thought nothing could be worse than having my mother murdered, but what if the killer had turned out to be my father? I would have needed a lot more than food to keep me going.

As Nick backed us out of the parking space, another text came in, this one labeled "Geoff Choi," saying Teodor was adamant about wanting to talk to us right away.

"Is that still her?" Nick asked.

"No, it's Geoff," I replied absently.

"Geoff?" He frowned as if trying to recall who Geoff was. The truck came to an abrupt halt. "You mean Dr. Choi?"

"Yeah," I replied, eager to get to the hospital and talk to the victim's brother. I tapped out a *Thanks a bunch!* to Geoff Choi.

The truck wasn't moving. I looked up from my phone into Nick's angry gaze. "How long have you two been texting each other?" he asked.

"Since we met with him," I replied. "He found me on social media. He's been keeping me updated on Teodor's condition. Plus, he sent me links to this one artist who makes Harry Pott—"

I stopped talking when Nick's fists tightened on the steering wheel, his knuckles turning disturbingly white. When he closed his eyes, I was certain he was trying to muster some patience, but unsure why he needed it now. "Do you not realize he wants to fuck you?" he said in a voice that was both angry and condescending.

So much for the patience mustering.

And his bluntness threw me for a loop. I'd heard him say curse words before, which was no big deal. I said them myself.

But I wasn't used to him saying the f-word specifically in reference to me and what someone wanted to do to me.

There were two qualities I particularly liked in Nick. One was that he seemed to appreciate that I was an intelligent person and respected me for it. The second was that he had a smidge of old-fashioned gentleman in him. Enough to be charming without being a macho jerk.

But there had been nothing in his question that was either respectful or gentlemanly.

"He's involved in the case, Nick," I said in the same tone of voice he'd used with me. "What's your problem?"

"My problem is that every time I turn around, there's another guy after you."

"That's ridiculous," I replied.

"No, what's ridiculous is that you encourage them all."

"What are you talking about?"

"I'm talking about Eli, the stalker you're chummy with, and Julian, who you have over for dinner, and now 'Geoff', who looks at you like he wants to eat you for lunch!"

"I told you I didn't invite Julian over," I said loudly. "And I can't help how Geoff looks at me!"

Wait, had I gone from the girl boys made snorting noises at to a woman with four men interested at once? Even if I traveled back in time to declare this to my sixteen-year-old self, I wouldn't believe me.

Of course, I only really cared whether Nick wanted me. However, I was still a little confused about the one time we'd gone to bed together, and what happened right after with "honey"—aka "baby girl"—on the phone. Then the next day Nick snapped back into protective mode like we were a couple.

Could he be one of the jerks who doesn't really want you long-term, but wants to keep you on the string to butter his ego until someone more exciting comes along? That would make him...

*A Brandtt. Ick.*

He expelled a loud breath. "Maybe you can't control their behavior," Nick said, the parental tone back in his voice. "But you can control the messages you're giving them! Have you told Julian you're not interested in dating him? Have you told Eli to stop following you around? According to LeeAnne, he was at the circus with you! And does Geoff know we're fucking? Maybe these guys wouldn't keep bothering you if you didn't keep treating me like I'm no more than a business associate."

Now I was pissed. Nick was calling me a tease, and apparently, now, what we did was "fucking," rather than making love.

Why was he worried about the messages I was sending instead of the message he gave me when he acted all lovey-dovey with another woman on the phone before I was even out of his bed?

I didn't have the courage to bring that up, though. A part of me was afraid to know the truth. If Nick told me he was seeing me and someone else at the same time, I'd have to cut him loose and just the thought of losing him made me want to go to Eddie's and buy all the Mexican sweet bread he'd stocked for the week.

"What about you?" I asked. "Are you going around giving women the *right* message? Were you honest with Jemima Harte when you flirted with her? And what about Suzee Driver from the Microtology Center? Or GracieAnne? How did you know she was in town? She made it clear she has a thing for you, but you're obviously keeping in touch with her. Then there was Marla." I lowered my voice to a dumb-guy tone. "Duh, sure, she's a beautiful woman staying in my house, but I'm not sleeping with her."

Nick twisted in my direction and gestured toward me with both hands. "*You* were a beautiful woman staying at my house and I wasn't sleeping with you!"

"I'm not a tall blonde who looks freakishly like your ex-wives!" Ha! I was proud of myself for that one!

Wait, had he called me a beautiful woman? That was nice...

*Beep-beep-beep!* The horn sounded behind us.

Oh. We were still sitting in the middle of the parking lot.

Nick hit the gas, his tires screeching at the quick take off, and neither of us said another word.

# CHAPTER TWENTY-SIX

**Rika**

So... Nick and I also didn't speak when we parked at the hospital thirty minutes later. Or when we walked into the hospital.

I had the room number in my texts, and Nick went where I went, emitting his angry-broody energy.

I tried to remind myself that I didn't have to be affected by his mood, but it wasn't easy.

The hospital halls seemed endless when we weren't speaking. I was glad when we finally found the right room, and, as any P.I. worth her salt would do, I peeked through the long pane of glass to see what was going on before entering.

Nick watched me, a judgy look on his face. I'd gotten the idea that he didn't like peeking or eavesdropping, but, as far as I was concerned, those actions were the "private" parts of being a private investigator. You had to snoop into people's lives sometimes to get to the truth.

A blonde woman was in Teodor's room. I could only see her from the back, but she seemed to be messing around with his IV. She wasn't dressed as a nurse, though.

I pushed the door open without knocking. Erissa spun around quickly. "Oh, hi, you guys," she said cheerily.

Nick put out his hand while saying, "Nice to see you again."

"Was there a problem with the IV?" I asked.

"Oh, no. I was just checking it," she said. "Teodor's in a lot of pain and he thought it might be empty." Her eyes shifted from me to Nick to me again as if trying to decide whether we believed her. "I, um, used to be a nurse," she added.

We both nodded like we believed her—and maybe Nick did —then we looked at Teodor.

"Oh," Erissa said. "I guess you haven't officially met. Tay, this is Rika Martín and her partner Nick..." She seemed at a loss for his last name.

"Ow-*een*," I said, figuring I owed him for all the times he'd introduced me as Rika Martin instead of Martín.

Nick didn't say anything. He just lifted his hand and rubbed the back of his neck, which I was apparently a pain in right now. *Good.*

Erissa frowned like his surname didn't sound right to her but let it go. "They're the private investigators I told you about," she finished.

"Forgive me for not sitting up," Teodor said as he shook our hands from his bed. "It will be a few more days yet because of the surgery."

"How are you?" I asked. I couldn't imagine what it must feel like to lose your twin, much less your conjoined twin.

Teodor sighed. "The doctors say I am doing well." He pointed to his heart. "But here, I am broken. My brother is gone and I don't know what pain is from the surgery and what is from..."

"The loss?" Erissa prompted.

"Yes. The loss," he agreed. "For thirty-three years I was never alone." He looked longingly to his left side, where his twin would have been. "My brother was with me, everywhere I went, everything I did. And now..." He let out another huge sigh.

"I thought you wanted to be separated from your brother," Nick said.

After examining his face, I realized he'd morphed into courtroom mode. I pressed my lips together and waited to see what happened.

Teodor blinked at him. "Physically, yes. I wanted a normal life with the woman I love. I didn't want to be attached in that way. But I always thought I would be near to him. I planned to keep him living with me while he was doing the physical therapy, then move him back to the other side of the duplex when he was more independent."

Erissa gave her head a quick shake. "You were what?" she asked, obviously shocked. "He was going to live with us? Then you were going to move him into my rental property permanently?"

"We were planning to get married," Teodor said. "You have two bedrooms in your house. I thought he would live there with us and, when he was ready, move back to our side. It was a perfect arrangement."

"'Our side'? And by 'our side' you mean the one you and Grigore have been living in?"

Teodor nodded at her, a befuddled look on his face.

Erissa's head tilted as if her brain was suddenly too full of thoughts to be held upright. Her mouth hung open for several seconds before she said, "When were you going to tell me this?"

"Tell you?" Teodor said. "I thought it was understood. He was my family. My twin."

"But he had a lot of family!" Erissa's voice pitched louder. "Why couldn't they take care of him?"

"He was not their twin," Teodor said simply.

Erissa straightened, pulling her head back. "Were you using me?" she cried.

A fleeting look passed over Teodor's face, but I couldn't get a read on it before it disappeared into the next emotion. Now,

Teodor was the one looking shocked. "Using you?" he repeated. "I do not understand what you are saying."

His English had seemed pretty fluent to me, even with the Romanian accent.

Erissa's gaze left Teodor. I followed her line of sight to a spot on the gray wall and since there was nothing of interest there, concluded that she was mulling over what she'd just learned.

Suddenly, she focused her razor-sharp gaze on Teodor. "Were you using all of us?" She seemed to be thinking aloud. "From when the documentary crew contacted you?" She paced across the room, behind me, then back toward the bed. "You told me the documentary producer, hospital and doctors got together and got you this major surgery for free. That production assistant Izzy called me about the offer I had on Craig's List for a handy person to live rent-free while helping fix up the house. Then you charmed me into falling for you so you and your brother could go from attached at the hip to attached at the living room wall!"

Teodor tried to sit up, grimaced in pain, then settled for curling the pillow under his neck. "I don't understand why you are angry!" he shouted. "We love each other and are going to marry. Grigore would be your family, too. You should take care of family!"

I glanced at Nick, noting his discomfort. If I weren't with him, he would have already told the feuding couple he would give them some time alone and left.

*Wuss.*

Lucky for me, I was used to drama, having grown up with my formidable grandmother and aunts who tended to just open their mouths and let the drama fly.

Well, actually, it was usually Lita and Tía Margo—and sometimes Mrs. Ruíz—who provided the drama. Tía Madi just threw in the occasional phrase to egg them on for her own amusement.

Erissa stood for several long seconds, staring at Teodor, her lips pressed together.

I could see where they both were coming from. In my family, the notion that you take care of family, no matter what, ran strong.

My aunts and grandmother hated Tía Margo's ex—Uncle Kurt— with almost every ounce of their beings, but, if he caught a debilitating disease, Lita would move him in and have Mrs. Ruíz nurse him back to health. He was still the father of two of her grandchildren, after all, therefore, family.

I couldn't blame Erissa, though, for wanting her fiancée to herself and for trying to make sure she wasn't being scammed.

"Baby," Teodor said. He reached out but Erissa took a step back and folded her arms in front of her.

She was no longer responding. It looked like we wouldn't learn any more from this spat.

"Teodor?" I said.

He laid his rejected hand on the white hospital blanket. "I'm sorry," he said. "How can I help you find my brother's killers?"

"Can you tell us about the night before?" I asked.

Teodor pressed his lids shut and took in a deep breath. "We watched television. I was working on an old radio an antique dealer had left to be fixed. Grigore was working on a cuckoo clock from the same man." Teodor paused and sighed. "I was excited about the surgery, but I was selfish. I wanted a life with the woman I loved, and Erissa didn't like Grigore."

Erissa huffed. "It had nothing to do with liking or not liking him!" she said. "Trying to make love with your twin giving me the stink eye—"

*Hm...* She hadn't mentioned Grigore's "stink eye" when we asked her about intimacy before.

"He was reading his books!" Teodor cried.

"You didn't see it! You were always on the bottom!"

Nick cleared his throat, reminding them we were in the room. I didn't appreciate this, considering how curious I was about how this sex with one conjoined twin, but not the other thing worked.

Erissa glanced at him, then crossed her arms again.

"So..." I prompted. "You were fixing things and watching TV..."

Teodor nodded. "Everything was fine. We were watching Hollywood News Hour and the commercials began. Then Grigore turned to me and said he didn't want the surgery."

"I told him he was just having cold knees."

"Cold feet?" Nick said.

"Oh, yes, I always get that mixed up. Why cold feet? Do American's feet get cold when they are worried?"

"It's just a saying," I told Teodor, wanting to get the interview back on track. "We don't know where it came from. After you told Grigore he had cold whatever, then what happened?"

"He didn't say anything, but I thought things were okay. He was a quiet person. Then, a few minutes later, I had my earphones in my ears—yoga music to help me get ready to sleep and feel calm about the surgery. While I was brushing my teeth, I realized Grigore was on the phone. I took out my earphones and heard him telling someone he didn't want to get the separation. We started arguing about it. Extra doctors had flown in to observe and assist the surgery, the hospital and surgeons were giving their time free! When would we ever have another opportunity like this if he refused?"

"Then what happened?" Nick asked.

"He agreed to have the surgery and we went to sleep. That's the last I remember. The police said I was awake the next morning when they brought us to the hospital, but I don't remember any of that day."

That sounded a little too neat. "How did you convince him to change his mind again?" I asked.

"He was saying he would be crippled and alone. I promised him I would always take care of him." Tears shown in Teodor's eyes. "He was a part of me."

"Don't you think it's strange that you didn't awaken during the attack?" Nick asked.

"No." Teodor shook his head sadly. "Having another person connected to you from birth causes your brain to..." He seemed to be searching for the right word, "...filter out what the other person is doing. I was night owl. Grigore was morning person. We were used to each other reading, typing on computer, or even repairing things while the other slept. That is why we could both sleep sitting up. If I was still working and Grigore felt sleepy, he just went to sleep..." A tear ran down his face. "I wish I had awakened. Maybe I could have stopped them."

I steeled myself for the next question I had to ask. "Have you seen the, um, murder weapon?"

Teodor wiped his eyes on the sheet even though there was a box of tissues at his bedside. "The police showed it to me," he said. "A picture."

"Did it belong to you or Teodor?"

He shrugged. "We shared all our tools. We always were working on projects and fixing things since we were children. We had collected many tools that were given to us. We may have a hundred screwdrivers if you count the tiny ones."

I glanced at Nick. His eyes were narrowed. "How many larger ones do you think you had?"

"I don't know," Teodor replied. "I don't even remember where most of them came from. They were everywhere, in toolboxes, around the house..."

"And you really can't say for sure if you'd seen or used that particular one before?" Nick's tone was skeptical.

"It was a medium, red-handle screwdriver," Teodor said, frustration obvious in his voice. "I have used screwdrivers like it before, but I can't be certain that one was ours."

"Is there anyone who might have wanted Grigore dead?" I asked. "Anyone who was angry with him? Weird circus fans? Disgruntled customers from your repair business?"

"My father and Xavier were angry with both of us because we were ruining the act, they said. But more angry with me than Grigore. And how would it help them if we were dead?"

Nick leveled his gaze with Teodor's and I knew what was coming. "What about you?" Nick said. "You were angry with him."

"Yes, we often argued," Teodor said. "It is hard to be two people in one body. But he was still my brother. Besides, killing him would be the same as killing myself."

*Unless your girlfriend had witnesses on the scene to make sure you didn't die,* I thought, but didn't say.

But after the visit to the medical examiner's office, I was pretty sure Teodor wasn't the trigger man, so to speak. I slid my eyes toward Erissa to see if she looked guilty, but she still seemed pissed about the plans Teodor made without her approval.

"Thanks for your time," Nick said. He was clearly done with this, even if he didn't seem satisfied with Teodor's answers.

It bugged me that he'd tried to end the interview on his own again, but he was probably right. Teodor either didn't have much information for us or wasn't going to give it up.

I was still mulling things over when I turned to follow Nick. As I reached the door, a thought occurred to me. I turned back. "Just one more thing," I said. Teodor lifted his eyebrows at me. "Is there a computer you use? Or a smartphone?"

"No, I have dumb phone," he replied. "It was very cheap. I use Erissa's computer sometimes."

"The one the cops took," Erissa said.

I nodded at her then turned my attention back to Teodor. "Have you ever done a search on how long it takes a second conjoined twin to die after the first does?" I hated to ask such an insensitive question, but I was just doing my job.

Teodor looked genuinely confused by my question. "Why would I do such a thing?" he asked. "I've known since I was child that, as long as we were joined, we would die together. Maybe not in the same instant, but..." He shook his head. "I should be dead. I should have died with him as God intended."

Erissa raced to his bedside. "Don't say that!" she cried. "Don't ever say that!" She threw her arms around Teodor, then loosened her grip when she realized she might be hurting him.

"We'll leave you two alone now," Nick said, ending the interview on his own for the second time in the last five minutes.

Had he already forgotten our discussion about this sort of thing? Maybe I should have chosen a less alpha partner.

He opened the door and stood aside while I walked through it.

I could hear Teodor and Erissa sobbing together as we left.

$$\sim$$

## Nick

The second we left the room, I put my arm around Rika's waist and said, "We need to talk," into her ear.

Her body tensed under my touch. Definitely not what I wanted to happen when I touched Rika.

I released her and we walked silently toward the waiting area I'd seen around the corner from the elevators. I needed to talk to her about the case, but, after her response to my touch, it was hard to focus on the murder.

Was the one and only time we'd been together not good for her? My ego wasn't willing to accept that explanation. Not yet anyway. Despite how it might look—considering the three divorces—I was pretty sure that if you called every woman I'd ever slept with, the one thing they'd all agree on was that I was good in bed.

And, lying in bed with Rika, our breathing still ragged from the unprecedented sex—at least for me—I was sure we'd both found the person we were supposed to do this with for the rest of our lives.

Believe me, I know how dubious that sounds from someone with my past, but I truly experienced something with her I never had with another woman.

Sure, sex had been fun and pleasurable in the past. But having Rika in my bed brought my emotions to the surface in a way I didn't know was possible.

I loved her.

I'd said the words to other women, but I had no idea what I was talking about. That was clear as day now.

We got to the waiting room and I sat on the small couch. Rika opted for the chair positioned at a right angle to the sofa.

I rested my forearms on my thighs and leaned in toward her. "I'm thinking it's possible Teodor and Erissa set this up."

Rika's gaze had been on my hands, but at that statement, her eyes lifted to meet mine. "That's what I said at the beginning of all this, but you kept defending Erissa!"

"Yeah, but—" I started to argue, not wanting to admit I'd been wrong.

"But of course, it sounds better when it's your idea." She sat back and crossed her arms. "Why've you changed your mind now?"

"Them."

She drew her eyebrows together in a puzzled look I didn't see often but was fucking adorable. I came *this* close to leaning in and kissing her forehead, which I was sure was forbidden after our "professional" conversation.

"Them?" she repeated.

"When referring to the murder, Teodor said, 'Maybe I could have stopped *them*'."

Rika thought for a moment before replying. "Lots of people use 'they' and 'them' when they don't know the sex of the person they're talking about. Maybe he just picked up the habit while learning English." She didn't look one hundred percent convinced of her argument. "He's pretty fluent, but it isn't his first language. It could be a misspeak. Why is this enough to change your mind?"

"I've deposed a lot of witnesses and cross-examined them in court. Most people say 'he' when they don't know who the murderer is."

Rika shook her head dismissively. "On the specific cases you worked in Texas they said 'he'. You don't know what a person from another country would say, or even another state."

She had a point. But I still thought I did, too. Men committed far more murders than women did, and I was pretty sure that was true worldwide. It made a certain amount of sense that the default when talking about a murderer was typically "him."

Besides, my suspicions hadn't been raised by just one word. "Before that, he asked how he could help find his brother's *killers*. Plural."

I saw the spark in Rika's eyes and knew I was getting somewhere, so I continued, "When I add that to the fishy way Erissa acted—hiring you, then practically harassing you about what time you'd be at the twin's place..."

"And the cops thinking she killed her husband..." Rika added. "Damn it! I knew it! We're not going to get paid!"

"Didn't you collect something from her already?"

"Yeah, she sent me five hundred dollars, but that's not nearly enough for solving a murder case and it's not like the LAPD is going to pay us our fee."

Rika flopped back in the chair, her face pointed almost to the ceiling, her eyes closed.

She rubbed both temples with her index fingers like she was trying to wind up her brain. "So, we have two sociopathic narcissists—Anatolie and Xavier—both of whom were angry with the twins, one of whom may, or may not, have sicced his tiger on me. We have Constata, who threw knives at us and seemed to love Grigore but does wear a crucifix. And we have Erissa and

Teodor," she said. "What we don't have is any solid evidence against anyone."

"We've got to be missing something," I replied.

Rika pulled her phone out of her back pocket and checked it. "Well, it looks like the LAPD is missing it, too. Julian says they've dusted everything they took with them for fingerprints. They're tracking down the owners of the items the twins were fixing to rule out their prints, but they think it's a dead end. The lab is having a hard time with DNA samples. Teodor has verified that the mattress was already very used when they got it. They were sleeping on it without a bottom sheet." She shuddered. "Bleh. Men."

"Hey, I always have a sheet on—" I began.

Rika held up her hand to stop me and read from her phone again. "It's going to take weeks to sort out fingerprints and DNA and none of it looks likely to pan out. They subpoenaed Teodor and Grigore's phone records, but have had to go back to the judge because it turned out the phones were in Erissa's name."

It hit me that this information was probably coming from Julian rather than Najila. "Why did he bother to text you with zero information?" I asked, jealousy gnawing at my gut.

"When he texted me 'good morning', I asked him for an update."

Damn it. I wanted to punch Suriano in the middle of his pretty boy face. "He texted you 'good morning'?" I asked, unable to keep the edge from my voice. I imagined Julian with a bloody face and broken nose and decided I'd like him better that way.

"Yeah," she said. But her mind was still elsewhere. "He usually texts me either 'good morning' or 'good night', depending on what shift he's working."

"You mean..." I could feel some ancient, primal testosterone flooding my bloodstream. Way more powerful than modern-day testosterone. "You mean," I tried again, "Julian has been texting you every day?"

She nodded as she seemed to be checking other things on her phone. "Mm-hm."

"Since when?"

She looked up as if just entering the conversation. "What?"

"When did Julian start texting you every day?"

"Um..." She shrugged. "After we ran into him, I think. You know, at the Microtology Center, right after you got to town." She said it like it was no big deal another man was thinking about her so much, he wanted to greet her each morning and tuck her in at night.

I'd had enough. This wasn't the place, but I couldn't stay in this limbo where I didn't know if she was all in with me. "Rika—"

"Oh, sweet!" she exclaimed. "Geoff just texted that the documentary crew is here in the hospital. Eighth floor conference room." She hopped up and took off toward the elevators.

I sighed and followed her.

# CHAPTER TWENTY-SEVEN

**Rika**

When we walked up to the conference room door, we paused and peeked through the little square window to see whether we were in the right place.

There were five people sitting around the table—Doctors Choi and Duarte, a middle-aged white man with a short salt and pepper beard to match his wavy hair, a petite white girl with her hair dyed neon green, and a youngish mixed-race guy with super cool dreadlocks that stuck up, then swooped down, hanging to just below his shoulders. I wondered if I could get my hair to do that. Then I remembered the ringlet disaster.

"I don't know if I can sign off on this," Dr. Duarte was saying. "When it was a documentary about the separation of conjoined twins, that was one thing, but now—"

"It's still a documentary," the man with the beard said. "It's just a different kind."

Nick knocked on the door.

Why would he do that? We could hear really well from the hall. It was the perfect opportunity to do some eavesdropping and find out more about the documentary crew!

"Nick!" I whispered through ground teeth, but the man was already waving us in.

Nick opened the door and I went through first. "Hi, I'm Rika Martín," I said, before Nick could take charge again. "And this is my partner Nick Owen."

The bearded man stood and stuck his hand out. "I'm Stan Swartz, the director," he said. "Dr. Choi told us about you. Have you met Dr. Duarte?"

"I'm glad to see you again," Dr. Duarte said as she stood. I noticed today's cross was a bona fide crucifix with a very unhappy Jesus on it. I automatically tried to superimpose it onto the image in my mind of Grigore's hand, but it was impossible to compare the two this way. Besides, a surgeon had too much to lose to go around murdering her patients.

A documentary producer on the other hand...

I glanced at Stan, trying to gauge his level of desperation, then turned my attention back to Dr. Duarte.

She'd rounded the table, and, instead of offering her hand, she gave me a hug. Immediately, she felt like family to me. Now that I'd held her in my arms, I was sure she wasn't the killer, even if she was several inches taller than me, meeting the minimum height qualifications to be the killer...or worse, a model.

But, what can I say? I pretty much always feel better after a hug and Dr. Duarte had a nice energy about her.

"Oh, are we hugging?" Dr. Choi said. He popped out of his chair and came around the table toward me.

Nick stepped into the path between us. "Just the ladies," he said.

Dr. Choi chuckled and said, "Nice to see you again, Rika. And your bodyguard, too." He flashed me a mischievous half-grin.

The scowl on Nick's face said he didn't think there was anything to grin about.

"You're the ones who found them, right?" Stan was saying.

"Damn, I wish we'd gotten footage of that," he murmured, probably to himself.

Dr. Duarte gave him a scolding look he didn't seem to notice. "It's truly nice to see you, again," she said to me and Nick. "Teodor wouldn't be alive if you two hadn't heard him calling out and broken in to save him. Not everyone would do that."

*Uh...* Nick and I gave each other *What the hell? Did you tell them that story?* looks. Then I realized it was probably Erissa. If she still wanted to be with Teodor, it didn't look good that she was having him investigated. But why didn't Teodor correct the story? Maybe he and Erissa really were in this together.

Then I remembered that Teodor said he didn't recall anything after going to bed that night.

"Well, this is my cameraman—" Stan started to say.

Dreadlock guy, who Stan had gestured toward, cleared his throat.

"Sorry," Stan said to the guy before turning back to us. "This is my *visual artiste*, Jeb."

*Jeb?* Of all the names in the world, "Jeb" would have been the last name I would have guessed for this guy. Plus, it was a terrible name for an *artiste*.

"Rad threads," Jeb said, pointing at my Marvel superheroes as toddlers tee.

That's when I noticed he was wearing a black t-shirt with a huge red *Spider-Man* logo on it. "Thanks, yours is awesome, too," I said. My eyes drifted back to the young woman, who was wearing a vintage *The Flash* hoodie. "Oh, wow, yours, too," I added, glad to be surrounded by my peeps.

"This is my right-hand man, Izzy," Stan said as he nodded toward her.

She was closest to us, so she stood and shook my hand. "My real name's Isabel, but that's lame," she said.

I wasn't convinced Izzy was a better name than Isabel but kept that to myself.

She thrust her hand out to Nick. When he took it, she asked. "Are you, like, with anybody? 'Cause you're really hot."

My head did a quick involuntary shake. Did she just hit on Nick right in front of me? I mentally retracted my compliment about her shirt.

Nick's lips parted in surprise—at her bluntness, I was sure, since he already knew he was hot—then he regained his composure. "I'm not on the market right now," he said. "How about I call you if that changes?"

Instead of stepping off, Izzy lifted onto her tiptoes and whispered loud enough for me to hear, "However good your girlfriend is, I'm better," she said confidently. "I'm very bendy."

Nick's lips quirked up in the corners as he fought to suppress a laugh. "I'll keep that in mind," he said.

*Butthead.* He could have proclaimed his undying love for me —okay, maybe I blew that possibility by insisting he act more professional. But anything was better than making me—I mean her—think he might call her.

"Have a seat," Stan said, so we sat. "We're trying to see if we can salvage the documentary. Do you mind waiting for a few minutes while we finish up?"

"No problem," Nick said. "Do you want us to step out?"

If the conference room chairs didn't have arms on them, I would have jabbed my elbow into his ribs. Stan had already invited us to sit down. Why would we want to leave the room and miss out on their conversation? We might learn something valuable.

Maybe I needed to schedule a training for Nick—Private Investigations 101.

"It's fine!" Dr. Choi jumped in. "I'd hate to miss the opportunity to be in the same room with Rika Martín." He said my full name with the kind of enthusiasm people usually reserved for celebrities. My heart beat faster and I couldn't stop the corners of my mouth from turning up.

At least until I felt the tension emanating from Nick's body. I slid my eyes toward him, feeling a bit smug about the turn the conversation had taken.

He'd managed to blank his expression, but I knew by the set of his chin that he was not happy.

Well, at least that was something. I wondered, for the first time, what would have happened if Nick hadn't taken that call. Or if he hadn't left me alone in his bed while he was on it.

"Damn, have we fallen into a real-life dating app?" Jeb asked.

I chuckled, but everyone else ignored him, which I thought was unfair because that was kind of funny.

Dr. Duarte glared at Dr. Choi. The look said she was not okay with his flirty behavior in a professional setting. As a middle-aged female doctor, she'd likely had to put up with more than her share of stupid man behavior. It was probably even worse when you know the men aren't stupid, just choosing to be jerks. "As I was saying..." she began again. "I signed off on a medical documentary about separating conjoined twins, not this thing you want to do now."

Dr. Choi turned towards me. "The Med Channel doesn't want it anymore," he explained. "They only do happy endings."

"But we have an offer from Murder TV," Jeb said. "They have two different series they could put it in, depending on whether or not it's still unsolved when they air it. They have a lot more viewers than Med anyway."

"It's not called 'Murder TV'," Stan said, clearly annoyed.

"It might as well be," Dr. Duarte replied. "I don't like the idea of exploiting the twins—"

"Why do you feel it's more exploitive now than it was before?" Dr. Choi asked. "Because you might get less screen time?"

"Screen time?" Dr. Duarte replied. "That's disgusting, Geoff."

Geoff Choi shrugged and chuckled, clearly not caring what Dr. Duarte thought of him.

She continued, "The documentary we agreed on was in the interest of science."

"It's not like it was a 'How-to' video," Geoff argued. "And even if it was, how often does 'science' need to know how to separate adult conjoined twins fused at the hip?"

"Okay..." Stan put the backs of his hands together in front of him, then pushed them outward as if separating a couple of boxers. "Let me just bottom line this for you guys. We've spent a year and a lot of money—my personal money—on this documentary."

Izzy pointed a pleading gaze at Dr. Duarte. "I swear Stan was about to have a stroke when we heard what happened. If Dr. Choi hadn't given him a sedative and asked if we couldn't just sell it somewhere else, I think he'd be in the hospital."

Dr. Duarte didn't appear to be swayed by Stan's near stroke. Maybe because, as far as we knew, Izzy was not qualified to diagnose one.

Jeb leaned toward Dr. Duarte, resting his elbows on the table, looking deeply into her eyes. "Dude," he said soulfully. Dr. Duarte blinked rapidly, apparently not used to being addressed as "Dude."

Jeb went on. "I totally get that your heart's in the right place, but I've never really understood the whole 'exploitation' concept. 'Cause, like, we're all exploiting each other every day if you think about it. You need people to get sick so you can make a living. Is that exploiting their pain or healing them?"

Dr. Duarte had clearly not gotten this philosophical about her occupation before. Her mouth dropped open, but she didn't reply.

"And, like, I need Stan to pay my salary so I can buy weed." When everyone's brows lifted, he added, "And, you know, food and stuff. But Stan needs me to capture the magic. Who's exploiting whom?" He shrugged. "We're both exploiting each other, right? I mean, if we all stop exploiting each other, civilization, as we know it, is over."

Nick, the doctors and I all looked at each other.

This was confusing. Jeb had made a profound observation, but he'd done it in a voice that was somewhere between surfer dude and valley girl.

"And what about Teodor's bonus?" Izzy said as she gave Stan a sideways glance.

I was sure the bonus hadn't existed until this second. I was beginning to understand why Izzy was Stan's "right-hand man."

"Bonus?" Dr. Duarte repeated.

"Yes," Izzy said. "Teodor gets a big bonus once the channel actually buys the documentary."

I noticed she didn't give an exact amount. She and Stan would have to get their heads together and figure it out when the rest of us weren't around.

"Oh," Dr. Duarte replied. "I didn't think about it affecting his income."

"That's understandable," Izzy said sympathetically. "You're a doctor." She shrugged, then reworked her face into a fake-pained, expression as though apologizing for what she was about to say. "You probably don't have to worry that much about money, but Teodor is an unemployed ex-circus performer who's just lost his twin, his acrobatic partner, and his repair shop partner. I'm sure he'll need recovery time to get used to doing everything differently. And if he has to worry about money on top of—"

Dr. Duarte lifted her hand and Izzy stopped talking. "I understand," the doctor said. "I wouldn't want Teodor to suffer financially after all he's been through. I'll sign."

Stan, Izzy, and Jeb released a collective sigh of relief.

Geoff Choi seemed to have already lost interest in the conversation and grinned flirtatiously at me.

My face heated and I couldn't help but smile back. Sure, he

wasn't Nick, but he was hot and I hadn't had hot people flirting with me my whole life like Nick had.

An alarm went off and Geoff Choi checked his phone. "Well, you already have my signature," he said. "I need to go do surgical rounds." He stood, walked over to where Nick and I were sitting, and said only to me, "Let me know if there's *anything* else I can do for you." Then—I swear on my vintage 1975 Lynda Carter Wonder Woman doll—Doctor Geoff Choi took my hand from the table, leaned over and kissed it.

Yes, *kissed* it!

*Holy mother of Zeus!*

The rest of my body grew as hot as my face until I felt like one giant blister. A strange sound came out of my throat—sort of a strangled giggle.

I wasn't sure how much of my reaction was from embarrassment and how much was from the fact that a hot guy had never, ever kissed my hand before. Come to think of it, no guy had ever kissed my hand before, hot or otherwise. And did I mention this guy was TV doctor hot? I never would have thought I'd react so ridiculously to a cute doctor kissing my hand, but now I knew. I was a silly, silly girl.

I glanced at Nick to see if he'd noticed my reaction. Maybe it wasn't as bad as I thought.

Nick's face looked hard, like it was carved from stone, which was way worse than regular scowly Nick.

Now, I felt both embarrassed and guilty.

Dr. Duarte was suddenly there. She, literally, elbowed Geoff out of the way and hugged me, but not before giving him a look that said she didn't approve of his behavior and was trying to figure out who she could report him to. "Goodbye, Rika, Nick," she said as she reached across me and shook Nick's hand.

As the doctors walked out the door, I heard her say, "Really, Geoff, we're at the hospital."

And just before the door slammed shut behind him, Geoff

replied, "I'm not the one who hugged her."

*Good one!* I thought, still feeling kind of giddy, despite the embarrassment.

Nick cleared his throat. "So, you've been following the twins around for a while?" he asked Stan.

"Yeah, for the last eight months. I know the director of the hospital and he contacted me to tell me there were plans being made for an unusual separation. We approached the twins and they agreed to let us document what they were going through."

"Can you think of anyone who'd have it in for one or both of them?" Nick asked.

Stan considered the question. "Well... I'm not sure how to answer that. One or both of the twins got into arguments with several people while we were with them, but I don't see how it would benefit any of them to murder Grigore or Teodor."

"Sometimes it's just about emotion," I pointed out. "Anger, revenge, love gone wrong..."

Izzy looked at the time on her phone and I got the feeling she thought they had better things to do. She rattled off a quick list. "Xavier was pissed about them leaving the circus. He and Teodor had an angry argument. Anatolie was livid that they were ruining the act. He and Teodor had a screaming argument. Constata was very upset that Grigore wouldn't be traveling with the circus anymore. She and Teodor ended up yelling at each other, then she cried and told Grigore this wasn't good for him, and that he was abandoning her there with a bunch of assholes and he needed to refuse to get the operation, then—"

"Then that crazy old bat threw a knife at the twins," Jeb interrupted. "We were pretty impressed by the way they ducked in unison. Teodor jerked his head to the right, Grigore to the left. The knife went *feeyoo*—" He made an air sound with his mouth while his hand mimed throwing a knife.

Izzy perked up. "It went right between them! They may have had practice dodging Constata's knives, though. People claim that scar on Palba's hand is from an argument she and Constata had about a costume. They say Palba's hand was resting on the table and Constata jammed the knife right into it!"

Nick and I looked at each other, eyebrows raised. Constata's crying over Grigore had been convincing, but if she considered Grigore's leaving a betrayal...

"Which twin was she aiming for when she threw that knife?" Nick asked.

*Good question, Nick.*

Stan flipped his palms up in a *Who knows?* gesture. "It's hard to say. I mean, their heads were right next to each other."

"She could definitely put somebody's eye out," Jeb added.

I thought about the hole where Grigore's eye used to be and shifted my gaze toward Nick. His was focused on the table like the evidence was laid out there, in front of him.

He wasn't a guy who would relish putting an elderly woman behind bars. After watching the expressions change on his face for several seconds, I became convinced he was thinking about how he'd defend her if she were his client.

I sighed. No matter how smart he was, Nick wasn't cut out for this job. He was too goodhearted.

Not that I'm a sociopath. I can feel empathy for a lot of people, but I had trouble mustering up sympathy for someone who took another person's life from them.

From their families.

"Besides the people Izzy listed, who would gain or lose because of the separation and who would gain or lose from the death of one or both twins?"

Stan, Izzy, and Jeb sat pondering the question.

"Was there life insurance?" Nick prompted.

"Oh!" Jeb cried. "I know the answer to that one. The twins decided they should get life insurance on each other, in case the surgery left one of them alive and one dead. Teodor said it would be a way for the one who died to keep taking care of the other."

Nick sat forward in his chair. "Teodor will be able to collect life insurance on his brother?"

"No, dude. I wasn't finished," Jeb replied. "The life insurance company turned them down. Didn't like the pre-existing condition or the circus job."

I wondered if the twins had tried other insurance companies when the camera wasn't around. They were still young. Surely there was a company who'd give them insurance, sight unseen. If a form asked whether they were in good health, they could say "yes." They had to be in great shape to do what they did.

Maybe we'd been thinking of this all wrong. What if Erissa and Teodor didn't murder Grigore because he didn't want the surgery? What if it was planned months before? That way, Teodor and Erissa could claim the money and live out their lives together in luxury.

"Honestly, if I were writing this story," Stan said, "I'd be deciding between Anatolie, Xavier, and Constata as the killer. One's a hothead who flies off the handle about practically anything. One's a guy I could totally see plotting revenge. One will knife you first, ask questions later."

That was certainly true. Nick and I had experienced it firsthand.

I felt like it was time to leave, even though I hadn't gotten as much as I'd hoped for from these people who'd followed the twins around for months. On the other hand, we had found out that Constata was generally a stabby person—not just a frightened old woman—and that the twins had been trying to buy insurance.

I gave Nick a *let's go* glance and we both stood. I thanked everyone. Nick shook their hands, but when he got to Izzy, she held it for an extra moment, caressing his hand with her thumb.

I imagined using my Assassin's Creed wristband on her. But, in my imagination, the blade was not made from plastic.

Nick peeled his hand away, but not before giving Izzy one of his sexy Nick Owen smiles, the kind I thought should be reserved for me and me alone. He got to the door first and was holding it open, waiting for me to go through when something struck me. None of the documentary crew had mentioned that they had a lot to gain or lose where the twins were concerned.

I turned. "Just one more thing, Stan," I said. "I have this weird OCD problem. I need to know what's at the bottom of chains or it drives me crazy the rest of the day." I pointed to his neck. "Do you mind me asking what that is around your neck?"

He looked surprised, then shrugged and pulled it out. An antique gold crucifix dangled from the end of the chain. "It's a family heirloom my grandmother gave to me. She was my favorite person in the world. I wear it close to my heart, even though I identify as Jewish like my dad's side of the family."

"Okay, thanks!" I said cheerfully.

Once we were out the door, walking toward the exit, Nick said, "What the hell? Are there always this many people wearing crucifixes in L.A.?"

I considered the question. Having spent my life around mostly Catholic Hispanic people, I'd seen so many crosses and crucifixes, I wasn't sure I even noticed them anymore. At least before this case. "I don't know," I replied. "Aren't there a lot of people who wear them in Texas?"

"A lot of women I know have dainty little crosses around their necks, but not with the half-naked man being tortured to death on them."

"Yeah," I said, thinking aloud. "Maybe it's a retro-trend or something." Although fashion trends weren't normally started by middle-aged directors or elderly wardrobe women. At least, I didn't think they were.

"That clue seems like a dead-end, but if we find an insurance policy..."

I chuckled. "Follow the money."

He nodded. "Follow the money."

# CHAPTER TWENTY-EIGHT

**Nick**

When we pulled up in front of Rika's grandma's house, Latin music was streaming out the open windows.

We got out of the truck, then Rika came around to where I was standing on the sidewalk. "Is this a party?" I asked.

She snorted—but let the record show, it was the cutest snort I'd ever heard.

"Depends on your definition of a party," she said. "Come on before you miss it."

As we walked up the porch steps, she turned and put her finger to her lips. She opened the door, walked in just a couple of feet and stopped. I was right behind her, curious to find out what was going on.

The pleasant aroma of home cooking hit my nose at the same time my brain tried to comprehend what I was seeing. Multiple pots and pans sat bubbling on the stove. The Miami Sound Machine was blaring from a speaker, encouraging people to shake their bodies and do that Conga. And the two grandmotherly women in the kitchen were intermittently stirring pots while dancing to the music.

To be clear, they weren't just bopping their heads while music played. They seemed to have a loosely choreographed routine happening that involved waving their cooking spoons in the air at specific times, dancing a complete circle around the kitchen and rotating their hips with impressive agility.

I couldn't stop my eyes from flicking down to Rika's very nice backside as I wondered if she could move her hips like that. Then I imagined her moving her hips like that while horizontal in my bed.

*Yeah, I think I'm a pretty good guy, but I'm still a guy, so sue me.*

When I forced my gaze up again, I noticed an expression pass over Rika's face. She'd been smiling as she watched them dance. But, for at least a moment, it wasn't a smile of pure joy. There was something else in her eyes.

Regret, maybe, that her grandmother didn't have enough times like this since losing her eldest daughter? Anger about all that was taken from them?

Then "The Macarena" came on, and the kitchen got wilder as the ladies tried to outdo each other on the hip-swiveling part. Rika and I burst out laughing.

Mrs. Delacruz's head jerked toward us, but instead of appearing embarrassed, she called, "Paprika! This was your favorite! Remember? Come dance!"

Without a word to me—as if she'd forgotten I was there, in fact—Rika ran to the kitchen. Her back was to me as she moved in to complete a dance circle with the two older women. Seconds later, I found out she *could* move her hips like that!

I'd seen bachelor party strippers dressed in G-strings that were less seductive than Rika was in jeans and a t-shirt.

By the time the song ended, my brain had completely lost control of the rest of me. "Rika?" I said.

Mrs. Delacruz turned down the speaker. "Hi *Neeek!*" she and Mrs. Ruíz called in unison, then they burst into what I could only guess were endorphin-fueled giggles.

"Rika," I tried again. "Don't we have insurance research to do?" As if I could possibly have insurance on my mind after that show.

"Oh, duty calls," she said breathlessly as she headed for her room.

"How long before dinner's ready?" I asked.

"Thirty minutes," Mrs. Ruíz replied.

I followed Rika into her bedroom, shutting the door behind me. Wrapping my fingers around her arm, I turned her toward me. Her gaze was surprised and curious, but not for long because I slid a hand to the back of her head and kissed her.

She kissed me back, thank God. In fact, she lifted herself to her tiptoes as she took control, thrusting her tongue into my mouth.

Her palm came up under my shirt, pressing against the bare skin of my back.

It was on.

Without breaking contact, I managed to reach out and turn the lock on her door. Then I moved her backward, braced a knee on her bed and took us down.

When my aroused nether region made contact with hers, she moaned into my ear.

I didn't care where we were anymore or when dinner would be ready, or if I ever ate dinner again. Every nerve ending, every pore, every organ in and on my body needed to be close to her —naked—now.

I whipped her t-shirt off, tossing it away.

Her breathing was as ragged as mine. Now, it seemed ridiculous I'd ever had doubts about us.

I brushed my lips against her neck and she giggled. I had to pull my head back to see the expression on her face.

Her eyes were shining, her lips turned up in that smile I couldn't get enough of. In that instant, I knew that Rika's laughter, Rika's giggles, Rika's snorts, were the best sounds I'd ever heard.

She was so damn beautiful in ways I'd never even considered before I met her. If I could only get her to be as free and relaxed with me as she was in the kitchen...

*I love you.* The words swelled up in my chest, nearly forcing their way out, but caught at the base of my throat.

If I said those words would it make things better for her? Or would it scare her away?

For the first time, it bothered me that my stellar courtroom instincts didn't seem to carry over into my personal life much, if at all. I needed to know what she needed. I wanted to understand how to make Rika and me an "us."

I kissed her neck, then ran my tongue along the top of her breast. How could this simple white bra she was wearing be the hottest piece of lingerie I'd ever seen?

Maybe because it contrasted beautifully with her naturally tanned skin.

I tugged the top of one cup down and slid my tongue over her nipple. She let out a staccato "oh-oh-oh," before sucking in a shaky breath.

The sound made me hard so fast, I thought the fly on my jeans would burst. As I attended to her other breast, I managed to undo the button on her jeans, caressing the skin underneath with my thumb.

"Nick," she murmured as I ran my tongue from her belly button to the top of her bikini underwear.

Her hands slid into my hair. Next thing I knew, she had handfuls of my t-shirt and she was tugging on it. I reached back between my shoulder blades and helped her by yanking the fabric upward. She finished the job, but now that I was shirtless, I wanted her topless too. I moved back up, reached around, undid her bra clasp, and slid the straps off her arms.

*I love you.* This time I'd nearly said it to her breasts.

Glancing up, I couldn't miss the sensual expression on her face. Her lips parted. Her eyes full of aroused expectation.

I kissed her hard and deep, then pulled her jeans off and flung them to the floor.

Her body stiffened and she grabbed her pillow, pressing it to the area between her breasts and her bikini underwear. If she were shy, wouldn't she cover her breasts instead?

Whatever. She still seemed willing and that was good enough for me. I got rid of the rest of my clothes in a flash as she scooted up the bed.

"Paprika..." I murmured into her ear. "I I—"

The doorbell rang twice, followed by several loud knocks.

Rika tried to sit up, causing us to bump foreheads. "Ouch!" we both said at the same time.

"Someone's at the door," she informed me unnecessarily.

No. *Hell* no. We were not stopping now. "Probably one of your aunts," I said as I tried to lift the pillow from her abdomen.

"They never knock," she replied. "Everyone has a key. They just walk in."

"Probably a neighbor wanting to borrow a cup of sugar."

"God, how old are you?" Rika said. "Nobody borrows a cup of sugar, anymore, if they ever did."

That actually hurt my feelings a little, not that I'd ever admit to it. Did being ten years older than someone put you in a different generation than them?

*Maybe you should bing it*, a sarcastic voice in my head suggested.

"Paprika!" Mrs. Delacruz called.

"Shit!" Rika whisper-yelled as she looked around the room. "Where are my clothes?"

And just as important, where were my clothes? Maybe if all my blood hadn't rushed south during the Macarena, I would have been more aware there were other people around and we might need to find our clothes quickly.

We each grabbed our jeans, started to put them on, then realized they weren't ours. We made the handoff and pulled them on at record speed.

I found Rika's bra on the floor and handed it to her. She started to struggle with it, then just tossed it on the bed and pulled her shirt on.

I got my shirt back on and shoved my feet into my sneakers.

As Rika headed for the door, I reached out and raked my hand down her hair, thinking it was only right considering I was the one who messed it up.

When we walked out, Rika's Aunt Madi was lounging on the couch, phone in hand. Instead of looking into her phone, however, she was watching us, a knowing smile on her face.

*Great.* When had she come in? And had she heard us before the doorbell rang? I'd been so wrapped up in what we were doing, I had no idea how loud we'd gotten or when the kitchen music had quit playing.

*Your fly's undone,* Madi mouthed as she gestured toward my crotch.

*Shit!* I checked my zipper, only to find it wasn't undone at all.

I gave her a pissed off look and she burst out laughing.

We approached Rika's grandmother, who was standing at the open door, definitely not laughing. "These..." She waved her hand toward Detectives Hertz and Winchell, palm up, a disgusted look on her face, "...*people*...want to speak with you."

Rika's expression matched her grandmother's. Mrs. Ruíz, cooking spoon in hand, watched from the kitchen.

"We need to discuss the latest murder you're involved in," Detective Hertz said. I noticed her hair was loose instead of back in a ponytail and she was wearing makeup.

Maybe she had a date lined up after work.

I tried to imagine the man who would ask Detective Hertz out. It wasn't that she was unattractive, bone structure-wise. But she had what I guess you could call "resting bitch face," and the bitchy attitude to go with it, but not in a fun way.

Rika's grandmother lifted her gaze to meet those of the much taller woman. "What does that mean—'*latest* murder' she's involved in?" Mrs. Delacruz asked, knowing full well what Hertz meant. "Do you mean the murder that you accused her innocent father of? Or the murder of her mother when she was a little girl...still unsolved?"

Hertz rolled her eyes and Winchell blew out a loud huff. "We told you, we weren't on the force then," he said.

"But they still have the evidence. The case was never closed. You could go back and look at it anytime, yes? It's called an old—" She shook her head, then turned to Madi, brows raised.

"Cold case," Madi said.

"Yes, a cold case," her mother repeated. "I see them on TV. They get solved all the time by new detectives who were not on the case before..." She shrugged. "But I guess the new detectives have to be smarter than the old ones, not more stupid."

Winchell turned to Hertz. "Maybe we should just get a warrant and toss this place again. We can take her granddaughter to the station for questioning."

Mrs. Delacruz's hand moved to one of her hips as she gestured dramatically with the other. "And maybe I should file a complaint with your boss about how you come and harass the families of murder victims."

"Or maybe we should just haul you in for obstructing justice," Winchell replied.

Normally, I would have given in to the urge to step in and save Rika's grandma, or any woman if Gabe is to be believed. But somehow, I felt Mrs. Delacruz liked fighting her own battles.

"Or maybe, I will call the TV stations," she said. "They still have reporters working there who covered my daughter's murder. One of them is an anchor now. Another is a news director. When they come, maybe I should bring out all my plaques from the homeowner's board—crime fighter of the year—for..." She turned toward Madi. "How many years?"

Madi's eyes met Winchell's. "I don't know, but the box is too heavy for me to lift. Regardless, between the neighbors and all the church activities you volunteer for, we could have three hundred people here with signs when the reporters come. Or maybe we should all meet up in front of the station...?"

Hertz sighed and checked her watch. She definitely had a date later and was mentally tallying how long it would take her to get changed and get wherever she was going, I was sure of it.

Winchell opened his mouth, but she laid a hand on his forearm and he closed it.

"Let's start over," she said in a more pleasant voice than I'd heard her use before. Her civilian voice, I figured. "May we please come in and talk to your granddaughter and Mr. Owen for a few minutes?"

"After the way you destroyed my house with your searching? No. If my granddaughter chooses to talk to you, you can speak outside."

It occurred to me that, as scary as Mrs. Delacruz could be, she was also kind of awesome.

"Miss Martín?" Hertz said.

Rika glanced at me, then stepped out onto the porch. I followed and shut the door behind us.

"How did you come to find the body... um, bodies... um, twins?"

I didn't want Rika to feel she had to support the lie Erissa told, so I jumped in first. "We were hired—"

Rika laid her hand on my forearm, just like Hertz did to Winchell. I didn't appreciate being "handled" in the same way as that dumbass, but I let her take over.

"I met Erissa Fisher at a Starbucks," she explained. "She thought her boyfriend might be cheating—"

Both detectives leaned in. "Her boyfriend Teodor?" Hertz asked, her surprise clear. "But—"

Rika waved her off. "Yeah, I know it sounds weird, but she and

Teodor claim conjoined twins get used to tuning out each other's activities. Anyway, she hired me to go to the duplex on the day she said he would be gone and search for evidence."

"Are you saying this search just happened to coincide with Grigore Vatamanu's murder?" Winchell asked.

"Yep. She claims it's a coincidence, but..." Rika shrugged.

"Has she done anything else suspicious?"

"You first," Rika said. "Do you have any physical evidence pointing to her or anyone else?"

"We're not supposed to discuss an ongoing investigation," Hertz said.

Rika cocked her head as if thinking. "Yeah..." She dragged the word out. "I don't think I'm supposed to either. Erissa hired me to find the killer."

Damn, I loved this woman. I couldn't help but smile.

After giving me a dirty look, Hertz checked her watch again. *Must be some date.* "Look," she said. "Our captain's getting impatient. He said we can't clock out for the night until we have a suspect, and I've got something to do."

"A date," I interjected.

"With a gigolo," Winchell said dismissively.

"He's not a gigolo," Hertz replied. "He's an athlete."

Winchell snorted. "You paid for him at the bachelor auction."

Hertz looked as though she wanted to tase her partner. She bent in closer to Rika and spoke in a conspiratorial tone. "Look, we've got nothing right now. The DNA could take forever. Their bedding was old and full of stains, their side business caused them to have tons of random fingerprints on the items in their house, except for the murder weapon, which was wiped clean before his brother woke up and touched it, assuming he's telling the truth about that part. If you can give me anything I can take to my captain right now so I can make this date, I'll owe you one."

I watched Rika's face change as Hertz's words sunk in. My mother would have called her expression "pleased as punch." I was pretty sure she'd waited her whole life to hear those words from a homicide detective. It was like something out of a TV show.

"Okay," Rika said. "I—" she glanced at me. "*We* don't have much either, but Erissa was extremely specific about what time I had to be there. She re-confirmed my time of arrival over a dozen times. It seemed a little much at the time, but after we found Grigore dead and Teodor in danger of dying, it seemed pretty suspicious."

"So, you think your client is the killer?" Hertz asked.

"I haven't made that determination," Rika said. "There's also their father, who was livid about the twins leaving the act and, after I asked the circus owner a few questions, he may or may not have sicced his tiger on me, depending on who you ask. That documentary director had a lot to lose, too. I don't know who committed the murder, yet. I'm just trying to help you go on that date." And trying to help herself get a marker she could cash in later with Hertz, but, of course, I didn't say that aloud.

Hertz nodded. "Yeah, okay, thanks." She seemed genuinely grateful. "That'll do for tonight."

I noticed Rika left out knife-throwing Constata and wondered if it was because she felt sorry for the old woman or because she felt Constata was more of a suspect than I did and didn't want to give it away. She also didn't mention Eli. That guy was fishy as hell, and I wasn't kidding when I told Rika he might commit a murder just to make her job more interesting.

Hertz turned and jogged down the steps. When she got to the car, she saw that Winchell hadn't moved. I noticed the stubborn set to his jaw. Was he jealous of her date?

"Let's go!" she cried.

"Coming," Winchell replied as he ambled down the steps without a word to us.

Margo's car skidded to a stop in front of the house. She practically flew out of the car and race toward us. "Who?" she cried. "Is it Madi? Mamá?" She was breathing like she'd run all the way here.

"No!" Rika said. "Everyone's fine. They just had questions about the case I'm working on."

Margo's hand went to her chest. Her eyes closed as she took in deep shuddering breaths to calm herself.

Damn. This family had been through a trauma they could never forget to the point where they were constantly waiting for the other shoe to drop.

I guess it's easy to go through life believing "it" will never happen to you, whatever "it" is, until it does. From then on, you know how vulnerable you are.

The cop car started up. Winchell was driving and wasn't in the hurry his partner was. He might be jealous, but he'd better watch himself. I was sure Hertz would kick his ass if he caused her to miss her chance to date a professional athlete.

At the sound of the motor, Margo turned and gave the detectives a murderous look. As they drove away, her shoulders dropped. She wiped both eyes with the backs of her thumbs.

"I fucking hate cops," she muttered as she opened the door and went inside.

My mind searched for something to say that would lighten the mood. "I think that was the first time I've heard Margo curse," was all I could come up with.

Rika nodded. "She doesn't curse...normally. Unless things are really..." She let her voice drift off and I left it at that.

# CHAPTER TWENTY-NINE

**Rika**

When we walked in, Tía Margo was in the kitchen, her arm around my grandmother's shoulder as Lita stirred the contents of a pot. Mrs. Ruíz was at the cutting board.

"What are we having?" Tía Margo asked, peering into the pot.

"We are brrrranching out!" Mrs. Ruíz said with the flair of a boxing ring announcer.

"Vegan Vegetable Curry!" Lita finished for her.

Tía Margo squinted harder. "But isn't that beef floating around in there?"

"Yes," Lita replied. "We tasted it and it was missing something, so we added the beef."

Tía Madi, who was sitting in her spot on the couch, snorted. "You can't call it 'vegan' if it has beef in it."

"It's the name of the recipe we found on the internet," Mrs. Ruíz said. "We want to give them credit."

"I'm pretty sure they wouldn't want credit for this," Tía Margo replied. "And what if we brought actual vegans over and you called it Vegan Vegetable Curry? They'd be horrified to find out they'd eaten meat."

Lita waved a hand in the air, shaking her head. "Don't bring any vegans into my house," she said. "I feed people who come to my house, and vegans are too much trouble. I understand the vegans don't want to eat animals, but you can't even feed them cheese! Why not cheese? The cow is still fine."

"I still don't understand why they don't eat meat," Mrs. Ruíz said. "Do they think cows and chickens have a bucket list they haven't completed? I lived on a farm when I was a little girl and not one of the animals planned to become a scientist or take a cruise to the Bahamas. All they did was stand around eating all day." She threw up her hands—one of them still holding a knife—in an *Am I right?* gesture. "Show me a chicken who can put on a bikini or find a cure for cancer and I'll stop eating meat!"

Nick threw his head back and laughed his full-throated manly laugh, which, I swear to God, made my aunts, Mrs. Ruíz, and my grandmother stop what they were doing and watch him. Mrs. Ruíz even licked her lips like she could taste him from where she was standing.

But who could blame her? Nick was super-hot on his worst days. When he smiled like he was smiling now...

I glanced toward my bedroom wistfully before my brain took over again. What were we thinking, trying to do the nasty right under my grandmother's nose?

Maybe I could make an excuse and sneak off to Nick's hotel room tonight. Despite seeming over me the last time we did it, he certainly seemed into me today. Or, almost into me, to be precise.

Much of the time, I still had trouble believing someone like Nick Owen would want me for anything long-term when he could have any woman, including Mrs. Ruíz, apparently.

To be honest, I felt I was closer to Eli's league than Nick's. And, at least, I knew Eli wouldn't dump me if I gained some of that weight back. I couldn't imagine tall, hunky Nick Owen with the heavy version of me, not in a million years.

The door opened and Sofia walked in carrying Gucci. She handed her off to Nick.

"What's for dinner? I'm starved," she said.

"What did you do to my dog?" Nick asked. It was a legitimate question. His Maltese was now cotton candy pink and wearing a tiny purple hat with pink polka dots on it.

"We have a birthday party every month for the dogs who were born—or adopted—in that month," Sofia explained. "All our clients are invited and the dogs get to play together. The hair dye will wash out in one or two shampoos."

"Did it have to be pink?" Nick asked.

"It did," Sofia smirked. "Just so I could see that look on your face."

Tía Madi cracked up. I smiled. When those two gave someone a hard time, it was a clear sign they liked and accepted that person, and I really wanted my family to like Nick.

Nick scratched Gucci behind the ears and put up with a dozen of her tiny kisses before setting her on the floor. She made a beeline for the kitchen. "Dance Gucci, dance!" Mrs. Ruíz said as soon as the Maltese was underfoot.

Once Gucci had twirled round and round on her hind feet, Mrs. Ruíz rewarded her with a piece of beef from the 'Vegan' Vegetable Curry.

"Here, Sofia, set the table," my grandmother said. She handed Sofia the plates and went back to the stove.

Sofia handed the plates to Nick. He chuckled and started setting the table, clearly willing to do whatever it took to keep his dog sitter happy.

Madi motioned me to the couch to look at a cool Instagram post.

The door opened again. "Hey, y'all!" LeeAnne cried as she came in. "Look what I found in the driveway." She gestured toward the front porch.

Julian walked in.

*Oh, jeez.*

I glanced at Nick. He was standing still as a statue, his plate-filled hand hovering in the air over the table, his eyes trained on Julian.

Smiling warmly, Julian strode toward me as I stood to greet him. He came in for a hug, punctuated by a kiss on my cheek. "Thanks for inviting me," he said. He handed me a rectangular box.

Behind me, I heard a plate hit the table, much louder than usual.

"Hi...Julian." I said. Then I almost added, "What a surprise to see you," but what sense would that make after he thanked me for inviting him?

I cut my eyes to my right where Tía Madi was sitting. My blasé aunt had perked up, her attention one hundred percent focused on my predicament.

I sank onto the other end of the couch.

"Julian!" my grandmother practically squealed. "So nice to see you!" She hustled out of the kitchen and threw her arms around him.

While he greeted her with a polite kiss on the cheek, as expected, I checked out the box in my lap. It looked like...

I lifted it to my nose and inhaled.

*Chocolates.*

These would not be going into the trash.

*But they should,* the Jilly Crane counselor in my head replied.

*But they won't,* my tongue and stomach cried simultaneously.

Again, we ended up at the table with Julian on the end, inches away from me. I was sitting perpendicular to him to his right, Nick was next to me on my right.

As we ate, I could feel waves of anger rolling off Nick. But I couldn't bring myself to embarrass Julian in front of everyone by telling him I didn't invite him, either time.

*Plus, you don't want to give back the candy.* I bitch slapped the

Hungry Hungry Hippo who lived inside me, but she didn't seem affected in the least.

Lucky for me, several celebrities had come into the boutique where LeeAnne worked this week, therefore, she did most of the talking. I picked up my fork, accidentally rubbing my upper arm against Nick's. He didn't make eye contact. The pang in my chest was so sharp, I sucked in a startled breath.

Julian, on the other hand, was too willing to make eye contact and, every time he did, noxious guilt flooded through me.

The curry dish tasted good, but my throat was refusing to swallow it.

It was hard to think of anything other than my discomfort, but when I came to, LeeAnne was saying, "...so Angelina Wilde wants me to be her doggy stylist!"

"*Doggy* stylist?" my aunts, Lita, and Mrs. Ruíz said in unison. Sofia didn't seem to find the notion shocking at all.

"Yeah, it's just part-time for special events, but you never know what it could lead to!" Her eyes shone as she looked around the table at my family members. "Less than a year ago, all I had was a pipe dream about living in L.A., being a stylist to the stars and, thanks to y'all, my dream is coming true!"

My eyes cut to Nick, expecting him to point out that being a dog stylist was not the same as being a stylist to the stars.

He didn't even seem to be listening. He just stabbed one piece of meat after another with his fork and chewed, as if he was in a hurry to finish the meal.

Then suddenly, he grabbed his phone from the table and stood. "I'm sorry, but I have to take this," he said to the table at large. He walked out the front door. Gucci chased him, then skittered backward when the door swung closed behind him.

She stood, staring at the door, making frustrated growling noises.

For the next ten minutes, whenever there was a lull in the conversation, I was aware of Nick's voice out on the porch. I strained to hear what he was saying, but could only detect the tone—surprised, then gentle and reassuring in a voice I was certain he wouldn't use on a man.

My attention was diverted when Sofia's phone dinged. She checked it and typed something into it.

I realized Nick had stopped talking outside and, seconds later, I heard his truck start up.

*No! Julian should be the one leaving, not Nick!*

My phone vibrated. I lifted it from the table and clicked to the text messages. There was one from Nick.

*I need to leave town to check on something important. Should only be gone a day or so. Sofia says she can keep Gucci. Be safe. Take tomorrow off and don't go sleuthing without me.*

Oh, my God! Nick was leaving me? He said it was just for a day, but maybe this was his way of letting me down easy. First a day, then it would stretch to a few days, then a week, then a month...

Where was he going? And more importantly, who was he going to see?

The woman on the phone, that's who. And knowing Nick's modus operandi, if she seemed to need him more than I did, I'd probably never see him again.

What little food I'd eaten sat heavy inside me.

Maybe it wasn't just about something or someone needing Nick's attention. Maybe he used the phone call as an excuse to leave.

*Damn.* Maybe he was convinced I was into Julian, considering how often "I" invited him to dinner.

*Please come back to me, Nick!* I desperately wished I were psychic, even though I didn't believe in psychics.

Closing my eyes, I forced myself to take three long calming breaths.

I touched my phone. The screen lit up and I reread Nick's

message. Then, I closed my eyes again, attempting to slow my thoughts like my Jilly Crane counselor taught me.

Breathe in. *He said he'd only be gone a day or so. That means he's coming back.* Breathe out.

Breathe in. *Nick's coming back... Nick's coming back... Nick's coming back...* Breathe out.

"Are you okay, Rika?" Julian asked.

I opened my eyes to find him holding a spoon full of *natilla* halfway to his mouth. My grandmother was walking around the table serving the custard to everyone.

Why would she make *natilla* now? Christmas was over weeks ago.

Then I remembered the little Colombian restaurant near the community college where I met Julian. A bunch of us went there that December to celebrate the end of the fall term. Julian loved the *natilla!*

Were my grandmother and Julian communicating on a regular basis? Did she ask him about his favorite Colombian foods? She assumed everyone had a favorite Colombian dish, despite the fact that most Americans didn't know what Colombians ate.

Julian finished his dessert, along with the cup of coffee my grandmother had provided. I was only vaguely aware of LeeAnne's chattering, my aunts' interjecting comments, and the clattering of dishes as Lita and Mrs. Ruíz carried on their own conversation in the kitchen.

This was beyond awkward! Maybe Nick was right about me leading guys on. Well, he hadn't said it exactly that way, but that's what he'd meant.

I glanced up to find Julian still gazing at me expectantly, like he thought I was about to burst out in song or do a standup routine. I dug into the *natilla* and I wondered if there would be enough left over for a missing-Nick, late-night binge.

Sofia stood, deposited her plate in the sink and picked Gucci up off the floor. "We need to clip your toenails," she said to the clueless pup.

I considered Sofia for a moment. My cousin had a bomb-shell body since junior high. To me, her interactions with guys had seemed effortless. If she liked them, she went out with them. If she wasn't interested, they disappeared and didn't come back.

But I'd missed out on all the love lessons I assumed most people learned in junior high and high school. And it's hard to think of yourself as leading guys on when you don't truly believe you're desirable. Where was the line between being friendly and being too friendly? Was there a remedial class I could take? I kicked ass in class.

Wait a minute! This wasn't all my fault! Julian and I were fine as ex-classmate buddies before my grandmother started interfering. At least, I thought we were fine.

I uncrossed my legs under the table, then crossed them the other way, trying not to show how anxious I was for Julian to leave. Couldn't he feel the tension?

I examined his body language. He looked completely relaxed. One might even say he looked at home in my grandmother's dining room. He was cute, in great shape, employed, and had Lita's stamp of approval, as clear as if she'd tattooed it on his forehead. I could almost imagine a life with him.

And that life was very, very boring.

That's when I realized, sooner or later, I was going to have to hurt Julian's feelings.

He checked his phone. "Better get going. I'm working tonight."

*Well, thank you, Thor!*

I stood to see him off. He moved like he expected me to walk him out, but I halted several feet from the front door. If I stepped outside, I was afraid Julian would try to kiss me for real, then I'd have to decide whether to let him or push him away, which seemed like a worse rejection than telling him I was involved with someone else.

I'd have to use the word "involved" because I wasn't sure which of the more specific labels applied.

"It was nice to see you again, Julian," I said, hoping the formality of the phrase would give him the hint that we weren't going to be an item.

"Thanks for inviting me," he said.

I tried the truth out in my head—*I didn't invite you, Julian.*

Wouldn't any man feel humiliated if he responded to a dinner invite, ate the food, then was told by his hostess that she hadn't actually invited him?

I couldn't bring myself to say it.

He hugged me and gave me a kiss on the cheek, then waved to my family, thanking them and blowing kisses to Lita and Mrs. Ruíz.

They captured the kisses in their hands, then pressed their palms to their cheeks like a couple of synchronized swimmers, but without water or those weird nose plug things.

Once I'd shut the door and watched to make sure Julian's car was pulling out of the driveway, I turned around and addressed the room at large.

"Why does Julian keep thinking I'm inviting him to dinner?" I asked loudly.

All chatter stopped. Every pair of eyes in the living-dining-kitchen area darted to me, then shifted and peered at my grandmother expectantly.

*Just as I suspected.*

"Lita?" I said. "Why does Julian keep thinking I'm inviting him to dinner?"

My grandmother, the one who could stare down a puma, didn't make eye contact. Instead, she focused all her attention on folding a dishtowel.

I tried to imagine how Lita was masquerading as me when

communicating with Julian. "Did you...hack into my social media?" It was hard to imagine, but the only explanation I could come up with.

"Hawk?" Lita said.

"Hack," I repeated.

"That's what I said," she replied, confirming this was an accent issue and had nothing to do with birds of prey.

Beyond frustrated, I threw my hands up in the air, "*Abuelita!*" I yelled, hoping her full title would jar the truth out of her.

"Okay, okay..." She waved her hands in surrender. "I just call him and say, 'Rika left in a hurry, but she asked me to call you and invite you to dinner'. That's all."

Tía Margo chuckled wryly and tilted her head toward me. "I guess sometimes old school works just as well as high tech."

Madi aimed a mischievous grin at her mother. "Are you going to confess your lies to Father Francisco when you go to church?" she asked tauntingly.

"It wasn't a sin," Lita argued. "It was a good deed."

Margo's smile disappeared. "Mamá!" she said in a scolding voice. "Was it a good deed for Julian, making him believe Rika is interested in him when she's not? Or was it a good deed for Rika, who's madly in love with another man and having trouble expressing her feelings for him, but now also has to break Julian's heart?"

I had mixed feelings about Margo's little speech. I didn't realize she'd deduced that much about my situation with Nick. I felt emotionally exposed. On the other hand, my grandmother needed to hear the truth about her meddling and its effects.

Lita huffed out a big breath. "Nick is a good man, but he's not for Rika. He carries a lot of luggage."

I was confused. "Yeah, I guess he's pretty strong, but I don't understand what luggage carrying ability has to do—"

"Baggage," Margo said. "She means emotional baggage."

"Oh..." I felt silly for not catching onto that one. I'd lived with my grandmother most of my life.

Lita walked solemnly to where I was standing and enveloped me in a hug. "Paprika, after everything you've been through in your life, you deserve something fresh and clean."

Was she calling Nick stale and dirty? Maybe it was time to take her for another eye exam.

"I know he is handsome..." she continued.

"And tall," Mrs. Ruíz added.

Lita nodded. "And tall. But he's older and he's been around the clock too many times."

"You mean 'block', Mamá," Margo said.

"No. I mean clock," Lita insisted. "He's much older, so he's been around the clock too many times. What does it matter how many times you've been around the block?" We all looked to each other for a logical argument, but no one came up with anything. Lita continued, "You deserve to start out with someone your own age and—"

"Make your baggage together," Mrs. Ruíz finished for her.

Lita gave her a look that said, *Silencio!*

Mrs. Ruíz pressed her lips together.

My grandmother was standing with her face inches from mine—my aunts and I automatically defaulted to Latin personal space requirements in her house, rather than American ones—and she was willing me to agree with her and decide I was in love with Julian after all.

I appreciated everything she'd tried to do for me in my life, even the misguided stuff. I knew she always had the best intentions for me. But I couldn't be with Julian for her.

"Excuse me," LeeAnne said. She hadn't moved from her spot at the table and she'd been so quiet during this discussion, I almost forgot she was in the room. "I don't wanna butt in on your family business..."

Everyone turned to listen to her. Lita and Mrs. Ruíz looked

puzzled at her statement. Probably because there was no such thing as "butting in" to them. If they could hear a conversation and had something to say about it, they said it.

"I've known Nick my whole life," LeeAnne continued. "And he's been a great guy, always. When his daddy died, he watched out for his mamma and little sister...and even me. I guess he realized I didn't have anybody to..." Her eyes drifted toward a memory before she cleared her throat and continued. "That whole thing about the three divorces... I know that makes him sound like an a-hole, but there were other forces at play."

*Other forces at play? What does that mean?* But I didn't say anything because LeeAnne was already having trouble getting her point across. I'd never seen her this sentimental about Nick.

"I don't know how Nick sees it, but from where I stand, those women were liars and users." She looked at my grandmother. "A girl could do a lot worse than Nick Owen. And I've never seen him look at another woman the way he looks—" She stopped herself before she finished the sentence, like she was afraid she was going too far, maybe stepping on Nick's toes.

I'd never thought LeeAnne cared about stepping on Nick's toes before this. In fact, I would have sworn she enjoyed it, but she seemed to understand how high the stakes were for us and didn't want to muck it up, I guess.

"He's just a really great guy and any woman would be lucky to have him," she said. "That's all I'm gonna say about it."

# CHAPTER THIRTY

**Nick**

I drove toward the hotel to pick up a couple of things before heading to the airport.

For the second time this week, Julian had shown up for dinner, ostensibly in response to an invite from Rika.

What the hell was I supposed to think about that?

It's true that we never officially said we were exclusive. But a big part of me felt like Rika and I together were inevitable, in the best possible way.

Yes, there'd been mixed messages and odd behavior along the way. And she gave off a "yes, but not yet" vibe a lot of the time, so I figured I'd use the job to get to know her better and the time to get in good with her family, who she was obviously very close to.

I guess the last part was a bust because her family seemed to like Julian as well, or even better, than me.

Regardless, when I got back, I needed to have an honest, private talk with her and get some clarity.

*If* she'd cooperate. I always had the feeling she was hiding a big part of herself from me, and I didn't understand why.

As I followed the parking signs at the airport, I reset my brain to the issue at hand.

My sister DeeAnne had finally come clean about what was going on. Kyle, her ex, seemed obsessed with revenge and still wouldn't leave her alone, even though they'd been divorced for months.

A couple of weeks ago, he'd started sending her the boudoir pictures they'd had taken for their second anniversary. I didn't know anything about them at the time, of course. I guess it's not the kind of thing a girl wants to talk to her brother about.

But, when she'd called me at Mrs. Delacruz's house, she explained that, while the pictures were very tasteful in the context of private photos to be seen by a married couple, they were still very sensual and not something she'd ever post on social media.

Her job involved work with and on behalf of kids, not to mention that she'd always been modest about her body, even when our mom was pushing her to "jazz" up her high school wardrobe, which, in Mom's lingo meant sex it up.

Now, Kyle was threatening to start posting the photos online. He was smart enough not to word his messages as threats, but when someone says things like, "the guys on the Screw My Ex site would love this one," it was clear what he meant.

While I certainly got how hard divorce could be, I never understood men who were obsessed with getting revenge on a woman they once exchanged vows with. Despite passing away young, my dad had made sure he instilled a respect for humans in general and he modeled respect towards my mother, even if he was frustrated as hell with her.

My mom's instructions to me, regarding the fairer sex, were geared more toward superficial acts of chivalry, like opening doors and finding something to compliment them on.

For the first time, I wondered if my dad ever regretted marrying my mom. Did they have anything at all in common?

My ten-year-old brain hadn't known it needed to record every interaction for future examination. What kid expects to lose his strong, always reliable dad before his eleventh birthday?

From the moment we found out he was gone, I knew it was my job to take care of my little sister. I helped her with her homework. I taught her to play sports well enough to keep other kids from making fun of her, although she never took to any of them. I tried to soften the blow when Mom forced her to do things she hated, like performing in pageants and going out for cheerleading.

I chuckled as I remembered how upset I'd gotten when word of who the junior high cheerleaders would be the next year made it over to the high school, minutes after they were announced. When I went over to walk DeeAnne home from school that day, I tried my best to channel my dad and started saying what I hoped were the right things to console her.

After several seconds of silence and with a very guilty look on her face, she confessed that she'd screwed up the routine on purpose because she'd never wanted to be a cheerleader in the first place. Then she begged me not to tell Mom.

Under no circumstances would I ever have told Mom. In fact, to this day, she was convinced there was a conspiracy—instigated by a teacher she used to compete against in pageants—that kept her daughter from taking her rightful place on the squad.

I was proud of my little sister. I saw her practice the routine with my mom, and she had it down pat. It takes guts to purposely humiliate yourself at school, even if it helps you meet your long-term goal.

Truth be told, I was always proud of DeeAnne. She didn't accept the small thinking she was often surrounded by in our little town. She fact-checked, thought things through for herself, and came to her own conclusions, all without a sensible parent around to guide her. And, since she graduated from college, she'd worked at non-profit organizations helping refugees, the homeless and now kids.

She was one of the most awesome people I'd ever known. There was no universe in which she deserved to be harassed by her creepy ex-husband.

What made Kyle's actions even harder for my attorney brain to fathom was that he had no demands. There was no end game. Certainly, no win-win situation. He was a smart guy. He knew he'd done too much now for DeeAnne to ever consider getting back together with him. Why was he doing this?

Revenge. She left him and his ego couldn't accept it.

But no man was going to take revenge on my baby sister while I was still alive and kicking. And this had gone too far to fix with a civil conversation.

I might not have a sleeve full of cyber tricks to pull from like he did, but I had one big thing in my favor.

I knew I could scare the crap out of Kyle.

Meanwhile, I'd convinced myself Rika had already gotten into all the trouble she was going to for this case. She'd be fine for the twenty-four hours I'd be away.

As I turned into the parking lot, the thought crossed my mind that I might spend the next few decades trying to talk Rika out of doing dangerous things on her own.

And, if that was the cost of admission into her world, permanently, I was okay with that.

~

**Rika**

The next morning, I sat at my computer, feeling a little lost.

Despite my dream of being a lone P.I., I guess I'd gotten used to having Nick working with me.

And I really wished I had him around today, so we could bounce ideas off each other.

I was frustrated with the investigation.

There were certainly suspects in Grigore's murder. In fact, he knew people from all over the world who seemed capable of killing without remorse, thanks to that sociopath Xavier and his circus of assholes. But nobody there was a real standout suspect.

When I awakened this morning, I had a text waiting from Julian. The cops had virtually nothing to go on, so, they'd called Erissa in for questioning again.

While Erissa had been at or near the top of my suspect list all along, I thought it was a mistake for the cops to question her before they'd gathered more evidence. I was pretty sure they hadn't even gone through her phone records yet or they would have been at my door a lot sooner, wanting to know why she called me repeatedly in the days before Grigore was murdered.

I wished I had the power to pull the phone records of everyone at the circus. Oh, and the documentary crew, too. Although Erissa had the most to lose, emotionally speaking, if Grigore refused the operation, Stan had the bigger financial and career investment in the separation.

As sketchy as she seemed, a part of me felt like Erissa was too obvious as a suspect, with her convenient timing and dead first husband. But, in real life, weren't most murderers the obvious suspects? Wives, husbands, girlfriends, boyfriends...

However, I still felt I needed to do surveillance on Stan.

Unfortunately, I didn't have the right equipment, yet, to do anything other than follow him around in the car. I could really use a parabolic microphone that would pick up sound from hundreds of feet away. Then, I could sit in my car and listen to what was being said inside Stan's office or his house.

I didn't get hands-on murdering vibes from Stan, though. He seemed like the type who would hire someone else to do his dirty work.

That brought me back to phone records. At this point, Stan would have already paid the hitman. They would have no further reason to communicate, but phone records could point me in the right direction.

How did one go about meeting people who worked for cell service companies?

As if on cue, my cell phone rang. When I looked at the screen, I was surprised to see Geoff Choi's name.

"Hey, Rika, how's it going?" he said when I answered.

"Eh, so-so," I replied honestly.

"Are you still working on Grigore's case?"

"Yep," I said. "But I don't feel like I'm getting anywhere."

"I might have information to change that."

I sat up straight. "What do you mean?"

"Well, I'm no investigator," he began. "But I saw Stan a few minutes ago. The medical examiner just released a report. Somehow Stan had gotten it, along with imaging they supposedly took of Grigore's body."

My ears perked up at his choice of words. Wait, how did Stan get access to the x-rays in an ongoing investigation?

Must have paid somebody off.

"Supposedly?" I repeated.

"Yeah, we did CT scans, MRI's, and pretty much every test we had at our disposal on the twins. We knew their bodies inside and out. But, the scans from the M.E. are..." He paused as if considering whether he should be telling me this.

"Are...?" I prompted.

"They're not Grigore."

This was unexpected. Could there be a mix-up?

Then, it hit me that someone at the M.E.'s office probably took Stan's money and gave him the images from an old case. That way, they wouldn't, technically, have divulged information they shouldn't.

When I didn't reply, Dr. Choi continued. "Stan left me the report and there are irregularities there, too."

*Irregularities? Hm...*

"What kind of irregularities?" I asked.

"I'll tell you what," he said. "Come to dinner with me tonight and I'll fill you in."

The invitation took me by surprise. "Dinner?" I said as if I'd never heard the word before.

"Yeah. I figure if I'm giving you information, I might as well get a meal with a beautiful woman as a reward."

I wondered what beautiful woman I was supposed to bring along before I realized he was referring to me.

*Holy mother of Zeus!* An intelligent, handsome surgeon who shared my love of everything geeky was asking me out on a date!

My face warmed and I felt the flattery down to my toes.

I mean, I didn't have feelings for Dr. Choi, at least not the major kind I had for Nick, but what could it hurt to have dinner with him? He might be able to shed light on the case. Plus, it would be the perfect time to get him to hook me up with his geek gear supplier. He'd only sent me one contact so far—the one who made the awesome Hogwarts model—but I wanted them all. I couldn't afford much now, but maybe after a few more cases...

*And*, this was the perfect night for dinner with the doctor since Nick was out of town and wouldn't be eating with us at Lita's house. Maybe going to dinner with someone like Geoff Choi would help give me the confidence boost to really go for it with Nick.

Maybe I'd be so high off Geoff's flirting, I could tell Nick how I felt about him.

There was really no reason to refuse the offer.

"What time do you want me to meet you at the restaurant?" If I took my own car, it would remove the awkwardness of riding in the car together and temper his expectations, in case he was expecting me to give him more than a couple of hours of my time over dinner.

"How about seven o'clock at The Ferns?"

"Sure," I said. "I'll see you then."

"Great!" he replied. "It's a date!"

# CHAPTER THIRTY-ONE

**Rika**

I walked into The Ferns, feeling self-conscious, my head swiveling around for any sign of Dr. Choi.

I was glad he gave me a heads up on where we were going and really glad I'd decided to wear the brand-new dress one of Nick's exes had left behind in his house in Bolo—long story.

This was a classy restaurant. The dress was body conscious with animal print done in a classy, sophisticated way. My only worry was whether the pounds I'd gained might make it look sad-tight instead of attractive-tight.

Anyway, this restaurant was fa-a-ancy. I'd gone to a few nice places in New York, after Brandtt started making his *Real Millionaire Bachelors of New York* fake reality show money, but never in Los Angeles.

My grandmother was always cooking and neither Brandtt nor I had any money when we started dating in L.A. Our cheap dates bothered Brandtt. He thought he was destined for a more glamorous life. Not me, though. I wasn't into expensive things, unless you counted geek gear.

Come to think of it, I'd been in more good restaurants in

Colombia than in Los Angeles since my dad became a head chef at one, then another high-end restaurant in Bogotá. But the times I'd gotten to visit him there seemed like nothing compared to the time I should have spent with him.

That sad, icky feeling started growing inside me, but I swallowed a couple of times and it went away, as it almost always did.

Tía Margo always said you weren't supposed to "stuff" your feelings. I never told her, but I disagreed. Because, really, who wants to be around a person who talks about her dead mother and absent father all the time, especially once that person is an adult?

Why was I even thinking about this now?

*You feel you don't belong here and your anxiety is spiking,* the Tía Margo who apparently lived in my head pointed out.

I felt warmth at my elbow and turned to find Dr. Choi next to me. He smiled and I instantly felt better. With ease and confidence, he strolled up to the desk and informed one of the hostesses he had a reservation.

Despite some confusion and whispering between the hostesses, both dressed in white shirts, black vests and black skirts, Dr. Choi didn't seem the least bit disturbed.

His stance said, *I'm not worried. I'm a surgeon, and I'll speak to your manager if you screw up.*

That may be a lot for a stance to say, but I could tell the hostesses recognized it and were not interested in testing him.

A minute later, we were following a white, middle-aged man with the posture of a butler to a gleaming table made of dark wood.

There was a moment of awkwardness when the man and I started to pull my chair out simultaneously. I quickly let go and allowed him to do his job.

Once I was seated, I looked up to find Dr. Choi smiling widely at me. "I didn't think you could be more beautiful," he said. "But the firelight reflecting on your hair...it sets you aglow."

*Aglow*? Did I know any other men who used the word "aglow"?

This was a mistake. Despite the posh ambiance, I'd imagined more of a casual dinner with conversation about the case and a bit of geek talk—enough to find out where he was getting his awesome stuff.

This, however, felt more like a seduction scenario.

Of course, I hadn't been involved in a ton of seduction scenarios. After I lost that extra person I was carrying around on my body—jeez, bad metaphor considering the case I was working—I had Brandtt until he broke up with me. Then I'd been hung up on Nick and had started gaining weight back, so I was pretty sure I wasn't giving off a hit-on-me vibe.

However, if I let Dr. Choi buy me an expensive dinner, would he expect something in return?

*Think, Paprika. Take control of the conversation.*

I decided I'd pay for my own dinner, steep as the cost was going to be. "Well, thanks for meeting with me, Dr. Choi," I said, trying to set a professional tone.

"Geoff," he said. "Call me Geoff."

"Okay," I said like it was all the same to me. "Thanks for meeting with me about the case."

He tilted his head a bit, his lips arranged in a sexy half-grin. "The pleasure is all mine. Regardless of the reason."

This guy did not mess around! He was pouring on all the charm, which would probably have been super-hot if:

a) I wasn't such an awkward nerd and b) I wasn't already head over heels for the coolest, hottest, funniest, and generally greatest guy in the galaxy.

"Um...thanks," I replied. "That's...nice of you to say." Was that how a normal woman would respond? I wasn't sure.

"Nothing nice about it." Now there was no smile. He was looking deep into my eyes and sort of smoldering.

I had no idea what to do with a smoldering man, especially a smoldering man I wasn't planning to sleep with. For the first time, ever, I wished I had the numbers to text those girls who made fun of me in high school and ask how to put out this fire.

Honestly, cute as he was, I'd assumed he'd be more of a nerd, like me, not some pickup artist. I wondered if he'd been born with that kind of confidence or if it came with the stethoscope.

The waiter came over and Dr. Choi—I mean Geoff—ordered us a very expensive bottle of merlot, which only stressed me out more.

I checked the menu, mentally tabulating what my half of the wine bottle plus one of these extremely overpriced entrees would cost.

A minute later, the waiter came back and poured the wine. Then he stood, staring at me with a look that said, *I make more here in a night than you do in a month, but we'll pretend you belong here 'cause that's my job.*

But what he said was, "Can I get you started with an hors d'oeuvre, miss?"

"No!" I blurted. "Um, I mean, no thank you. None for me. I'll be too stuffed to finish my dinner." I smiled apologetically at him. I'm not sure what I was apologizing for, but, as I may have mentioned, I was really stressed out.

"Okay," Geoff said. "I guess we'll just order now, if you're ready."

"What can I get for you, miss?" the waiter asked.

I'd already scanned the menu and decided on the chicken rosemary, the least expensive thing on the menu, which wasn't saying much. While Geoff ordered, I prepared to try again to take control of the conversation.

The second the waiter walked away, I said, "So, you had information for me about Grigore's scans?"

Geoff leaned back against his chair and stretched his torso. "This case has you wound too tight," he replied. "Have a glass of wine. Relax. We can talk business later."

I took a sip of my wine, then sucked in a deep breath, feigning relaxation. But I had no intention of relaxing while in the company of pickup artist extraordinaire Dr. Geoff Choi.

I started to feel like I was staring into his come-hither gaze against my will. I forced my eyes to avert themselves. He could be a vampire, and I didn't want to make it easy for him to mesmerize me.

My shifty eyes traveled down his neck to his tie. I'd been so nervous, I hadn't noticed he was wearing his Millennium Falcon tie clip.

I stared at it enviously, even though I had no use for a tie clip. But whoever made it was head and shoulders above most crafts-men. I wasn't normally a jewelry person, but if I had a pair of earrings or a necklace made by the same person, I'd wear the hell out of it.

"I love your tie clip," I said. "It's really detailed. Where did you get it?"

"Well..." He pressed his lips together smugly. "I know a guy."

*Aha!* I knew he knew a guy!

"Can you hook me up with him?" I asked.

He paused as if thinking about it.

I leaned in toward Geoff, while wondering if his guy made other things too, like a death star. Or a White Walker sword. No, a Furious Power Fist from *Fallout Four*! If I had a power fist, I wouldn't ever need a gun!

"I've got a better idea," he said. "Let me know what you're into..." His eyebrows flipped up, then down, suggestively, "...and I'll get it for you."

I might not be the most experienced person when it comes to men, but I wasn't an idiot. I could see by the unmasked lust in his eyes that Geoff wasn't going to give up his guy without getting a particular something in trade from me.

There went my dream of having my own personal artisan. No

matter how much I admired the work, I wasn't going to prostitute myself with Geoff over some model spacecraft.

Oh, well. Who knew when I'd have enough money to buy a custom piece anyway?

My eyes went back to his tie clip, gleaming like a freshly minted quarter. It was very 3-D, with the strips that originated in the middle and continued out in four different directions—north, south, east and west—raised above the sections around it, in sort of a cross shape.

It struck me that I'd been too narrow-minded in thinking of the shape on Grigore's palm as a crucifix all this time.

There were probably lots of jewelry designs that involved lines crisscrossing each other. Maybe, when Nick came back, we should look at the photo of Grigore's hand and brainstorm about what else could cause an imprint like that.

"Are you still with me?" Geoff asked.

"Oh, I was distracted by your tie clip again. Can I take a picture?" I could show Nick what I meant instead of telling him. I wondered if those documentary geeks had anything like this. Then, I reminded myself again not to settle on the idea of a crucifix or a Millennium Falcon. I needed to consider anything people wore on their torsos or around their necks with crisscross patterns on them.

Suddenly, I recalled the cool ankh necklace Dr. Washington was wearing the day we met with her. I tried to mentally superimpose it onto Grigore's hand.

"Sure, you can," Geoff replied. "But make sure you get my face in it. Don't want you to forget about me."

I smiled at him and snapped the picture. He'd turned his head just a tad when I took it, clearly knowing his photographic angles as well as Brandtt did.

I was pretty sure Geoff Choi was a dawg, but if I weren't a goner over Nick, I might actually try a one-night hookup, for a change. Of course, that was easy to claim when I had no intention of following through. In reality, the idea of sex with someone I barely knew gave me major anxiety.

"So, what were the irregularities you noticed in the scans?" I asked. That was supposed to be the reason for our dinner, after all.

He lifted his eyebrows. "Scans?" His face said he had no idea what I was talking about.

"You said there were irregularities...?"

He burst out laughing. "That was just an excuse in case you needed to get away from that big bodyguard of yours."

"Do you mean Nick?"

"Yeah, your business partner who wants to be more. I get that sometimes women have to do things to get what they want... You know, lead a guy on. If they're rich but stupid, they don't deserve to have the money anyway. No judgment."

I was suddenly aware of my blood pumping, hot, in my veins. He'd just called Nick stupid and me a gold digger.

Geoff Choi was getting less attractive by the minute.

I guess I'd never considered how many jerks I'd meet being a private investigator. This case had been full of them, but I hadn't expected Geoff to turn into one. Maybe I'd given him too much credit for being a super cute geek.

Since it didn't look like I was getting any information about the case or his craftsman, there was no reason for me to be here. Geoff was a jerk and, after his rude comments about Nick, I wanted to throw a drink in his face and storm out.

But then everyone in the restaurant would be staring at me in this snug dress, judging me, while Geoff chuckled and gave the businessmen at the next table a look that said, *Women! What are ya gonna do with them?*

All right then, I was going to take control of the conversation, eat my dinner, and drive away, hopefully never to see Geoff Choi again.

"I've been thinking of trying my hand at those models, like

you make," I said. "Do you have any tricks of the trade? Yours looked perfect!"

He nodded, apparently agreeing with me about their perfection. "I'm very particular about the things I use," he said. "For instance, if there's glue included in the model kit, toss it out. It's crap. I use cement glue."

My brain rewound and played his words again, coming to a screeching halt at the word "cement." Did he mean regular cement glue or the brand Sea-ment we'd found in Grigore's bedroom?

"Just any cement glue?" I asked.

He shook his head, his lips turned up, clearly enjoying imparting his wisdom on little ol' me. "There's a brand spelled S-E-A-M-E-N-T. It's the most waterproof. Figured if I ever had one of those kids that throws everything into the toilet, I wanted my stuff to be waterproof so I wouldn't have to kill him."

There was something about the look in his eyes when he said the last seven words...

My eyes flicked back and caught on his tie clip. If my memory was correct, it could be a match.

The waiter showed up with our plates, laying mine gently in front of me before going over to Geoff.

"Oh, my purse is vibrating," I said. "I'm sorry. I have to check this." As the waiter refilled our water glasses, I pulled out my phone, tapping quickly to the photo of Grigore's palm. I tried to memorize every line before I said, "Oh, no big deal," and put my phone back into the purse.

Then I checked the tie clip again. How many people could Grigore have known who owned something that was this close a match to the imprint?

But wouldn't Dr. Geoff Choi have much more to lose by murdering Grigore than he could possibly gain? Starting with his medical license and ending with being the bitch to whoever was heading up the Asian gang in prison. He was way too pretty not to end up somebody's jailhouse girlfriend and I was sure he knew it.

But what were the other possibilities? That one of the documentary crew saw Geoff's pin and asked where he could get one? I couldn't imagine Jeb or Izzy wearing a tie, much less a tie clip.

Geoff had started eating. I lifted my fork from the table and picked at a mini potato on my plate. I was uncomfortable with the silence. "You were telling me about your models," I reminded him. "Tips and tricks?"

I watched him swallow. "Oh, yeah," he replied. "I guess I'm kind of extreme about it. I have a special room with the best air purification system to keep the dust out. I handle everything with gloves to keep the skin oils from affecting them. My ex-wife used to make fun of me for being overly meticulous."

I couldn't blame him for that. I'd want to take every precaution, too. "Plus, you're less likely to leave fingerprints if you decide to commit a crime while cleaning your..." Something flashed in his eyes that sent a shiver down my vertebrae. "...your, um, stuff." I made myself laugh. My comment had started out as a joke, but it didn't feel like one anymore.

"Can you excuse me for a minute?" I asked. "Just need to hit the powder room." Powder room? Since when did I call it a powder room? Did anyone ever call it a powder room, outside of old movies?

I hoped he hadn't found my words suspicious. He had the money to charter a plane if he wanted to, and I didn't want to be the one to make him bolt.

I snatched up my handbag—which was actually one of Sofia's nicer bags—and headed for the bathroom.

When I got there, I locked myself in a stall and pulled up the picture of Grigore's palm again, then compared it to the picture I'd taken of Geoff's tie clip.

The multiple non-linear indentions on Grigore's palm that fell in between the parallel lines, and also where the lines came together in the middle, could easily have been caused by the tie clip. In fact, now these raised areas seemed to fit the bill much better than Jesus-on-the-cross would have.

I flipped back and forth, back and forth, looking for a line that would prove the impression hadn't been made by that clip, but couldn't find any. They matched exactly. The only question was whether they were the same size. The pictures weren't to scale. I thought about the Sea-ment glue. How common was the stuff?

Tapping the icon for my favorite store app, I searched to see if I could find it.

It wasn't there.

I went to several home improvement store sites and searched.

It wasn't there either.

I did general Bing and Google searches *Sea-ment Brand* and *Sea-ment Glue*. The search engine kept adding results that included c-e-m-e-n-t which was not helpful.

Finally, I put the words in quotation marks and a listing popped up for what appeared to be a tiny company with a home page that said you could only buy the genuine article from their website.

The price was ridiculous. Teodor and Grigore wouldn't—probably couldn't—spend this kind of money to fix random items they were given to repair. Most people wouldn't spend this kind of money on glue for any purpose.

I tapped into my message app and found a text from Nick. *I'm on a plane. About to take off. Back tonight. See you first thing in the morning.*

I started texting, then backspaced to erase what I'd written. Was I being paranoid and ridiculous? Why would a surgeon risk everything to kill a patient?

I slid my phone back into my purse and unlocked the stall door. Then I remembered the strange expression on Geoff's face, at two different times since we got to the restaurant. My gut said something wasn't right about him.

Pulling my phone out again, I texted, *This may sound crazy, but I'm having dinner with Dr. Choi and I think he might be the murderer.* I was going to leave it at that, but, just in case, I added, *Evidence: tie clip and palm print, uses Sea-ment brand glue for models.* I started to put the phone away but realized if Nick thought there was a possibility Geoff was a killer, he'd be trapped on a plane, worrying about me.

*Don't worry,* I added. *I'm in my own car. I won't go anywhere with him.*

Once I was out of the stall, I did some deep breathing and checked my face in the mirror. I smiled at myself to see if it looked convincing. Then I walked out the door.

# CHAPTER THIRTY-TWO

**Rika**

I kept staring at the sky, at the starship Enterprise as it hovered over me. I was standing in that spot, right outside of Bolo, Texas, where I found the body, months ago.

Had I gone back in time?

But it was daytime—I twisted to look behind me—and there was no dead body.

When I turned back toward the old highway I'd called "Zombie Road" last summer, things got even weirder.

Five people were kneeling in a row in front of me, palms extended. Nick was holding a little velvet box. Julian, his badge. Geoff Choi had a tiny model of the USS Enterprise that looked exactly like the one in the sky. Eli held a tranquilizer gun, but not like you'd normally hold a gun. It was lying across his palms like a gift, much like the others. And, next to Eli, was Yoda, holding his lightsaber.

Did he beam down from the Enterprise? That didn't make sense. They weren't even from the same space movie franchise.

"Oxy," Eli said.

"What?" I tried to ask, but my mouth wouldn't cooperate.

"Where's my Oxy?" The expression on Eli's face hadn't changed, but his voice was demanding. Did he want to trade me the tranquilizer gun for drugs?

Wait, why would he think I had any Oxycontin or Oxycodone or whatever?

"You'll get it when we've finished for the evening." That was Geoff's voice, but his mouth hadn't moved.

*Weird.* But maybe his other hobby was ventriloquism.

"I need it now!" The voice was like a boom, loud enough to wake the dead.

And me, apparently.

I struggled to lift my eyelids. When I got them open a crack, I saw Geoff in his doctor's coat. Next to him was a man so tall and skinny, it was like I was seeing him in one of those funhouse mirrors.

"If you yell at me again, you won't get any at all," Geoff said to him.

I closed my eyes, wondering if I'd awakened from one dream just to find myself in another. I opened them again and let them scan the room before nausea forced me to close them.

What was that? Vertigo?

I tried to inventory what I'd seen—Geoff and the tall man, a bunch of random hospital equipment, boxes...

Maybe I was in a large storage room?

There was a strange tingling sensation in the nerves of my head and neck. I tried to lift my hand to touch my face but realized I couldn't feel my arms or legs.

Had I been in a car accident? Was I paralyzed?

Panic welled up in my chest, but I pushed it into my stomach, wishing I had a doughnut to cover it with.

*Retrace your steps, Paprika.*

I remembered being in Nick's hotel room, in his bed. That was nice. Better than nice, it was earth-shattering.

Did I pass out from the awesome sex and get taken to the emergency room?

But Geoff Choi was an orthopedic surgeon, not an ER doctor. Maybe Nick shattered something besides Earth with his phenomenal bedroom skills, like my legs or my pelvis or something else that would require Dr. Choi.

No. Nick and I were together weeks ago. Or days ago, maybe.

Everything was fuzzy.

I pried my eyes open again and saw that I was covered by a sheet.

Did I have clothes on underneath?

I focused on various parts of my body to see if I could feel the band of my bra or the elastic in my underwear. But I couldn't feel much of anything.

A picture flashed in my mind. Geoff Choi was smiling from across a table. The table was set beautifully, like they are in fancy restaurants.

From the back of my brain, one of those voices I was always locking away was trying to tell me something. Bells were going off.

*Ping... Remember...?*

*Ping... Remember...?*

*Ping...*

I remembered.

At the restaurant, I'd decided Geoff was the killer.

*Holy mother of Zeus!*

What if I was dead? Maybe he'd killed me and put the sheet on me, and I was just waiting for them to cover my face and take me to the morgue.

Or would he need to dump my body somewhere else? Surely an unregistered corpse would send up a lot of red flags in the morgue.

Okay, I was pretty sure I wasn't dead because dead people can't ponder or remember or reason.

The only reasonable assumption at this point was that handsome geek Dr. Geoff Choi was a murderer and had done something to put me in this state.

Damn, I hated it when my people went bad. He was even a cute geek. What a waste!

The men's voices moved farther away. A door closed and I thought I was alone in the room. After lifting my eyelids to check again, I decided to start at my feet and work my way up to see if anything on my body was operating.

Concentrating as hard as I could on my toes, I watched as they wiggled under the sheet.

*Yes! That's always a good sign on medical shows.*

Then I tried to move my ankles.

*Nothing.*

My legs.

*No dice.*

My arms?

*Not at all.*

My fingers?

*Yes!* My fingers, like my toes, were in working order.

Finally, I turned my head one way and then the other. I lifted it off the gurney. Or maybe it was a bed. I wasn't sure if there was a difference and never thought to bing it before.

Regardless, my most extreme extremities were in working order, but nothing else.

And, finally, my memory finished clicking into place. I knew where I was. The wing of the hospital we'd seen closed off and under construction from the first day we came.

I was screwed.

I turned my head again, looking for inspiration, something I could use to get out of this mess.

That's when I noticed the IV tube coming out from under the sheet, leading to a bag that was hanging on a stand next to the bed.

The end hidden by the sheet must be plugged into one of my veins. I had no idea what drug I was dealing with, but, if I could just stop the IV from dripping...

I considered swinging my head back and forth, if my neck cooperated, to try to knock the stand over. But there was no guarantee knocking it over would dislodge the needle from my vein.

I decided to run a tool assessment to figure out my options.

*Hm... Tools at my disposal—fingers, toes.*

That didn't take long.

What could I possibly accomplish without having access to my arms or legs?

Only one idea came to mind.

I tapped each fingertip on the bed, bent my fingers, then squeezed them into a fist. They seemed to be working normally. But were they strong enough?

Only one way to find out.

Leaving my right where it was, I focused on my left hand, lying next to my hip. With my index finger, I stretched upward, clinging to my hip with my nails, pulling my hand up onto it.

Next, I advanced my middle finger past the index finger and dug in. It seemed to be working, but I couldn't tell for sure since I couldn't feel the arm.

I lifted my head and watched as I repeated the same pattern —index advance, middle finger advance—two more times under the sheet.

It was working! My hand was past my pelvis, dragging my arm along behind it.

Tilting my head back, I looked at the door. I was still alone.

Moving as fast as I could, I kept my fingers crawling toward their goal. After what seemed like an eternity, but was probably only a minute, the fingers of my left hand ran into my right arm.

It took all the strength I had in them to crawl along the skin until I found where the IV was connected to me.

My fingernails found the edge of the tape that was securing it and I learned it's much harder to pull tape off without the momentum of arm movement. I poked the sheet up, making it into a tiny tent.

Now, I could peek inside. I found the edge of the tape that was holding the needle in place. I scratched at it with my thumbnail until enough lifted, and I was able to grasp it awkwardly between my index and middle fingers. I managed to tug at it until it came off, but the needle came with it.

*Blood!* I poked my right thumb up, to keep the sheet hovering above. If the blood soaked through to the top sheet, they'd know something was up.

Meanwhile, I used my left thumb to apply pressure to the hole the needle had come from in my right arm.

Luckily, the needle was still under the sheet. There was a chance he wouldn't notice.

Now what?

I had no idea how long it would take this stuff to wear off.

The door squeaked behind me. I shut my eyes, trying to come off as a serene sleeper, instead of a desperate potential escapee.

I hoped my blood wasn't soaking through the top sheet.

"How are we doing?" Dr. Choi asked. It was hard to think of him as Geoff now. Geoff sounded too innocuous. This was one of those movie-style, evil-villain doctors I was dealing with. "I know you're awake," he said. "You're breathing like a scared rabbit."

*Crap.*

As I opened my eyes, the tingling I'd felt in my fingers and toes spread to my hands and feet. That was fast, but I tried to keep the hope out of my gaze.

"Can you talk?"

I wasn't sure I could talk, but if I could, I didn't want to sound too strong. "I... I think so," I said in a scratchy whisper. "Was I in an accident?" Maybe if he thought my memory was gone, he wouldn't murder me.

"Nice try," he said. "But this little drug I've been working on doesn't have that side effect, does it, Nail?" He glanced toward the tall guy. "I treated Nail, here, for an injury and he got addicted to pain meds. I give them to him after he helps me out. He's also my guinea pig for my own concoctions."

"Nail?" I blurted. I mean it was a weird name.

Dr. Choi turned his back to Nail and leaned over me. "His real name is Nelson, but his coach at the college says he's dumb as a doornail, so that's become his nickname. It fits him, don't you think? Long skinny body... Big head..."

I examined Nail to see if he looked like the kind of guy who would turn on his dealer to save a life. He had pasty white skin, blonde hair and vacant blue eyes, which were glued to Dr. Choi like a well-trained dog's.

Nope. I wouldn't be getting any help from him.

"Nail is seven foot one," Choi continued. "Guys like him used to throw me in lockers and trash cans when I was in school. Now..." He smiled viciously at Nail. "Now, he's my bitch, aren't you, Nail?"

Nail nodded enthusiastically. "Yes sir, Dr. Choi."

*Great.* I was a dead duck.

Dr. Choi grabbed a clipboard and came back to my bedside.

"What kind of drug are you trying to make?" I asked.

I wanted to regain the use of my appendages before he tried to kill me. I had to at least put up a fight. Even if the police didn't question him about my disappearance, Nick would, and I wanted Nick to know I didn't go down easy.

I'd never kept my fingernails long, but, if I really dug in, they were probably long enough to put some gashes on Choi's face—a face that wasn't nearly as handsome now that he'd kidnapped me.

He huffed. "Originally, it was going to cure cancer," he replied. "But that didn't work out. If I can't come up with another medical use, it could always become the next black-market date rape drug." He didn't sound like he was kidding. He checked his clipboard. "Okay, I need you to answer a series of questions involving the drug's effects. Do you remember your name?"

"Rika." I figured talking was better than murdering. My forearms were tingling, but not my calves. Maybe I could find a way to drag this questionnaire out for a while.

"Your full name," Dr. Choi insisted.

"Rika Martín. Could I have a glass of water?"

"After you finish answering my questions."

"My throat is too dry," I said miserably. "I need water. Or maybe I can just go back to sleep and I won't notice." I let my lids fall heavily over my eyes.

"Nail go get her a cup of water with a straw," he said.

Nail hustled out of the room.

"Now," Dr. Choi said. "Give me your full name. The one that's on this." He pulled something from the clipboard and flashed it at me—my driver's license.

It was my turn to huff. I didn't go around telling everyone my real name and I certainly didn't want to share it with this psycho, but my ankles were tingling and when he'd moved the clipboard, I'd seen several papers on it. Maybe his third degree would allow me time to get mobile.

"Paprika Anise Martín," I said. "My dad is a chef."

Dr. Choi burst out laughing and couldn't seem to stop. The sound of it could be described as "maniacal."

"My dad's an OBGYN," he said when he finally finished laughing. "Can you imagine if he used the same reasoning to name me and my brothers?"

I nodded. "I know, right?" My ankles and calves were starting to tingle.

"We'd be named...what?" He lowered his voice, clearly mimicking someone. "These are my sons—Uterus, Vagina, and Endometriosis."

I forced a chuckle. It was hard to believe this clever man was a cold-blooded killer. He had such a good sense of humor.

I reminded myself I needed to waste as much time as possible. "Why would he name two of you after organs and one after a medical condition?"

"He doesn't particularly like me," he replied.

*Maybe he had a feeling you were going to turn out to be a kidnapping, homicidal maniac*, I thought, but did not say. "They'd be lousy names anyway," I said. "Maybe if the names weren't so Latiny. I know! You could be Dr. Birth Canal Choi."

He burst out laughing again. Once he started laughing, he seemed to have trouble controlling it. Maybe he suffered from some sort of mania.

Finally, he pulled himself together and got back to the task at hand. "Have you lost feeling in any part of your body?" he asked.

"Yeah, like the whole thing," I said snottily. "I thought that was the point."

He chuckled. "It wasn't originally, but I guess it is now." Why did he sound so jovial?

*Nutcase.*

"But, clearly, you can use your mouth," he said.

"Okay, I can feel my head and neck and move them a little. Everything else is numb."

"Awesome!" he replied.

Nail came back and stuck a cup of water near my face. He held it still as I lifted my head, grabbed the straw between my lips and sucked in the cool liquid. I figured it couldn't hurt to be hydrated in case I had a chance to escape.

Dr. Choi went on to ask me dozens of questions, wanting to know my whole medical history as if he was planning to treat me, instead of murder me.

Could I be the one who was confused about what was happening here?

Maybe I hit my head. Maybe Dr. Choi was a bit eccentric but hadn't killed anyone. Maybe I was here for a legitimate reason, but the injury and drugs were making me think crazy thoughts.

I shifted my eyes to Nail.

*No.* This could not possibly be legit. Legit doctors didn't hand out opiates to people they knew were addicts, not to mention referring to their patients as bitches.

And if I were going to hallucinate, I'd be seeing Nick or, at least Liam Hemsworth, not a spaced-out, oddly proportioned college basketball player.

Dr. Choi glanced around the room, then got one of those doctor's stools and rolled it near the bed. "So...?" He smiled mischievously. "Don't you want to know how it all went down?"

I closed my eyes and told myself to hold it together.

As long as Choi and I weren't talking about the murder, I could hang on to the possibility that he hadn't committed the murder or, at least, didn't know that I suspected him. Under those circumstances, there might be a chance, however minute, that he wouldn't kill me.

But now...

"I'm not sure what you're talking about, but I'm getting tired again," I opened my eyes halfway. "Seriously, did I hit my head when I passed out? I don't remember much about the last couple of days."

"Hmph!" he scoffed, definitely not believing me.

*Damn it!* I should have added acting classes into my course schedule. Why didn't I think of that?

"It's a little late to start minding your own business," Choi said. "Besides, I pulled off a pretty perfect crime and you're the only person I can tell about it."

It sounded like my options were either let him brag to me about killing Grigore, then get murdered, or get murdered sooner. "Well, I have been curious," I said. He seemed pretty arrogant. I wondered if flattery would get me somewhere. "I thought it was Erissa or one of the circus people, but none of them seemed like enough of a mastermind to pull this off."

Choi nodded thoughtfully. "Mastermind..." he murmured to himself as he smiled dreamily. "Yeah."

Wait, was I imagining the tingling in my knees?

"Tell me everything," I said. If there's one thing I knew I could do, it was ask questions. And every question could get me a step closer to mobility.

"Hm... Where should I start?" he mused.

"How about why?" I offered. "It's the thing nobody seemed to understand. In fact, I got the impression that if anyone was destined to be murdered, it was Teodor, not Grigore. Why did you go after him?"

"Why?" In a flash, Choi's body went tight, his face bright red and angry. "Why?" He stood and paced the room. "I was the lead surgeon on a conjoined twin separation! Do you know how often an orthopedic surgeon gets a chance like that?"

"But you are a surgeon," I said. "Most people in the world—"

"Dream of being an orthopedic surgeon?" he finished.

Okay, he had a point, but it still was quite an accomplishment and he did earn enough money to get the primo geek gear. "You're still a surgeon," I said.

He rolled his eyes, then closed them and flopped one hand out, palm up in what seemed like frustration. "Do you know what my oldest brother does for a living?"

His eyes were still closed. I wasn't sure if the question was rhetorical.

He opened them and glared at me.

Okay, not rhetorical. "No," I said. "I don't know what your brother does."

"My *oldest* brother is a brain surgeon."

"That's cool," I replied. "You guys must have a lot to talk about at Thanksgiving."

"Cool?" He paced to the end of my gurney and back again, his hand spread across his forehead as he rubbed his temples with his thumb and middle finger. "You think that's *cool*? That my brother is a neurosurgeon while I'm a glorified *sawbones*?"

Uh-oh. I'd always been fascinated with the complexities of sibling relationships since I didn't have any brothers or sisters. They had a profound effect on people. I was pretty sure I couldn't fix a lifetime of Choi feeling "less than" in time to save myself from getting murdered.

Maybe I could steer us into a less emotional topic, like semantics. "To be fair," I said. "I think 'sawbones' was used for all surgeons, not just—"

"Do you know what my other older brother does?" Choi interrupted, clearly not as interested in antique slang meanings as I was. "He's a cardiothoracic surgeon. Do you know what that means?"

"He operates on people's hearts?"

*Damn it! Someone tell me I'm not about to be murdered because of a bad case of sibling rivalry!* Such an ironic fate for an only child.

Choi was rubbing his temples harder. "Fucking brothers didn't even leave me a decent organ to work with," he muttered. "Plus, my professors had it in for me at med school. Probably jealous about my looks."

"Yeah, that must have been it," I agreed. *Or maybe, like your father, they noticed you were batshit crazy.*

"But it was all going to be better." He started pacing again.

In my peripheral vision, I noticed Nail had broken a sweat and his hands shook like he was starting withdrawals. Maybe he'd attack Choi if we dragged this out long enough.

Of course, then he might feel the need to shut me up for witnessing the murder.

"I was going to star in a documentary," Choi finished dreamily.

"I think, technically, the twins were the stars," I blurted.

He frowned at me, then his lips turned up and the dreamy expression returned. "But I would have been the hero of the film," he said. "My parents love documentaries. And neither of my all-mighty brothers have been on TV."

He looked at me expectantly so I nodded. I realized my upper arms and the fronts of my thighs were tingling.

*Keep him talking, Paprika.*

"But I don't understand," I said. "The surgery hadn't been canceled. You could have still—"

Choi waved his hand around, erasing my words from the air. "As far as everyone else knew, Grigore had a case of cold feet, which happens all the time with surgery. What they didn't know was that Grigore called me again around three o'clock in the morning. He said he didn't want the surgery, had never wanted it and, for once, he was going to stand up to his brother. He said he wouldn't sign the consent forms. Wouldn't even come to the hospital."

"So, you went over and killed him?"

He shrugged. "I guess I kind of lost it."—*Kind of?* — "They were good with their hands," he continued. "I'd brought a few collectibles over for them to work on. An old Victrola. A mid-century Mickey Mouse watch. A space heater shaped like R2D2..."

"That sounds awesome!" I said, forgetting for a split second that I would never live to see the space-aged space heater.

"It's super cool!" he said. Then he gave his head a quick shake. "Anyway, when they were taking me out to show me some things they had in the shed in the yard, I noticed their back door wasn't locked and commented on it. Reminded them they were living in L.A. now. They laughed. Said they didn't have much worth stealing. When I came back to pick up my stuff, I noticed it was still unlocked."

"Well, it was kind of their fault, then," I replied. "This is Los Angeles. Who doesn't lock their doors? I think there's a defense in there somewhere. You know my partner is an attorney—"

"What?" Choi yelled. "Do you think I'm stupid, too?"

"No!" My hands tried to fly up and help me explain, but I forced them to settle under the sheet. "I'm just saying that anyone who leaves their doors unlocked in this city is asking for it, that's all."

He shrugged and gave his head another quick shake. Was that a tick? "Either way, they deserved it," he said.

"So, did you want Teodor dead, too?"

"At the time, yes. He'd kept his brother under control for thirty years, but when it mattered to me the most, he screwed me over!"

Choi's "me-me-mes" had him sounding like a major narcissist. People only existed to meet his needs. Unfortunately, I couldn't think of one way it would benefit him to leave me alive.

"I was going to be humiliated," he said. "Having to tell colleagues who had flown in to participate or watch the surgery that they'd come for nothing. I just wanted them both to disappear."

"Why didn't you use the screwdriver on Teodor, too, then?"

"I was pretty traumatized by the thing with Grigore."

The *thing* with Grigore? He made it sound like they went to a party together and Grigore got drunk and gave a waiter a wedgie.

Grigore was a patient who didn't want a surgery that could put him in a wheelchair. What was hard to understand about that?

"You were traumatized?" I repeated.

"Yes. He woke up and tried to fight me off. Ripped the surgical gown I'd put on to protect my clothes."

"The blue kind?" I asked.

He nodded.

I knew that scrap of blue paper was an important clue! But Nick made that comment about not being able to solve every case with a scrap of paper and made me doubt myself.

I composed a quick mental note reminding me not to trust Nick's instincts over mine in the future...if I had a future.

"I got freaked out because I wasn't sure how much noise we'd made in the struggle," Choi continued. "I just wanted to clean off the handle with the antiseptic wipe I'd brought with me and get away before anything else went wrong.

"But you unplugged Teodor's phone so he'd die too."

"Yeah, I saw it on the way out. Like I told you, he'd controlled Grigore his whole life, but now when it was most important..."

*To you,* I thought. *Most important to you, you nutty narcissist.*

"And I kind of liked the idea of him waking up, realizing he was dying and then going for the phone..." He mimed a person picking up a phone, then flailing around in desperation when it didn't work. He chuckled again, but this time his laughter grew and grew until he was holding his midsection.

*Goodbye narcissist. Hello full-blown psycho.*

"Now, I'm glad he didn't die, though," he went on. "I can still be in a documentary. I didn't think of the idea until later that day, when I was talking to the documentary crew."

"Yeah, that'll be really cool," I agreed. The tingling had moved up into my hips and shoulders. While Choi was talking, I'd started running tests on my system, flexing muscles in my legs and arms. I could feel everything but my abs and maybe the middle of my back.

The excitement of becoming ambulatory soon was short-lived because I still wasn't sure how I could escape Geoff Choi and his pet giant.

"So, I'm over all this talking," he said. "I'm a man of action. Have I satisfied your intellectual curiosity?"

Oh, no. I did not want to find out what happened after the talking stopped!

"The glue!" I blurted. "I found that Sea-ment glue in the twins' bedroom. Was that yours?"

"Yes!" he said. "I put it in my shirt pocket as I ran out of the house. It was stupid. I had a fantasy about killing one twin, then gluing the others' lips and eyelids together and sticking around to watch what happened. You know, I thought it would be entertaining, but, once I'd fought with Grigore, it was too dangerous for me to stay."

Dread engulfed me. Not just from the mental image Choi had invoked of the twins, but because it clarified what was about to happen to me.

Choi was in his element here. This room wasn't being used for anything but storage. I heard no noises from the hallway, which meant I was probably right about being in the wing of the hospital that was undergoing renovations. This was Friday night. Choi had at least until Monday morning before any construction crew showed up. He wasn't going to kill me quickly or let me drift off into a happy sleep as my mind and body quietly shut down.

A psycho like him was going to want to have a little fun first, and he'd want me wide awake for it.

# CHAPTER THIRTY-THREE

**Nick**

Despite having been on the plane back to L.A. for a couple of hours. I was still second-guessing how I'd handled the Kyle situation.

I'd spent the whole trip to Seattle mentally listing the possibilities and debating the pros and cons.

Initially, I'd considered threatening him with legal action, which would be the obvious go-to, considering my background. But I kept circling back to Kyle's personality.

He was smart. He'd worked for several of the top tech firms, getting major promotions and raises each time he changed jobs. If legal action was the only deterrent, I wasn't sure it would stop anything.

Kyle would think he could out-maneuver me on the internet and cover his tracks somehow. And getting him any real punishment for putting his ex's racy pictures on the internet would be unlikely in criminal or civil court.

However, there was one thing I knew about Kyle that might get him to lay off DeeAnne: He was a wuss.

I'd learned from the bits of time I spent around him during

their marriage that there were computer geeks who loved sports, who worked out, who ran marathons and biked hundreds of miles.

Kyle had friends like that. However, Kyle was more of the stereotypical geek shown in movies. He spent almost all his time on the computer and didn't enjoy any physical activity, unless you counted what his characters did in video games.

In fact, DeeAnne once told me he found me intimidating, even though I'd been nothing but nice to him while he was married to my little sister.

But now, he was bullying her, and I decided to fight fire with fire.

I wish I had a picture of Kyle's face when I showed up unexpectedly at his door. Another guy was there—a friend or roommate, I assumed—coming out of the hall behind the living area. He took one look at my body language, flashed me the peace sign, and retreated into a bedroom.

Of course, if he'd been rooming with Kyle for more than a week, he probably wished he could beat the shit out of him by now.

In the end, I didn't need to lay a hand on my sister's ex.

Standing closer to him than I normally would, forcing him to look up at me on the porch, caused the color to drain from his face. I pushed past him into the living room and made him open his computer and delete all photos of my sister. This was much easier than I expected because, although his apartment was a mess, his computer files were perfectly organized.

The next part, I'd have to thank Rika for. I'd learned a lot spending time with her, including the multiple ways geeks backed up their files.

I'd spent my time on the way to Seattle reading about the different cloud services and memorizing their icons. So, once Kyle deleted the files from the computer, I pointed to any icons that looked similar to the cloud symbols for the various companies that provided the service and made him open them all for me.

Sure enough, the pictures were there, too. I tried not to look too closely. DeeAnne wasn't naked, but who wants to see their baby sister in sensual poses while wearing lingerie?

Once those were erased, I stood over Kyle and asked, "Where else?"

This was where my old attorney skills came in handy. I was bluffing. I didn't know he had the pictures stored anywhere else. I only knew that Rika had three different ways of backing up her files.

"Where else what?" he asked, but his shifty eyes gave him away.

I started pulling the drawers to his desk open. The top one held a box with labeled thumb drives. Instead of looking at the labels, I decided to take them all in case Kyle had purposely mislabeled one with DeeAnne's pictures.

"What the fuck, man?" Kyle had said. "You can't just take all my—"

I leaned down, wrapped my hand around the scruff of his neck and gritted out, "Where else? This is your last chance."

"External hard drive," he gave up immediately. He gestured to a small component sitting behind his laptop. I'd seen Rika with something that looked exactly like it.

I took it and held it as Kyle stared at it like a kid who just got his ice cream cone taken away by a bigger kid.

"Here's the deal," I said. "I've hired an investigator to do name and image searches on a regular basis. If he finds any of these pictures or anything derogatory with my sister's name attached, I'll be back." Kyle wasn't making eye contact, which I decided to take as a good thing. "Do you remember what I did for a living?" I asked.

He didn't respond.

"I got defendants out of murder charges. Doing a job like that gets you thinking about how you'd do things differently...better." That part I'd made up. I'd never considered how I'd murder another person, but Kyle didn't need to know that. "If you hurt my little sister one iota more than you already have, I'll hurt you. And I'm not talking a small hurt. I'm talking unrecognizable. Then when you're almost gone, we'll start the disposal process. Parts of you will be burned. Other parts melted with chemicals. Anything that won't burn or melt, I will pulverize until it's just dust in the wind."

Okay, I wouldn't do most of that stuff. In fact, the last sentence was inspired by an old Kansas—the rock band, not the state—song. But the important thing was that Kyle believed I would do it.

And he believed me, if the sudden scent of urine in the air was to be taken as a sign.

When I left DeeAnne, I told her to call me immediately if Kyle made any contact or caused her any more trouble. I was pretty sure I'd made the desired impression, but I hadn't spent enough time with Kyle over the years to be able to predict his behavior.

I felt the plane descending and glanced out the window, noting the lights of L.A. spread out below.

I wished it wasn't so late. I missed Rika, which must mean something. The only other living person I remembered missing was my sister.

But what was she playing at with Julian? She claimed she wasn't inviting him over, but he sure thought she was, and she hadn't done anything to disabuse him of that idea.

Was it an ego thing? Did she want us competing over her?

The possibility irked me. But then I considered the fact that I'd competed for much less valuable things. Maybe I just needed to step up my game and prove to her that I was the one. She was worth it.

The plane landed and, as it taxied toward the gate, I picked up my phone to let her know I was back.

There was a notification telling me she'd texted me just after I got on the plane. I hoped after she saw my text about coming back, she'd texted a *Yay!* or *Can't wait to see you,* or even a message about who she wanted to interview tomorrow.

Instead, I saw: *This may sound crazy, but I'm having dinner with Dr. Choi...*

Dinner? I was out of town for a day and she was already having dinner with another man?

My heart sank, then squeezed painfully in my chest.

*...and I think he might be the murderer.*

All the breath left my body. She thought she was at dinner with the murderer?

But Dr. Choi? I didn't like the guy for obvious reasons, but why would a surgeon risk murdering a patient? Rika's imagination must have gotten away from her.

Then I read the next text.

*Evidence: tie clip and palm print, uses Sea-ment brand glue for models.*

Was she saying that she was sure Choi's tie clip matched the imprint on Grigore's palm? And we did find that tube of glue around Grigore's side of the bed.

My heart slammed against my chest. If Rika was with the murderer and he had an inkling that she was on to him...

There was one more text.

*Don't worry. I'm in my own car. I won't go anywhere with him.*

Maybe she was home safe by now.

I clicked over to my favorites list and tapped her name. Then I waited as her phone rang and rang and rang.

**Rika**

I was watching Choi open a box Nail had brought in at his request. I wasn't sure what everything in there was, but seeing it had brought clarity about what my future held.

There would definitely be torture. Maybe rape? Dismemberment?

My entire body began to shake. I glanced at the sheet, hoping Choi couldn't tell, in case shaking would clue him in that the drug was no longer coursing through my veins.

I thought of my mother. Had death been quick for her? Or did she have the same moment of realization I did about the monster who took her?

Choi gazed into the box as if he was daydreaming about what he'd do with the contents.

The first thing I identified was a silver-colored mallet. I'd seen a much smaller version used by plastic surgeons on TV doing nose jobs. I couldn't imagine what one this size was meant to break.

There was another heavy metal object that looked like it belonged on someone's garage workbench or, at least, it would if wasn't so pristine and shiny. I'd seen this before, too, when I'd happened upon a show on the Med Channel. It was a rib spreader.

Bile rose in my throat.

"Have you seen one of these before?" He reached into the box and held up a white object that reminded me of some sort of space weapon. "It's a surgical stapler," he said gleefully. "I'm partial to the ones with the pistol grip." He put the nose of it into the pocket of his doctor's coat, then pulled it out and pantomimed shooting around the room, making "pew, pew, pew" noises like he was the sound man for Battlestar Galactica.

How did I not realize how crazy this guy was when I first met him?

*You were blinded by his pretty smile.*

God, I hated to think I was so superficial I could be completely thrown off by a handsome face.

*And his awesome geek gear.*

Okay, that was understandable.

"I almost forgot," he said. "I need to unhook you from the IV. I want to make sure you can feel what I'm doing." He turned away. "Nail, where are the restraints?"

*Restraints?*

If they got any sort of restraints on me, it was over. My muscles tensed. I eyed the mallet, wondering if I was strong enough to do any damage with it.

Nail pushed away from the wall, presumably to retrieve the restraints.

Then, I heard a squeak behind me. My head jerked to the side as the double doors swung open.

Hallelujah, it was Nick!

"Rik—" was all he got out before Nail smashed him in the jaw with his huge fist. Nick swayed and I could have sworn he was trying to fight off unconsciousness. But he crashed to the floor, hitting his head with a thump.

My body jerked and I sat up, wanting to go to Nick.

Luckily, Choi and his henchman were focused on their latest victim and didn't notice me. Choi squatted next to Nick's beautiful body and checked for a pulse.

*Please be alive, Nick!*

Then, I realized, if he was alive, I might have to get both of us out of here.

They weren't expecting this turn of events and would have to decide how to deal with two of us instead of one. Maybe I could find an opportunity to...to...

Damn it! I still couldn't think of what to do!

"Still alive," Choi said as if to himself. He looked up at Nail. "I'm going to need more garbage bags."

*Garbage bags?*

I stifled the cry that tried to escape my throat at the thought of my Nick being dismembered and shoved into trash bags.

"I'm going to run to my car," Choi said. "Stand outside these doors and guard them. No one should be here at this hour, but if someone shows up, do what you did to him."

Nail nodded and followed Choi out.

As soon as the double doors flopped shut, I scrambled off the gurney. Blackness tried to overtake me and I almost conked out. I held still for several seconds while it passed.

"Nick!" I whisper-yelled.

I ran my hands over his skull and found a lump, but no blood. He could have a concussion or be bleeding internally. I shoved those thoughts out of my head, trying to focus on the good things—mainly that he wasn't bleeding to death and the knowledge that he'd played football for years. He was a pretty tough guy.

I tried again. "Nick," I whispered as I attempted to smack his face without making much noise.

*No response.*

I lifted his arms and flung them around.

*Nothing.*

I reached under his shirt and pinched his nipple as hard as I could.

*Zip.*

Nick was going to die and it would be all my fault!

I heard Choi's voice in the hall. I jumped back on the gurney and tried to straighten the sheet out over myself.

When he and Nail entered, he was holding a brand-new box of thirty-three-gallon garbage bags. He went to the back of the room and pulled out another gurney that had been collapsed and stored sideways between the boxes and the wall. He brought it over and set it next to Nick.

"It'll be easier to get him on it this way, then raise it up," he said to Nail. "Bring me the extra IV bag."

*Oh, no. No, no, no, no, no! How can I possibly get Nick out of here without the use of his arms and legs?*

Not only could I not carry him, but I was pretty sure I couldn't drag his six-foot-plus body more than a few feet. And he was all muscle! I'd always heard muscle weighs more than fat.

"I can't," Nail muttered.

Choi straightened and looked up at him threateningly. I'm not sure how a person gets the confidence to look threateningly at a person twice his size, but it was the one thing about Geoff Choi I wished I could emulate. "You can't?" he said. "And why is that?"

Nail's feet shuffled. He looked intimidated. "When I was getting stuff out of the car, I dropped it."

"Are you telling me my life's work is splattered all over the pavement outside?"

Nail hung his head. "Yeah."

Choi's face contorted and for the first time, I could envision him plunging a screwdriver into Grigore's eye. Nail was lucky his eyes were out of reach.

"Do you even know how to use your opposable thumbs?" Choi asked. He closed his eyes and spent thirty seconds massaging his temples as he had before. Suddenly his eyes popped open and he looked at Nick. "Okay, then, I guess we'll have to use the restraints on him." He glanced at me. "Maybe we can find tubing or something for her. She's tiny. It shouldn't take much to hold her."

*Tiny? Did he just call me 'tiny'?*

I glanced at the "gun" he'd thrown back into the box and imagined stapling his balls to his forehead while they were still attached to his groin, of course.

It only took the two of them a few minutes to get Nick set up on his own gurney, his wrists and ankles secured to the frame with Velcro straps. Then, they raised his gurney up to the same height as mine.

He was inches away. I wanted to reach out and touch him.

Make sure he was still warm. Try to wake him up.

What if he was in a coma?

Choi was staring into his box of horrors. "Know what this is?" The joviality was back in his voice. He held up an instrument with a power cord attached. It had a round blade at the end. "It's meant for cutting off casts, but I was thinking maybe I could see what else it cuts." He pressed the button and made a "vroom-vroom" sound with his mouth since the saw wasn't plugged in. "It would be cool to dissect a live person, don't you think? They only let us work on dead ones in med school."

He wanted to dissect us alive? How many parts could he take out before we passed out or died? As curious as I was about almost everything, I did not want to see myself dissected, and Nick...

*Holy mother of Zeus!* If Nick got dissected it would totally be my fault!

"Oh, and I can do a little brain surgery on you—I'll bet you've got a gorgeous one!" He smiled flirtatiously. "And open-heart surgery on this guy." He started pointing back and forth between us. "*You* get a surgery and *you* get a surgery!"

Was that an Oprah imitation?

He stared at Nick. "He's really too tall to be trusted. Looks like one of those jocks, big man on campus types. I saw how you looked at him. You realize he isn't right for you, don't you? He's not one of us."

Damn Sofia for blowing smoke up my ass! Even this crazy person knew Nick was out of my league.

Okay... time for a brain reset. I had no time to think about whether I had a future with Nick while there was a very good chance neither one of us had a future. I couldn't push what was happening into my gut and cover it with carbs. I couldn't lock it away in the back of my brain. I needed to be hyper-focused and watch for any opportunity to escape.

"Doc," Nail said pleadingly. He was even paler and the sweat was trickling down his face. "I need the oxy."

Choi huffed and dug around in his pocket. He pulled something out and handed it to Nail.

"Just two?" Nail asked.

"For now," Choi replied.

Nail went over to a corner where he proceeded to wrap the pills in a paper towel, smash them with his foot, and snort the powder. He lowered himself to a seated position on the floor, leaned his head back and made little humming sounds.

Choi turned back to me. "Druggies," he said. "Can't live with them, can't kill them... because then who would carry the bodies around?" He burst out laughing. "I should have been a standup comedian," he informed me between giggles.

His laughter stopped suddenly. "I've got an idea!" he cried. Then he hustled out of the room.

I looked at Nail, who seemed to have checked out for the time being. He sat in the same spot humming unrecognizable tunes to himself.

"Nick!" I hissed. "Wake up!"

Nick didn't move.

*How do you rouse a head trauma victim?*

I decided to try the mom approach. "Nicholas Bernard Owen!" I said in a terrible imitation of a Texas twang.

He still didn't respond.

What else did I know about Nick? I needed something his brain would feel absolutely compelled to respond to.

That was it! I closed my eyes and said the words in my head with just the right intonation. Then I opened them and said. "Hey, no balls!" This time, I thought my voice sounded surprisingly close to LeeAnne's. "You just gonna lay there and take it, NO BALLS!"

That was kind of loud. I glanced at Nail, who was still humming.

When my gaze went back to Nick, his eyes were open. He

blinked up into the bright operating room lights before turning his head and seeing me.

"What the fuck?" he asked. He tried to lift his hand and realized it was attached to the bed frame. "What the fuck?" he repeated. He struggled against the restraints, writhing and jerking, like an animal in a trap, but the straps were thick and the Velcro was strong.

"What the fuck?" he said, yet again.

I hoped Nail hadn't brain damaged him down to a three-word vocabulary.

I tried to condense what was going on to the crucial facts. "Geoff Choi has you restrained and he thinks I'm still incapacitated from medicine he gave me, but I think I'm okay now. Nail, there..." I gestured towards him, "is the one who knocked you out. Choi just left the room temporarily."

Nick looked at me like I was an idiot. "Why aren't you running away? Get the hell out!"

Was he already starting an argument with me?

*Jeez! Lawyers!*

On the other hand, maybe it meant he wasn't too brain damaged.

"First, I'm pretty sure Nail can outrun me, oxy or not—"

At the sound of his name, Nail opened his eyes and looked at me. "Shhh!" he said. Then he closed his eyes and went back to humming.

"Oxy...what?" Nick whispered. But we had limited time to formulate a plan, so I ignored him and went on.

"Second, Choi is a total psycho. There's no way I was leaving you here with him. He wants to dissect us while we're alive."

"But, if you can move, why are you still lying there?" he asked.

"I didn't want to tip them off that I'm mobile until I had a plan. Did you bring your gun?" He was wearing his bomber jacket. I hoped he'd tucked the gun into the back of his jeans before he came in.

"No, I don't have my gun," he said like it would be ridiculous to bring a gun to a kidnapping.

I squeezed my eyes together and sighed. "Why didn't you bring your gun?"

"I came straight from the airport," he said. "Besides, Choi's not that big. I knew I could take him."

"It didn't enter your mind that he could have a henchman? Evil geniuses have henchman! It's like a requirement!"

"Sure, if you're making a low-budget, crap movie."

I lifted my head off the bed to glare at him. "All kinds of movies have henchman. Darth Vader is Emperor Palpatine's henchman!" I thought about the bump on his head. "But I'm giving you a pass on that one because you have a head injury." After all, he had come to save me.

He rolled his head to look straight into my eyes. "Rika! This isn't a movie!" he whisper-shouted. "This is real life. Real trouble."

"Which brings us back to my original question of why you didn't bring your gun?"

"I told you, I came straight from the airport!"

"So, that gun training you thought was so important—"

"Really?" Nick said. "You need to be right about this, now? What did you bring to protect yourself with?"

"When the night started, I was just on a date!" I said.

Nick's eyes darkened and his jaw suddenly looked like it was made of steel. "I hope a date with a doctor was worth all this," he said angrily.

"People! People!" Geoff yelled, clapping his hands like we were elementary kids he was trying to hush. "This was supposed to be about me."

He was back. And he had a large plastic bag hanging from his wrist. What were the chances it contained something I needed right now, like a couple dozen donut holes or a box of lemon coolers? Normally, Double Stufs were my go-to cookies, but I felt they'd weigh me down too much in this situation.

"Glad to see you're awake, counselor," Choi said to Nick.

Nick narrowed his eyes threateningly, which I thought was silly considering he was incapacitated.

Choi reached into his bag and pulled out something shaped like a scalpel, but with an electrical cord attached. "This thing is really cool," he said. "It cauterizes while it cuts, so you don't bleed out. It could make the fun last a lot longer." He gazed at the scalpel admiringly.

"So many more options now that your love interest, here, has shown up. Like, should I disembowel you while he watches or do I disembowel him while you watch?" He lifted a finger in the air as if a new thought had struck him. "It doesn't matter! You'll both be awake and watching the whole show. Don't worry. If you pass out, I'll have Nail wake you up again. Wouldn't want you to miss anything."

He was trying to scare me, but it wasn't fear, but anger that whooshed through my body, turning my blood hot.

This lunatic was not going to cut into Nick's beautiful eight pack! Not if I had anything to say about it.

Choi started whistling "Whistle While You Work" as he moved two rolling steel tables over next to Nick's bed. He pulled the saws and the drill and a few other things from his box, arranging them on the tables just so. Then he pulled a heavy-duty electrical cord—the kind workmen often use—from the back of the room, plugged the scalpel into the cord and the cord into the wall.

He went back to the table and moved each of the tools of his trade ever-so-slightly until they were all lined up as perfectly as possible. Once everything was to his satisfaction, he picked up the cauterizing scalpel. "What do you think, Nail?"

Nail was standing in the corner, now, letting the two walls prop him up. He raised his eyebrows. "Huh?"

"Should I dig right in on this guy or cut a few toes off her first?"

Nail cocked his head like he was considering the options.

I lifted my head to look at my toes, careful not to move them and tip Choi off. They were still covered by the sheet, but, for the first time, it hit me that there were no shoes or socks on them.

"Do you remember how pretty they are?" Choi walked over and lifted the bottom of my sheet. "Maybe I can keep them in a jar in my man cave."

Nick's fists clenched as he strained against the Velcro. "You so much as break a toenail," he said. "I'll fucking kill you."

Wow. Nick sounded like a badass from an action movie. Too bad he wouldn't be able to back up those words.

"The dude," Nail said dreamily. "Can you really take his guts out while he's watching? Cause that would be cool."

"Why not her guts?" Choi asked. "We wouldn't want anyone thinking we were sexist."

"Well, I was hoping you'd let me have a little fun with her before you started slicing her up."

*Fun* with me? Now *my* fists clenched under the sheets.

"I'm not running an escort service here!" Choi yelled. "This is your job. Haven't you heard the term 'Don't shit where you eat'?"

"Yeah..." Nail said slowly. "But I never knew what it meant."

So, bottom line was, if I got rid of the murderer, I'd still have a rapist to contend with. I wasn't counting on Nick's help. He'd been unconscious minutes ago. Even if I managed to get his restraints off, who knew what would happen when he tried to stand up?

"Let's see if my scalpel has heated up," Choi said cheerfully, as if he hadn't been yelling at Nail seconds before.

I heard my phone's ring tone—the zombie sounds—but they were farther away than usual. Where was my phone?

Choi cocked his head, listening. "What's that sound?" he asked Nail.

"What sound?" Nail asked.

Choi motioned to him to follow as he headed to the door. He stood and listened. "What the hell is that?"

"Zombie?" Nail offered.

Choi rolled his eyes. "You're an idiot. You go check that hall." He gestured to the right. "If you don't find anyone there, check to the left. I'll check this one." He pointed straight ahead. "If you run into anyone coming this way, knock them out and bring them in here."

Nail seemed surprised. "Another one?"

"If we're doing these two, we might as well make a party of it," Choi said. "Don't worry. No one will ever suspect me, and the bodies will be dissolved before those idiot homicide detectives figure out which way is North."

"Why would they need to know which way is—?" Nail began.

Choi interrupted. "Just do what I told you."

They both slunk out of the room looking to their right and left for the origin of the noise.

"Okay," Nick and I said at the same time.

"When Choi comes back—" I began.

"You won't be here," Nick said. "Run. Take the left hallway and get the hell out before Nail comes back to check it."

I sat up suddenly, then had to breathe through a wave of nausea. It dawned on me that I was wearing a hospital gown.

*Ew!* I wondered which of the creeps had undressed me.

"I'm not leaving you," I said. "If he murders you, it will be my word against his and who do you think Hertz and Winchell will believe?"

I slid off the side of the gurney. As my bare toes touched the floor, blinding pain sliced through my head. My stomach lurched and I turned away, not wanting to barf on Nick.

"Damn it, Rika, if you can, pull these restraints apart and run! I'll stand at the door and deal with—"

"Like you dealt with them when you came in?" I gritted out.

Maybe I needed to add "unreasonable and grumpy" to Choi's side-effect list.

"Rika!"

Wobbly on my feet, I held onto my mattress, then Nick's, as I moved to his side. I was at the bottom of his gurney, near his boots. I grabbed the nearest restraint and pulled.

Wow. Either I was much weaker than usual or this was mega-industrial strength Velcro.

"Rika?" Nick said. "Are you okay?"

"He drugged me," I said in case his brain had been too addled when I tried to tell him before. "I couldn't move when I woke up."

An expression I'd never seen before crossed Nick's face. I thought I knew his angry expression. But I guess I'd never seen him livid. "He *drugged* you?" he asked incredulously. "Did he...?" He didn't finish his sentence, but I knew what he was thinking because a voice in the back of my head had been trying to ask me the same thing.

"I don't know. That's not my main concern right now," I replied in a no-nonsense voice.

I shook out my hands. I hadn't realized how cold they were before, but as I shook them, I could feel my blood warming them.

I grabbed onto the tab of his restraint again and pulled, hard.

The Velcro came apart as I fell backward against my gurney from the effort.

When I straightened, I realized the nausea had calmed. My head still throbbed, but my arms felt a lot better. I started toward the closest restraint, which was holding Nick's right foot.

"Rika, just get my hand loose," he said.

That made sense. Then he could get himself free. Why didn't I think of that? Had the drug affected my logic? I changed direction and that's when Choi came back through the doors.

Surprise registered on his face. "What—?" He glanced at the IV stand, then back at me. "You can move already? How long have you been unhooked?" he asked. He seemed more concerned about data on his drug concoction than he was about me being loose.

I shook my arms out, then jogged in place to make sure my legs were working. "I just unhooked myself a second ago," I lied.

Did he really think I was going to help him with his little science project after he kidnapped and drugged me?

He was on one side of Nick's gurney. I was on the other side. I tried not to see Nick's face in my peripheral vision. I couldn't be distracted right now. Choi's face had taken on a predatory look.

He started to come around the gurney, but as he got near Nick's head, I moved back toward his feet. He changed direction, but, as he made it to the mid-point, at Nick's waist, I moved so I was directly across from him.

Suddenly, Choi pushed at an angle and Nick's head came towards me, while Choi tried to run around his feet. I rushed to Nick's head and pushed, which forced Choi to move up by Nick's head again, in case I made a run for the door.

I glanced at Nick's wrist, but if the wrist restraint was as tough as the ankle restraint, I wouldn't be able to get it open before Choi was on me.

We were in a stalemate for a while, swinging Nick's gurney back and forth, me using it as a buffer against Choi.

After several minutes of this, Choi and I ended up back where we started, directly across from each other over Nick's midsection.

I glanced at Nick to check on him. He was silent, his eyes glued to me.

Why just me? Why wasn't he looking at Choi?

Then, I knew. Nick was watching to see when I'd make my move. I also knew that no matter what that move was, Nick would try his best to back me up, restraints or not.

I cut my eyes toward the exit, wishing more than ever I had longer legs. Choi smirked. "You know I run marathons in my spare time, don't you?"

No, damn it, I did not know that! But his revelation only helped solidify my plan. I channeled my inner chubster, grabbed the side of the bed and ran forward, driving the gurney into Dr. Choi's midsection. He half ran, half stumbled backward until he hit the wall. I threw all my weight—past and present—against the bed.

He didn't hit his head as I'd hoped, but he did let out a blood-curdling scream. "Stupid bitch!" he yelled. "You could have broken my spine!"

I wasn't sure if that meant I could have, but didn't, or if it meant his spine felt like it could be broken but he wasn't sure yet. I certainly hoped it was the latter.

While I kept the pressure on, he tried to wedge his hands in between his torso and the bed frame. He was also jerking his body strangely.

Then I saw the reason. His foot was caught at an odd angle between a box and the wall. Whatever was in the box must have been heavy. His foot couldn't push it away, though I could see he was trying.

Nick saw the opportunity. "Rika!" he called. "Get me loose!"

I shoved my hip against the gurney and stretched toward Nick's left hand. Choi let out a primal grunt that turned into a low-pitched bellow as he threw himself to the side and knocked the box that was trapping his foot off the other box it had been sitting on.

I realized what was about to happen and started running backward, just before Choi started pushing the bed toward me.

I jumped—or maybe stumbled—out of the way as it slammed into the wall. The momentum caused him to stumble, his torso falling over the bed.

I grabbed the nearest weapon, in this case, a rolling pole with some sort of monitor on the top. Choi was only a few feet away. I had no time to consider other options. I picked it up near the wheels and swung as hard as I could.

The monitor cracked against Choi's skull and he fell to the floor. I jumped over him and reached for one of Nick's wrist restraints.

Then, suddenly, I was going in the opposite direction—backward instead of forward—and worse, I was going down. I twisted around to find Choi's hand on my leg, pulling me to him. I put a hand out to try to stop him, but he was stronger.

My hospital gown rode up higher as I landed in his lap, one leg out straight, the other stuck underneath me. I could hear Nick struggling against his restraints behind me but knew he couldn't help me. In fact, what I did now could determine whether the two of us would end the night in those garbage bags.

I needed a way to neutralize Choi without a weapon or any noteworthy physical strength. The anatomy charts I'd studied—online, of course—flashed into my mind.

Testicles would be the most obvious way to go, but I was sideways, on his lap, so that would be hard to manage. If I went for his eyes, he'd probably block me before I got to them.

Solar plexus.

The solar plexus, right under the sternum. One of the most vulnerable places on the body, if I could just...

I faked a left-handed, two-fingered eye poke. Choi grabbed my wrist, just as I expected. That's when I pulled my right arm back and punched forward as hard as I could into the top of his gut.

Air whooshed out his mouth. He dropped my wrist, his hand going to his chest. Panic-stricken, he tried to suck in a breath but couldn't.

*Score!* I'd knocked the wind out of him, just like I'd hoped to!

I jumped up and used my leftover adrenaline to rip the Velcro off Nick's other ankle. Then I turned toward his head and made for the wrist restraints. Just as I got there, the doors opened...

And Nail strolled in.

# CHAPTER THIRTY-FOUR

**Rika**

Nail looked at me quizzically, then scanned the room until he saw Choi crumpled on the floor.

He grinned. "You do that?" He sounded impressed. "Man, you're going to be a crazy fuck!" Then he lifted me off the floor, shoved me against the wall and started messing with the front of his shorts.

Panic swept through me. Never in my life had I felt I was seconds away from being a victim of...

My mind stopped short, not wanting to even think the ugly word. I was practically a rag doll in Nail's giant hands.

For the first time, I really, truly felt it.

I was small. Tiny even, just like everyone said.

Heaving the thought away, I made myself take in a deep, full breath.

A new feeling passed through me.

Determination.

I might not be able to stop this, but my attacker was not going to leave unscathed.

I started to struggle. Nail pressed his upper body against

mine, compressing me between him and the wall. "I see how you made Choi your bitch," he said into my ear. "And now I'm gonna make you mine."

Behind Nail, I could hear what I was certain were the sounds of Nick struggling against his wrist restraints, but I had little hope that he could escape the wide Velcro bands.

Meanwhile, my legs were still dangling in mid-air. I wasn't about to wrap them around Nail's waist and make this easier for him. I tried kicking and kneeing him, but I couldn't swing my legs back far enough to get the momentum to do damage.

He just pressed his thighs into my legs, forcing one to the outside of his, and wedging the other between his thigh and the wall.

I tried repeatedly to get my thumbs to his eyes or give him an uppercut to the chin, but, even under the influence, he had the strength and reflexes of an athlete. He batted my hands away like he was swatting flies.

"Ready for the fuck of your life?" he said as he tried to get my gown and his shorts to cooperate while continuing to hold me up.

Fury rose up inside me, spreading through my limbs like electricity.

Like *power.*

I lifted my forearm and wedged it against his neck, trying to force him to drop me. I stared him straight in the eye. "Go. Fuck. Your*self.*"

The smile left his lips and his eyes grew deadly. "Know what we're gonna do now?" he asked. With a swipe of his hand, he knocked my elbow away. "We're gonna find out if a person can really be banged to death."

I corkscrewed my body as hard as I could, nearly forcing him to drop me, but he readjusted and had my back flat on the wall again within seconds.

*Damn it!* I couldn't stop this. And, maybe worse, I couldn't stop Nick from witnessing it. I closed my eyes, resisting the temptation to look to Nick for help he couldn't give. I didn't want him to feel guilty about this.

The sound of Nail's zipper caused a fresh dose of adrenaline to shoot through me. I had to try one last time.

As he leaned his torso back and started trying to lift my gown again, I smashed my right elbow into his nose, which made a loud cracking sound. At the same time, I torqued my body as hard as I could to the left.

Suddenly, I was falling to the floor. I landed on my ass and scrambled to my feet.

But before I could get away, Nail's hand was in my hair, pulling, unaware of the scalp of iron that ran in my family.

I swung my arm back, then forward, sending my fist toward his crotch, but he jerked out of the way and all I got was his hip.

He retaliated by wrapping my hair over his hand several times until he was practically holding me by the scalp. He twirled me around and jammed the front of my body into the wall. I turned my head just in time to protect my nose, but my cheekbone hit the concrete so hard I saw stars.

Nail ran a hand over my ass, even as blood from his nose dripped onto my shoulder. "Guess what?" he said. "I like it even better from the back. In fact, while I'm back here, maybe—"

He was interrupted by a sound behind him. It started off as a growl but turned to a roar.

I leaned to one side and looked past Nail to see Nick lift his feet in the air, then throw his torso forward so hard, he landed on his feet, his wrists still attached to the bed. At the same time, the two metal supports that ran the length of the gurney hit the floor and bent. This meant Nick was standing in the middle of the room with a bed on his back.

Nail followed my line of sight to Nick. "Dude!" he said in an oddly enthusiastic tone. "You look like some kind of turtle transformer!"

"Get your hands off her," Nick gritted out as he advanced on my attacker.

Nail stepped back and turned his attention to Nick. "What are you gonna do about it, Turtle man?"

What *was* he going to do about it? His wrists were still bound to the bed rails.

Nick took a step forward, dragging the bed along with him. Then, suddenly, he jerked to one side and spun, smashing the side of the gurney into Nail.

Nail fell backward and slid several feet.

I heard a groan and turned to see Choi trying to get up. I grabbed the monitor pole and swung again, but he was expecting it this time. The monitor made a smacking sound as he caught it with his palm.

He reached forward and grabbed the pole and we ended up in a tug of war over the makeshift weapon. I decided to go old-school and use a tug-of-war tactic I used on Sofia when we were little.

I pulled back as hard and as far as I could. "You think you're stronger than me, bitch?" Choi said as he moved his right hand over his left, clamped on and pulled harder.

The second I felt the increased tension, I released my end. Choi pulled the monitor straight into his chin.

Holy crap! That's what I'd been hoping for, but I didn't expect it to work as well on a grown-ass surgeon as it did on my five-year-old cousin.

He made a "fu—" sound in the split second before it smashed into him, then his head cracked against the floor and he passed out.

I spun around, just in time to see Nail, hunched over, plowing into Nick with his shoulder like a football tackle.

When Nick smashed backward into the wall, the remainder of the bed frame exploded. He checked his arms and saw that he still had a four-foot piece of pipe Velcroed to his left hand. He seized it with his right hand so fast, I almost missed it, then smashed it on Nail's head just as he was starting to straighten.

"Ow!" Nail raised his hand to check the side of his head.

It didn't seem like much of a reaction considering how hard the hit sounded. Then I remembered he was on at least two pain killers.

He stood, stretching to his full height. I realized if I was going to jump on his back to help Nick, I'd missed the opportunity. He was too tall.

Nick turned the pipe and jammed the end of it into Nail's midsection, but Nail managed to grab his end and tried to shove it into Nick's chest. But Nick saw it coming and ran backward, then stepped aside at the perfect time. The end of the pipe hit the wall with Nail holding it, visibly jarring his body.

His face contorted, turning red with anger, then purple.

This was bad. Nick had held his own so far, but I'd seen what one punch of Nail's giant hand could do when he caught Nick off guard.

I ran a quick assessment of the situation.

Nail had an extreme height and reach advantage, the reflexes of an athlete, and was around twenty years old. He was an addict, but I didn't think the quantity of drugs in his system would slow him down much.

Nick was fifteen years older, but also had lightning quick reflexes. Plus, he had brains on his side that might enable him to fight smarter.

This could go either way, but probably not without a lot of damage to Nick.

I glanced around for inspiration, my eyes catching on the tables of surgical tools. As I grabbed the staple gun, I saw Nail smash Nick against the wall.

"Nooooo!" I screamed as I stumbled over to them. I pressed the stapler to the exposed skin where Nail's shorts had slid down and pulled the trigger.

This did not have the expected result. Stupid as it sounds, I'd expected to see the kind of thick staple I'd seen come out of normal staple guns, not the smaller surgical one now stuck at the base of Nail's spine.

Nail let go of Nick and reached back to dislodge the staple. I figured distraction was better than nothing and managed to get a couple more staples in him before he leaned over and wrenched the instrument from my hand.

A split second after his head came down, Nick wrapped an arm around his neck from behind. This put Nail's long body in an awkward position, his back almost parallel to the floor, his knees bent.

Nick's muscles bulged as he squeezed tighter, but Nail wasn't giving up. He started bucking and kicking his long legs backward, but Nick managed to keep him bent and mostly avoid the kicks.

When the bucking and kicking didn't work, Nail began squirming and writhing like a giant worm. Both men were sweaty at this point, and I knew Nick couldn't hold onto him much longer.

I ran over to the table of horrors again. The cauterizing scalpel was still plugged into the long extension cord. I held my hand an inch above it and felt the heat radiating.

I ran back to the men, the extension cord trailing behind me.

Nail had managed to swivel to the side. Nick still had his arm looped around the guy's neck while the two of them sort of arm-wrestled left-handed, between their bodies.

I cringed as I leaned in and swiped at Nail's calf with the scalpel. A chunk of smoking skin fell to the floor.

The sight nearly made me toss my Oreos.

He turned, trying to face me. "Sh—!" was all he got out before Nick jerked his arm tighter. Nail's eyes were bulging as he kicked backward at me.

"Stop kicking," I said, surprised at the calm tone of my voice.

He didn't stop kicking. So, I flung my scalpel hand in his direction, making a deep slice above his knee.

"F—" was the only sound he made. He stopped kicking, but reached up behind him, grabbing at Nick's head.

I stuck the scalpel between his legs and watched as the crotch of his basketball shorts melted away. "Stuhgg!" he squealed.

My eyes shifted to Nick's face. And even with a seven-foot basketball player struggling in the crook of his arm, Nick's gaze, when it met mine, was warm and encouraging, infusing me with fresh energy.

I looked up into Nail's wild eyes. "You need to be still," I said. "Unless your crotch wants the same treatment your legs just got." He stopped fighting Nick and froze, his legs wide.

After I let my eyes travel to his crotch, I met his gaze again. I spoke in my softest, sweetest voice. "Who's the bitch now?" I raised my brows questioningly, trying for the same mild expression I might use if my phone battery died and I needed to know the time of day.

Nick loosened his arm a little to allow our captive to speak.

"You crazy, fucking bi—!"

Nick's arm tightened again and cut off his air. "Wrong answer," Nick said.

I pressed the scalpel to the inside of his thigh, which melted some fabric that was still hanging there before it made contact with his skin. A stream of noxious smoke rose from the spot it had touched.

"Guhhl!" Nail cried.

I pulled the scalpel from his thigh and held it under his crotch again. "Can't lie," I said. "I'm feeling pretty powerful right now. I mean, I don't think this could cut your leg off or anything, but I'm thinking I could do a lot of damage to this thing." I stabbed my finger into his boxer briefs where I thought his penis might be. "I'll bet I could take it down a few notches," I added.

"Instead of a foot-long, it could be more of a fun-size. And, who doesn't like tiny things?" I smiled again.

Suddenly, tears were streaming down Nail's face. My heart softened and for a moment I felt bad for him...

Until I recalled what it was like to be assaulted and nearly raped, that is. "I'm going to ask you again," I said. "Who's the bitch now?"

Again, Nick loosened his grip. Nail sucked in more air than I'd thought one person could hold, then panted out several breaths.

I raised my brows and lifted the scalpel a half-inch.

"Me! Nelson!" he croaked out. "I'm the bitch!" Nick released him and he fell to his knees, which put us eye-to-eye. "I'm the bitch," he repeated as tears flowed freely from his eyes. "I'm the bitch."

I cocked my head like I was channeling Chino. "Yeah," I said calmly. "And now that we've got that straight, I guess you're ready for prison."

Nick yanked the restraints off his wrists and made makeshift cuffs out of them for Nail. All the fight was gone from the guy. He just stayed there on his knees, bawling like a baby as Nick bound his hands behind his back.

"Do you have your phone?" Nick asked.

"No, but I heard it earlier," I said. "It may have fallen out in the hall."

Nick glanced at Nail, whose shoulders were slumped as he blew on one of the injuries to his leg. He seemed completely checked out.

"I don't have mine either," Nick said. "I don't remember what happened to it after I followed the tracker here. I'll check the hall and see if I can find one of them." He gestured toward Nail. "If he tries anything, castrate him."

As he left the room, I ran his words back through my mind.

Did he say something about a tracker leading him to me? Or was he just talking about the GPS leading him to the hospital?

But, how did he figure out I was at the hospital?

As I carried the cauterizing scalpel—which I now thought was way better than a gun—back to the table, I found Choi still crumpled where I'd left him, on his side, half of his face on the floor. His eyes were closed. I leaned down, trying to determine if he was breathing.

Sure, he was a vicious criminal, but I didn't really want to be responsible for killing another person.

The contents of his pocket caught my eye.

It was Nick's phone. It must have fallen out of his pocket when Nail knocked him out. I reached in with two fingers and pulled it out, then turned toward the door. "Nick," I yelled. "I found—"

My foot refused to move forward, probably because something was wrapped around my ankle again.

*Damn it!*

I swiveled my head slowly, not really wanting to see what was happening. When my gaze reached Choi's face, it was turned up towards me, bruised on both sides. His eyes stared up at me murderously.

What was this, a teen horror movie where no matter how many times they whack the psycho, he keeps coming back to kill them?

Whatever. I'd had enough.

I snatched my weapon of choice from the table and turned toward him. My first thought was to put a slice into the hand on my ankle.

Then I realized something. Dr. Geoff Choi was a surgeon with wealthy relatives. They could afford a whole team of attorneys. His bruises would fade and he'd go into court in a spiffy suit with his million-dollar smile and his million-dollar lawyers and beat the rap. Or file an appeal and be freed on a technicality.

I knew I had an obligation to make sure no future women were tricked, drugged, and murdered by this handsome lunatic. He needed to look like the maniac he was.

I changed direction, last minute, and pressed the scalpel to his face.

# CHAPTER THIRTY-FIVE

**Rika**

Nick and I were sitting in the hallway on chairs someone brought us, waiting for the police and EMT's to sort out whether they were taking Choi and his henchman to the functioning part of the hospital—yes, they decided they had to—and who they were sending along to guard them until they could be booked. That's where the discussion came in.

I'd managed to get my dress back on before the cops arrived. The homicide detectives—not Hertz and Winchell, thank Zeus—asked me why I'd changed as if that made my story suspect.

But I had trust issues with cops since I never knew when they might decide to throw me into the car and take off with me. After all I'd been through tonight, I was not about to be put in the backseat of a police car practically naked, so they could just suck it.

I didn't normally use the term "suck it," even in my own head, but I was exhausted and sore and those were the only words that came to mind. I thought I did pretty well by not letting them escape my mouth when the cops questioned me.

We'd been triaged by the EMT's. Nick didn't show any signs of brain damage and we mostly had bruises that would heal on their own.

Nick had even managed to find my phone before the cops arrived.

After I finished checking my calls and texts to make sure my family members weren't worried about me, I remembered what he'd said about "tracking."

"How did you know I was at the hospital?" I asked.

He lifted his phone, a superior look on his face.

I bugged my eyes out at him, too exhausted to play games.

"Remember that link you sent to help me find you when the gangbangers were chasing you and LeeAnne a couple of weeks ago?"

"Yeah?"

"I thought that app might come in handy again, so I bought it and downloaded it to my phone. It somehow synced up with the link you'd sent in my texts and added your phone to my list of targets."

"Targets?" I repeated.

"Their word, not mine."

"You've had the ability to track my phone for weeks?"

"Yeah, but I only remembered after I got your texts, then couldn't get ahold of you."

We sat quietly while I considered how I felt about Nick knowing where I was at all times. Sure, it probably saved my life tonight, but it also removed my ability to ever tell Nick a white lie about where I was going.

I noticed his expression had darkened. He was watching me and not in a good way.

"What?" I said irritably, beating him to the—grumpy —punch.

"I left town for one day and you went on a date with someone else."

He wasn't asking me a question. He was just saying it aloud, as if he needed to get it out in the open to weigh its importance.

My lips parted, expecting my brain to give them something to say, but, as I said, I'd been through a lot and couldn't find the words to explain to Nick that what he'd said was both true and not true at the same time.

I mean, yes, I went out to dinner with Geoff Choi, but it wasn't a date, date. I had no intentions of having a relationship with him, no matter how handsome he was.

Nick continued. "First you invited Julian to dinner with the folks, and now—"

I made a growling sound in my throat. "I told you, I didn't invite Julian!"

"It's getting harder to believe you about this stuff." He scanned me top to bottom. "And you wore the dress *I* gave you on your date." His voice was soft, but with the hard edge of something else. Jealousy? Anger?

*Disappointment.*

I had disappointed him, and Nick was the last person in the world I wanted to disappoint.

But wait a minute... "You flew off to who knows where to see a woman," I threw back at him.

His eyes closed. He shook his head like I was the unreasonable one! "My little sister Dee was having a problem with her ex."

*His sister? Crap!* I opened my mouth to apologize, but a glance at the dress changed my mind. I pinched the fabric between my thumb and forefinger to direct his attention to it. "Well, in case you've forgotten, this was a hand-me-down from one of your ex-wives! It's not like you went and picked it out for me."

"If I had picked it out, would you still have put it on and gone on a date with another man?"

"I—" *Hm...* Would I have? It was the only thing I had for such a fancy restaurant, and, even if Nick and I were in a clear, solid relationship, I wouldn't have thought of it as cheating. I wasn't interested in Geoff Choi, at least not that way.

"Never mind," Nick said. "I just got my answer."

"Nick! It wasn't a real date!"

"Did he ask you to dinner?"

"Well, yeah."

"And he clearly told you what kind of place he was taking you to if you got this dressed up. Do you think men typically ask a woman out to a fancy restaurant where he can see her all done up and sexy if he's not interested in fucking her?"

Well, that was blunt. I wasn't sure how to reply.

Nick blew out a derisive snort. He shrugged. "I guess a doctor *is* an upgrade from a lawyer."

*Oh my God! He did not just say that!*

"Is that really what you think of me? That I'm just out trying to snag the best trophy husband?"

"You wouldn't be the first woman to do it. Not even the first one I've fucked."

Rage boiled up inside me. How dare he compare me to his airhead exes! My hand flew up of its own accord to slap him in the face.

He caught me by the wrist.

The skin on my chest burned and the heat spread up my neck to my cheeks.

I was not a person who slapped other people in the face because she didn't like what they said. It was so retro—in a bad way—like a scene from an old black and white movie.

I yanked my wrist away and focused on the gray floor as I tried to breathe away the rage and embarrassment. Why had I lost control?

Because I'd fallen for Nick that first day, when he'd made a joke at the police station in Bolo. And because, if he'd asked last summer, I would have stayed with him.

Yes, I totally would have stayed with him in that silly one-horse town where I'd been unjustly arrested, labeled the "Grey Widow" and humiliated in court, not to mention almost being killed more than once.

The ball was in his court, but he let me leave and never contacted me. Just went on with his life like I'd never been in it.

The humiliation had drained away, but the anger had blossomed into a big red fireball in my abdomen. "It's not like *you* ever asked me on a date," I blurted.

His eyes turned stormy, then narrowed as he stared at me like I was a lunatic or a bitch or a bitchy lunatic, I wasn't sure.

"I invited you to stay in my home. I cooked meals for you. Got you whatever you needed." He looked into my eyes like he was trying to find something—or someone—in there. "I kind of thought that trumped a date."

"It's not the same!" I said.

"No, I think it's a far cry better."

"But that was..." I searched for a fitting word, "...charity."

"Charity?"

"Yeah, I was your client and needed a place to stay."

Nick's elbow came up as he rubbed the back of his neck. I knew what that meant. I was wearing on his last nerve. I was the proverbial pain in the neck, turned literal.

"So, you went out with Geoff Choi because I never asked you on a date?"

"No, I went out with Geoff Choi because he said he had information on the case, including scans that didn't mesh with the M.E. report. Jeez, not everything's about you." However, we both knew Choi could have emailed me the images or we could have met at his office in broad daylight. I decided to come clean. "Plus, I noticed he had the nicest geek stuff in his office I've ever seen. I wanted to find out about his supplier."

"Oh..." The disappointed look was back in his eyes. "So, you were using him."

"I wasn't using him!"

But before the words were out of my mouth, I knew Nick was right. I might not have been after Geoff as a trophy husband or for cash or jewelry, but I was using him to get what I wanted.

In my defense, his Millennium Falcon was the most detailed I'd ever seen. My online and con friends would totally get that.

Unfortunately, Nick wouldn't.

Okay, maybe I was looking at this from the wrong angle. Nick was clearly unhappy that I'd gone on a date with another guy, which meant our time in his hotel room hadn't just been a convenient hook-up for him.

Was this proof that Nick wanted us to be exclusive?

I mean I'd wished and hoped and sometimes I even thought I knew, but those times were fleeting. Probably because of my own insecurity.

I tried to imagine Nick and me as a couple. Weird that I'd never really imagined it before. I'd never gotten past daydreaming about him touching me and kissing me and having his way with me. Or my way with him.

The new image in my mind still didn't seem quite right. Nick was tall and handsome and confident. I was shortish, chubby, and my confidence was mostly centered on my brain.

*Remember? You're not chubby anymore*, said a voice in my head that sounded a lot like my old Jilly Crane counselor.

I tried to fix the picture in my mind, unsuccessfully, but it didn't matter. Hot, smart, funny Nick Owen wanted to be in an exclusive relationship with me.

"You could still do it," I blurted. "Ask me on a date, I mean."

Nick stared at me, his head tilted slightly. He looked at the ground. Then he sucked in a deep breath. "I don't know that I want to do that right now."

As his words sunk in, an awful feeling slid through me.

*He's changed his mind.*

He didn't want me that way anymore. He thought I was like his exes. He thought I was a user, and maybe I was.

I didn't think there was anything else I could say to make him see me differently. I was about to lose him from my life over the dream of fancy geek toys.

I swallowed hard, trying to get the lump out of my throat. Tears burned behind my eyes and I had to blink lightning fast to keep them from pouring over my cheeks.

What if he decided to go home to Bolo?

"You're not leaving L.A., are you?" I asked. There was a pleading edge to my voice I didn't like. But I had to know.

"I'll need to give it some thought," he said. Then he got up and walked out.

# CHAPTER THIRTY-SIX

**Rika**

I was on pins and needles, waiting for Nick. I paced the empty living room wondering where my grandmother had gone off to before I woke up, but glad she wouldn't be here when Nick arrived.

We didn't have a case to work on, and there'd been no reason for him to come by and get me this morning and no reason for me to call or text him.

The truth was, I was afraid to contact him. If he'd decided he didn't want to spend time with me, I didn't want to know about it, even if I had to stay on pins and needles permanently. People say it's always better to know, but, in my experience, that doesn't hold true, at least when it comes to loved ones.

As it turned out, my wishes were irrelevant. Around one in the afternoon, Nick texted me that he was coming over and had something to talk to me about.

Since then, I'd been trying to prepare myself for the words I knew were coming. He was going to dissolve our partnership. He was going to leave me.

The most I could ask of myself was that I let him go with

dignity. In other words, I didn't want to cry like I did when I left him in Bolo.

I was so anxious, when the knock finally came, I nearly jumped out of my skin.

Once I opened the door, Nick strode in, his face serious.

"Is this about us? Our partnership?" I blurted.

"What?" Nick said as if his mind had been a million miles away from our issues.

I met his gaze and realized how self-involved I'd been. He looked freaked out. And, any number of things might have happened since I saw him last.

"Is your mom okay?" I asked.

"Yeah, she's fine," he said.

"Your sister?"

"She's fine too."

The question I needed answered most rose up in my throat again. *Is it me? Are you leaving me?*

But before I could embarrass myself further, Nick sighed and said, "It's my cousin Eliza in Bolo."

"You had a cousin in Bolo?"

"She was a few years younger. My mom's brother moved away from Bolo for a better job while Liza was in elementary school. After that, I didn't see a lot of her. She moved back just a few months ago. Her family still owned property in Bolo and she needed a cheap place to stay. Her and her baby girl. She'd reached out to Dill, who owns the Dill's Dollar Stores in Bolo and other stores in neighboring towns to see if he had a job for her. She'd just started working for him in the Bolo store a month ago."

I noticed the verb tense. She *had started*, not she's *working at.* "What happened?" I asked.

"She..." He closed his eyes as his abs tightened and his torso curled in a little. I realized the full force of whatever happened was just hitting him.

"Sit down, Nick," I said firmly.

425

He didn't argue. He sat on the couch, elbows on his thighs, staring at the carpet like he'd never seen it before.

"She was murdered," he said. He looked up at me and the raw shock and anguish on his face made my chest hurt.

I sat next to him. For better, and sometimes worse, Nick was a protector of women. This was the kind of crime he couldn't understand in a million years.

"Shit," he said in a near-whisper. "In my mind she's still ten years old."

I threaded my hand through the space between his arm and thigh and laced my fingers in his. He stared at my hand then, without looking at me, lifted it and pressed it to his cheek.

"Mom's a mess. On the phone, she kept jumping around between being horrified for her niece, terrified there was a killer on the loose, and enraged in general. She's convinced that if it's left to the local authorities, the murderer will never be brought to justice, and I can't argue that point."

So, this was it. The thing I knew would take Nick away from me, even if I didn't know exactly what the thing would be.

Once he settled into his huge, comfortable house in Bolo again, he'd never come back. Maybe he'd decided being a litigator wasn't his thing, but being a P.I. wasn't ever on his list of potential occupations. There was no reason for him to come back to L.A., especially now that I'd disappointed him.

What was I thinking? I should have let him sign us up for one of those fancy offices. Then, maybe, he'd feel obligated for the next few years, at least.

*Obligated. Isn't that hot?*

I believed Nick was attracted to me, but, as I always tried to remind myself, he'd been attracted to lots of women.

And, now, he'd seen me in my natural habitat. In my geek clothes. Living in my grandmother's house. In a bedroom full of nerd decor that he probably found childish.

But, what could I do? Tell him not to go be with his mom at a time like this?

I took in stuttering breaths, trying to tamp down the fight or flight reaction my body was having to the idea that Nick was leaving me. My heart banged miserably against my ribs.

I had no choice but to be a grownup about this, even if I wanted to throw myself across Nick's lap, wrap my arms around his waist, and tell him I couldn't imagine living without him.

"I'm really sorry this has happened to your family, Nick." I thought about how my mother's murder had affected my family. Everyone's life changed drastically and the ripple effect...

But this wasn't about me. I needed to be strong and not make this hard on Nick.

"When are you flying out?"

Was this the last time I'd ever see him?

So much for my dignity. A million tears welled up in my throat, threatening to choke me as I frantically swallowed them. I needed a bag of Double Stuf Oreos, stat. No, not a bag. A case. Maybe I could find a wholesaler online. If the warehouse was across town, I could stop for some of those Mexican *empanadas* at Eddie's, then drive through whatever Krispy Kreme donut locations were on the way.

A bomb had been dropped in my stomach and the only way to neutralize it was with carbs. Lots and lots of carbs.

I tried to focus on the yumminess of the treats, instead of the anguish of Nick leaving me.

I decided, again, I was not going to cry. I wasn't going to make him feel guilty. This relationship never could have worked out, anyway. Whether I was hot or not, chubby or slim, I wasn't in Nick's league. I would never be a person who could move through the world with ease and confidence. And wasn't that the only kind of woman who made sense with Nick Owen?

I realized he hadn't answered about when he was flying out.

My hand was still in his. He squeezed it, sending a flood of warmth mixed with regret coursing through my body. "When am I flying out," he murmured to himself. Or maybe to our hands because that's what he was staring at.

Suddenly, his gaze snapped up to meet mine. His eyes were as beautiful as ever, but I could read the sadness and maybe worry in them. He seemed to be searching for something in mine.

"I was hoping *we* were flying out," he said.

This book is over, but the story continues in the next Martin and Owen Mystery—*Dead Hair Day*. Go to NinaCordoba.com to sign up to get my newsletter with book release notifications or to contact me. You can also stay in the loop by visiting my Facebook page @NinaCordobaAuthor. I'm always happy to hear from readers and I appreciate your support.

# ACKNOWLEDGMENTS

I want to give a special shout out to my Nina's Inner Circle group for not only encouraging me with your enthusiasm about my books, but also for acting as beta readers, post sharers, poll takers, and clarifiers (when I need to know if readers in other states or countries will understand what I just wrote).

Since writers spend so much time alone wondering if anyone in the world will want to read all these words we've agonized over, the best thing that can happen is to find a supportive group of readers who really get you and love your work. You are kind, wonderful people and you're worth more than gold to me.

Also, thank you to the fabulous Brenda Bennett for being both my assistant and my manager. Your spreadsheets and graphs give me the heebie-jeebies, but I'm so happy to have found you!

## YOU'RE WELCOME

I'd like to send a special "You're welcome" to the real Geoff Choi, who met me once, found out I was a writer, then hounded me to put his name in a book. (Salesmen! Sheesh!)

So, I made you a handsome doctor, just like I promised, but maybe you should redact the last few chapters of the book before you show it to your parents.

Made in the USA
Middletown, DE
30 April 2022

65045889R00245